The
Prince
of the
Skies

Also by Antonio Iturbe

The Librarian of Auschwitz

The
Prince
of the
Skies

ANTONIO
ITURBE

TRANSLATED BY
LILIT ŽEKULIN THWAITES

MACMILLAN

First published 2021 by Macmillan
an imprint of Pan Macmillan
The Smithson, 6 Briset Street, London ECIM 5NR
EU representative: Macmillan Publishers Ireland Ltd, 1st Floor,
The Liffey Trust Centre, 117–126 Sheriff Street Upper,
Dublin 1, DOI YC43
Associated companies throughout the world
www.panmacmillan.com

ISBN 978-1-5290-6333-2

135798642

A CIP catalogue record for this book is available from the British Library.

Printed and bound by CPI Group (UK) Ltd, Croydon, CR0 4YY

MIX
Paper from
responsible sources
FSC® C116313

Visit **www.panmacmillan.com** to read more about all our books
and to buy them. You will also find features, author interviews and
news of any author events, and you can sign up for e-newsletters
so that you're always first to hear about our new releases.

To Susana, who flies with me

The music which was playing over the sound of the engine as these pages were emerging was 'The Bricklayer's Beautiful Daughter' by William Ackerman.

CHAPTER 1

★

Le Bourget Aerodrome (Paris), 1922

ANTOINE DE SAINT-EXUPÉRY

HE PULLS THE JOYSTICK BACK toward his chest and the biplane lifts in search of a bank of clouds over Paris. The Caudron C.59 shudders, the Hispano-Suiza motor snorts. He soars through the white clouds, then pulls on the metal cable and forces the plane to climb an air mountain until it's doing a handstand in the sky. The vibration of the fuselage carries through to his hands and from there, to his entire body.

Sublieutenant Saint-Exupéry shivers, intoxicated with vertigo, and smiles with the infinite satisfaction of the mad, of children absorbed in their games: no notion of risk or time, immersed in a world that belongs solely to them, because they have made it to their own measure.

While on the ground, the Caudron C.59 plane is nothing more than a cumbersome 700-kilo lump of wood, full of screws, rivets, and solder. It looks pathetically fragile as it rolls along on its little bicycle wheels, dragging its heavy frame—an overgrown child, chest puffed out, rattling precariously on its wire feet as it starts to trundle down the runway. The smallest stone in its path could knock it off balance, causing it to overturn spectacularly. But then the miracle happens: The heavy rolling hulk takes off from the ground, lifts itself toward the horizon, ascends and then suddenly banks slightly, agilely, gracefully even. It's made a mockery of its destiny as a whale stranded in its hangar.

Antoine matches the plane itself. On the ground, both his big body, which forces him to move awkwardly, even clumsily, and his head filled with daydreams, totally ill-equipped to handle the most mundane aspects of daily living, convert him into a confused, tottering penguin futilely flapping its wings and unable to reach the sea. But up in the sky, he's a totally different person.

He becomes weightless.

He moves the rudder to the left and the nose of the plane abruptly rolls in that direction. He smiles. He's fulfilled every child's dream: to make toys real and reality a game.

He traces a braid in the air. He loves feeling that giddy tingle which elevates him beyond mediocrity; realising that he's left all the vulgarity of the barracks on the ground, together with those officers who yell until the veins stick out in their necks.

Antoine only raises his voice on those happy nights when he's had too much burgundy or pastis and he launches into songs which start out cheerful and end up melancholy. When he gets angry, he falls silent.

> *How sterile it is to say*
> *What silence already knows . . .*

The plane sways in the air and Antoine sways too. He is a great admirer of the poet Mallarmé, and to show his support, he himself occasionally writes verse.

He has already performed a thousand pirouettes in the air, but that's not enough. It's never enough. For him, life always feels like a suit that's too tight. He adjusts the throttle and the machine loses momentum until it comes to a standstill. A plane hanging motionless in the sky becomes a lump of metal definitively attracted by a violent gravitational force. The plane stalls and goes into a spin. A small group of spectators on the ground follows the spine-tingling nosedive with an accompanying "Ohhh!" which wants to be cheerful but sounds nervous. An eternal few seconds later, Antoine abruptly pulls on the joystick and levels the plane into a glide which shaves a field of poppies.

He's taken advantage of the absence of most of the officers of the 34th Regiment this Sunday afternoon to mount his own little air show. His favourite childhood game at his family's Saint-Maurice-de-Rémens mansion, full of nooks and crannies, was, in fact, devising plays he staged for his siblings. He was both the playwright who wrote the scripts and the over-the-top actor who performed them. His family could never tell whether he was a serious child or a clown. They were incapable of confirming which was the real Antoine: the one who would stand mesmerised in front of the window on rainy afternoons watching the drops racing across the glass, or the one who turned the attic upside down and then suddenly appeared disguised as a buccaneer or an explorer shouting ridiculous phrases in order to amuse his sisters and cousins.

He asks himself that very question. *Who am I? The court jester who shakes his bells when he's with others, or the silent introvert I am when I'm on my own?*

A vibration in a wing pulls him out of his daydream. He shouldn't become distracted when he's flying, but his thoughts soar when he's in the air. He turns his head for a few seconds in a reckless attempt to catch a glimpse of his friends who are watching his aerobatics, but they are mere pins stuck into the ground.

There they are—Charles Sallès, Bertrand de Saussine, and Olivier

3

de Vilmorin . . . But when he performs his most outlandish spins, he's performing for only one person, the girl who never leaves his thoughts.

He recalls the first time his cousin took him to visit the lavish house on Rue de la Chaise where Madame de Vilmorin was already then hosting one of the most intellectual salons in Paris.

A waxen-faced butler had shown them to a room with quilted sofas and walnut bookshelves to wait for the two Vilmorin brothers to finish getting ready to accompany them to an ice cream parlour on the Champs-Élysées. And then he'd heard the music. It was a violin being played with a mournful slowness, the bow moving ever so slowly across the strings without the note ever disappearing entirely. The notes had been so frayed that they hung in the air as if snagged and, rather than a melody, they had seemed more like its echo.

The music had pulled him upstairs and he'd reached the third floor in a trance. The second door off the hallway had been ajar, so he had poked his head in.

A young girl in purple pyjamas had been playing, reclining against cushions of various colours on top of a bed covered with a blue satin quilt. Her chin had rested so softly on the chinrest that the violin had almost become a pillow. A governess with a white cap had been sitting on a chair by her side and had fixed her gaze on the intruder. But instead of throwing him out, she had gestured for him to wait and put a finger to her lips to tell him to be quiet.

Hypnotised, he had contemplated the girl's red hair, her green eyes, her pale hands. She had been playing with a mixture of indifference and concentration, which had forced her to focus on the far end of the fingerboard, where her own fingers were playing at jumping rope.

He remembers fervently begging the god of all things beautiful never to let that melody end as long as he lived.

When it had finished, the governess, Madame Petermann, had begun to clap with scant enthusiasm, and had arched her brow as a sign that he should do the same. And he had, of course, loudly and enthusiastically. After carefully laying her violin inside the case on top of the quilt, the girl had given him a smile. That smile could stop time. At least it had stopped his, and all the chronometers in his life had been reset to zero.

"I don't think we've been introduced . . . ," she had said, and Antoine had blushed as if the girl's red hair had been reflected in his face, and he'd started stuttering.

"I beg you to forgive me bursting in, mademoiselle. It was the music that made me lose my discretion . . ."

"And you are . . . ?"

"Oh, of course, forgive my lack of manners! I'm Antoine de Saint-Exupéry. You must be Olivier's sister. I'm a friend of his; we study together at the Académie Bossuet."

"I'm Louise de Vilmorin."

"My apologies for appearing in your room uninvited. I'll leave now."

"Oh, don't fuss. A hateful condition of my hip bones forces me to keep to my bed, and my bedroom serves as the salon where I receive my visitors. I adore visits!"

"Could I come and see you one day?"

"You can ask for an appointment," she had replied without enthusiasm. But at the sight of the young man's look of desolation, she'd added coquettishly: "Or you can just sneak in during my music practise."

A voice had called him from the depths of the house: "Saint-Ex! Where the devil are you?"

"Your brother wants me; I have to leave. I'll be back!"

He'd barely said it when his enthusiasm was replaced by concern. "But will you remember me when you see me again? My face is so ordinary!"

She had looked at him with an inscrutable smile which could have meant either complacency or disdain.

"Who knows. I'm forgetful."

"It doesn't matter!" he'd replied quickly. "I'll definitely remember you, Mademoiselle de Vilmorin. I'll remember for both of us!"

In the cockpit, he laughs now at his own awkwardness. He presses down on the throttle pedal, opens the flow of fuel, and moves the joystick so the plane will perform a zigzag in the sky. Shortly after he had met her, he had to report for his obligatory military service and enlisted in the air force to make his long-held dream of flying a reality. After several transfers, he was posted to Casablanca, and during that period of training and discomfort, he was accompanied by the memory of Louise, a love that kept growing at a distance.

His return to Paris and a posting to the 34th Regiment quartered at Le Bourget filled him with delight at being back in a city full of theatres, bookstores, boulevards, and get-togethers with his friends . . . but in particular at the opportunity of revisiting the house on Rue de la Chaise. He needed to see her again.

He asked André de Vilmorin over and over again to be received by Louise, but André was tired of seeing all his friends stammering pathetically when confronted by his sister, even being prepared to line up in the small visitors' room in the naïve hope of begging a few moments of attention from a girl who allowed herself to be idolised without losing that gesture of disdain with which she dismissed her suitors as soon as she tired of their presence.

One Thursday morning when he thought it would never happen, a private entered the office, where Antoine was scribbling lines of poetry in his spare time, and gave him a note which informed him that Mademoiselle de Vilmorin would receive him.

The next day, he barely ate, moving the noodles around on his plate, leaving them virtually untouched. He got dressed with the utmost care: He put on the only suit he owned, which he'd managed to get the barracks laundry to iron for him in exchange for a half pack of cigarettes, and carefully arranged his hair, combing it up high with brilliantine. He left early for the Vilmorin residence because he needed flowers, lots of flowers, the most beautiful flowers in France. He would have loved to be the Merovingian King Childebert, who built an entire rose garden for his queen in the centre of Paris. Louise de Vilmorin deserved nothing less.

He walked to a very high-class flower shop in Rue Charron, which had a display in its front window as enticing as a candy store, and asked for an enormous bouquet of colourful flowers. When the sales assistant told him the price, he went pale. That month his mother had made the payment on the coat he'd been buying on installments since the previous winter, and he'd barely managed to eke out his military pay to the end of the month, leaving him with just a few coins. He couldn't hide his embarrassment from the sales assistant as he told her he'd thought better of it. Back out on the street he sighed, defeated. He'd been the happiest man in the world for twenty-four hours and now he was back to being the most wretched.

As he reached the corner, it occurred to him that he wasn't far from the flower market on Île de la Cité. It was a grand hothouse with a mossy smell and the feel of a train station in among the bustle of barrows from the food market and soldiers on leave buying flowers for apprentice seamstresses on the Right Bank of the Seine.

He emerged with a small bunch of lilacs and happy again.

The butler, dressed in a vest with golden fringes, opened the front door with professional indifference and pointed to the small reception room with a gloved hand. An unpleasant surprise was waiting for Antoine: two other young men were already sitting there. There was clearly a queue to court Louise de Vilmorin!

His rivals were impeccably dressed in pinstriped suits. One was carrying a gilded vase full of exotic flowers and the other was weighed down by an enormous box of cakes and assortments bearing the logo of Dalloyau, an exquisite pâtisserie on Rue du Faubourg Saint-Honoré with the finest cream pastries in Paris.

He hid his little bouquet behind his back before they noticed it. He now realised that his posy was too common, inappropriate for a refined young lady like Louise de Vilmorin. He greeted the two men with a nod and propped himself against the doorframe with the unpleasant feeling that he was a vagrant in this elegant house and that at any moment they would realise he was an imposter and the butler would throw him out on the street.

It's true that his family belonged to the old aristocracy of Lyons and that he had spent his childhood in a small castle with a thousand doors. But that was too many doors for the paltry heating. As a ruined count, he felt ridiculous using his title. He loathed his cheap flowers and angrily squeezed their defenceless stems.

The butler announced that Mademoiselle de Vilmorin was awaiting them in her bedroom, and the three of them headed upstairs on their pilgrimage. Antoine let the others go ahead and, when no one was looking, crushed the flowers into the pocket of his jacket and made a half turn to leave while he still had time to avoid making a fool of himself. But as he was turning around, he saw that the sphinx-faced butler was following them, so he continued up the stairs.

Louise was sitting on her bed with her back against the headboard and two enormous cushions supporting her arms. Her beauty was in her weightlessness; there was something that made her float above everything.

With a triumphant smile, one of the boys approached to hand her the weighty vase overflowing with ribbons, bows, and flowers. Instead of stretching out her arms to receive it, she extended a politely indifferent "thank you" and turned to Madame Petermann, who stepped forward to accept it with an annoyed expression on her face and deposited it on the bedside table next to two similar floral arrangements. The other gentleman stepped up to give her his sweet delicacies; she gave him the same brief smile and thanked him. Without the slightest sign of taking the box with the huge purple bow, she looked at the governess, who accepted the package. Louise propped herself up on one elbow to see the third visitor, who seemed to be concealing himself behind the other two.

"Are you playing hide-and-seek?"

Antoine blushed and took a few steps forward.

"Ah, it's you! The Count Saint . . . Saint what?"

"Saint-Exupéry! How nice that you remembered me after all this time!"

She looked at his empty hands, and in order to hide them, Antoine stuck them into the pockets of his jacket. His words came out flustered.

"Forgive me, I wanted to bring you a gift . . ."

As he began to gesticulate, his nervousness made him pull his hands from his pockets, and with the movement of his gigantic paws, a shower of lilac petals flew out. They scattered throughout the room, forming a cloud which hung briefly in the air before landing softly on the quilt.

Louise's bored expression changed for the first time.

"Are you a magician?" she asked.

"M-my apologies . . . ," Antoine stammered.

"Don't apologise," she replied with a glimmer in her eyes that made them seem even greener. "I love magicians."

"A corporal in my squadron in Casablanca taught me a few card tricks."

"Put on a show for us!"

"I, err . . . I don't have a deck of cards."

"Madame Petermann, could you go and find us a deck?"

"Mademoiselle, you know I have orders from Madame de Vilmorin not to leave you alone with gentlemen."

Louise, used to being in charge, turned to the other two young men, who were observing the conversation as if turned to stone.

"Why don't you two go in search of Monsieur Dupont, the butler, and ask him to bring up some cards from the bridge room?"

Reduced to the role of secretaries, the two dejected young men left the room, and returned followed by the butler carrying a deck of cards on a silver tray.

Antoine performed his tricks. He guessed the card she deposited in the middle of the deck, and repeated the trick with one of the gentlemen, who collaborated reluctantly. Not long afterward, the two gentlemen left, defeated.

"Do you know any other magic?" asked Louise, tired of card tricks.

"I know the works of Mallarmé . . . He performs magic with words!"

"Tell me something . . . what do you think of Baudelaire?"

"He's capable of the most sublime and the most grotesque."

"Come back tomorrow and explain that to me better. I love poetry."

Her smile was full of promise and their love affair began from there.

If only Lou-Lou, as he now calls her, could be here this Sunday afternoon to see his aerial feats, but her painful hip still hasn't recovered and she has to rest a little longer. He performs his aerobatics to continue surprising her with tales of his exploits. She can't abide boredom! With cheerful impulsiveness, he becomes a trapeze artist in the sky over Paris.

As soon as he lands, he gets rid of his goggles and the military flight suit he put on over his shirt and Sunday trousers. He hurriedly fixes his tie as he walks along the edge of the runway toward the waiting group. Sallès strides to meet him, arms open wide.

"Saint-Ex, you were magnificent!" And he grabs him by the arm with camaraderie. "I salute a crack aviator!"

Bertrand de Saussine claps and whistles and Antoine reciprocates with an exaggerated bow. Olivier de Vilmorin, however, impeccable in his tweed jacket and silk tie, keeps his arms crossed, the expression on his face severe.

Antoine looks at his friend and future brother-in-law.

"Those manoeuvres of yours . . ."

"That last turn was an *L* . . . An *L* for *Lou-Lou*! I did it in her honour. Will you tell your sister? You should tell her; she won't believe me!"

"You shouldn't be doing that."

His bitter tone surprises Antoine.

"I shouldn't trace her letter?"

"You shouldn't perform such idiocies. Don't you understand? You're going to kill yourself one of these days!"

Antoine takes him arm affectionately, but Olivier, irritated, shakes himself loose.

"It's nothing more than a game for you! You're an egoist. Those 'great aviator' pirouettes . . . What about my sister? What future awaits her? To be a pilot's widow before she's thirty?"

Bertrand tries to defuse the situation.

"Come on, Olivier! Saint-Ex knows what he's up to, right?"

Charles Sallès gestures ambiguously. He once flew as a passenger with Antoine, who let go of the joystick and pretended he was playing the maracas.

Antoine has fallen silent. It happens to him sometimes: Suddenly, the lights go out.

Olivier de Vilmorin softens his tone and addresses the others: "My mother's worried. Do you know what my older siblings call Saint-Ex?"

"No."

"The condemned man."

The Vilmorin family are like a fortress. Descended from Joan of Arc, they are aristocrats and millionaires. And who is this Antoine de Saint-Exupéry? It's true that he has an ostentatious surname and even the title of count, which he is embarrassed to use. But he is an aristo-crat from the provinces, his father is dead, he's known to have only one winter suit and one summer one, with shiny patches on the elbows. He's doing his obligatory military service with the air force, and says he wants to dedicate himself to a profession which is as seemingly useless as it is pointlessly dangerous—an aviator. Olivier knows that his mother is uneasy about this fiancé that her daughter has found herself, when she could have future government lawyers, sons of ministers, and heirs to the greatest fortunes of France falling head over heels for her, all of whom have made a futile pilgrimage to the house on Rue de la Chaise since she was of courting age. But she has chosen this ungainly young man with nothing to offer. Lou-Lou and her damned whims!

Charles Sallès intervenes to ease the silence.

"If Saint-Ex is a condemned man, he has the right to a last meal! Let's celebrate it at the Café des Deux Magots!"

Antoine emerges from his lethargy.

"Yes! My treat!" he says happily.

As soon as he's said it, he realises that he has just a few miserly francs in his wallet to get through the rest of the month, but that's not important right then. He can get to the end of the month by eating all his meals at the barracks mess, and if he's in dire need, he can always ask his mother, a nurse in Lyons, for some money and reimburse her when he gets his next pay packet.

Montmartre is the painters' and sculptors' quarter, but the writers' stomping ground lies between the Latin Quarter and Saint-Germain-des-Prés. That's why Sallès, to paper over that somber moment, has proposed the café in the heart of Saint-Germain, a spot which has an irresistible attraction for Antoine and for Louise herself, who also writes poetry.

As they take the Pont Neuf across the Seine in Saussine's Citroën,

Antoine repeats what he tells them every time they go there: Mallarmé, Oscar Wilde, Apollinaire . . . they were all regular customers.

"But Verlaine more than anyone . . . he was the Socrates of the Deux Magots!"

Although they've all heard the story many times, they listen to him with pleasure. They know that as long as Antoine is talking, everything's fine. He's especially good at storytelling, a power of seduction that turns his flying anecdotes into fascinating tales.

The four young men wave at the waiter, dressed in an apron down his ankles, and settle in at a table under one of the two figurines of the Chinese wise men for which the establishment is named. Fifty years earlier, when the former proprietor decided to convert his fabric and novelty store into a restaurant, he kept the decorative statues of two Chinese men in meditative poses. Nobody remembers any more how they came to be there, nor what they represent. Antoine loves to invent biographies for them.

"I maintain they were Marco Polo's commercial go-betweens in China when he used to travel in search of silk and fabrics. What do you say?"

"But if they were mere fabric dealers, why would they call them wise men?"

"My guess is we're dealing with two Si-Fan masters," ventured Sallès.

"Si-Fan? What the hell is that?"

"What? You haven't read the Fu-Manchu novels? Well, the Si-Fan secret society is silently infiltrating everywhere. Its members are assassins who move like shadows and are trained to kill without a sound."

"You're wasting your time, Charles. You ought to read more serious things," Bertrand reproaches him.

"That's nonsense!" Antoine can't help blurting out with excessive vehemence as he gets up from his chair and pounds the table. "How can you ask literature to be serious? If literature is serious, it becomes nothing more than a notarised document!"

He says this so forcefully that an embarrassed silence falls over the room. Customers at other tables stare at him and Antoine is mortified. Olivier changes the subject, but Antoine has become taciturn and tells them he's going outside for some fresh air.

In fact, it's not fresh air he's after, but solitude. On the terrace, all the tables are empty—that languid, late-Sunday-afternoon abandonment when night falls without warning. He turns up the collar of his jacket and lights a cigarette, trying to warm himself with the embers. Traffic on the boulevard has died down, barely any pedestrians remain, and a cold wind lifts the edges of their jackets.

An elderly man dressed in an old three-quarter-length drill coat is leaning on a long, thin stick that looks to Antoine like a Zulu lance. The man turns to him.

"Don't you think it's extraordinary?"

Antoine looks in front of him and all he can see is an empty sidewalk, a few cars, and a cyclist riding past in profile.

"What's extraordinary?"

"The streetlamp!"

And then it dawns on him: the cap, the drill coat, and that stick which, in reality, is a pole that in times gone by must have had a wick on its tip.

"Are you a lamplighter?"

"Yes, sir, I am."

"But we haven't had gas lights in Paris for years."

The man makes a wry face.

"And don't I regret it. You know something? When I was working, my job often tired me out, and I could only think about getting home and going to bed. The lamplighter was the last one to go to bed after lighting all the lamps at night and the first to get up at the break of day to put them out."

"Lighting and putting out . . ."

"That's it."

"And it wasn't a boring job?"

The man looks at him, genuinely perplexed.

"Boring? What a strange idea!"

"What I mean is, didn't it become repetitive?"

"Repetitive, sure, of course. That's how it had to be. First one lamp, then another, and another after that. First one street, and then another, and another, and another. And so on . . ."

"And you didn't find that tedious?"

"Tedious? What do you mean? It was my work, I had a mission: Light the light and put it out. If I hadn't lit them every night, someone could have fallen into a pothole and broken his legs, or worse. An honest couple might have been assaulted without anyone realising it. I was responsible for the light. First one lamp and then another and another. And so on. And at dawn, the reverse: put one out and then another and then another after that . . ."

"But now that you're retired and the streetlights are electric, you must be happy; now you can sleep as much as you want."

"No. I now realise how happy I was when I was going round the whole city. First one lamp and then another, and another one after that . . . and so on."

"So what are doing here at this hour?"

"I continue to go round the city making sure all the lights are working. If there's a burnt-out bulb or a vandal has broken one, I jot it down in a notebook and the next morning I tell them at city hall so they'll fix it."

"And do they pay any attention to you?"

The man looks sad.

"Hardly ever."

Antoine feels the urge to get up and embrace him, but he holds back because at school they taught him the norms of social behavior, one of which was not to hug strangers in the street at night. He can't recall if, in that book of good manners, an exception was made for lamplighters. He just can't understand a planet on which no one finds two strangers fighting in the street odd, but many are scandalised if they see two strangers embracing.

"I'm going to go on with my rounds."

"Sir?"

"Yes?"

"With your permission, I'd like to be your friend."

CHAPTER 2

★

*Service Aéronautique Barracks, Istres
(Southern France), 1921*

Jean Mermoz

A PLATOON OF RECRUITS IS struggling to dig a ditch under the watchful eyes of Sergeant Pelletier, who is scrawny and swarthy—a sardine left on the grill too long. In a voice redolent of muddy trenches and cheap alcohol, he demands they work harder, and threatens to confine them to barracks and hang them by their balls from the flagpole.

"Goddamn slackers, mommy's boys! You'd have shit yourselves in the war. And I'd have made you eat your shit."

One of the boys slows down momentarily. Pelletier walks toward him and deals him a blow which resonates across the whole camp.

"Four days' detention."

"Sergeant . . ."

"Six!"

When they've comfortably reached a depth of two metres, the sergeant signals for them to get out of the hole. Some climb out with difficulty, exhausted after several hours of digging. Pelletier makes them stand in formation in front of the rectangle they've dug in the ground. The young men, most of them newcomers to military service, can feel the sweat pouring down their backs and their temples throb from their effort. The odd one has wobbly legs. The head of the unit plants himself in front of the soldiers and smiles for the first time all morning.

"Now fill it up again."

Some close their eyes in despair. One somewhat overweight boy in the front row sighs. With two strides, the sergeant stands in front of him and demands his number.

"Four days' detention."

Pelletier scrutinises the rest of the platoon and the recruits stare at the horizon to avoid meeting his rabid eyes. But one of them looks directly at him with an uncompromising stillness.

"Any problem with my order, recruit?"

"No, sir! At your command, Sergeant!"

The sergeant reads a form of insubordination into his look and his resolute tone. But there's no question the recruit has made no punishable gesture and his response has been firm and virile, as the sergeant demands. He checks out the young aspiring soldier from head to toe with suspicion: He's a good six inches taller than the sergeant and almost a foot broader in the shoulders, and Pelletier notices that he's gripping his shovel with so much force that his biceps are visible under the sleeves of his uniform. He feels an instinctive aversion toward this recruit because he realises the young man isn't afraid of him.

"What's your name, recruit?"

"Mermoz, sir! Jean Mermoz!"

He can't punish him for having a military attitude. The sergeant nods and looks at him with the eyes of a hunter watching a rabbit evading his shotgun, but also with the greedy glint of someone waiting to savour that moment down the track when the prey is in his sights again and he blows it to smithereens.

18

As they toss the earth back in, with hands blistered by the handles of their shovels, Mermoz gazes toward the far end of the Istres camp where half a dozen biplanes sit quietly on the runway. He hears his stomach growling because the midday meal isn't enough to satisfy his hunger, but he also notes another emptiness: flying. That's why he enlisted in the air force, willing to face the incredibly long four-year commission.

One day, having never been up in a plane, he felt that inner urge that takes us down a particular path at a crossroads of life. He had a somewhat bohemian, even indolent youth, filled with lengthy afternoons reading poets who wanted to be rebels and roaming the streets of Montparnasse around the Avenue du Maine, where he lived with his mother, a good woman embittered by life. One afternoon, leaning on his elbows looking down on the Seine which was overflowing its banks, he saw an enormous floating log being dragged along by the current. And he saw his own life reflected in that swollen water-soaked log.

He wasn't going to let the years drift by like that log. He swore to himself that, no matter what happened, he wouldn't allow himself merely to be carried along: He'd swim upstream. He'd never be a piece of water-logged wood. He needed a challenge to achieve this, something that would put him in charge of his own destiny. And that was when he looked up into the sky for inspiration and saw the clouds. He nodded his head in agreement and laughed out loud, not at all concerned by the looks he was being given by the pedestrians crossing the bridge just then. He'd get up there, higher, faster, further than anyone.

He enlisted in the air force to become a pilot, but reality wasn't in step with his dreams of adventure. Istres turns out to be a dead end where they've sent many of the infantrymen who survived the Great War which had ended three years earlier: people with no vocation, some decorated solely for their cruelty. Accustomed to feeling important in the mud of the battlefield, they are nobodies in the antiseptic normality of peace. Some of them, like Sergeant Pelletier, can't bear the arrogance of the pilots in their leather bomber jackets who fancy themselves heroes of the skies. During the Great War they played with their flying pieces of junk while the infantrymen swallowed mud and blood in trenches that had become slaughterhouses.

Mermoz tries to avoid the oppressive atmosphere of the barracks, but he can't escape his own frustration. Weeks pass and they still haven't started their training as airmen. They just move stones to no end, dig pointless ditches they then have to fill in again, or carry out exhausting marches lugging heavy backpacks filled with pieces of metal. Many sense their vocation flagging. The odd one has already given up and transferred to the infantry corps, and can be seen every morning inside a sentry box on guard duty, free of all obligations save keeping boredom at bay. But Mermoz accepts these punishment activities impassively and even encourages his comrades to cope with them in good spirits.

"We're doing healthy exercise. We'll be as strong as oxen!"

He takes advantage of free afternoons, after the long sessions that leave others exhausted, to work on his boxing in the camp gym. He hits the bag methodically, uses a skipping rope, and exercises with an enthusiasm that amazes his companions.

The pay is minimal and he has to save for drinks at the Sunday dances in Istres. But his body demands more food than the miserly barracks meals. You can get a quarter of a litre of hot chocolate at the commissary for six centimes. It's not much, but you can soak bread in it until you're full. He realises right away, however, that his lunch box only fits half a baguette. One afternoon he fronts up to the soldier serving the rations and holds out an empty cookie tin he found in the storage room. The soldier stares at the tin in amazement.

"I've misplaced my regulation lunch box. I have to make do with this until I get a new one from the commissary."

The soldier takes another look at the metal container and then studies him. The tin is twice the size of the regulation lunch box. It's such an obvious ploy that it's clear the recruit is not trying to deceive him. He's asking for his complicity without a "please" or any sign of humility, merely claiming what is his. The container is duly filled with thick chocolate.

At the dance in the city he tries to suppress a different hunger as an orchestra of four wizened musicians scares away the Sunday torpor. It's not hard for Mermoz to attract the attention of girls weighed down by the boredom of a city where nothing ever happens. He's a handsome young man, well built, virile, and always polite. He changes girls more often than his socks.

One afternoon in the ballroom where the men and women play cat and mouse, a very slim girl crosses in front of him, her eyes more excessively made up than is customary in a prudish provincial city and her hair cut in the garçon style. The mothers, grandmothers, and aunts who are the virginity police of their daughters, granddaughters, and nieces, put their heads together and gossip.

Mermoz doesn't like girls who are all skin and bones, but he likes this one because of her nerve, because she swims against the current. He walks toward her with the resolution that usually makes the local seamstresses fall in love with him. The vanity of a new conquest makes him puff up inside like a stuffed turkey. What he doesn't know is that she spotted him the moment he entered the room, and sashayed past him as soon as she decided that she was interested in this soldier with the blond crew cut.

Mermoz takes her by the arm and whispers a compliment in her ear. She fakes a slight blush, letting him think he's winning her over.

The curfew at the barracks is nine o'clock on Sundays. That doesn't leave much time to take girls to the *pension* La Martinique where, for a few centimes, the receptionist lets him have a room for a short stay. Some days, when he turns up without any money, the receptionist lets

Mermoz put it on a tab, and never complains about late payments. On other occasions, Mermoz doesn't have time to go to La Martinique, or the girls are scandalised by his intentions. Sometimes he gets manual relief after assuring the girls with a hearty laugh that they won't lose their virginity this way. But on this particular afternoon, not half an hour has gone by before Madeleine is crossing the threshold of the room at La Martinique with him, and a minute later, her clothes are off. Without the slightest hint of shame, she crosses the room to get her bag and takes out her compact.

"No need for makeup, you're gorgeous as you are."

She smiles. She has a soft spot for naïve boys. She shows him the metal box which doesn't contain face powder, but rather, a small brass tube and some white powder.

"What's that?"

She looks at him knowingly.

"This, dear, is your passport to paradise."

CHAPTER 3

★

Paris, 1923

Antoine de Saint-Exupéry

The Génestin rolls down the crowded Boulevard de Clichy. André, the oldest Vilmorin brother, sings the praises of the new family automobile and explains how the new power-assisted brakes invented by Paul Génestin can stop a car travelling at 110 kph in 26 metres. Charles Sallès, seated next to him, agrees. Reclining on the seat behind them because of her hip problem, Lou-Lou watches the bustle on the street.

"I'd love to go to the Moulin Rouge," she exclaims, pointing toward the cabaret with its windmill, the sails of which, at this hour of the morning, are motionless.

"I can't picture you at an old-fashioned cancan show," Charles says to her.

"Oh, Charles, darling . . . you're really the old-fashioned one!" And everyone in the car laughs at Lou-Lou's cheek. And she has the final say: "They haven't done the cancan for years. They now concentrate on cabaret . . ."

"You wouldn't like it, Lou-Lou . . . ," Saint-Ex chimes in.

"Why?"

"It's a brothel for the most uncouth nouveaux riches in Paris."

"Saint-Ex, don't use such language in front of my sister! It's offensive to a young lady!" André admonishes him.

"Fine, fine . . . I take back the brothel bit. It's a tearoom where no one drinks tea."

As Charles and Lou-Lou burst out laughing and André shakes his head as if Antoine were a lost cause, the horse-drawn cabriolet in front of them suddenly brakes. The horse pulling it kicks out its back legs and the load tips out. André is forced to brake abruptly too.

"When will they rid Paris of these carts!" he shouts angrily.

A mountain of melons has rolled onto the sidewalk and a mayhem of pedestrians has formed, a mix of gentlemen in hats and spats observing, people from a nearby food market rushing to help the young boy with his spilled merchandise, and crooks taking advantage of the confusion to disappear with melons under their arms.

Loud cries of "Stop, thief!" can be heard.

The traffic has come to a halt and horns start to honk.

"Paris is impossible! This traffic jam will last forever. I'll turn around and we'll try to get there via the square."

"Wait," says Lou-Lou. "We're only a step away from the Viennoise. We're getting out here."

"The doctor says you mustn't walk."

"Who says I'm going to walk? Aren't there enough gentlemen here to carry me?"

Before her brother can open his mouth to protest, Louise already has the car door open.

"Wait! Do you always have to be so impatient?"

"I can't waste a minute. Life is too valuable to fritter away, right, Antoine?"

He vehemently agrees.

"If they auctioned a minute of life at Christie's . . . how high would the bidding go?"

"I reckon two thousand francs. What do all of you say?"

"Much more!"

"I bid twenty-five hundred!" shouts Sallès.

"Three thousand!" And Lou-Lou raises her hand energetically.

André snorts, wavering between amusement and irritation.

"Okay, okay! But wait a minute, I'll leave the car at the curb."

"Quick, André, hurry!" Antoine urges. "We're losing thousands of francs."

In the trunk is the litter which they've used occasionally to take Lou-Lou for a walk in the countryside during the worst moments of her illness. It's a portable carrier which the Vilmorins bought from an importer of Eastern goods. It consists of a thick, varnished pole of cherry wood from which a small bamboo hammock hangs, shaded by a stiff piece of cloth above. Charles extracts the contraption and positions it next to the door. Lou-Lou accepts her fiancé's hand to help her get in and lie back.

Antoine and André, one up at the front and the other at the back, have the honour of carrying her, resting the cherry wood pole on their shoulders like porters. Charles Sallès is in charge of clearing a path through the throng until they reach Rue Lepic.

"Make way! Make way, please," he shouts with energetic authority, theatrically playing the part of barker. "We're carrying a very illustrious lady."

People step to the side for them, with Sallès resolutely leading the way followed by two young gentlemen carrying an exotic palanquin bearing a young redheaded lady gazing into the distance, her chin raised to show off her long, elegant neck.

The waiters attending the tables of the Brasserie La Place Blanche, their trays loaded with glasses of red currant juice and cups of tea, stop and stare. Curious workers wearing aprons pushing carts along the street, gentlemen in bowler hats, and female workers in long dresses crowd around to see this lady who travels quasi-airborne through the city, transported by her retinue as if she were a modern-day Cleopatra. A gendarme who has arrived on the spot to organise the confusion made by the cartload of melons sees the approaching litter and presents his respects to the lady with a military salute, convinced she must be the daughter of a diplomat from some remote country. Lou-Lou returns the gesture with a slight tilt of her head, and the policeman places himself in front of Sallès, imperiously ordering people to move out of the way.

In this manner, he clears a path for them as far as the corner, and escorts them to Rue Lepic, where, on the street level of the Beau Séjour hotel, the Viennoise pâtisserie exudes a delicious aroma of butter and toasted flour over several metres. Antoine and André carefully lower the palanquin. The policeman departs with another military salute. Antoine chivalrously offers one arm to Lou-Lou, while Sallès offers her another. The four of them, who have so far contained their mirth to add gravitas to their arrival, enter the pâtisserie roaring with laughter.

CHAPTER 4

Air Force Barracks, Istres
(Southern France), 1921

Jean Mermoz

THE WEEK HAS LASTED ONE hundred days. Each day has lasted one hundred hours. Sergeant Pelletier has made them sweep the landing strip—only used for an hour a day—up to three times daily.

He's made them march up and down in formation: one-two, one-two, one-two . . . mark time, mark time . . . Any error can mean punishment—cancellation of Sunday leave—and they all sweat as they strive not to make a mistake.

Mermoz is impulsive, but he doesn't bear a grudge. These weeks, however, have solidified a dark anger inside him which blocks out everything. Something else is happening to him that has never happened before: His hands shake.

Wednesday, they're given the opportunity to select their posting. Of the forty who volunteered for the air force, only five have chosen to go on. The others have accepted a posting in the infantry, which means they'll spend the rest of their military service in some quiet administrative branch, perhaps at another base where they'll never see Pelletier again.

But Mermoz hasn't given up.

At five o'clock, the sergeant orders them to fall in and tells them he has a special job for the aspiring pilots. First, he orders them to march at the double to the far end of the base, close to the perimeter wall. Then, he orders them to raise a metal trapdoor in the ground. When they do so, a black hole with a ladder is revealed and they are hit by a nauseating smell.

"The base's cesspit hasn't been emptied for weeks. I want it spotless. If you leave just one bit of shit, I'll make you clean it with your tongues."

He points to a cart with some baskets into which they have to dump the excrement.

"Any questions?"

"No, sir! At your command, Sergeant! . . . Where are the shovels?"

Pelletier guffaws.

"Shovels? You can't waste military equipment on these tasks. You've got shovels at the end of your arms. Hop to it, you slackers!"

Mermoz goes down first and a fellow sufferer called Corsault tells him to cover his face with a handkerchief. The methane expelled by the cesspit could cause them to black out and die in the least honourable way imaginable.

To avoid nausea and retching, Mermoz keeps telling himself that being there, in the middle of all that shit, is a victory. Because he hasn't given up, he hasn't taken a backward step.

Three of the five soldiers become ill and climb out of the well before they finish the job. Pelletier takes disciplinary action against them for disobeying orders and they lose any chance of being accepted into the pilot program. Corsault and Mermoz ride it out to the last basketful. As they hold their breath, they try to think only of their hope of learning to fly. They never thought such a pure dream could take them to such a filthy place. A captain heads their way to check out what they're doing and Sergeant Pelletier informs him that he's brought a pair of soldiers to clean out the pit.

The captain watches them emerge with empty baskets. Hands black, clothing black, faces black. They stink.

"Have you cleaned it out completely?" he asks them.

"Yes, sir!"

Pelletier screws up his black eyes.

"If you've lied to the captain, I'll throw you in stockade till your hair turns white."

The two soldiers remain at attention, but they don't believe Pelletier will go all the way down to check, and stain his pristine uniform.

"I have a very precise way of finding out if you really have cleaned everything as you were ordered." And there's something almost sly in his smile. "If it's true that you've done a thorough clean, you'll have reached the bottom and so you'll be able to tell me what colour the tiles are down there."

"We can't, Sergeant . . ."

In the silence that follows, Mermoz looks Pelletier in the eyes; Pelletier salivates, anxious to snatch his prey.

"We can't say what colour the tiles are because there aren't any. The bottom is cement."

There's fire in Pelletier's look.

"Is that true, Sergeant?" asks the captain, wrinkling his nose at the smell of the soldiers.

A bitter antagonism still visible in his expression, Pelletier has no option but to agree.

"Then order these boys into the showers, and they are free of any remaining duty until tomorrow."

"Yes, sir," he replies with badly disguised irritation. "You heard the captain. Dismissed!"

The two race off happily toward the showers; the other soldiers stare perplexed at the two walking shit heaps.

Friday, Mermoz consults the printed order of the day hanging from a hook by the door of the sleeping quarters, and sees the entry he's been waiting so long to read: "Private Mermoz will begin his pilot training on Monday. Report to the quartermaster at the aerodrome after reveille." His cry of jubilation can be heard throughout the base.

That afternoon, he bands together with Corsault to play poker with a recently enlisted innocent from a good family who fancies himself a great player. They gang up so that when it's Corsault's turn to deal the cards, he manages to give the jokers and face cards to Mermoz, and Mermoz reciprocates when it's his turn. In this way, sometimes one wins and sometimes the other, with the result that the youngster doesn't suspect they're screwing money out of him on both sides.

Since he has an overnight pass on Saturday, Mermoz takes advantage of his winnings to invite Madeleine to a restaurant he thinks elegant, where they serve a delicious trout stuffed with bacon. When she leaves half her trout uneaten, Mermoz fishes it off her plate onto his own, and empties the bottle of wine. He never gets his fill. When he asks her if she'd like dessert, she gives him a "good girl" look with those excessively painted eyes that give her a ghostly air. The dessert she's after isn't on the menu. That's served in the cats' alley, as they refer to the dark street behind the shutter factory, where they usually find someone to sell them the white powder. When they reach the Bouches-du-Rhône hostel an hour later, their eyes are shining and their blood is on fire.

Back at the base, thinking about the start of his apprenticeship makes up for everything that's happened in the past. However, the theoretical classes soon grow tedious, and the bulk of the mornings are given over to scrubbing the greasy hangar floor and repairing damage to the burnt parts of the planes which have survived the First World War. The Nieuports and the Morane-Saulniers are flying coffins. One of the duties the novice pilots have to carry out every couple of days is attendance at the burial of a student or pilot.

Finally, the first training flights with an instructor arrive, and then the day when Mermoz is to climb on his own for the first time into one of those flying coffins which have broken so many young lives. Most people would be terrified at the idea of entering one of these pieces of junk with wings and a single engine that breaks down every three or four flights, but he's happy when he finally turns the ignition key and sets his plane in motion down the tarmac.

Mermoz feels powerful. He and the plane vibrate in unison as if they were one and the same. His euphoria is extraordinary: He shouts, he laughs, he shivers.

CHAPTER 5

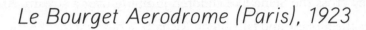

Le Bourget Aerodrome (Paris), 1923

ANTOINE DE SAINT-EXUPÉRY

THE SUNDAY DROWSINESS IN THE barracks of the 34th Regiment of the air force makes it easy for Antoine to convince young Lieutenant Richaux that they should take the Hanriot HD.14 out of the hangar.

"I'll pilot and we'll see the Seine from the air," he tells him.

"We should have entered it into the daily flight log approved by Command HQ. You're not following standard procedures."

"Regulations are what frighten me the most in this world, Richaux." Second Lieutenant Saint-Exupéry's bug eyes beseech him with a look somewhere between plaintive and seductive. "Regulations are the death of imagination."

Richaux shrugs. "It's your call."

At that, Antoine's expression switches from sadness to joy.

They walk to the robust biplane normally used for training flights. It has a wooden frame covered with fabric, two open cockpit bays, tandem-style, and the upper wing serves as a roof. Antoine gets in the back, excited by the prank, and they take off abruptly, as if they were in a hurry. They climb rapidly over the city.

Antoine laughs. He can't resist the temptation to check out the plane's versatility, making it bank and then zigzag through the air as if they were skiing among the clouds. Richaux feels his stomach contract, everything contract, but he's not going to make his flying companion happy by telling him he's scared. Antoine shouts with pleasure.

They cross the Seine like children jumping over a stream. Antoine steadies the biplane and falls silent. Richaux is puzzled that he can't hear anything from his rear companion.

"Why aren't you talking now, Saint-Ex?"

"Because I'm thinking."

"What are you thinking about?"

He gets no answer. On the way back to Le Bourget, as they approach the aerodrome to land, a cracking sound fills them with concern. They fear the worst and that's just what happens: The engine stops when they're eighty metres above the ground and there's no way to abort the landing.

Richaux screams. Antoine shrieks. The nose touches the ground and the propeller snaps off with force, the plane tips over, one of the twin wings breaks, they feel an almighty jolt amid the chaos buffeting them. Their bodies are violently battered. There's a loud bang, then grinding, the bodywork snapping, pain. Then everything dissolves into darkness and silence.

CHAPTER 6

★

Villemin Hospital (Paris), 1923

Antoine de Saint-Exupéry

The light is white and the smell antiseptic. Antoine knows, or somehow senses, that hours or days have gone by; that it's not Le Bourget; that his body isn't lying in the wreckage of the plane. He doesn't dare open his eyes. What if he were to discover that he's dead? He prefers not to know. You're not dead until you're aware of it. And if he is dead . . . will they have sent him to heaven or to hell? He can't resist his curiosity. He raises the shutters that are his eyelids and sees Charles Sallès sitting on a stool beside him.

"Sallès . . ."

"Nurse, the patient in room five has woken up."

"Where am I?"

"Where do *you* reckon?"

"If you're here, it can't be heaven. And it must be a good hell, with music and attractive girls."

"You've got it in one! Villemin Hospital isn't exactly heaven. It stinks of disinfectant! But there are some fabulous nurses, you'll see . . ."

Antoine tries to laugh but his whole body hurts as soon as it moves. He's struck by a worrying thought and suddenly becomes serious.

"And Lieutenant Richaux?"

"He'll be fine, but he'll have a sore head for a few days. He's fractured his skull."

"I'm so sorry!"

The nurse comes in and signals to Sallès to leave the room.

"The patient needs rest."

Sallès winks at his friend and nods mischievously to draw attention to the nurse's figure. She pretends she hasn't noticed and sets about checking the patient's blood pressure.

As she squeezes the bulb which inflates the armband, she looks at him, bandaged from head to toe.

"A plane crash, right?"

"A somewhat bumpy landing."

She shakes her head in disapproval.

"You're the third injured pilot I'm taking care of. I just don't understand you people. It would seem you're not worried about dying."

"Death . . . that seems to be the world's biggest concern."

"And isn't that how it should be?"

"Maybe we should concern ourselves less with death and more with life."

The nurse leaves the room shaking her head and muttering, "Pilots . . . no one can make them see sense."

The next morning, having recovered somewhat, he writes a few reassuring lines to his mother, which include some affectionate words and the odd joke so she can see he's feeling fine, and the little drawings with which he always decorates—or spoils—his letters. And as on other occasions, he ends with a promise to mend his ways, a request for some money and a plea: "Maman, love me a lot."

Antoine has suffered a concussion, multiple traumas, and bruises. But more than his ribs, it's the consequences that start to cause him real pain: He's taken a plane without permission, he's wounded a fellow officer, and he's destroyed a machine which is the property of the military. He mentally prepares his plea and writes in his head a report that will inspire his superiors to be benevolent.

He puts together a thousand and one arguments, and they all seem convincing to him despite the gravity of his offense. He's so concerned about what his squadron leader will say that he forgets that the tribunal closest to home is the one which always judges us most severely.

Marie-Papon de Vilmorin makes a dramatic entry into his room without saying a word, her nose way up in the air, and plants herself a metre from his bed, her arms crossed. She looks like Lou-Lou: She's just as tall as her sister, her eyes somewhere between green and brown, but her hair is dark rather than red and her features are more harmonious. She's beautiful, but she lacks Lou-Lou's ability to bewitch an entire tribe with a look.

An air of antagonism enters with the straight Vilmorin nose. Antoine attempts a smile through the hole in the spectacular bandage around his head, but she doesn't reciprocate. It's as if she were riding an ice floe.

"I come bearing a message from my sister."

"How is she?"

"Quite upset, thanks to you. Louise wishes to inform you that, following a conversation with my parents and my siblings, she has decided there is no way that this can happen again. If you wish to formally ask for her hand in marriage and continue with the engagement, you must abandon this absurd madness of being a pilot."

"What are you saying?"

And he sits up in bed even though he hurts all over when he moves.

"I believe I've made myself perfectly clear."

"Stop being a pilot?"

"Absolutely!"

"That's not possible!"

"What sort of serious profession is it anyway? My father says that no respectable person would dedicate himself to something like that."

"And what does Lou-Lou say?"

"I've just told you! She's the one who asked me to come and tell you! She's too upset to come herself, but she doesn't want to spend the rest of her life anguished, waiting to see if her husband will crash today or tomorrow morning."

Antoine falls silent, lost in thought.

"Either your aerial follies or my sister. You choose."

Head held high, she makes her farewell through gritted teeth and departs, leaving the swish of her dress hanging in the air behind her.

He'll have several days of convalescence in the hospital to ponder his decision. But is there actually anything to mull over? The love he feels for Lou-Lou is everything. How can he give up the love of his life?

Impossible to lose Lou-Lou . . . But can one live without flying? Is there anywhere else where it's possible to find that happiness that comes with cutting the chains that bind us to the ground and heading skyward, unburdened? That weightlessness . . .

He turns over suddenly in the bed and a shooting pain in one of his ribs reminds him that he's bruised and battered on the outside and now also broken on the inside.

How can one choose which to give up, eating or breathing?

He's angry. Not with his fiancée, because she's probably right to complain. It's more that he feels misunderstood. As far as he's concerned, flying doesn't involve any anxiety, and he doesn't even consider it particularly dangerous. Those who stay on the ground know nothing about the connections you establish up there, how much you feel master of your machine and the moment, how rock-solid you feel supported by thousands of cubic metres of air . . .

Since the first time he set eyes on Lou-Lou, he prayed constantly that she would notice him, that a miracle would happen and that divine creature would fall in love with an impoverished, ordinary character like him. He smiles with a hint of bitterness. God punishes us by listening to our most fervent pleas. Now Lou-Lou loves him so much she can't bear the idea that he might kill himself in an accident and won't allow him to climb into a plane again.

He flails around among his tangled hospital sheets as desperately and uselessly as the amputated tail of a lizard.

But his love for Louise de Vilmorin impels him upward as much as flying. Her red hair is a balloon that elevates him with her. With her by his side, life ceases to be ordinary. There's nothing to decide; the decision has been made. Lou-Lou demands him safe and sound beside her. Isn't that marvelous news? He's the luckiest man in the world! How could he possibly have felt so miserable a moment ago? Millions of men would give their right arm, maybe both arms, to be in his place. He'll stop flying and make Lou-Lou happy.

Her happiness will be my happiness . . . He tells himself again that he's very fortunate. And yet, huge tears fall from his eyes.

CHAPTER 7

★

Bourlon Tile Factory (Paris), 1923

ANTOINE DE SAINT-EXUPÉRY

A PILE OF YELLOW FOLDERS sits on top of the table. The window of the office where Antoine works, in a section with three other book-keepers, overlooks an inner courtyard. Accustomed to seeing the world from a height of 3,000 metres, to Antoine this tiny window doesn't seem to look out over anything much. When he leans out of his office build-ing he sees another identical building in front of him. The city is a set of identical dominoes.

He reflects on the days after his departure from the hospital. It would have been easier if they'd discharged him from the army for tak-ing out a plane he wasn't entitled to fly. But they informed him that his punishment was two weeks' detention. The lightest possible punish-ment, little more than a friendly scolding.

He can't rid himself of the confused expression on his commander's face when Antoine told him he was leaving the army.

"Have you become frightened after the accident?"

"Definitely not, Major!"

"But you're crazy about flying . . . perhaps excessively so."

"Yes, sir."

"So are you no longer interested in flying?"

"No, sir. Nothing would make me happier than to climb into a plane right now and take off."

"I've got it! You've found work as a civil pilot with a better salary."

"No, sir."

"Well what, then?"

He remembers how he blushed as he replied. "I'm in love with a woman whom I'm going to marry. I can't love two things at once."

The following weeks had been strange. The doctor said that it couldn't be because of the bruises and the crack in his rib, but there was still no question he was having difficulty walking; he could hardly lift his legs. It was as if a strange gravitational force had trapped him and prevented him from lifting his feet.

He'd been forced to ask his mother for help because he was running out of money. In fact, he decided to accept the invitation of Yvonne de Lestrange, his mother's cousin, whom he calls his aunt, to move into her house to save himself the expense of renting a room.

Lou-Lou, by comparison, had been radiant, and her joy was his. She'd spend the day imagining the house they would live in one day, which she pictured as a sort of castle with the latest in art deco furniture and an attic where they would organise poetry readings. She would get irritated when she asked him if he'd prefer silk or cloth curtains and he'd answer without giving it any thought.

Throughout those weeks, he'd had to put up with a certain hostility from some of the Vilmorin siblings. He got wind of the fact that they called him "the lazy pachyderm." His future mother-in-law suspected he was a fortune hunter who wanted to live off the Vilmorins. So finding a job became a necessity that tormented him.

Lou-Lou had gone away for a few weeks' holiday. Thanks to his mother's efforts and the money he'd made from the sale of a Kodak camera, he'd paid for a ticket to spend a few days in Geneva with her . . . and Madame Petermann.

He'd travelled to Switzerland with a suitcase full of poems he was writing to her. They were all passionate, some more tender, others more brazen, perhaps even slightly erotic.

Eventually, a well-connected friend of the Vilmorin family had found him a job paying 800 francs a month in the office of a tile manufacturing company.

So he now has a folder full of invoices open on his desk. He looks at it closely, but lists of numbers exhaust him. The fives look like arrogant, fat men and the ones like skinny, conceited men. Without realising it, instead of ticking off the inventory, he sketches little drawings in the corners of the paper: first a tree, then a snake, and then, in the blank section at the very top of the page, a cloud. That's where things get complicated. Clouds are the most difficult things to draw. Not everyone can do it. He considers this to be a serious matter that only children have managed to solve. They draw clouds that look like the soft, woolly coat of a lamb.

He tries to imitate the children. The cumulonimbus clouds float on the top part of the page. Then he pauses to consider his work and smiles. The vertical strings of figures have stopped being numbers and have turned into rain falling torrentially from the clouds. At the bottom, he draws a field of flowers.

The head of the department, a man always dressed in a black suit who converts every day into a funeral, enters Antoine's tiny office slightly dragging one leg locked by osteoarthritis in the knee. He walks to the desk carrying folders that seem to weigh as much as tombstones. Initially he looks pleased to see Antoine concentrating on his work, but suddenly he's on the verge of losing the folders and even his grey hair.

"What are you doing?" he asks with alarm.

"What are you referring to, Monsieur Charron?" Antoine replies with a naïveté that rocks the old accountant.

"You can't cover those inventories with doodles!"

Antoine pulls his head into his shoulders like a tortoise. The boss doesn't know if this new employee, recommended despite demonstrating no sign of an accounting background, is pulling his leg. He can't understand these spoiled young people with no interest in working . . . They want everything handed to them on a plate! But he holds back from saying this because his new employee's recommendation comes from an important client, a very respectable person. People with money always seem respectable to Monsieur Charron.

"Stop making a mess of the inventories or I'll have to report your behavior. This is a serious company. Numbers are important—they represent money and you can't play with that. Check the sums, tally the numbers. If you want to become someone in this company, you have to be responsible."

The head accountant, a man who has left the best years of his life among the dust of filing cabinets, limps off. Antoine, puzzled, watches him leave.

Numbers definitely strike Antoine as a game for financiers, while rain is definitely serious and important. He gazes wistfully at the inventory. He rubs out the drawings until all that's left is a dirty shadow, and makes his way into the desert of numbers.

There's a surprise waiting for him outside at five o'clock, when work is over. Lou-Lou, much recovered these past few weeks, or perhaps tired of her role as the lady of pain, is waiting for him on Rue du Faubourg Saint-Honoré together with Madame Petermann, of whom he refers behind her back as "frozen face."

Lou-Lou waves to him and he shakes off the feeling of failure. He plants himself in front of her and takes her hands. He makes a move to brush his face against her cheek, but Madame Petermann stretches her neck and emits a bulldog-like growl. Laughing, the young couple sets off, a few paces in front of her. They go as far as Place Montholon, where there is a spacious garden area with linden and cherry trees dominated by two enormous oriental plane trees.

In his mind's eye Antoine can still see the moment, a few weeks earlier, when he formally asked for Lou-Lou's hand in marriage. His mother had sent him an antique piece of family jewellery from Saint-Maurice which had survived various pawnshops and other catastrophes: a ring with two modest little diamonds, in need of a new setting. He recalls how the Vilmorins examined the ring every which way with the earnestness of professional jewellers, which struck him as crass. Their reluctant approval made it crystal clear, in case there might be any doubt, that they consider the Saint-Exupérys to be aristocrats very much down on their luck. And he hasn't told them that his mother, a real countess, has to work as a nurse in the regional hospital to support herself. There's absolutely no way he wants them to speak of his mother in a condescending manner.

Lou-Lou, on the other hand, accepted the ring full of joy. She immediately put it on her finger and held out her hand very theatrically as if she felt favoured by it. If she thought it wasn't grand enough she never let it show. And he loved her more than ever. Lou-Lou's voice drags him from his thoughts.

"You're happy with your new work, aren't you? It was very kind of Monsieur Daniel-Vincent to recommend you for the position. They'll make you section head in no time, you'll see."

He agrees, with little enthusiasm. It irritates him that he only got the job thanks to the recommendation from a friend of the Vilmorin family.

"Aren't you comfortable there? Aren't they good to you? I can have a word with Monsieur Daniel-Vincent."

"Don't even think about it! They treat me very well in the company. They're friendly and patient with my ineptitude. It's just that . . ."

"Do you have a nice office? Maybe that's why you're not feeling comfortable. What if we were to buy a plant? Or better yet, a cage with one of those multicoloured tropical birds."

"I don't think my boss would be pleased if I had a bird. He wouldn't find it serious enough."

"I'll convince him. It's important to be surrounded by beauty."

"My office is two metres by two metres. I guess Monsieur Charron would say that it's a serious office."

"But you told me you had a window."

"True, but when I lean out of it, what I see is the back of another office block identical to mine, and an office clerk identical to me. I don't know if it's a window or a mirror."

"A mirror?"

"I hate mirrors! They're incapable of inventing anything."

"They do also show us who we are."

"Mirrors are the executioners of fantasy. If I were the president of France, I'd ban mirrors in public spaces."

"You're mad, Antoine! You don't want to see the truth."

"The truth is hardly useful for anything. It's sad. We have to invent something that's better than the truth."

"Lies?"

"Perhaps . . ."

"Lies are better than the truth?"

"They're more human. Truth is what we can't change. Truth is death! We die, nothing can change that, it's been imposed on us. Lies, on the other hand, we can construct to suit ourselves."

"I prefer poetry's truth, Antoine."

She grasps his hands and Madame Petermann's cough can be heard from behind them.

Lou-Lou talks to him about the house she'd like them to have once they're married, one with enormous balconies and a metal railing, as is the current fashion, with very thin, almost see-through curtains which will flutter when stirred by the wind. Antoine laughs.

"You don't want a house, you want a yacht!" But her chatter lifts his spirits.

CHAPTER 8

★

Palmyra (Syria), 1922

JEAN MERMOZ

A PLANE APPROACHES THE ASPHALT landing strip dusted with sand. Nobody sweeps the runways here. It's ridiculous to contemplate the sight of a veteran with a broom as if he were a house-proud home-maker. They're all veterans in Syria, from the moment they set foot on this base in the middle of the desert.

The crosswind is strong; the plane sways and zigzags over the land-ing strip, on the verge of overrunning it and overturning. The pilot, a sergeant wearing a uniform adorned with a garish yellow neckerchief, climbs out of the cockpit gesticulating and yelling.

It's an emergency, but it has nothing to do with the forced landing he's just performed, because that's pure routine.

"Am I in time for the game?"

There's a game of poker in the pilots' room. And it's serious. As the commanding officer sent round an order forbidding the playing of cards for money, they bet with bottles of wine. When the sergeant comes in, the smoke is so thick you could cut it with a knife and spread it on a slice of bread.

"The visibility in here is worse than in a sandstorm!"

Mermoz greets him from behind a row of wine bottles, some of them empty. He's starting his military duties the next day, so he decides to retire from the game and give up his spot to the recently arrived sergeant. He leaves the room clutching six bottles of wine and once outside, tosses bottles to his comrades as he walks past, which they have to catch in midair.

"Drink to my health!"

He ends up handing out all of them.

As soon as he passed his pilot's exam in Istres, Mermoz went to the base office and asked for a transfer to Syria as a volunteer. A sergeant handed him a form to fill out and sign. One of the boxes asked why the request was being made. There were several blank lines for his response, but he summarised his reason in two words: "to fly."

In Palmyra, Mermoz has finally managed to satisfy his hunger for flying. When he takes off in the plane, he feels that things are sorted. He flies with a sleepy mechanic sitting in front of him, but he's in charge of the plane's controls. There's nothing else in the world, nobody else to please, nobody else to obey, nobody else to hate. Flying is complete in itself, perfect, nothing more is needed, nothing is missing. He flies low over the desert and looks down at his shadow projected onto the sand. *That is me.*

CHAPTER 9

★

Bourlon Tile Factory (Paris), 1923

ANTOINE DE SAINT-EXUPÉRY

IN HIS CLOSET-SIZED OFFICE, ANTOINE anxiously watches the clock on the wall. Its second hand advances slowly, limping exactly like Monsieur Charron. It takes a year to tick round one minute. It takes a thousand years to get to five o'clock.

Lou-Lou is waiting for him, accompanied by her brother Olivier and several friends. They walk to Boulevard Saint-Germain and all happily squeeze together around a table in the Brasserie Lipp, a colourful art nouveau establishment. The ceilings are decorated with themes from mythology and the lamps above their heads have shades like fluttering butterflies. The waiter, whom they know, brings a tray on which there is a jug of water with lemon slices and another with Alsatian wine.

Antoine loves Chez Lipp with its hustle and bustle, its Hapsburg sausages, and its beer topped with thick foam, served in glasses as big as trophies.

"Bring us some marinated herring!" orders Henri.

"And sausages with sauerkraut!" suggests Olivier.

"With double sauerkraut!" adds Antoine.

"We have to talk," Lou-Lou whispers in his ear.

"Yes, yes. But first we have to drink a toast, right, Bertrand?"

"And what are we toasting?"

"We're toasting that today is today."

"Just that?"

"That seems little to you, Henri? It's the most extraordinary thing. Nothing is better than this moment right now."

"A toast!"

Antoine urges everyone to fill their glasses.

"Come on; hurry up! We can't waste a second! This moment, everyone together around this table, is priceless! Let's not waste the smallest portion of it!"

Henri nudges him with his elbow and points with his chin at the waiter.

"Have you seen his hair?"

"What's wrong with it?"

"Look carefully! He's drawn rows of hair with charcoal on his bare patch to cover it up."

"That really is a bald attempt at being an artist!"

They roar with laughter. Henri has tears in his eyes, and Bertrand is on the verge of spilling his wine on his sister, Renée de Saussine.

Antoine glances at Lou-Lou out of the corner of his eye and sees her slowly lighting one of her Craven "A" cigarettes. She has a way of lighting cigarettes that reminds him of modern-day film actresses, only she does it much better. Actresses imitate gestures; Lou-Lou invents them.

She looks at him, stands up carefully because of her delicate hip, and heads outside limping slightly. She has a hypnotic way of moving.

Outdoors, with the end of summer, the night is fresh, and people are strolling along the boulevard with birdlike abandon.

"Antoine . . ."

"I've always been intrigued as to where the people we see passing by are actually going. They pass in front of our lives momentarily and then disappear. Where do you think, Lou-Lou?"

"I've no idea . . ."

"They know nothing about us. Doesn't that seem incredible to you?"

"Antoine . . ."

"If we were to die right now, they wouldn't even be aware of it."

"Antoine, the doctors don't think I've recovered fully from my hip condition. We should delay the wedding."

"Delay?"

"Postpone it."

"The most important thing is your health, of course. Delay it by how much? Two months? Three?"

She inhales so deeply on her English cigarette that it burns right down.

"I don't know . . ."

Lou-Lou is staring fixedly at some point at the end of the boulevard, but in reality, she's only staring into the depths of the night. Antoine realises that she doesn't want to look him in the eye, and his chest fills with broken glass.

What does she mean by "I don't know"? Shouldn't she have said that the doctors "don't know"? And the way she said it, it sounded as if the delay were a relief.

He's thinking all this as she lights another cigarette in silence. He doesn't dare open his mouth. If he formulates the fateful question— "Are you unsure about wanting to marry me?"—it might summon an answer he definitely does not want to hear. Not only does he remain silent, but he presses his lips together tightly, because if you open the door the cat will get out.

The two of them go back inside in silence. Antoine looks at the mirrors at the back of the room and sees himself, Lou-Lou, and the others as if he were seeing them from the outside. A group of happy, well-dressed young people talking incoherently and drinking wine from crystal glasses.

Who are they?

They bring him the Grand Marnier mille-feuille he's crazy about and he doesn't even look at it. That happy "today" they were toasting just a few minutes ago has vanished. He has no idea why people have a stupid obsession with dreaming about the future: He would give everything to have stopped time just a few minutes earlier and stayed living forever in a present where Lou-Lou was laughing, in a time where she hadn't said "I don't know."

CHAPTER 10

Bourlon Tile Factory (Paris), 1923

ANTOINE DE SAINT-EXUPÉRY

IN THE TILE FACTORY, ANTOINE has found a use for the inaccurate invoices that are going to be thrown out: making paper planes out of them. He already has an entire squadron in his desk drawer.

Lou-Lou has been very busy these past weeks with her music studies and physiotherapy classes. He's burning with desire to see her, but she's always busy. It's been days since he's laid eyes on her, and one of his friends tells him he's seen her with her crowd in the conservatory cafeteria and shopping in the Galeries Lafayette.

One autumn afternoon, he returns to his aunt's house as down in the mouth as the cigarette dangling from his lips. His aunt takes him by the arm and tells him she's going to introduce him to some guests. He doesn't feel like taking part in a social function, but Yvonne doesn't give him a chance to say no.

In the small salon, she walks him over to a group of men talking quite animatedly. One of them is a young publisher called Gaston

Gallimard, who's all the rage. Another is the writer André Gide, man of the moment, who amazes with his prose and scandalises with his open homosexuality. Antoine feels inhibited in the company of strangers and doesn't open his mouth. Gallimard, the publisher, accepts a glass of cognac and throws friendly gibes at Gide.

Just then, a guest who wants to be unconventional arrives fashionably late wearing a bow tie and, in his desire to be outlandish, enters the salon without removing his very tall hat. When the members of the social circle turn toward him, he doffs his hat and performs a flamboyant bow. Yvonne welcomes him and he again removes his hat in a theatrical manner. Gide and Gallimard are still deeply involved in their conversation, and the newly arrived guest, a writer who has achieved some success with his melodramatic short stories, seems put out because they haven't paid him the attention he deserves.

"And who are you, young man?" he asks Antoine.

"I'm Yvonne's nephew . . ."

"You must know who I am."

"Of course!"

"Next time I'll bring you a dedicated book."

"And how do you know which of your books I'll like?"

"You'll like all of them."

Yvonne returns just then to serve the new guest some tea. He makes her sit down beside him and, without any prompting, begins to talk to her enthusiastically about his new book. Antoine looks at him as if he were from another planet: The writer doesn't touch his tea or the tray of cakes and pastries; his sustenance is admiration. So, while the writer fills himself with the air he swallows as he speaks, Antoine stuffs himself with brioches. As far as he's concerned, poetry lies elsewhere.

*   *   *

Throughout the anxious weeks that follow, one way for Antoine to stop thinking about Lou-Lou's lack of replies to his messages is to write energetically: to conjure her up on sheets of paper from which she'll emerge like a handsome genie who comes out of the lamp and concedes all your wishes.

Throughout those days, he focuses all his effort into producing poetry with his fingers, but he only manages to put together a magnificent collection of crossings-out.

He also spends time thinking about his past flights and wonders if he could perhaps re-create them through writing. It does, however, require real effort to pin down that sensation of flight on paper. Words are not as light as they seem; they bear the weight of the ink drops. It's hard to make them take to the air. In the odd fleeting moment when his hand moves by itself, he senses the secret of writing: it's like dipping a bucket into a remote well in the middle of the desert and extracting water.

But he lacks the concentration to write. He gets up from his chair almost immediately and starts to pace back and forth. He goes down to the street and walks around the block. On one such afternoon as he's walking in front of a toy shop window, he sees an electric train going round and round in an eternal circle and thinks to himself: *That's me.* A few days ago, he managed to speak to Lou-Lou for a minute on the phone, but she couldn't talk anymore because she was in a great hurry—it was time for her tennis lesson. Whenever Antoine suggests that they meet, she replies cheerfully that they must, but that right now she has to rush off to one thing or another: a fundraising raffle, afternoon tea at an elegant house, a singing lesson, her family's box at the opera . . . He knows that Lou-Lou has to go hither and yon without spending much time anywhere, so that nothing will wither. She plays hide and seek with him all over Paris.

One afternoon, after several days with no news of her, he arrives at Rue de la Chaise without warning. He's the young lady's fiancé, but when he asks for Louise, the butler still asks disdainfully on whose behalf. It seems to Antoine that everything in this house conspires against him.

The butler informs him that Mademoiselle de Vilmorin is travelling and has left a letter for him. He doesn't want his face to show his astonishment so he makes a superhuman effort not to move a single muscle that would betray his anxiety. As soon as he's back on the street and around the corner, he hurriedly tears open the envelope.

The slightly inclined handwriting tells him that she has had to leave urgently for Biarritz to be close to her grandmother, who is indisposed. She'll undoubtedly spend some time there. *This will give us time to sort out our feelings,* she informs him.

Sort out our feelings . . .

He has to lean against the wall. He feels dizzy. He asks himself if feelings can be sorted, like a pile of linen in a cupboard.

His legs are wobbly. He walks home as if he were drunk.

Lou-Lou needs weeks to know what she's feeling. I only need a second to know that I'm madly in love with her!

He tugs nervously at his hair, but banishes the bad omens: *My love for her is so great that it will cover both of us.*

It takes him three nights of insomnia to write her an adequate reply. The scrunched-up balls of rejected sheets of paper form a mountain on the floor of his room. He wants to tell her how much he loves her, but he doesn't want to suffocate her. He knows that Lou-Lou needs space, nothing must contain her. He doesn't want to convey a sense of despondency because he doesn't want her to think that he's blaming her for his dejection. But at the same time, he doesn't want to feign an artificial happiness that will give the impression that her absence doesn't matter to him. He writes and he rips up, he writes and he rips up. Composing a letter is more difficult than writing a poem: With poetry, feelings influence the words; in this crucial letter, the words must carry his feelings through the air, hoist them up a mountain path like porters climbing Everest.

His Aunt Yvonne has already become accustomed to his habit of rushing like a wild boar to the little table where the mail is deposited and scrabbling through the letters as soon as he gets home from the office. For days, the wild boar retreats to his room downcast.

Finally, Lou-Lou's reply arrives and he races upstairs with the letter. He sighs before tearing it open: His happiness or misfortune lies within. He's expecting either something good or something bad, a yes or a no. What he receives, however, leaves him even more confused than he was: She talks about the weather in Biarritz; a trail dug out in the rocks beyond the beach, where the waves crash on stormy days; a book by Rimbaud she's finding fascinating; afternoon conversation sessions organised with neighbours and people from good families in the area; and horror stories told by a Romanian maid. There's not a word about their relationship. And she ends her letter with a neutral "Yours affectionately."

And the days go on like this, waiting for letters that don't come or which merely bring notes on local customs and manners and avoid the essential, crucial matter. Weeks become months and his initial nervousness is turning into melancholy. The squadron of paper planes has multiplied. The Bourlon Tile Factory invoices have never travelled to the filing cabinet so full of doodles.

Christmas is approaching and Antoine decides he has to go to Biarritz. He must assault the castle and rescue the princess. It's now or never.

He already knows the Vilmorins are difficult, and if he asks if it's appropriate for him to come and visit the family bastion, it might result in some kind of resistance. So he gives Lou-Lou just twenty-four hours' notice via a telegram, so the family can't dissuade him: MISS YOU. ARRIVE TOMORROW SUNDAY TEATIME TO SPEND AFTERNOON WITH YOU. ANTOINE.

He travels for many hours on a train that takes him slowly from Paris heading for the western Pyrenees, and stops at the Midi station in downtown Biarritz. He thinks how simple it would have been to fly. He smiles as he pictures the commotion he'd create if he suddenly landed in the garden of Grandmother Vilmorin's house. He half closes his eyes and he's flying, with Lou-Lou in the front seat of the cockpit, allowing the wind to whip her red hair every which way, with that fluffy gentleness of which dreams are made.

He's dragged from his thoughts by a murmur. A woman has sat down in the seats across the aisle with her five children. One of them tries to follow the trees with his eyes as they go past.

"Why are the trees running, Maman?"

"They're not running. We're the ones who are running."

"But they seem to be the ones running!" exclaims one of his brothers.

"Trees have roots and can't move. It's impossible for them to run. If your eyes tell you the trees are running, ignore your eyes."

The children nod. They understand.

Antoine smiles. That mother is Einstein. Physicists have begun to realise in this modern twentieth century what poets and children have always known: You can't see what's really important with your eyes. There'll come a day when, without realising it, physicists will be poets.

Summer holiday destinations like Biarritz have a drowsy air in winter. Closed restaurants and shuttered holiday houses transmit a nostalgia for the brilliant bustling days that have disappeared. Lou-Lou's grandmother's home is a mansion on the outskirts of town surrounded by a high stone wall covered with ivy, like Antoine's childhood home.

The young servant girl wearing a white cap bars his entrance but informs him that they're expecting him. In his imagination he thought he'd find Lou-Lou in the middle of the garden, alone, sitting sadly in front of a small white iron table bearing a teapot and two cups, and perhaps a book of Rimbaud's poetry.

Tea, in fact, is not being served in the garden but in a sumptuous salon with an empty fireplace and huge hunting pictures crowded with deer and gentlemen in red riding coats. Lou-Lou isn't alone; it seems to Antoine that there's a crowd—half a dozen people casually chatting. Rimbaud isn't present. Lou-Lou, in the middle of the group, is eating a Danish biscuit and gesticulating dramatically as she dominates the conversation in her lively way.

When Antoine enters the room, the conversation stops, and she gets up to welcome him. He gets the impression that these ladies and gentlemen greet him with scant enthusiasm. They make space for him near Lou-Lou and all eyes are on him.

"How are things in Paris? Any interesting premières?" Lou-Lou asks him.

"I haven't been going out much recently . . ."

Given Antoine's halting words, a young gentleman with an impeccably trimmed goatee, who introduces himself with a title Antoine forgets a moment later, begins to speak enthusiastically.

"What you can't miss is *Les Misérables* at La Pleiade. It's superb."

They are all very interested and ask the gentleman for details. And knowing that he's the centre of attention, he tells them all about the play in a witty manner and they all offer high praise for his explanations. Antoine finds it insufferably snobbish that he should comment on a work by calling it "superb." He looks at Lou-Lou and she wades in with a commentary of her own about an exhibition or an opera, and they all start talking animatedly because they've all been everywhere and seen everything. He's sitting in the middle of the group, and the words and conversations go back and forth around him without him being able to trap a single one. No loneliness seems as overwhelming to him as the one he feels sitting in the middle of these people. He misses the train that brought him from Paris, rocking him in a compartment where he could curl up and dream of his preferred encounter with Lou-Lou in the garden.

Lou-Lou tries to bring him into the conversation and asks him about topics that might interest her friends: Has any new restaurant opened? Are there any rumours about the announcement of municipal elections? Does he know any details of the scandalous divorce of the Duke and Duchess of Luchon? But he doesn't know anything. All he could tell them about are the filing cabinets in a tile factory and poems turned into balls of paper. He tries to make his frugality polite but he disguises his discomfort badly and ends up falling silent. Words don't come to his mouth; they aren't there, he can't find them. He wouldn't need words to tell Lou-Lou what he feels: He'd just have to pull down the zipper on his chest and show her his swollen heart, beating for her. But he feels caught in the trap of this elegant salon full of talkative people. He takes a sip of tea and it tastes likes moss.

The return train departs at seven, an overnight express which will leave him with just enough time to go from the station to his office the following morning, without even stopping off at home. He's thinking about this, when the conversation turns to the recent opening of a play by Pirandello.

"It was sensational," notes a woman sitting in one corner of the three-seater couch.

"Yes," the young man with the goatee backs her up. "Pirandello's works are pure philosophy."

At this, Antoine emerges from his reverie and springs up unexpectedly. His cheeks are red and he says loudly: "Pirandello practises the metaphysics of a doorman."

His angry outburst produces a silence. Those present cast a prejudiced eye over this heavily built stranger with a face as red as a watermelon, but nobody says a word. He waits for someone to rebut him; he can't bear it that people put playwrights like Pirandello—whom he considers skilled entertainers—on the same level as men and women of letters who search to unravel the meaning of life. Someone takes a sip of tea. Lou-Lou looks at him with an expression of total indifference.

"If you'd said Ibsen," he said wildly, "now there's an author who writes to make people understand what they didn't want to understand! But Pirandello?"

Antoine leaves his question dangling in the air and turns his head from one side of the group to the other, but no one replies to his vehemence and all remain fashionably silent. Amid the silence, broken only by the clink of teaspoons against china, he realises that in these gatherings it's bad manners to raise your voice or to contradict people strongly. Suddenly, standing in the middle of a ring of people who pretend to be concentrating on their cups of tea, Antoine feels ridiculous.

"Forgive my vehemence," he whispers as he collapses back into his armchair, glancing at Lou-Lou out of the corner of his eye. "Please forgive me. I don't know how to let things wash over me."

The only reaction he receives in reply is the odd, forced, polite half smile.

"My train actually leaves shortly. So I'll stop being a bother." He turns toward Lou-Lou. "Lou—Louise, will you see me out?"

Her gesture is equivocal.

"I'll be right back," she tells her guests.

They head for the garden where the Atlantic night is cooling Biarritz. *Alone at last!* Antoine had so many phrases ready to say to her. He'd gone over his most ingenious sentences for hours in the train—he wanted to show himself to be the most seductive man in the world. But now he feels he's in a bad mood after this excruciating afternoon, and he's been hurt by her, because she clearly doesn't reciprocate his love with the same zeal. Lou-Lou stops on the porch, her face and voice as cold as the night air.

"What's the matter with you, Antoine? Why are you behaving in such an absurd manner?"

"I don't like these people."

"You don't like them? They're my friends! You could have been more pleasant. The Count and Countess of Montluçon are the owners of the most important steel industry in the region, Monsieur Calmette is a government lawyer and it's rumoured he might be a minister soon . . ."

"Minister . . ."

"Yes! Minister of Justice!"

"Do you know something? When I was travelling here, a woman boarded the train with five children. I'm sure she didn't have any titles or property, but she was teaching her children, and me, very important things. Well-to-do people have never taught me anything."

"You're so intolerant . . ."

"It's true that I'm not tolerant! Tolerance offends me! I don't have the frivolity of your friends, which would allow me to treat everything like a game."

"You're certainly turning out to be disagreeable . . ."

"I'm an unpleasant type, that's true! Agreeable people, like that peacock with the goatee who makes a few superficial comments and believes he's very intellectual, really get on my nerves."

"Everything gets on your nerves . . ."

"Why didn't you keep the afternoon free for just the two of us?"

"You didn't even have the delicacy to ask me if I already had something arranged for this afternoon."

"I've come specially from Paris! I've travelled seven hundred kilometres to see you."

"I'm sorry you've come so far, but I didn't ask you to do it."

What's worst of all is that Lou-Lou doesn't even say this to him angrily, as if at heart, she doesn't care what he does or doesn't do. And that irritates him even more.

"I thought we needed to talk, right? You and I are engaged, or had you forgotten that, what with so many get-togethers with would-be ministers?"

"Have you travelled so many kilometres just to bring reproaches?"

And she looks at him again with those bewitching, penetrating eyes. He drops his head, like a child being scolded. He realises he's put his foot in it yet again. His rage deserts him and all of him deflates like a burst balloon.

"Lou-Lou, forgive me, please. I'm the most ridiculous person in the world. I'm sorry, I'm really sorry. I had no intention of being rude; it's just that these months away from you have been agony."

At that, she looks at him and for the first time for as long as he's known her, he sees her becoming really serious.

"And yet, you know nothing of my suffering."

"Lou-Lou . . ."

"Our relationship is no longer possible."

"But why?"

"Nothing is ever perfect for you unless it's exactly as you've thought it was going to be."

"I'll change! I swear! I'll like everything; your friends will delight me. I'll love Pirandello!"

"It can't be."

"Why not? I love you madly!"

"That's not true."

"How can you say that. Every fibre of my being is in love with you!"

"No, Antoine, you're not in love with me. You're in love with the idea you have of me. You're in love with the Lou-Lou you've created in your imagination. A moment ago, when I was sitting chatting and you didn't think I was paying attention to you, I noticed you were looking at me resentfully. Just at that moment, I wasn't who you wanted me to be. But I'm like them too: I can be frivolous, I like to have amusing friends, talk about opening nights at the theatre, fashion and décor . . ."

"I'll be delighted by fashion! I'll become a friend of your friends! I'll go back inside and apologise to them one by one. I'll do card tricks to entertain them!"

"Impossible . . ."

"I'll change! I'll never get angry, I promise! I'll be an ideal husband!"

Then Lou-Lou gives a brief laugh that sounds like a cough.

"But the point is that I don't want to be an ideal wife . . . I can't imagine anything more boring!"

Antoine's countenance changes.

"Marrying me strikes you as boring?" he asks her angrily.

Lou-Lou sighs. She looks him up and down with barely disguised weariness.

"Right now, it would strike me as truly boring."

Her tone is cutting; it hurts. Sugar has become salt. Gold has turned into sand. He nods and lowers his head. Lou-Lou's magic made him appear to be a prince, but the spell is broken and he's back to being the frog with bulging eyes he's always been.

Lou-Lou turns on her heel and goes back inside the house to her world of shining lights. He no longer knows which is his world. He wishes he really were a frog, because then he'd at least be able to stay in the pond and see her strolling through the garden at dusk. But his is another pond, constructed from invoices and tedium in a tile factory.

CHAPTER 11

★

Palmyra (Syria), 1923

Jean Mermoz

Following a plane crash and the subsequent rescue of both him and his injured mechanic after three days and nights trudging through the desert, Mermoz has been promoted to sergeant. And he's been given a posting normally reserved for a hardened veteran. Taking charge of medical flights is one of those challenges that, to him, are like the air he breathes. But a responsibility, too. There are only two doctors to service an area that covers thousands of square kilometres and he's the pilot who flies them back and forth, transferring patients who require hospitalisation in Damascus and supplying medication to those who need it. The work is draining. He can't remember the last time he slept five hours straight. But who wants to sleep?

Turbulence suddenly buffets his plane, and a moan of pain emerges from the rear section. He took off before dawn to transport a woman crushed by a camel. She has multiple broken bones and infected wounds, and requires urgent surgery. He can't risk further turbulence so he flies above the clouds even though it's dangerous and contravenes regulations. At that height, the compass is his only means of orientation and there can be deviations of many kilometres, which may lead to getting lost. But Mermoz has already spent so many hours flying these skies he feels he recognises every pocket of air.

As soon as he lands, the stretcher bearers rush toward the plane. Mermoz whistles at one of the airport employees and gestures urgently for him to come over with the fuel hose.

"What's the rush?"

"I have to go back to pick up the doctor who was left behind because there was no room for him in the plane. Or are *you* going to operate on this woman?"

"But aren't you even going to have some tea?"

"I'll have kerosene. Hurry up, I haven't got all day!"

When he gets back to the Palmyra base, mission accomplished, the sun is setting. He walks in front of the base tents like an automaton and his head feels as if it's about to explode. He should get some sleep, because in eight hours' time he's back on duty, but his headache is growing in intensity. He goes inside his tent and the Moorish rugs seem grotesque. Too nervous to sleep, he barely manages to nap for a few hours, and when he wakes up, he feels worn out, completely exhausted.

He puts his hand in his trouser pocket and takes out a small bag he bought in the Damascus bazaar with money he won in an illegal game of poker. The white powder.

He knows it could be the cocaine which is producing his mood slumps, but it's also what allows him to maintain his tempo. Another intense day awaits him tomorrow and he can't falter. He lays out a long line and inhales it down to the last speck.

After a breakfast of four eggs scrambled and a baguette, he feels euphoric.

"Let's go, go, go!" he shouts at the mechanics. "There's a mission to complete."

On his way back to the aerodrome at nightfall, he notices an excessive shaking when he takes hold of the joystick to turn toward the southeast. He checks the engine output; the revolutions are constant. He removes his hand from the controls; it's his hand that's shaking.

The eighty kilometres back to base seem eternal; he tries to stop the twitchy movements but he can't. His descent prior to landing is somewhat abrupt and the plane lurches in the air. He swears angrily. He loathes making errors and his shaking hands make him an unreliable pilot.

One of the ground crew comes over to joke with him. He's picked a bad moment.

"Don't you have any work? Take care of your own business!"

His companions are puzzled because he's usually entertaining and talkative. He shuts himself away inside his tent and holds his hand out flat: It's shaking. He smashes the hand against a low wooden table, which breaks. His hand aches from the blow but obstinately continues to shake. He rummages inside a baked clay jar and removes from its hiding place a bag of cocaine which still contains a generous snort.

He walks outside the camp perimeter, giving a desultory salute as he goes past the guard post. A few steps farther on, the desert swallows him up. He walks down a dune and, once out of sight of the sentries, takes out the little bag and looks at it. He doesn't need this fine powder to be Jean Mermoz. With all his might, he throws it as far away as he can.

He returns to the base and shuts himself away in his tent. He looks at his right hand; it's bleeding slightly and feels sizzling hot. He curls up on his pallet and, unusual for him, feels cold. He sleeps a few hours but suddenly he's awake and can't get back to sleep. He's shaken by a sudden anxiety and feels an unpleasant dizziness inside, as if a bottomless pit has opened up somewhere in his body. Everything is turning to ice inside him; the bed is rocking as if he were sleeping in the cabin of a boat caught in the middle of heavy seas. He grabs the edges of the mattress because he feels he's falling, and he holds back the urge to shout. Withdrawal symptoms overwhelm him savagely with their whirlwind twists and turns toward a drain down which his sanity is sliding.

He gets out of bed at daybreak and quickly dresses. He can't bear it any longer. The guard on sentry duty looks puzzled as Mermoz leaves the base headed for the desert. He thinks the dune in question is the first one on the left, although the wind shifts everything around. He calculates where he threw the bag and, urged on by his shakes, squats down to search for it. He crawls over the sand, digging with his hands and coming up empty again and again. When the wind picks up, he stops briefly, sweaty and panting. He opens his mouth and it fills with sand; he grits his teeth and it makes a grinding sound as he chews. Suddenly, he sees a silhouette on the ground. It's his own shadow, but it could be that of an animal sniffing the ground. He pounds the sand with his hands in despair.

What am I doing down here on all fours like a rat? I am a rat.

He stretches out a hand and holds it level. It shakes, and having hit the table with it, it's also swollen and bruised like that rotten tree trunk being carried down the Seine by the current. And that's not going to continue, it's definitely not going to happen. He stands up and, finally, shouts with all his might. It's a shout with no specific words, but which says it all: the stress of the past few weeks, his pride in being a pilot, his fear of fear, the frustration of seeing himself transformed into a puppet by cocaine. The desert wind carries off that interminable scream. He's a bit calmer afterward and finally feels exhaustion, a blessed weariness after so many hours of agitation, anxiety, and anguish.

He recalls the dirty look from the sinister character who used to sell him the powder in the narrow cats' alley in Istres. One night, Mermoz told him it was the last time, and the man laughed, spraying him with saliva: They all come back, he replied. Not Mermoz.

I won't return, you damned son of a bitch!

He'll never drag himself over the ground again, not for a bag of drugs, not for anything or anyone.

Never . . .

He clenches his fists and his own rage prevails over the cold and the dizziness. He walks back to the base. The guard sees Mermoz returning dirty and covered with sand, but there's such dignity in his upright walk, head held high, that the sentry doesn't dare address him beyond coming to attention and giving him a military salute. Everyone admires Mermoz, the iron sergeant; they don't know that inside he's shaking. Mermoz returns the salute and strides resolutely to his tent. Someone walking past him thinks he hears Mermoz mutter, "I won't return."

He collapses on his bed and starts to sweat. The trembling extends to his whole body. A friend who enters his tent is alarmed at the sight of him shaking with violent convulsions and goes in search of one of the doctors. The medical captain thinks it's epilepsy and injects him with enough tranquillizers to put an entire army to sleep.

When Mermoz wakes up the next morning, it feels as if there's an octopus inside his brain squeezing his head with its gelatinous suckers. Every one of his deranged cells is begging him for its ration of cocaine, his whole body is screaming at him deafeningly. He could have asked to be hospitalised, but prefers to combat the withdrawal symptoms by working double shifts, playing three times as many poker games, hitting the punching bag in the gym, emptying bottles of wine, and going to the busiest dens of fast living to smoke hookahs and link up with as many girls as come into range—and there are quite a few, as the young women are fascinated by the pilot with the body of an athlete. A Maronite girl who works in a café with musical entertainment dubs him "the blond angel."

One night Mermoz lands his hospital plane at the base after a trip of several hundred kilometres and an afternoon of debauchery in Damascus. As soon as the kitchen is alerted to the return of Sergeant Mermoz from his mission, they prepare a plate of ham with six eggs scrambled. Much to everyone's surprise, however, he tells them he's exhausted, isn't hungry, and is heading straight for bed. He doesn't get as far as his tent. He faints near the spare parts hut and doesn't wake up until two days later in the field hospital; he's collapsed and has been at death's door.

He has eight months of army duty left, and High Command decides to repatriate him to France so he can finish his military service more calmly, with an eye to having a rest before reenlisting. The lieutenant colonel in charge of the Palmyra region requests his presence in person at Command HQ to tell him that they're keeping his post open for him.

CHAPTER 12

★

Bourlon Tile Factory (Paris), 1924

Antoine de Saint-Exupéry

Antoine draws the tiny, pointed spike on top of Baron Munchausen's Prussian helmet. The baron is sitting on a giant ball and holding on to some reins as if the ball were a horse. Antoine draws his nose and his black calf-length boots. When Monsieur Charron passes nearby, he hides the sheet of paper under the cashbook. He also processes invoices now and again and notes the amounts down in the books, and that's enough for them to leave him in peace.

Sometimes he lifts his head and looks out the window, which looks out on another window in another building, where another head looks up from a desk and looks out. *Window or mirror?*

The night he returned from his awkward excursion to Biarritz, he wrote Lou-Lou a very long letter explaining everything: how important she was; detailed descriptions of all the good times they had spent together. He made her all sorts of promises of future happiness, even of wealth, because fortune always smiled on him, or so he believed. He left his aunt's house at daybreak and waited until the post office opened so his letter would be the first one dispatched. As he was walking to work, he was already regretting what he'd written: too long, too stilted, too much like a sermon. The next day, the same post office employee with oversleeves again saw the same tall, ungainly young man bringing him another letter. For three days in a row he sent a different letter and each one was intended to rectify the previous one in some way.

Lou-Lou took several days to answer, and then she replied to all three letters at once. Based on its size it was more a note than a letter.

After a brief opening where she addressed him as *Dear Antoine*, she explained with detached politeness that she appreciated his words but that their engagement had been *permanently cancelled*. She then continued that *of course, she'd be pleased if they could continue to be friends*. As he attempted to crumple the envelope with all his rage, he noticed something hard inside it: It was the engagement ring, which seemed smaller and older now, and with no shine, as if the gold had turned to brass.

The words *permanently cancelled* go round and round like a carousel in his head. It doesn't sound like Lou-Lou's way of speaking; maybe her older brother, a notary, composed those words for her. He had sent love letters and they were answered with a legal demand. He sees the Vilmorin family's hand in this, the mother who always looked at him with suspicion and those older siblings who were like a Roman legion.

And what is this business of "being friends"? *Rubbish! You can't be "friends" with someone you love.*

He tries to stop thinking about her green eyes, but it's like erasing the reflection of a face in water with your hand. Images surface of their trip to Geneva with Madame Petermann acting as chaperone, when the two of them wrote crazy letters together and invented rapturous poems. He asks himself how love can be so volatile and, at the same time, so heavy. It presses on him with an incredible weight.

He leaves his office and delays his return to his aunt's house on Quai Malaquais. He has nowhere to go, no one's waiting for him anywhere. As on other afternoons, he chooses not to cross the river via the busy Pont du Carrousel and instead uses the Pont des Arts, perhaps an overly pompous name for such a delicate bridge. A group of children who are happily jumping their way across the bridge make the whole structure vibrate and he feels a slight tingling in his feet. The feeling in his legs is just like the one he had in the plane when his life was vibrating.

These past few months, the regular get-togethers with his friends in the cafés and brasseries have been unbearably long and grey. He's like a wet blanket at these noisy gatherings; the champagne tastes like stagnant water. With Lou-Lou gone from his life, he feels as if the curtain has come down and the lights have been switched off. There's an empty theatre inside him.

The man who was always scribbling lines of verse on paper serviettes thought he'd find solace in poetry. After all, sorrow and unrequited love have always been succulent ingredients in the poet's kitchen.

After he returned from Biarritz, he went back to sitting at his little writing desk for hours trying to string together emotionally charged lines of poetry, but his hand would go limp and his pen would pump puddles of oil onto the paper. Poetry books seemed like imitation romanticism. He couldn't bear the cheap sentimental trinkets they offered.

He decides he's never ever going to write poetry again. He feels there was more poetry in that lamplighter he once encountered, who roamed the city looking after the streetlights as if they were bright plants, than in a hundred books of poems.

He starts to write prose. Poetry might arrive at the description of a moment, but prose constructs it. He's created a hangar on the desk in his room and is obsessed with using the reverse side of his pen when he writes.

He needs a change, so he checks the "Wanted" advertisements in the paper every day. They're looking for electricians, midwives, warehouse assistants, surveyors, accountants, and piano tuners, but they never list pilots. Aviation isn't an industry; it's just the audacity of a few reckless entrepreneurs, and his flying experience is limited. Every now and again the papers write about the death of one of those madmen determined to fly in metal machines.

One day he finds an advertisement from the Saurer truck company looking for sales representatives to travel throughout the French interior. The idea of returning to rural France takes him back to his childhood home in Saint-Maurice where, as dusk fell, there was a smell of wet earth and burning firewood.

When he tells Monsieur Charron that's he's resigning, Charron puts his head in his hands. He can't understand why someone would leave a comfortable accounting job in Paris to go and sell trucks on commission in dead-end backwaters. Antoine can't be bothered explaining to him that when you've lost everything, there's nothing left to lose.

CHAPTER 13

★

*1st Fighter Aviation Regiment, Thionville
(Northeast France), 1923*

JEAN MERMOZ AND HENRI GUILLAUMET

MERMOZ'S NEW POSTING IS AT the Thionville barracks, very close to the border with Germany. He arrives from Palmyra with sergeant's stripes and a kitbag full of experiences that make him very self-assured. As soon as he arrives at the base, he goes to present his papers. He gives the company captain a half-hearted salute, as he used to do in Palmyra where rank wasn't taken too seriously. The captain examines him from head to toe with a severe look.

They order him to proceed directly to the barbershop and the uniform store and then report again "in the regulation manner." Mermoz is taken aback. He thought he'd be received at the base like a war hero, that they'd invite him to sit down in the officers' bar to relate his adventures, but they treat him with bureaucratic indifference. His arrival has created a bigger stir among the troops. Some soldiers give him a routine salute while others look at him with curiosity. A group of six approaches him.

"Is it true that in Syria soldiers address the officers informally?"

"Are there Bedouins who eat the pilots they capture?"

Mermoz isn't in the mood for stupid questions from pilots who strike him as babes in arms devoted to routine weekly tourism flights.

"Ask for a transfer and you'll find out what's there," he answers cuttingly, with a wave of his hand to scatter them as if they were a flock of pigeons.

He's clocked-up almost six hundred flying hours; they wouldn't reach anything like that number, even if they added together the entire squadron's hours.

One of the pilots has stayed behind. He looks like a grocer with his chubby cheeks and nondescript face.

"Excuse me, Sergeant. I wanted to ask you how the new Nieuport 29 is coping with those extreme heat conditions?"

"Don't you have anything else to do?"

The first officer mumbles an apology and retreats. Mermoz is irritated by this swarm of ground pilots who haven't flown through a desert sandstorm, who haven't seen passengers die in their planes, who don't know what it is to have a tongue as swollen with thirst as the cadaver of a person who has suffocated.

The squadron leader, a young captain from a well-to-do family, who recently graduated from the military academy, informs him that they're going to carry out a training exercise in flight formation, the only one that week.

"You, Sergeant Mermoz, will lead them. They'll all have to follow your flight path. I want you to fly ten kilometres to the northern hill performing huge zigzags there and back. Also, throw in a few rolls so they pay attention while following you.

"Yes, sir!"

Smiling, he heads for the Nieuport 28, an elegant steel-grey biplane with a slim fuselage and two built-in machine guns sticking out from the rear. The 29 model he flew in Syria is still not available here. He puts on his helmet and grins broadly: *These Sunday pilots are going to learn a thing or two today.*

Seven aircraft take off, with Mermoz leading the way. First, he allows them to get into formation. They know how to do that well, and all remain equidistant in the sky.

All together in a tight formation, very good. As a flock of sheep, they're okay. Let's see if they're also of any use as pilots . . .

Mermoz opens the throttle fully and his Nieuport shoots off as he traces the first tight zigzag. He carries out an aerial slalom which breaks up the formation. At least three of the planes have gone out too wide in the swerves and lost seconds, which leaves them straggling and out of formation. But Mermoz doesn't slow down. He reaches the hill and, in an aerobatic move, steps on the pedal to turn the plane until it's flying vertically. He laughs. He already knows that when he stabilises the plane again, he'll be on his own. Five planes have been left adrift, slow on the uptake, trying unsuccessfully to follow in his slipstream.

A glance to the left, and Mermoz sees that one pilot has followed him in the turn.

One left . . . not for long!

He makes the next move, a double yaw at full speed, descending at the same time. The other Nieuport follows him. He pulls the joystick toward him and suddenly climbs a few hundred metres and then lets the plane take a nosedive without warning. As he's diving, he sees out of the corner of his eye that the other plane is falling alongside him, maintaining the appropriate distance.

People start to gather on the airfield, pointing at the sky where an aerial duel is taking place. The leader tries to detach himself from the second plane but it follows him precisely, reacting swiftly to the abrupt turns and maintaining an impeccable two-plane flying formation.

Mermoz starts to perspire. His intention to peel off from the rest of the planes is now crystal clear and, if he doesn't leave this novice behind now, it's going to leave him looking bad. So with the next zigzag he takes a wide turn, drops speed, then accelerates suddenly and dives to the left. The other plane completes the maneuver almost before Mermoz.

It's like he knows what I'm thinking!

He does two more nosedives and another ascending zigzag, and the other Nieuport follows him with precision and elegance. The time allowed for the exercise is long gone, so Mermoz lands. As soon as the engine stops, he gets down to watch the other Nieuport land gently to the applause of the many assembled soldiers. Mermoz's pride has been wounded, but the first thing he does is walk over to the plane which has followed him so expertly. He waits for the pilot to get down and remove his helmet. It turns out to be the first officer with the nondescript features he'd rebuffed earlier on.

"You were magnificent, First Officer. Allow me to congratulate you."

"Thank you, Sergeant."

"Forget the sergeant! We're colleagues. Call me Jean."

"Delighted. I'm Henri Guillaumet."

"By the way, Henri, about what you asked me regarding the Nieuport 29 in Syria, it worked like a dream. The 300 hp engine gives it double the power of these 28s. The fuselage is more dynamic and it's much smoother to handle. You'd love it. When you try a purebred like the 29, everything else comes across as a mule."

Mermoz regrets having judged his fellow pilot too hastily. When the remaining planes land, he waits for the pilots, shakes each one of them by the hand and congratulates them on their effort.

"You're all invited to the mess for a beer, paid for on a stupid sergeant's tab!"

As Mermoz walks to the hangar, the captain crosses his path.

"Captain, I know that I might have gone too far up there. You know how it is, you come alive . . ."

The officer looks at him unmoved.

"It won't happen again, Captain."

"I would hope not. This isn't a Roman circus." That said, the captain starts to laugh. "In any event, a little fun isn't so bad for people now and again."

The officer marches off and Mermoz gives a sigh of relief.

As he heads for the mess, someone hurries up behind him.

"Halt! That's an order!"

That irritating tone; that cracked voice. He closes his eyes and curses his misfortune, because even before he turns around he already knows whom he's going to see: *swarthy face, thin mustache that looks charcoal-drawn, raging eyes.* Pelletier . . .

"Stand to attention before an officer, imbecile!"

Mermoz focuses on the recently awarded lieutenant's stripes and reluctantly comes to attention.

"I knew it had to be you! What you did up there is enough to have you court-martialed. Do you think you can put soldiers' lives and military equipment at risk? What were you trying to prove? Your complete stupidity?"

Mermoz remains silent.

"Has the squad captain detained you?"

"No."

"You mean 'No, Lieutenant!' I'm going to report your irresponsible behavior as well as your disrespect toward a superior."

Rarely has Mermoz felt such a desire to smash someone, screw them up into a ball of paper and throw them into the garbage.

He bites his lip hard to stop himself from leaping on top of Pelletier, who marches off shaking his head in profound irritation.

Mermoz orders three tankards of beer just for himself at the canteen bar and downs each in three gulps. Half the pilots in the squad have refused his invitation, no doubt bothered by the way in which this recently arrived pretentious sergeant has shown them up. The other pilots are watching him, somewhat intimidated, all except First Officer Guillaumet, who is taking small sips of his beer as if he were drinking tea. Some of his companions congratulate the mild-mannered first officer for his flight, but he nods as if it weren't important.

"Guillaumet, how did you manage to follow the sergeant's line?" one of them asks, glancing over at Mermoz, wanting to highlight his fellow pilot's victory over that bigheaded sergeant.

Mermoz knows that it's only right for him to put up with the euphoria of these domestic pilots, who feel vindicated. Guillaumet half closes his eyes for a moment, as if he were falling asleep, and then quietly replies:

"What I did is easy, there's nothing to it. What's difficult is what the sergeant was doing. He had to think about every movement, make it up on the go and fly at the same time. I just had to imitate him."

Mermoz, who is already drinking his fourth tankard, pauses and looks at him with curiosity. First, Guillaumet has given him a lesson in flying. Now, he's giving him a lesson in humility. He wonders again if he has underestimated him.

"I propose a toast to First Officer Guillaumet." Everyone joins in enthusiastically, and with a timid smile, Guillaumet raises his own tankard, still almost full.

Mermoz had forgotten the cold of northern France. Thionville is a city whose thick, fifteenth-century walls, which at different times have held out both the French and the Germans, are incapable of stopping the invasion of the polar wind. He's out for a walk with Guillaumet and another first officer from the squadron called Garnet. They cross paths in the market square with many soldiers strolling in their grey over-coats. Mermoz has covered up his sergeant's stripes with a scarf so that the young soldiers aren't obliged to salute each time they go past him. Young women walking in groups of two or three glance at the trio as they walk by, and giggle. Just then, a soldier accompanied by a woman with curly blond hair strolls past them.

"Look out. It's Lieutenant Pelletier."

The three soldiers stand to attention as he goes by and the lieuten-ant lifts his chin arrogantly while the woman, not as young as she'd like to be, but with curves she makes a point of emphasizing by the sassy swing of her hips, seems to be amused by the pantomime with the salutes. Mermoz brazenly stares at her generous breasts. Pelletier seems not to notice, while she gazes back at Mermoz coquettishly.

"Let's get out of this square; there are too many peacocks out for a walk."

They make their way through less busy streets and when they see a light shining from a doorway, they head for it. It's a noisy, seedy little café where you drink wine in a short glass and anisette in a small cup. Mermoz orders a bottle of wine for the three of them, but with his thirst of an island castaway, he's already had nearly three glasses when the other two have barely had time to start theirs. He turns to a group of men leaning against the bar and asks them lightheartedly: "Where can you meet decent girls in Thionville, but without overdoing the 'decent' bit?" The patrons only know about the local brothels. Mermoz shakes his head and turns back to his friends.

"Paying for sex is like eating lettuce. It doesn't satisfy you."

One of the regulars, with more anisette than blood in his veins, takes offense at his comment.

"Who do you think you are, coming here to talk about the respect-ability of the girls of Thionville, loudmouth?"

Mermoz sweeps back his wavy hair, quite long by military standards.

The local challenges him with glassy eyes, and when Mermoz doesn't reply, he plucks up courage.

"What's the matter, big boy? Cat got your tongue? Chickening out now? Come outside if you dare." The man goes to the door. Guillaumet and Garnet stand up, but Mermoz puts a huge hand on each one's shoulder and pushes them back down onto their chairs.

"I'll be back in a minute."

He goes outside; the two officers look at each other. They don't know if they should wait inside the café as Mermoz said, or go outside to see what's happening. Since various patrons are already heading outside, they make for the door too, but they don't even have time to get there. Mermoz is already back wearing the same mocking smile he had when he left. He's needed only half the specified minute. They see the legs of the character who had challenged Mermoz sticking out from a garbage can on the other side of the street. He's waving them about fruitlessly, trying to get out.

There's still some time before curfew at the base and Garnet takes them to a rather run-down dance hall. An older man at the door, dressed in a worn-out tuxedo, allows them in for free. A small four-piece band is playing something resembling a polka. The dance floor is empty, but groups of young women and men are crowded around the bar, half the latter, soldiers.

Mermoz's expert eye sweeps the joint meticulously until he spots something that attracts his attention. There's a woman at the back of the room on her own. She's somewhat older than most of the young girls fluttering about. She's wearing a dark blue, knee-length dress finished off with a fringe and a necklace of fake pearls, and she's drinking a mixture of mint and water in a tall glass. There's something about her that rings a bell: *curly blond hair, high heels, striking breasts* . . . Mermoz smiles enigmatically. Guillaumet knows that when Mermoz laughs uproariously, everything's fine, he's just having a good time. But when he smiles, anything can happen. He follows the direction of Mermoz's gaze and it lands on a blonde at whom Mermoz is openly staring, until she notices and acknowledges it with an almost imperceptible nod of willingness.

"Excuse me, boys, but I have a matter pending on the other side of the room."

Guillaumet grabs him by the sleeve of his uniform.

"Don't go. She's Pelletier's girlfriend."

"You don't say!"

And then Mermoz does produce his contagious guffaw, which makes Garnet double over laughing too.

A concerned Guillaumet watches them leave together and their departure is also followed by several other curious pairs of eyes.

Days spent strolling with Cécile turn into dates. She drinks mint liqueur with lots of ice and he soon takes a liking to it as well. Their dates become a relationship fiery enough to melt that ice. She has lived alone since her mother died a few months ago; her father went off to war in 1914 and never came back. She survives on a small pension and the generosity of strangers. Mermoz doesn't know exactly what he feels for Cécile, but her lack of modesty fascinates him. Sometimes, he rings the doorbell and she opens the door naked, drink in hand, and somewhat inebriated.

"You're a bit tipsy."

"Well then, get a drink too!"

"You're undressed."

"So, get undressed too!"

One afternoon, as Mermoz is heading for the gate to go out on his exit pass, Lieutenant Pelletier plants himself directly in front of him. The whites of his eyes are yellow. His swarthy face is grey. Pelletier knows; Mermoz can read it in his furious look.

"I'm going to finish you off, you swine. I'm going to have you court-martialed and you'll spend the rest of your life in a military prison."

The lieutenant walks off leaving an icy blast behind him. Mermoz has been thinking about it for a while, but right then and there, he decides he's definitely not staying in the army. He can't stand the ridiculous hierarchy which enables an imbecile like Pelletier to trample over young men whose sole offense is their innocence.

He's had the addresses of a couple of civil aviation companies jotted down for a while already. He'll write to them in the morning offering to work for them as a pilot. He just has to put up with this for a little while more to see out his obligatory military service.

The following week he lands two two-day detentions: one for having dirty boots and the other for not saluting his superiors with sufficient energy. When the weekend arrives, Pelletier is standing at the exit gate and when he sees Mermoz heading his way he orders him to do an about face.

"We need a reinforcement duty sergeant in the workshop."

"What? On whose orders?"

"Mine! Two more days of detention for contempt."

Mermoz breathes deeply, clenches his fists until the nails dig into his flesh.

Pelletier becomes Mermoz's sticky shadow. Sanctions start to rain down on him for the most absurd reasons, and resentment builds inside Mermoz. Since he can't release it against Pelletier, if a soldier gives him a nasty look in the mess, he doesn't use his rank to admonish him, but takes off his combat jacket with his sergeant's stripes and comes to blows with him. If they tell him he has to shave twice a day, he refuses to do it. If they punish him for not having a haircut, he lets it grow longer. If they punish him for drunkenness, he goes to the mess the next day and drinks the bar dry.

The base has become a prison for him. Rather than a soldier, he's now a hostage of the army. What hurts him most about this constant punishment is that, having been placed in detention, he's been removed from the squadron and can't fly. Detention, on the other hand, he's resolved in his own way: When he feels like it, he jumps over the base fence and escapes to the city. Escaping like a fugitive protected by the shadows adds more emotion to his breakouts to see Cécile.

His relationship with her has been based on revenge from the start and so he doesn't know to what extent he really likes this woman. There's something perverted about it all: They're united more by hatred than by love.

One afternoon he gets to Cécile's house at the usual hour, but she doesn't open the door when he rings the bell. The last time he was there, she'd given him a key, and he uses it to gain access. He finds her lying on her bed, her face buried in the pillow.

"Don't look at me . . ."

She's sporting a black eye, a swollen cheek, and a split lip.

"He told me nobody laughs at him. He said really ugly things . . ."

Something explodes inside Mermoz. The floodgates give way and he feels rage overwhelming him. He rushes back to the base. He barges through the barrier like a tram with no brakes, so blinded that he doesn't care if the private or sergeant on guard duty reports that someone in detention comes and goes with impunity. It doesn't matter. Nothing matters anymore. He just wants to grab Pelletier by the throat and squeeze till there's no life left in him.

The soldier at the gate salutes him when he sees it's a sergeant. Mermoz asks him where Pelletier is to be found and the soldier replies that he's on the training ground. The officer on sentry duty looks out through the window of the guardhouse. He sees Mermoz stop long enough to pick up a rusty metal bar and then hurry on. Mermoz is blinded by rage and has a frenzied look about him.

The sentry rushes into the room where the soldiers awaiting their turn in the sentry box are resting and points to three of them.

"Each of you grab a rope and follow me. Do exactly as I say and don't ask any questions. Hurry!"

Mermoz is heading purposefully toward the training ground armed with the metal bar; he's not expecting to be attacked from behind.

They lasso him with the ropes as if they were trapping a wild beast. Catching him off guard, they force him to take several steps backward.

"To the flagpole!"

The soldiers throw themselves on him. Mermoz lands a punch on one of them and drops him to the ground. The other two encircle him, tying him up to the metal pole with the ropes. He struggles but is caught by surprise when he realises that the first officer holding down his arms to immobilise him is Henri Guillaumet.

"What the hell are you doing, Guillaumet?"

It's the momentary distraction Guillaumet needs to run the rope around Mermoz one more time and for the two soldiers to tie it at the back of the flagless pole.

Mermoz realises he's tied down and furiously tries to release himself.

"Let me go, you bastards! I'll split your heads open! I swear I will! As for you, Guillaumet, I'm going to kick you in the guts!"

Guillaumet tries to approach Mermoz, who kicks out at him. He walks behind him and gags him with a handkerchief to stop him shouting. Even so, Mermoz tries to bellow and to untie himself by jerking suddenly, so they're forced to run another rope around his chest, taking care to avoid his kicks.

Pelletier's scrawny figure is visible in the distance, about half a kilometre away, moving among the recruits. Mermoz sees him gesticulating and becomes even more agitated. He tries to yell, and bites on the gag. He insults Pelletier with words muffled by the cloth, swearing that he's going to kill him. Tied to the pole, he still flails and lunges violently, struggling like a wild beast caught in a net.

The three soldiers, terrified yet fascinated, watch the colossus desperately trying to break the ropes and tear the enormous steel pole out of the ground. They're not convinced he won't succeed.

Guillaumet orders the other soldiers to return to the guardhouse and they march off, looking over their shoulders, hypnotised by this mythological scene. Mermoz tenses his muscles and the ropes dig into his flesh.

"Untie me!" he mumbles imperiously through the handkerchief, eyes popping.

Guillaumet refuses with a shake of his head.

Mermoz grunts and gives another series of jerks at the ropes, trying to loosen them. In doing so, he rips the skin around his neck and starts to bleed. Guillaumet looks at him with concern and affection.

"If you go for Pelletier . . ."

"I'll kill him. I'll kill him!" Mermoz replies through gritted teeth. And he tries to free himself with more violent jerks.

"Of course you'll kill him, but he'll have beaten you. They'll lock you up for life."

"What does that matter? I'll have won."

"No! He'll win the game. Don't you realise? If you crack his head open with the metal bar, he'll be laughing in your face even as his brains are spilling out. He'll have achieved what he always wanted: you, rotting in a jail cell; you, unable to fly. In the end, he'll have gotten his way."

There's a moment's silence and finally, Mermoz stops flailing violently against the ropes.

"Don't make them happy. He doesn't deserve it. In a month's time you'll leave by that gate and out there you'll become a brilliant civil pilot while he'll stay forever on this base, bitter till the day he dies. If you really want to piss off Pelletier, do it by being indifferent."

Mermoz has become motionless against the flagpole, exhausted by his efforts. The tension in his hands relaxes at last, his fingers open slowly, and the bar falls to the ground with a metallic clunk.

Guillaumet draws the regulation bayonet which is always carried on guard duty, and cuts the cords. Mermoz, exhausted, his torn shirt spattered with blood and his face contorted by the strain, lets himself drop slowly until he's sitting on the ground.

The first officer picks up the metal bar and starts to walk back to the entry gate.

"Guillaumet!"

Guillaumet turns around and the two exchange a glance. There's no need for words.

Mermoz is removed from the squadron once and for all and assigned to a marginal section of the repairs workshop. The days go by, poker games take place in the barracks. And then, it's all over.

One morning, he puts on his white civilian shirt and the suit he can barely button because his shoulders have become so much broader. In the clothing dispensary, he hands over his belts, boots, uniform, the stained flight suit, his sergeant's stripes . . . A private hands over a receipt, and with the return of that bundle of clothes, Mermoz also leaves behind four years.

He heads for the exit to the base with its barracks, the quartermaster's and provisions stores, the warehouses . . . it all seems foreign to him already. When he's almost at the red-and-white barrier across the entrance, he crosses paths with a skinny person with a narrow mustache, and the eyes of a predator. Pelletier stops a few metres from him and Mermoz smiles. And his smile turns into that uproarious laugh he produces when he's feeling master of the world. He laughs and laughs.

He crosses the post without losing any more time because life awaits him. He looks around without stopping, and with each step the entrance to the base gets smaller.

He reaches the city and rings Cécile's bell. She opens the door dressed only in sandals and a necklace of coral beads.

"I'm off to Paris."

"I'm going with you."

She takes her suitcase out from under the bed. She walks over to the first drawer in the chest of drawers and starts to throw stockings and *culottes* into the suitcase.

"I think you ought to put on some clothes for the journey."

CHAPTER 14

★

Creuse (Central France), 1924

ANTOINE DE SAINT-EXUPÉRY

ANTOINE DRIVES A COMPANY CAR, a modest Sigma Zedel, along a winding road on which snow has started to fall. Snow creates its own mirages, and every so often he thinks he sees Lou-Lou walking across the sparkling whiteness of the fields. It brings to mind a phrase from a casual hiker called Thoreau, who said that the light which dazzles us is our own darkness.

When he found this new job a few months ago, Antoine felt enormous relief at abandoning his cubicle at the Bourlon Tile Factory. Employment with the Saurer truck company allows him to travel around various provinces of France, and provides him with a company car, a base salary of 1,200 francs and a commission for every sale, which could total as much as 25,000 francs.

He would have liked to have found work as a pilot but there are only enough stable airline companies to employ a few experienced pilots.

At least this new job prevents him from asphyxiating between the four walls of an office.

He's just visited a transport company near Limoges. They greeted him amicably but showed little interest. They barely allowed him to give his prepared speech about the virtues of the Saurer vehicles. They're good trucks but not the cheapest on the market. He tries to explain the merit of the trucks, but no one wants to know about worth anymore, just the price.

When he gets to Guéret, where he's based for the weeks he's doing the rounds of the Creuse *département*, he goes up to his room at the Grand Hôtel Central, throws his hat on the chair, and flops onto the bed, exhausted. Its name may be the Grand Hôtel, but it's actually small and gloomy, identical to any one of the budget hotels in which he stays during his roaming through the central part of France. He leans out of the window; Place Bonnyaud seems tiny.

The trees look like brooms . . .

They told him at reception that there's no mail for him, and he feels regret. Letters save him from melancholy, or plunge him into it, which is another way of fortifying himself. Charles Sallès occasionally writes to him, but the letters are mainly from his mother, and Renée, the sister of his friend Bertrand de Saussine. She writes the warm letters of a friend who is concerned about his situation. He calls her Rinette and politely woos her. He begs her tenderly to write to him more often. He doesn't love Renée, but he does love "love" itself. In that cold provincial solitude, letters are blankets that keep you warm.

Lou-Lou is a painful memory. He tries not to think about her, but it's like asking a fish not to think about the sea. He's met other girls in the past few months, at dances in the provinces of Montluçon and Dompierre-sur-Besbre, held in simple parish halls decorated with paper flags where they serve sticky blackcurrant drinks, but there's no jazz, no barman, no cocktails. And the mothers sitting on chairs lined up at the back of the room keep an eye on the local heartthrobs to make sure they don't get too close to their daughters during the waltzes. He sighs, and pictures himself awkwardly flirting without conviction with some insipid girl, in a last-ditch effort to frighten away Sunday loneliness.

The smaller his hotel room, the greater his distress. At night, when he turns out the light and closes his eyes, he calculates how much he'd need to earn to be able to buy himself a plane. First, he does additions and multiplications, keeping in mind the huge commissions he's going to earn from the sale of dozens of trucks, and pictures himself the owner of a small fleet of aircraft. Then he adjusts the numbers a bit more. In the end, he brings them down to reality and recognises that it's impossible.

When Antoine visits companies, as soon as the manager sees the arrival of the heavily built man dressed in an elegant but threadbare suit, stammering and apologizing with obsessive persistence for bothering him, Antoine already knows that the man isn't going to buy a truck, that he wouldn't even buy a pack of cigarettes from him.

"If you would be so kind as to listen, I'd set out in a detailed manner the characteristics and advantages of our Saurer trucks . . ."

He smiles to the best of his ability as he says it, but he can't hide the perspiration running down his neck.

"My apologies, but we're very busy right now."

"Another time, then."

As he drives, he tries to polish the speech he almost never gets to give in those cold transport company warehouses. Now and again, he thinks about the pilot in the story he started to write in his Aunt Yvonne's house. He'll be a decisive fellow. Since Antoine can't be one, at least his character will be. He sketches out some scenes and ends up digressing in his mind toward philosophical matters and other crucial questions: *Who are we? Where do we come from? How do you sell a truck?*

He writes better in his head than with his hands. What ends up on the sheets of hotel letterhead that he uses for his writing is a hodge-podge of scattered phrases. When he gets back at the end of those sterile days, tired from the kilometres travelled and the negative replies, his drowsy hand falls asleep over the sheet of paper. His last thought before he drops off each night is of Lou-Lou. The memories are nothing more than an obsession.

In Argenton-sur-Creuse, after driving over a peaceful stone bridge across a river overlooked by houses, he finds a tobacconist's that smells of American tobacco leaves. The salesgirl is tiny, her blond hair caught up in a ponytail, and she wears glasses. Antoine is captivated by this beauty in miniature, and walks out with a box of matches. After strolling through the silent town where nothing ever seems to happen, he returns to the tobacconist's to buy more matches so that the girl will get up from the stool where she's leafing through a magazine of knitting patterns.

During the two days he stays in the town he visits the tobacconist's so many times that his bedside table drawer is full of matchboxes. The last time he went back there to ask for another box of matches, the girl looked at him suspiciously, thinking he might be a pyromaniac.

He abandons the town, leaving behind the enchanting salesgirl who sells tobacco and matches in her tiny shop. Now that Lou-Lou is gone, his entire life feels like a match which flares for a moment and then burns out. Afterward, all that remains is a trace of black smoke.

CHAPTER 15

★

Paris, 1924

JEAN MERMOZ

PARIS IS A CITY WHOSE streets never sleep, full of countless cafés, men in fedoras with gold watches on chains, women with long necklaces and short hair who smoke their cigarettes through kilometre-long cigarette holders, shoe shiners who provide advice on how to invest in bonds, and brasseries with display windows packed with oysters on beds of ice that drip onto the sidewalk.

The first thing Mermoz does when he sets foot in the capital is stop in a store to buy an enormous wide-brimmed black hat and a cravat.

"What's with those clothes?" exclaims an amused Cécile. "You look like a somewhat notorious poet."

"The worst thing you can be in Paris is a run-of-the-mill person."

Seated in the only chair in their room, he steals a glance at his hat hanging from a hook on the wall, as he finishes yet another letter offering his services as a pilot, written as neatly as he can, given that the paper is lying on top of a chest. This letter is addressed to a Franco-Romanian company. He has to concentrate fully on the sheet of paper because the light coming in from the street is dim, filtered through windows so opaque that there's no need for curtains. In fact, he hadn't realised until a few days after taking up residence that there weren't any curtains.

He asked the receptionist, who laughed in his face.

"Curtains?"

Mermoz's immediate reaction was to grab the receptionist by the throat and cut off his laugh, but the poor wretch, who had teeth like piano keys, was laughing with such delight, as if he'd just been told the best joke ever, that Mermoz let him be. There was no question curtains were completely out of place in an establishment like the Hotel Réaumur, where no one ever stayed for long and modesty was an unknown commodity. You could hear fights and reconciliations and groans of every kind, including of love and contempt, through the paper-thin walls.

There's been little noise in his room for many days. The sheets on the bed he shares with Cécile are icy-cold.

Cécile slams the door as she comes in so he'll notice her presence—as if she could pass unnoticed in a room eight metres square. She arrives from the shared bathroom in the corridor, her lips painted red and her cheeks rouged. She rummages about in her things as if there really were something to rummage through. She takes out her shawl and a minuscule purse with a lot of empty space in it.

"Give me some money, Jean."

"Money? I don't have a centime. We already owe a week's rent, or didn't you realise that?"

"Damn! Didn't you say you were going to be a pilot and earn lots of money? If I'd known, I'd have stayed in Thionville!"

Mermoz shrugs.

"You can go back whenever you like. Thionville is still where it's always been."

"I'm off to have dinner somewhere."

"Without any money?"

"I'll find someone who'll pay for me."

The way she says it, she might as well be telling her doctor she has a cough.

When he finishes the letter, Mermoz carefully folds it. Tomorrow morning he'll go in search of work, something temporary while he waits for a reply from one of the aviation companies. He lies down on the bed, feeling an inner chill.

In the morning, he finds an office where they offer work writing addresses to match deliveries. It's in a basement and they pay 15 francs per 1,000 envelopes. There are about fifteen pariahs like him, hunched over, writing addresses in complete silence. Not a minute is wasted; each word spoken is one less address, a few centimes less.

He spends the whole day there and when he leaves, night has fallen already and he's tired, but he has a few francs in his pocket. When he gets back to the room with some bread and cheese for dinner, Cécile isn't there. He eats his share and leaves hers. An hour goes by and then another. Close to eleven o'clock, the only company he has in the shabby room is the plate with some slices of cheese and a piece of bread. He decides to eat all of it and then go out for a stroll to see what the night has in store for him.

When he gets back, it's past four in the morning and an awake Cécile is waiting for him. Her mascara is smudged and her clothes are wrinkled. Her breath stinks of mint liqueur.

She plants herself in front of him burning with rage.

"Where have you been? Who have you been with? Answer!"

Mermoz is not only silent, but he takes a few steps back with a look of disgust.

"Are you afraid of me?" And Cécile raises her hand theatrically as if she were threatening to hit him.

Mermoz could tell her the truth, but that strikes him as being too cruel. It's not as if he's frightened of her, or finds her affronted, faithful-wife scenes uncomfortable, if only because they are absurd. What makes him retreat is that alcoholic mint smell which he finds nauseating. He can't stand it. He can no longer stand anything about Cécile. He sets about gathering his things and throws them into the military kitbag he brought with him from Thionville.

"Get lost! I don't need you!" Cécile shouts at him.

And the more she shouts, the more she inundates him with her sickly-sweet minty breath, and the more he wants to get out of there as soon as he can, even if he has nowhere to go. He was going to start a new life in Paris and the only thing he's achieved so far is stagnation.

He wakes up the receptionist, asleep with his head down on the counter next to a plate of dried-out leftovers.

"Carillon . . ."

"Eh . . ."

"Carillon, I'm leaving the hotel. Cécile is staying."

"Ahh . . ."

Mermoz looks disapprovingly at the overly thin man with his large, beaver-like teeth.

"Listen. If any mail arrives addressed to me, keep it for me. I'll stop by now and again to pick it up. I'm expecting some important letters." He leans over the counter and gently pinches Carillon's cheek as he looks into his eyes with a tenderness that doesn't hide the strength of his resolve. "Don't let me down."

It's too late to go in search of a boarding house, and it's not worth paying for a night's accommodation for a few hours. So he makes himself as comfortable as he can on a bench, curling up to keep out the damp dawn chill. He sleeps like a beggar, but swears to himself that one day, he'll be looking down on things from the sky.

CHAPTER 16

Montluçon (Central France), 1924

ANTOINE DE SAINT-EXUPÉRY

PARIS TASTES OF COLD CHAMPAGNE, while the small cities you reach by secondary roads have the flavour of warm wine. It's always either too hot or too cold. Antoine is always too alone in the traveller hotels where all they serve for dinner is vegetable soup in slightly chipped, ceramic bowls.

He's been with the company for almost a year and he's sold one solitary truck. When he last visited headquarters, his bosses were understanding: These are bad times, the country hasn't recovered yet from the war. They all know it, they all agree, no one blames him, but he must sell some trucks or they won't be able to keep him on the books.

When the evening meal is over, Antoine prefers to end the day in some café that's still open so he's at least surrounded by people. Once there, he takes out his sheets with jottings, and erases more than he writes. His story about Bernis the aviator progresses very slowly. Antoine is like Penelope waiting for Ulysses, undoing at night what she has woven during the day. What he writes one day he tears up the next. When he rereads what he's written, it doesn't sound authentic to him. How's he going to narrate the life of a pilot when he's a truck sales representative?

He prefers to write letters, to his beloved mother and his sisters but mainly to Renée de Saussine, who's just a friend but who could be something more if she wanted to be. They're more like messages from a castaway than letters.

When he reaches Montluçon two days later, the only correspondence waiting for him is a telegram from Saurer's financial director. He's asking what sales expectations Antoine has. He drops onto the bed and stares up at the ceiling. He counts the cracks. If he were flying in a plane, his gaze wouldn't hit anything; there wouldn't be any ceilings.

The roads of the French interior are taking him nowhere. He decides to hand in his resignation and return to Paris, even if his only plan is a sheet of paper full of crossings-out.

CHAPTER 17

★

Paris, 1924

Jean Mermoz

Mermoz finds occasional work as a garage watchman or warehouse assistant, but he doesn't last long in any job. In an animal feed factory, they appreciated his broad shoulders and strength for carrying bags, but when they wanted to make him permanent, he quit. He can't allow himself to be tempted to put down roots and get accustomed to a grey life, because what gives him the strength to keep looking is precisely the precariousness of his situation.

He's stopped off at the reception desk of the Réaumur a couple of times a week during these months. Carillon's gaunt face shakes a negative each time he sees Mermoz coming through the door. The only news is that Cécile has gone without any notice owing two months' rent and she hasn't been seen since.

Two letters do arrive, one from the Franco-Romanian company and the other from Avions Hanriot. They have no vacancies right now, but thank him for his interest with the usual administrative courtesy.

One afternoon, he goes for a wander around Le Bourget aerodrome and drops in on an aviation company that transports freight. He wants to show them his military documents and his flight record of six hundred flying hours, but at the mere sight of him, the people working there frown.

He seems unaware of how he looks: He's lost weight because often the only thing he can afford to eat all day is a croissant and a café au lait. His hair has grown into a long tangle, and his overcoat, which frequently serves as a blanket on top of a bench on those nights when he sleeps outdoors, is wrinkled and stiffer than it ought to be.

"I'd like to speak to the manager?"

"He's not here."

"When will he be back?"

"Never."

He knows he has to find work so he can buy some new clothes and pay for a room. But now and again, the exhaustion defeats him and when he walks past a bar, he feels an irresistible thirst. Sometimes he shows his military papers to a group of patrons and talks about the decorations they promised him in Palmyra, and someone buys him a drink.

One afternoon, when he's leaving one such seedy bar, he bumps into an old comrade in arms from Syria.

"Max Delty!"

Mermoz claps him on the back and the man lurches back and forth like an empty wardrobe. He's not the strong, strapping young man Mermoz knew in Damascus; he's just skin and bones.

Max invites him back to his place, a tiny one-room apartment. There, he tells Mermoz about his illness, thanks to which he receives a miserly pension on which he just scrapes by. At one point in the conversation, Max stops, cringes, and clenches his jaw. The pain is back.

"The bottle on the table, please."

Mermoz hands him the bottle and when he unscrews the top, his nasal passages are assaulted by the smell of ether.

Max puts a few drops into a glass of water and drinks it. Soon after, he calms down, but he has trouble putting words together, as if he were suddenly drunk. He gets up with difficulty and, dragging his feet, takes three steps to the bed and flops down on it.

Ether is transparent, but has an opaque brilliance. Mermoz dissolves a little in water, as he has seen his friend do. Even in water, it has a bitter, burning taste and sticks to his tongue. A wave of inner heat invades him, his heart beats faster and his breathing quickens. Then everything slows down, and his mind starts to project chaotic images. He's dreaming, but he's awake.

Mermoz leaves the apartment talking to himself, captive of a delirium that makes him think he's in Syria talking with other pilots. Nothing is solid. His brain is a wet sponge. He gesticulates energetically and suddenly laughs without knowing why. People cross to the other side of the street when they see him coming. He suddenly feels a bewildering drowsiness and his eyelids are heavy. He lies down on a park bench and falls asleep under the stars.

As the weeks go by, bird shit is added to the wrinkles in his coat, and he tries to clean it as best he can with water from a fountain. He finds hourly work in a cleaning agency which sends him to filthy factories and warehouses to remove dirt by the basket load.

He drops in at the Réaumur reception desk several times a week. Carillon vigorously shakes his head, mouth open and teeth on display. Nothing.

He also visits Max Delty for silent get-togethers where they share their loneliness and the ether. Mermoz has a permanent taste of it in his mouth. He's conscious that he's falling into a drowsy weightlessness a little more each day, but he doesn't know how deep the hole is.

He finds out one morning a few weeks later as he's stirring a large, very hot café au lait served from an urn, the smell of which permeates the air in the welfare dining hall of Saint-Augustin church. Charity smells like boiled milk.

The woman in charge walks past his table carrying pieces of bread to soak in the coffee. She pauses for a minute.

"Good day, Jean. Nothing this week either?"

"Not much, Madame Lagardère."

"Don't despair."

"I never do."

The director of the charitable institution, Monsieur Agniel, has spoken with Mermoz. They can see that he's a well-mannered, educated young man with a good presence, and they're prepared to hire him as a driver to transport goods to their various regional offices. Mermoz knows he can't say no, but he hasn't yet been able to say yes. Monsieur Agniel looks at him with the proud beatitude of those who do charity work: They expect the people who receive it to show gratitude and accept unconditionally the work so generously offered to them. But Mermoz has an inkling—maybe an obsessive fixation sharpened by his ether-inspired mental confusion—that if he takes this work, he'll cover his basic needs, accept whatever fate he's been dealt, and stop looking for his real destiny.

He's thinking about all this as he walks toward the Réaumur reception desk. Perhaps this is the moment to decide what to do with his life. He pokes his head into the narrow vestibule. Carillon is asleep, squashed into his chair with his feet up on the counter, exposing the skinny shins emerging from his frayed socks. As he doesn't wake up, Mermoz whistles with all his might, and the man almost falls out of his chair.

Carillon looks at him crossly.

"A curse on your family! I was dreaming about a blonde with huge tits who was inviting me into her room. And just as I was about to go in, you wake me up!"

"I'm sorry, my friend. We're not having much luck with our dreams."

The receptionist agrees morosely, as if he'd just allowed the love of his life to get away.

"Don't suffer, Carillon, you'll find her again. She's inside your head, so there aren't many places she can hide. Go back to sleep, I'm already on my way."

"Perfect! Piss off!" The receptionist props his feet back on the counter. "Wait!"

"Now what? Does the blonde have a friend?"

"There's a damned letter for you."

He hands over an envelope with the return address of Latécoère Airlines. Mermoz anxiously tears it open. It's an appointment for a pilot interview at the Montaudran aerodrome in Toulouse in a week's time.

He inhales, and his chest expands as if it were a sail. He needs money for the train, for a haircut and to have his coat cleaned. He races to the cleaning agency and asks the manager to give him all the shifts he can, all the noxious companies, the most squalid ones, where no one wants to go. The public using the toilets in the Gare de Lyon station will be surprised over the next few days to see the cleaner, arm-deep inside the toilet bowls, whistling a tarantella as he scrubs.

CHAPTER 18

Montaudran Aerodrome (Toulouse), 1924

JEAN MERMOZ

MERMOZ WALKS FROM THE TOULOUSE railway station to the Latécoère Airlines facilities on the outskirts of town. The airfield is a huge stretch of level ground with runways chalked out in various directions to enable planes to land into the wind at any time. When he arrives at the aerodrome, he stops briefly and watches a Bréguet 14 take off until it's holding its own in the sky. He feels it's a good omen.

An employee takes him to the office of the director of operations, Didier Daurat. He steps firmly into the office where a man sitting on the other side of the desk underneath a map of Spain and the northern half of Africa with lines drawn on it watches him with calm indifference. He has an angular face, a dark moustache, and small black eyes.

"Monsieur Daurat, I've flown in Syria, I've crossed the desert dozens of times . . . I have six hundred flying hours to my name!"

The director looks at him without altering his expression.

"That's nothing."

His tone is neutral, but the words resonate loudly in Mermoz's head.

"Nothing?"

"Go and see the head of the workshops and he'll give you some mechanic's overalls. You start tomorrow."

"Mechanic? But, Monsieur le Directeur, I want to fly planes!"

"We'll see about that later."

Daurat returns to his paperwork. The conversation is over.

The boss of the workshop is more talkative. He tells him that two other rookies will be starting with him the following day, and suggests a place where he can stay.

"Most of the company pilots and mechanics are lodged at Le Grand Balcon. The daily rate for a room is four francs, and two and a half francs for the meals. It's run by three spinster sisters called Márquez, a little self-righteous, but kind. And they make the best cassoulet in the world!"

That night, dinner features wild boar stew. One of the sisters serves Mermoz a large portion. Mermoz's hunger, dormant during his months of impoverishment, suddenly reawakens at the sight of this delicious feast, and he devours the plateful before the woman has finished going around the table with the tureen serving all the others.

"Delicious, Madame Márquez! They'd kill to be able to serve a dish like this in the best restaurants of Paris."

The woman gives a satisfied smile.

"Would you like a little more?"

"If it's not any trouble . . ."

The woman serves him another generous portion and looks at him with the happiness of a mother watching her children eating with a good appetite. She continues to smile as she serves him for the third time and then decides to leave him the enormous tureen so he can serve himself as much as he wants.

His fellow diners, rookies who have recently started at the workshops, watch him in amazement. The man's stomach seems bottomless.

"If you keep eating like that, you'll turn into a mail sack!" one of them comments amicably.

Mermoz smiles as he continues to eat. Just as he's mopping up the last of the stew, the door of the dining room opens and a short, broad-shouldered man walks in wearing a leather bomber jacket that smells of the night and the cold. He has two circles imprinted on the skin around his eyes, the result of wearing pilot's goggles. One of the rookies hurriedly gets up and offers him his seat.

"That's Debrien. He does the Alicante route," the rookie whispers to Mermoz.

Another of the Márquez sisters rushes to bring a fresh pot of hot stew from the kitchen. An expectant silence has fallen; they all want to ask him something, and to hear him talk about the airline company, but nobody dares. Eventually, the novice who's been there the longest addresses him.

"How did it go up there today, Monsieur Debrien?"

The pilot slowly pours himself a glass of wine and answers as if he were miles away: "Nothing special."

"But we heard in the hangar that there was a fierce storm over the Pyrenees."

"Yes, well, the same as always."

Debrien continues to eat unhurriedly, and no one dares to keep questioning him. Six pairs of eyes are watching him, but he doesn't bat an eye; it could be that he hasn't even noticed. He's not there. He's still jumping over turbulent air at an altitude of 2,000 metres, feeling the trembling fuselage in his entire body and trying to prevent his hands and feet from becoming numb from cold.

Several of those around the table aspire to be pilots and dream— not without some trepidation—about those storms, which buffet the planes as if they were leaves battered by the wind. They really want Debrien to tell them everything, but it seems he has nothing to tell.

Mermoz looks at him and nods. He remembers how he was in Syria: Whenever he returned from his worst missions, he didn't want to talk after he'd landed. He understands this veteran pilot perfectly: *You've done your job, you're tired, you're back. There's nothing more to say.*

Mermoz goes up to the third floor. There's a hierarchy at Le Grand Balcon: pilots on the first floor; the rest of the employees and mechanics on the upper levels. He goes to bed and, despite the disappointment of being assigned to the workshops for now, he feels hopeful.

He's dreaming of wild boars when, in the middle of the night, he's awoken by voices. He hears the sound of hurried footsteps on the staircase and then the front door, so he opens the door of his room and looks out into the hallway. Another head is peering out of the room facing his, and the two of them wonder what's happening, but neither knows. Another head appears further along.

Eventually, one of their coworkers, Marcel Reine, comes up the stairs with a gloomy expression on his face and his eyes bright with alcohol.

"What happened?" they ask him.

"Those damned Márquez ladies!"

"But Marcel, they're saints!" they whisper in reply, laughing.

"Too much so," Marcel replies, annoyed. "There's no way to get up to your room with a girl."

"Did you try it?"

"I did it so carefully. As soon as they hear the front door open, they always call out 'who is it' from their room. I answered 'Marcel' and gestured to the girl to keep quiet. The sisters sleep on the ground floor with their door open, but there's no way they can see anything if they're in bed, with everything dark."

"And then?"

"Well, as we were going up that cursed staircase, which is so old it creaks, they counted the footsteps and did their sums. One of them leaned out in her nightgown to check the staircase and gave me a fierce dressing down. The girl ran out of the house as if she'd seen a ghost. I'm guessing I won't be seeing her again!"

His three companions laugh heartily. Reine pretends to be angry, but almost immediately bursts out laughing as well. They aren't pilots yet, but Mermoz detects the camaraderie of a squadron in this hotel.

The boss of the workshop is waiting for them at 6:30 the next morning. They are half a dozen young mechanics without much mechanical experience. He looks them over slowly.

"Pretty hands. Pity this isn't the Paris Conservatoire. Do you see those cylinders and that potash? The potash will be *your* instrument."

Mermoz sighs, but it's a happy sigh. If he has to scrub, he'll scrub. Better than anyone.

He doesn't think about ether again during the weeks of hard work and the sumptuous meals at Le Grand Balcon. The Márquez sisters' huge helpings have erased the leftover taste of ether in his mouth.

After three weeks, the boss assembles all the recently employed young men: Their cylinder-cleaning period is over. They look at each with joy.

"The time has come . . . to strip down engines."

The smiles disappear again. There are more sighs and the odd muttered complaint. Their boss looks at them good-naturedly.

"Being a mechanic is a fine job, boys. And in any case, you can't be a pilot if you don't know how the engine works. At least, not in this company."

Mermoz, resigned, agrees without complaining. If he has to strip engines, he'll strip them. He's convinced he'll fly again someday.

He and Marcel Reine have been seeing two young switchboard operators from the town hall the past few weeks and they have a date with them. After dancing in a dance hall till their boots split, Mermoz suggests ending the night in his room where he's been keeping a bottle of spirits in a safe place for a special occasion.

"And that special occasion is right now!"

The girls say yes, but Reine frowns and leans over to whisper to his friend: "You're mad! There's four of us! The Márquez sisters will be onto it instantly!"

Mermoz laughs. His guffaw puts out any fire.

They walk to Rue Romiguières and reach the front door of Le Grand Balcon. Reine is reluctant, because the hotel proprietors treat them like sons, even when it comes to their excessive conservatism regarding female friends, and he doesn't want to upset them. But Mermoz is a very determined leader of the party. He takes out his key to the front door, but before he opens it, he turns to Marcel and says quietly: "Do whatever I do."

He carefully steps inside and the others follow on tiptoes. When they reach the foot of the stairs a sleepy voice emerges from the sisters' room:

"Who's there?"

"It's Jean."

"And Marcel."

"We're both back."

"Good night, boys."

"Good night."

Mermoz squats down in front of one of the girls and gestures that he'll give her a piggyback. She climbs up on his back and, once she's secure, he slowly begins to go up the stairs, one step at a time. Reine smiles and hastens to do the same.

In this way, the two of them get to the third floor with their pretty cargo using no more than the required number of footfalls. The only problem is controlling the girls' laughter.

Working as mechanics in the hangars at Latécoère Airlines for almost two months is starting to become tiresome for young men hungry for adventure.

One afternoon, Daurat, the director, wanders in as he has in the past, his hands behind his back and the eternal cigarette dangling from his lips. The apprentice mechanics are loosening and tightening screws. And, as if in passing, he addresses them:

"You're summoned to the airfield tomorrow at 0700 hours."

Daurat continues on his way unperturbed and the six of them exchange glances. First, one of them drops his wrench, then the one next to him, then the next one . . . They create a musical scale of wrenches landing on the cement floor. The moment of truth has arrived.

That night, during dinner, one of the most experienced and admired company pilots, Rozès, turns up.

"Monsieur Rozès, we're going to sit our pilot's test tomorrow," they tell him as soon as he sits down at the table.

"So I heard . . ."

"Do you have any advice for us?"

"Fly well. Monsieur Daurat is very demanding; he's hard to please. The Latécoère workshops are full of mechanics rejected as pilots."

"But what can a director in his office know about flying a plane!"

"You know absolutely nothing!" Rozès replies angrily.

Everyone falls silent. The only sound to be heard is the veteran pilot slurping his soup until he puts his spoon down beside his bowl.

"Monsieur Daurat survived the Battle of Verdun. He was a distinguished pilot in the Great War and decorated for his bravery. Make no mistake about him: He's flown more hours and risked his life more times than anyone."

Nobody talks on board the tram taking them to the airfield before the sun has even risen. When they get there, still half asleep, Daurat is standing on the landing strip giving instructions to some workers who are filling the tanks with fuel. Legend has it among the airline employees that the director sleeps on top of his office desk, and when it's cold, he covers himself with the map from the wall.

Daurat walks over to the young men and they instinctively stand at attention.

"I want to see a good takeoff, a couple of turns to the left, another couple to the right, and a good landing."

They all nod. The veteran pilots position themselves against a fence to watch the event.

The first candidate takes off nervously, the wings wobble in the air, he makes a few rough turns and zigzags as he lands. The veterans shake their heads regretfully rather than negatively. Daurat, smoking a cigarette, watches impassively as the aspiring pilot climbs down from the plane with the same nervousness he demonstrated during the test and stands in front of him with a hopeful smile.

"You're not suitable. Get your belongings and stop by administration to pick up your salary."

Mermoz and the others watch him walk away dejected in the direction of the workshop hangar where they have their lockers. A shiver runs down their spines.

The next candidate is a likeable, foul-mouthed Corsican. He winks at them and walks resolutely toward the Bréguet 14. His takeoff is flawless and his turns are a bit wide, but acceptable. He miscalculates his landing. He touches down a bit late, a third of the way down the landing strip, and the plane comes to a stop twenty or thirty metres beyond the marked-out lines, so he almost reaches the waste ground. He's made an error in his calculations but he's handled the controls well, so the other candidates aren't sure about the verdict. The veteran pilots, on the other hand, are in no doubt whatsoever. They turn toward Daurat, but it's impossible to read anything in his serious expression as he smokes. When the Corsican reaches him, Daurat looks at him:

"No."

"But I only made one mistake!"

"One mistake is enough to lose a plane or a life."

"Anyone can have a bad day!"

Daurat takes a final drag of his cigarette.

"The prestige of the airline is based on the mail arriving every day. My work consists of making sure that bad days don't exist."

Despite everything he has seen and heard, there's not even a shadow of a doubt in Mermoz's mind. He stands very tall as he walks to the plane, calmly putting on his helmet and goggles. He settles himself in the Bréguet's open-air cabin and leans back against the seat's leather cushion: He feels at home again. Minutes earlier, he had noticed a prickly sensation in his stomach, but now all he feels is peace.

His takeoff is perfectly balanced and he remains on a straight line close to the ground until he performs a turn, American-style, and then the plane, nose pointing to the sky, soars up like a rocket, rising easily. He feels in complete control of the machine. He does a turn to the left and then immediately to the right, climbs even higher and performs a perfect figure of eight. He does an S-shaped approach to the runway and the plane rolls gently to the absolute center of the white circle. He gets down from the plane happy to have experienced again that feeling of fulfillment during the flight. Marcel Reine gives him a thumbs-up.

A smile on his face, Mermoz walks up to Daurat who is standing next to his assistant, a young man with round glasses who seems permanently frightened. The director gives Mermoz a dirty look:

"Do you think you're in the circus?"

Mermoz's smile disappears instantly.

"We don't hire acrobats here!"

Mermoz has flown like the best professional pilot and has demonstrated what he's capable of; he doesn't have to put up with this reprimand in front of everyone. He thinks it's unjust. And that injustice brings to the surface the dark rage he carries inside him.

"They'd appreciate my talent in another company."

He yanks off his leather helmet and rudely foists it on the director's assistant, who absorbs the blow on his chest as if it were a rugby ball thrown from the other side of the field.

Mermoz, in a huff, strides to the workshop to pick up his things and get out of there. He doesn't know where, but that doesn't matter. Something will come up.

Furious, he opens his locker and removes a comb, a shirt, and a pair of old boots. He hears calm footsteps behind him.

"You're leaving?"

Daurat removes a cigarette from his case and lights it.

"Of course I'm leaving."

"Right . . ."

"As soon as possible."

"You are undisciplined, arrogant, self-satisfied . . ."

"Yes, sir, I am. I'm very, not to say extremely, pleased with myself."

"You're ill-tempered . . ."

"No, sir. It's just that I loathe injustice. I know I flew well."

"Right . . . Conceited, indeed. You'll have to sort that out."

And then Mermoz's angry expression gives way to bewilderment.

"What? You're not going to fire me?"

"We'll see. Go back to the landing strip. Climb slowly to two hundred metres, turn gently, descend, and land from further away. Use the pedal for the turns and the joystick to go up and down. That's how we work in our airline company: pedal and joystick. We're not trapeze artists, we're mailmen."

Mermoz turns and almost bowls over Daurat's assistant, who's coming in the door with the helmet in his hands. Mermoz frantically grabs it and gives him a friendly pat on the shoulder so strong that the poor man's glasses almost fly off.

"Bouvet, get the suppliers' invoices for next week ready for me."

"But aren't you going to stay for the test?"

Daurat draws on his cigarette and stares at the brilliant orange embers for a few seconds. He glances at his assistant with that weariness inspired by people who need to have everything explained to them. He half turns and heads for his office. He has no need to watch Mermoz's test; he already knows that he's a pilot.

CHAPTER 19

★

Paris, 1925

ANTOINE DE SAINT-EXUPÉRY

ANTOINE HAS RESIGNED FROM SAURER and seen the relief on the faces of his bosses. He's gone down in company history as the worst salesman ever—one solitary truck. He has no idea what he'll do next, but his shirt pocket is bulging with the brown envelope containing his pay and the world has opened up. He's walking at a good pace, because the gang is waiting for him at the entrance to Prunier, a recently opened restaurant where they serve the best seafood in Paris. It's becoming harder on each occasion to get them all together, but Charles Sallès and his Russian girlfriend are there, together with Renée de Saussine and other friends.

He's already given notice that the meal's on him, and that puts him in high spirits. The last time he was in Paris, his friend Hervé had to pay for everything because Antoine didn't have a centime.

They all approve of the very modern round lamps and the bar where the caviar, scampi, and lobsters are displayed. The waiter appears and Antoine signals that he's in charge of the smiling group.

"What will it be, sir?"

"My God, what a question! Champagne and caviar, of course!"

Antoine has brought his deck of cards. Hervé's cousin and Charles's Russian girlfriend are a new audience for his magician's tricks. People enjoy them, and he likes to please.

He hands the cards to Renée, and when he's sure she has them in a safe place, he approaches Sallès in a theatrical manner and shows everyone that he's taking the three of diamonds from the pocket of Charles's jacket.

His friends smile, caught up in the movement of his hands. Everyone, that is, except Charles's girlfriend, who stares at Antoine absolutely engrossed. Earlier, when the introductions were taking place, Charles had asked them all not to refer to her as his girlfriend under any circumstances because, according to the theory he cheekily presented to them, as soon as commitment begins, the fun ends. The girl, who is wearing lots of makeup, stares at Antoine and in her accented French, tells him that she also knows how to manipulate cards. And then she takes out a deck of tarot cards and asks him if he wants his fortune told. Amused, they all raise their voices and shout "Yes" enthusiastically.

After laying out the cards and focusing all her attention on them, she fixes her Slavic eyes on Antoine and informs him that he's going to get married very soon . . .

"But I don't even have a fiancée!" And as he says it, he blushes slightly while glancing out of the corner of his eye at Renée de Saussine and thinking of Lou-Lou.

"It will be to a young widow whom you'll meet soon," the fortune-teller assures him.

Antoine's eyes open so wide in astonishment that they bulge like a sea bream and everyone laughs.

"Let's toast the future Madame de Saint-Exupéry! Whoever she might be!" Hervé exclaims.

"A toast!" Antoine celebrates, also laughing by now. "Waiter, more champagne!"

Sallès taps him on the arm.

"Come and have a cigarette outside."

At this hour Rue Duphot has little traffic. His friend takes a deep drag of his cigarette and he gazes toward the colonnade of the Madeleine.

"It's about Louise. She's in Paris at the moment."

"She's a Parisian. Why wouldn't she be?"

"There's more. I hear she has a fiancé."

"Bah, that doesn't mean a thing! Louise collects admirers like others collect stamps."

"I've heard it's serious."

"Serious?"

"That's what her brother said."

Antoine's jaw drops so far that his cigarette falls.

"Who is it?"

"Nobody knows him. He's an American friend of the family. He's almost forty and they say he owns mines in Brazil."

Antoine starts to walk down the street.

"Hey, where are you going? What about dinner!"

Antoine leaves. He spends the next twenty-four hours in bed, his mind whirling like an egg-beater: *Is he going to let a forty-year-old crock compete with him for Lou-Lou? It's definitely a family decision; they only think about business and money. How could she have fallen in love with an American? She can't stand hot dogs!*

Antoine can't sit back and do nothing. He draws up several outlandish plans and chooses the most bizarre of them all. He leaps out of bed, gets dressed quickly, and rushes down the stairs three at a time.

He goes to the Saurer workshop and manages to speak to a worker he met during his apprenticeship. At first, the man looks at him very suspiciously when Antoine asks to be taken for a ride in the biggest truck available. He becomes less suspicious when Antoine starts to take out banknotes. When he explains that he wants them to take the truck down Boulevard Raspail and then into Rue de la Chaise, the man looks at him as if he's mad and suggests with a hand motion that he fork out a few more bills.

Antoine has shaved, splashed on some cologne, and put on his best suit. He's bought a colossal bouquet of white flowers with what's left of his severance pay. His plan is simple, but he thinks it will be effective: He'll have the truck stop under Lou-Lou's window, the driver will lean on his horn forcefully several times, and he, Antoine, will climb on top of the cabin, which will be level with her bedroom. When she leans out, she'll find him in front of her window with a million flowers asking that they start all over again from scratch.

It all unfolds according to plan, although the truck has more difficulty than anticipated driving down Rue de la Chaise, which is not very wide. It even has to take over some of the sidewalk. When it stops in front of the Vilmorin residence, Antoine starts to climb up the outside of the cabin till he gets to its roof. He's told the driver to wait till he gets up there and stamps on the roof, and then to sound his horn. It won't be necessary. The truck has blocked the street and the other cars have already started to blow their horns loudly, so he has to hurry. From up top he can see that there's already a row of three cars and two bicycles. The street becomes a horn fanfare, even louder than he had planned. *Perfect. No way she'll miss that!* He sees movement in Lou-Lou's room. For a moment, he's worried that it will be Madame Petermann who will come out and mess things up, but he's in luck: He sees a flutter of red hair. Lou-Lou's the one who, alerted by the deafening racket from the street, walks toward the balcony to open it and see what's happening. The balcony door opens and Antoine trembles with excitement.

"Surprise!" he shouts with all his might.

Lou-Lou emerges and encounters Antoine on top of the roof of a truck cabin level with her balcony, holding an enormous bunch of flowers, all in the middle of an infernal traffic jam. But Antoine is the one who gets a surprise: Lou-Lou is wearing a wedding dress. A dressmaker, her eyes magnified by very thick glasses, appears behind her, carrying a tape measure and a pincushion. Lou-Lou looks annoyed.

"What are you doing dressed as a bride?"

"What do you think?"

"So it's true, then. You're going to get married?"

"That's pretty obvious. Goodbye, Antoine."

Irritated, Lou-Lou turns around, goes back inside and slams the glass doors. The woman in the tortoiseshell glasses follows after her, eager to smooth out some pleats.

Outside, the horn concert intensifies. The owners of some of the vehicles have stepped out of their cars and are hurling all sorts of insults at Antoine. He looks at the flowers as if asking their forgiveness. He stretches out his arm, and easing the bouquet between the bars of the railing, he deposits it on the balcony floor. He'll be the first to give her a wedding present.

He clambers back inside the cabin of the truck, oblivious to the shouts of the drivers. The nervous truck driver starts his engine right away.

"What a ruckus we've caused! Did your girl at least like the surprise?"

Antoine has a lump in his throat and he only manages to answer with a clown's gesture. The driver gives him a sideways glance.

"Where do you want to go now?"

"Far. As far away as I can."

CHAPTER 20

★

Barcelona (Spain), 1925

JEAN MERMOZ AND HENRI GUILLAUMET

MERMOZ STOPS IN FRONT OF one of the flower stalls on the Ramblas in Barcelona that tinge the avenue with bright colours and asks the stallholder in the blue apron to sell him a white carnation. Since Mermoz doesn't speak Spanish or Catalan he points with his finger. Once the flower is in his buttonhole he pauses in front of the window of a pastry factory to see how he looks in his new suit. The building has copper doors embossed in a fanciful manner with those coloured bits of tile so characteristic of the Catalan capital.

Barcelona with its grid design and modernist buildings strikes Mermoz as a city of small entrepreneurs and traders, in which severe moral rectitude declines as districts get closer to the sea and pedestrians make their way into the red-light district, full of sailors, prostitutes, the most notorious cabarets, and bustling gambling dens.

After a test flight to Casablanca and back, Daurat has assigned Mermoz to Barcelona to cover the section of the air route that flies over

Spain. A pilot carries the mail on the first leg from Toulouse to Barcelona. As soon as he lands on the strip set up on the southside of the city across the Llobregat River, the mailsack is transferred to Mermoz's plane which, without losing a minute, takes off for Málaga, with a stopover in Alicante. The next pilot is waiting in Málaga, and he'll cross the Strait of Gibraltar to continue the aerial relay which will end with the mail arriving in Dakar, Senegal, in record time. Letters from France to Africa, which used to take weeks or even months to reach their destination, now arrive in three days.

Mermoz has more money now, but goes out less frequently. He hardly drinks and has eliminated all drugs from his life. Flying is enough; it calms his nerves, and the exhaustion from eight or nine flying hours in a row saps his energy.

He catches the suburban train which takes him to the small town of El Prat and from there he cycles to the Latécoère Airlines hangar. He has time to sit on a wooden bench until he hears the hum of an engine in the air and prepares to welcome his colleague.

When Rozès climbs down from the cockpit, Mermoz rushes over to shake his hand. The recently arrived pilot raises his goggles and gives a friendly wave. There isn't time for more; as Daurat repeats ad nauseam: The mail is sacrosanct. The mechanic helps Rozès transfer the sacks to Mermoz's Bréguet. Mermoz immediately takes the controls and lines up on the runway for takeoff, heading for Málaga. As soon as Mermoz has reached sufficient altitude, Rozès will take off in the opposite direction to return to Montaudran, and that night he'll have a silent dinner in Le Grand Balcon.

Mermoz, surrounded by a jumble of starlings and low clouds, has left the wetlands of El Prat behind. The climate in Barcelona is unstable; sunny Andalucía lies 1,000 kilometres to the south. The Mediterranean air corridor to Valencia is calm, but as he approaches Alicante, he flies into the heavy gusts of air flowing down the Aitana Mountain range.

Next he has to fly over the promontories that present an obstacle at the Tiñosa headland. Despite hugging the coast, he's buffeted by gusts of wind from the Alhamilla and Gádor ranges, winds which carry with them the irritability of the Penibaetic Mountain chain. A few kilometres farther on, he's hit by the icy breath of the Contraviesa Mountains, chilled by the eternal ice of the Sierra Nevada. Flying over Spain is like flying over the edge of a saw.

As Mermoz flies over Lújar, close to Motril, the snow and sleet from the nearby Mulhacén Peak, over 3,000 metres high, thickens until the world disappears. Hail shrapnel noisily drums on the fuselage and the ice pellets smash into his face. He feels the cold making its way through his leather jacket and flannel shirt and his teeth chatter. He clenches and unclenches his fists so his hands won't go numb. The Bréguet's power to ascend isn't enough to lift it to the top of the stormy mass and fly above it. He must fly into the squall, and go through it, remaining at its mercy, but there's no way he can hate the storm, because what it demands brings out the best in him.

When he lands in Málaga, it's pouring. It doesn't matter, because he was already soaking wet one hundred kilometres ago. He watches the workers transferring the mailbags to a colleague's plane parked under an awning, and he feels satisfied. Those letters are expected by people eager for news of their loved ones or who want to know the outcome of a business deal on which their well-being might depend, or the answer to a declaration of love, a birth, a death. The pilots are carrying bits of people's lives inside envelopes.

Rozès occasionally brings him a present from Toulouse. There might be a bottle of Pernod or a French newspaper waiting for him in the office at El Prat aerodrome when he returns from Málaga.

On his return train trip from El Prat to the city, he reads a copy of *Libération* which is two days old. His attention is drawn to an item about the long-distance military flight known as Military-Zenith, an annual air race of almost 3,000 kilometres. The interest of the press in such races, where people gamble foolishly with their lives in order to establish records, strikes him as idiotic, although he does think they're useful for testing new models. Nevertheless, he's delighted when he sees that the winner is a sergeant by the name of Henri Guillaumet. He looks at the accompanying photo and there's his former comrade, dressed in his uniform and holding a bouquet of flowers, surrounded by half a dozen officials with bigger smiles than his. Guillaumet is the only thing he misses from his years in the military.

It's already very late when he reaches the Pensión Frascati, a small hotel which charges affordable rates—full room and board starts at ten pesetas. It's centrally located on Calle de las Cortes, a few hundred metres from Plaza Cataluña and facing the modern Ritz Hotel where a doorman in a maroon suit and matching top hat is permanently stationed. The pensión has one other advantage: The wife of the owner is French.

When he enters, the wife gestures him over to the reception counter where the keys are housed in a wooden beehive.

"They called you from head office in Toulouse. You are to call Monsieur Daurat in his office as soon as you arrive."

"But it's ten o'clock at night!"

"All he said was: 'As soon as he arrives.'"

Mermoz makes his call from the little booth to the office number, although it's too late for anyone to be there. It rings once, twice . . . it doesn't get to the third ring.

"Yes."

"Monsieur Daurat?"

"Speaking."

"It's Jean Mermoz. I didn't think I'd find you in the office."

"Listen. Riguelle is going to take a couple of weeks' holiday. You'll have to cover his absence."

"But I already have my shift."

"Now you've got two."

Riguelle flies the same route as Mermoz on alternate days. This means Mermoz will have to double his flying shift: 800 kilometres to Málaga; sleep overnight on a rickety bed at the airport. Then, the same number of kilometres back to Barcelona at first light the next day with the mail that has arrived from Casablanca. And back to Málaga again the following morning.

Not many people could handle such a grueling pace. But Mermoz can.

When he arrives in Málaga or Barcelona, they serve his meals on trays rather than plates, because he has such a voracious appetite. The manager of the commercial zone at the Málaga airport knows that Mermoz loves the paper cones full of small fried fish they sell at mobile stands in the city, and occasionally he asks one of the owners to come to the airfield to set up his stall there. The first time he did it, the proprietor of the stand, a very short Andalusian with impressively large sideburns, asked the manager how many customers he would be serving.

"One," was the reply.

"You're off your head!"

It was quite an effort to convince the proprietor to come out to the isolated airfield at that hour of the night with his deep fryer, his coarse flour, and his little fish to serve a single, solitary customer. When Mermoz, his stomach empty and his hands frozen stiff, climbed down from his plane after nearly ten hours of aerial leapfrog and saw a fried-fish stall in the middle of nowhere, he thought he was hallucinating. But hallucinations don't smell of olive oil.

The manager told Mermoz he could have as much as he wanted. He went over to the stand and the man handed over one of his waxed-paper cones full of a hot, crunchy mixture of small anchovies and the odd piece of dogfish. Mermoz poured the entire cone into his mouth as if it were water. He asked for another. And then another. When he'd gone through seven cones, the owner, dumbfounded by this fried-fish shredder, had to beg his forgiveness for having run out of supplies.

After refuelling his protein tank, Mermoz would collapse on top of the bed they had ready for him in the aerodrome outbuildings and fall into a deep sleep.

One night, when Mermoz gets back especially late to the Pensión Frascati in Barcelona, he finds a message from Daurat to call him urgently. It's nearly midnight; a strike by the transport union had converted his return trip from El Prat into a long odyssey accompanied by anarchist CNT picketers. Despite the late hour, he tries to call Daurat's office.

"Yes."

"Monsieur Daurat, I have a message to call you."

"Rozès's father is dying. He's asked for leave to go and see him."

"I'm sorry to hear that. So, has he gone?"

"I said he'd asked for leave, not that I'd granted it. We've got mail to deliver. I'm not going to authorise his leave until I have a substitute."

"And who's that substitute?"

"You."

"What? I'm already doing Riguelle's job as well as mine!"

"I see . . ."

Silence follows on the other end of the line broken by the static from the connection.

"What do you see?"

"I see you don't feel able to do it. Barcelona-Toulouse is like a bike ride, but if you can't, you can't. I appreciate your sincerity. Consistency of the postal service is too valuable to jeopardise, if you aren't sure you're prepared to transport the mail."

"But who said I wasn't prepared to transport the mail reliably?"

"I thought that's what you were saying."

125

"No way. I just . . . Dammit! Of course I can transport the mail to Toulouse!"

"You'll have to get up earlier in Málaga, leave at first light, and arrive in Toulouse before sunset. The stopover in Barcelona will only be to refuel. The next day, the same thing in reverse to Málaga."

"No problem."

"I'll hand over your hours to accounting so that they're paid punctually."

"What difference does the money make to me, Monsieur Daurat! I won't have a damn minute to spend it!"

"Good night, Mermoz. Now go and rest."

Mermoz says goodbye and as he hangs up, he wonders whether Daurat encouraged him to rest because he's worried about him or about the mail arriving at its destination safe, sound, and on time. Although, in reality, it amounts to the same thing.

Doing the work of three pilots becomes something of a habit for Mermoz. When his colleagues get back to their jobs, he's the one who wires Daurat asking him to assign him to any vacant route, and when he flies, it is with the same gluttony as when he eats . . . or makes love, or boxes in a gym on Avenida del Paralelo whenever he has time. He wants to expand his horizons and asks Daurat several times to be posted to the Casablanca route, but his long, handwritten requests are refused with a blunt "no."

At least he's given a week's vacation and he takes advantage of it to return to Paris. The city sparkles, and with a good suit and money in his pocket, it's a different place altogether. He is the same as he was when he was sleeping in a park with a filthy coat covered in bird shit; it's the others who look at him in a different way, and that fills him with a degree of resentment.

Mermoz savours a whisky-laced coffee on the terrace of the Promenade. It's his third. Instead of going to the theatre, he sits on terraces and watches the world go by. He likes to watch the women in particular. He's fascinated by the very slim ones with their shoulder-length hair and swan-like necks, as well as the plump ones with their generous breasts, who smile as they walk past. He marvels just as much at the blue-eyed blondes who look like Nordic goddesses, as at the long-haired brunettes with their brown, catlike eyes . . . He sees something beautiful in all women, without exception. From his seat in the stalls, he notices a pedestrian on Rue la Fayette strolling past the tables whose walk seems familiar. He wouldn't have recognised the style of dress or the haircut—he seems even shorter than before—but that way of walking is his signature.

"Guillaumet!"

And when the person comes to a dead stop and turns on his heels with the military precision of someone who's spent hours marking time, Mermoz encounters the same good-natured face from back then. He gets up and gives him a dramatic embrace. Before Guillaumet can object, he's already sitting at the table with an enormous whisky-laced coffee.

"I read about your victory in the Military-Zenith. You must have left a pile of smug officers feeling disappointed."

"To be honest, there was one officer, Lieutenant Challe, who was very generous and lent me his plane when mine suffered an irreparable breakdown."

"I don't want to know anything about the armed forces. It's full of injustice."

"That's why I discharged myself."

"Civil aviation is a totally different case."

"And what have you been doing with yourself all this time?" asks Guillaumet as he looks at Mermoz's impeccable woollen suit, his cloth overcoat, and his fashionable new hat. "I can see already that you're doing well."

"I escaped, yes. But I've spent time in the gutter."

"I don't believe it!"

"It's true, my friend. I've been hungry, I've eaten in charity halls and slept on the streets. In this city of thousands full of so many things, I've been as alone as a man can get."

"So why didn't you come and find me in Thionville?"

"Go back to Thionville to give Pelletier the pleasure of seeing me dragged down? Never! It wasn't easy, but they finally took me on at Latécoère Airlines. Now I'm living between Barcelona and Toulouse, and I'm in charge of the Spanish route. The company has great plans; the southern route in Africa will expand very soon."

"And what does it transport?"

"The most precious cargo in the world: letters. Business letters, love letters, letters between parents and their children . . ."

"I've never flown over Africa."

"You'd love it. You're in your plane and it's as if they'd placed the world down below just so you can fly over it."

Guillaumet smiles, his eyes bright not so much because of the whisky as Mermoz's words. There's a type of inebriation that only aviators know.

"They need good pilots who love their work at House Latécoère . . . Come with me to the airline!"

CHAPTER 21

★

Paris, 1925

ANTOINE DE SAINT-EXUPÉRY

LOUISE DE VILMORIN WAS MARRIED on the 7th of March. They didn't invite Antoine, which saved him from having to decline. For a while now, all his experiences have left an unpleasant taste in his mouth, as if he'd drunk the water from a vase of dead flowers.

For weeks, he wanders the streets of Paris on leaden feet. His pockets have holes in them. He has to write to his mother again for money and that makes him even more gloomy; he feels like a child lost in an enormous city. He walks and walks aimlessly, vaguely hoping that when he turns the next corner everything will change.

And if something were to happen around the next corner?

Nothing happens.

But if it happens around the next one?

His wandering footsteps often lead him to prowl along Rue de l'Odéon where the best bookstores are to be found. His favourite is La Maison des Amis des Livres, and he particularly likes the wooden box they put out on the street through which he can rummage with barely a pause in his roaming.

One afternoon when he returns from his walk, his aunt's house is buzzing with people. He's about to slip away upstairs when she calls him and asks him to come into the living room for some punch. The fruit cup handed to him by a servant with a silver ladle tastes divinely alcoholic. He thinks he'll have just one cup but ends up having three.

Among the invited guests is a man who is as tall and stocky as Antoine, but more athletic. His name is Jean Prévost and he's not a rugby player but rather the literary editor of an influential review, *Le Navire d'Argent*, financed by the publisher Jean Gallimard. Prévost has an intense voice and a polite, if emphatic, manner. His abrupt flourishes and gestures with closed fists reveal a passion for boxing.

"And what do you do for a living?" he asks Antoine.

"I was a pilot."

"Of cars?"

"I was an aviator."

"Tell me about it! Is it scary?"

"You're too busy up there to remember to be afraid."

"So what do you feel up in the sky?"

Antoine stops to think. Without realising it, he closes his eyes.

"The vibration."

Prévost shows a lively interest.

"What do you mean?"

"The planes are made of wood; they're like a child's toy and the engine makes them shudder constantly. The plane vibrates and you vibrate with it. Forgive me, I don't know how to explain it."

"Well, I like your way of explaining it."

If Jean Prévost has developed anything in his work, it is a capacity to recognise when someone is a born storyteller. He knows: This young man has that gift. A few minutes later, when he extends his huge hand to say goodbye to Yvonne's nephew, he looks him in the eye and tells him very seriously that he ought to start writing.

"I do, on occasion, Monsieur Prévost. I'm working on a story about a pilot."

"I'd be delighted to have it for my review."

Le Navire d'Argent has just been established, and it is the most important literary review of the moment. Gide himself publishes in it, and that strange Irishman, James Joyce. When Antoine goes up to his room, he starts to dance clumsily around the small writing desk. He wants to get back to writing immediately to finish the story of his aviator, Bernis, but he's too excited. Better than that, he starts writing letters to his mother, to Rinette, and to various friends telling them about what has happened. In his own way.

The most important editors of Paris are burning with a desire to read my writings!

The euphoria gradually evaporates over the next few days. Thinking up stories is less tiring than writing them.

One afternoon, he visits a former teacher of his from the Académie Bossuet, his old high school. Père Abarnou always felt sympathy for this student who at times applied himself, but who was almost always distracted, and who occasionally disguised his extreme shyness with petulance.

As they share an overly milky tea, Antoine explains his despondency; he's lost track of the only profession that satisfied him. The priest raises his eyebrows, rubs his greying beard, and then tells him he's going to speak about Antoine to a friend of his called Beppo. Beppo is an associate of Pierre-Georges Latécoère of Latécoère Airlines.

"Have you heard of them?"

Antoine professes his ignorance.

"They're trying to establish global transport routes for mail," the priest explains, and Antoine feels a stirring of excitement. "I don't know if you'd find this work satisfying . . ."

"They transport the most precious cargo in the world: letters. They're actually flying postmen! It would be the best job in the world!"

"You'd have to move to Toulouse."

"There's nothing tying me to Paris anymore, Father."

Antoine leaves the imposing building of the Académie Bossuet and takes a deep breath when he reaches the street. It's only a possibility. He knows it won't be easy for him to be accepted as a pilot given his limited flying experience. But he looks up and down the street and sees no one, so he takes advantage of this to perform a few steps of a dance of his own invention. A woman watering her geraniums watches him, her glasses sliding down to the tip of her nose.

CHAPTER 22

Barcelona (Spain), 1925

JEAN MERMOZ AND HENRI GUILLAUMET

MERMOZ SMOKES A CIGARETTE UNDER the hangar's external canopy as he watches the rain come down. One of the airline's inspectors, who oversees the operation of the various stopovers along the route, pokes out his bald head, swollen bags under his eyes.

"Come inside, man! It's cold out there!"

Mermoz gives a hearty laugh. The man looks at him with incomprehension and turns to go back inside. He knows nothing about what happens at an altitude of 2,000 metres travelling at 180 kilometres an hour.

The purr of an engine emerging from a mass of black clouds gives advanced notice of the arrival of the mail from Toulouse. Visibility is poor, less than fifty metres, but the plane appears perfectly aligned with the landing strip and, without the slightest wobble of its wings, lands gently on the ground. Mermoz nods. There aren't many pilots who fly with such complete control of their machine, so he knows he's going to take over from Guillaumet.

The mechanic races toward the plane with a black umbrella.

"Where's he going with that umbrella?" asks the inspector of finances.

"Daurat's orders."

"Ah! I see he looks after his pilots."

Mermoz makes a face. The man doesn't know Daurat. The umbrella isn't for Guillaumet, who's climbing down totally drenched from a cockpit full of rainwater. The umbrella is to protect the mailbag in the hold.

Rather than heading for the shelter of the barracks, the first thing the wet and shivering Guillaumet does is go over to embrace Mermoz. They exchange the dampness and the joy of crossing paths at an airfield.

"Is everything okay, Henri?"

"All good and on time. Monsieur Daurat gave me a letter for you."

He removes a wet envelope from the inside pocket of his leather jacket and Mermoz reads it as they walk.

"The boss is asking me to carry on to Toulouse with the mail tomorrow and present myself in his office."

The next day, the sun is going down in the west when Mermoz lands at Montaudran. Again in the rain, and again freezing cold. Two workers run to get the bag with the mail from Africa, which has travelled in record time to the point where people are starting to hold these flying postmen in high regard. But Daurat never tires of repeating the same thing every time a journalist wants to interview him about the postal miracle: "It's no miracle," he grumbles, "just a job."

The director has a report on his desk about Marcel Drouin, a veteran mechanic who knows everything there is to know about engines. Bouvet, Daurat's assistant, informs him that Drouin is waiting outside, and Daurat tells him to bring him in. Daurat settles into his seat and lights a cigarette. The mechanic is over fifty and losing his hair in fits and starts.

"Go ahead, Drouin."

"I've received notification that I'm to be demoted from my current position as head mechanic to assistant mechanic."

"Correct."

"Monsieur Daurat, it's true that I made a mistake with some connections. It can happen to anyone!"

"But it happened to you."

"I've been a mechanic for twenty years! You know I know my job better than anyone. You can't demote me to assistant! Everyone will make fun of me in the workshop."

Daurat studies him with a neutral expression which makes the worker uncomfortable. He just looks at him, neither irritated nor compliant.

"I assembled the first Latécoère plane. I've given my all to this company. If you downgrade me, I'll leave."

The director doesn't move a muscle or make even the briefest of remarks from behind his desk.

Dejected, Drouin turns around and retreats. "I'll request my payment from accounting."

After he's gone, Daurat takes the file with the report about the Drouin incident and leafs through the notes again, despite knowing them by heart. Just before takeoff, someone noticed that the Bréguet's electric wiring was connected the wrong way around. Drouin says he knows his trade better than anyone and the trouble is, he's right. If a mechanic makes a mistake out of ignorance, it's bad, but he can learn and won't repeat the mistake. If a mechanic who knows everything about an engine makes a mistake, it's because he isn't concentrating or has been distracted. And there's nothing to suggest he won't make the same mistake again. Overconfidence makes you lower your guard.

He mulls over the sheet of paper and thinks about Drouin's sad face. He's a good worker with more than twenty years in the job and an impeccable track record. Maybe he's being unfair to him.

Just one mistake . . .

He could tear up the demotion order that's causing Drouin to resign in a commendable act of professional pride. His resignation will perhaps lead to unemployment and the start of his decline. There aren't that many places an aircraft mechanic can work. It's possible he'll fall into a downward spiral that will lead him to despair, maybe to drink and ruin. So Daurat's decision may be devastating for Drouin. There's still time to tear up the order and throw it in the waste-paper basket, and a good man, honourable and hard-working, will recover his dignity. But the only thing Daurat scrunches up is the empty cigarette packet lying on his desk.

Bouvet timidly asks permission to enter.

"It's about Drouin, Monsieur Daurat. He's asked for his severance pay and the accountant has passed the form on to me for you to sign or decide something else—maybe to speak to him again."

His assistant glances at his boss with frightened nervousness over the top of his dark glasses. Bouvet has known Drouin since the latter had a full head of hair, and knows he's a good man. Daurat hunts for his pen in his jacket pocket and his assistant, cringing inside his cheap suit, summons the courage to say something.

"Monsieur Daurat . . ."

His boss stares at him with his tiny eyes and Bouvet bows his head. Crestfallen, he leaves with Drouin's signed severance papers.

Bouvet thinks I'm a tyrant. I am . . .

Daurat clenches his jaw. If he'd revoked the order, he'd have acted fairly with Drouin and his years of dedication. But he would have acted unfairly toward the airline's pilots. A badly assembled electrical circuit can cause the flow of fuel to be interrupted in the dead of night at an altitude of 4,000 metres, wipe out all the navigation instruments, and take a pilot to his death. It's true that he could have given Drouin a second chance. A second chance to wait and see if he made a second mistake. But what if, thanks to that second mistake, a plane crashed or a pilot died? Whose fault would it be? Would it be Drouin's fault? Or the fault of the person who authorised him to continue to make mistakes?

He doesn't know if he's been overly harsh.

Who knows . . .

CHAPTER 23

Toulouse, 1926

ANTOINE DE SAINT-EXUPÉRY AND HENRI GUILLAUMET

ANTOINE ARRIVES AT THE TOULOUSE train station on one of those autumn days when the sun is shining but not giving off any heat, when it dominates the sky but has no power. His nerves are making his gut vibrate like the strings of a guitar.

A modern electric tram takes him to Montaudran. A noise makes him turn around and he watches a Bréguet 14 take off until it's holding its own in the sky. He feels it's a good omen.

Thanks to his former teacher's intervention, Antoine was informed that he should present himself to the airline's director of operations, Monsieur Didier Daurat, and that whether or not he joined the company depended entirely on Daurat.

The office is austere, containing only maps and papers. The chairs are hard, no doubt to prevent anyone from remaining seated too long. Monsieur Daurat radiates an air of certainty which unsettles Antoine.

"Why do you want to join this company?"

"Because I want to fly . . ."

"Fine. But this is not a company that provides joy rides."

"I know."

"A joy ride company doesn't fly when it rains. It doesn't fly when it's foggy. Do you understand?" Daurat watches Antoine closely with his small, penetrating eyes.

"Perfectly, Monsieur Daurat."

The director of operations studies Antoine's pilot credentials.

"You have limited flying experience . . ."

"I was in the armed forces for three years."

"The armed forces in times of peace is a spa for rheumatics."

Antoine is about to say something, but he keeps his mouth shut. What little confidence he had has vanished. Daurat is right, his flying experience is minimal.

"Report for duty to the head of the workshop area tomorrow morning at 0600. He needs people for engine maintenance. That's all I can offer you right now, if you're interested."

"And in the future?"

"We'll see."

Daurat starts pulling papers out of a file and examining them. Antoine hesitates, unsure if he's to remain seated or if the interview is over. He wriggles in the chair until Daurat looks up, somewhat annoyed.

"Good day," he says dryly.

"Ah, yes! Forgive me, Monsieur Daurat! Good day!"

Cleaning engines with potash isn't the most exciting work in the world, but Antoine likes these hangars with their corrugated iron roofs on which the rain drums loudly, competing with the noise of the hammers, and he's amazed by the latest circular saws with their voracious but precise cuts. The planes are constructed by hand, one piece, one

139

screw at a time. The boss of the workshop, Monsieur Lefebvre, has an Austro-Hungarian mustache which turns up at the ends.

When the mechanics, grease up to their elbows, see the young man with his lordly manners and an aristocratic surname, and with a shirt and tie under his tight-fitting overalls, they're perplexed. He examines things with an odd intensity.

"What are you looking at with so much attention?" the boss asks him that first day.

"The way people are working with their hands. The precise sounds of what they're doing. It's as if I were in an orchestra rather than a workshop."

Monsieur Lefebvre gives Antoine a puzzled look and one of the mechanics in his grubby overalls starts to make mocking faces and to laugh at the new employee.

When Antoine begins to take apart cylinders, his hands aren't very deft, but he's well acquainted with fitting together engine parts. The 300 hp Renault engines aren't all that different from the ones he learned to take apart in the Saurer truck factory before he became one of their sales representatives.

He arrives back at his lodgings, Le Grand Balcon, that afternoon, tired but in a good mood. He'd asked for a room with a desk and they've given him one on the fourth floor. It has a large window that, from the rather jammed-in corner on which the building is located, overlooks the huge Place du Capitole.

Occasionally, he starts to write, but his concentration escapes through the window along with the smoke from his cigarette. He likes to watch the people coming and going into the cafés and brasseries lining the porticoed square that trams regularly traverse. From his window, he spies on the girls walking by in twos and threes as they laugh, whisper secrets to each other, and laugh again. There are also couples in their Sunday best, strolling hand in hand with that quiet look of those who have domesticated their love. He envies them.

There's a knock on his door. One of the Márquez sisters has an envelope for him. It contains a copy of *Le Navire d'Argent* and a note from Jean Prévost encouraging him to keep writing. His first story "The Aviator" has finally been published in this issue.

Antoine is pleased to see it in print; it feeds his vanity, if only briefly, to see his own name in ink. At the same time, however, it causes him a sadness of sorts: It's a finished work; he can no longer sink his fingers into its clay and give it form; it doesn't belong in his potter's hands anymore, in the same way that a child who has grown up no longer belongs in his parent's lap.

That night, one of the mechanics who works in his section sits down next to him at the common dining room table. When Madame Márquez deposits a china tureen on the table, the aroma of chicken soup saturates the room and the world seems a much friendlier place. A man quietly enters the dining room and wishes all the guests a good evening before taking a seat at a vacant table. He's wearing a leather jacket with damp patches on the shoulders and brings with him the cold of the high clouds.

"That's Henri Guillaumet. He does the route to Alicante," Antoine's colleague whispers. "They say he's the airline's most reliable pilot."

"How was today's flight, Monsieur Guillaumet?"

Henri Guillaumet's spoon stops halfway to his mouth, he looks up and gives a friendly smile. Then he continues to eat.

Nobody asks again. He's already given the answer: Everything has gone well, the timetable for each stopover has been met, there's nothing more to say. If the dampness of his jacket is due to a downpour he flew through over Barcelona, if his breath froze in the Pyrenees, if the engine coughed for hours, none of this is important.

The next morning, it's still dark when Antoine boards the tram for Montaudran. Guillaumet boards after him.

"Are you on duty today, Monsieur Guillaumet?" He feels bold enough to ask, as they are clearly heading in the same direction.

"Only as far as Barcelona."

"Only as far! You say it as if it were a stroll."

"You could describe it as that."

"But you have to cross the Pyrenees . . ."

The pilot anxiously consults his watch and his expression darkens. Flying over the Pyrenees doesn't worry him. What he's really concerned about is the trip to the airport on this tram, which is travelling so slowly it gives the impression it's going to fall asleep on the tracks at any moment.

Antoine introduces himself to Henri. "My friends just call me Saint-Ex," he adds shyly.

"Are you a pilot?" Guillaumet asks Antoine.

"I hope to be. I flew as a soldier, but for now I'm just an assistant mechanic."

"Don't worry. We've all had that job in this company. That's just Monsieur Daurat's way of making you prove yourself. You'll get your chance."

"Do you think so?"

"I'm certain. But, that said, you'll have only one chance. Don't fail. Daurat is fair, but he's merciless."

There's something indefinable about Henri Guillaumet that Antoine likes. Maybe it's his childlike smile.

CHAPTER 24

★

Toulouse, 1926

ANTOINE DE SAINT-EXUPÉRY, JEAN MERMOZ, AND HENRI GUILLAUMET

ONE NIGHT, RETURNING TO LE Grand Balcon after a hard day in the workshop, the mechanics' arrival coincides with that of a man with broad shoulders and blond hair, wearing a cashmere overcoat.

"That's Jean Mermoz," murmurs a mechanic reverently.

Antoine notices that Madame Márquez, who had dozed off in the chair in reception while knitting a sock with two huge wooden knitting needles, suddenly opens her eyes and starts to shout her sister's name.

"Odile! Hurry! Monsieur Mermoz is back."

The recent arrival smiles in what seems an enigmatic way to Antoine. There's something seductively affable in his expression that Antoine finds irresistible. The flustered women, hypnotised by the presence of this unquestionably superior guest, rush about the *pension* like headless chickens in their eagerness to get his room ready and serve dinner immediately.

Just then, Henri Guillaumet enters in his wet jacket, his hair a mess. When he sees the recent arrival, he walks over to him and gives him a big hug.

"How are you, Jean?"

"Fantastic. My only problem is the obstinacy of the doctors who treated me after the crash in the desert and my rescue from the Tuaregs. They think I should still be resting . . ."

"Well then, you ought to do it."

"Resting is what makes me ill."

Antoine, propelled by one of those inner impulses which sometimes cause us to take a risk, stands up and resolutely approaches Mermoz.

"My name is Antoine, Antoine de Saint-Exupéry."

"And that's been the case for some time?"

Mermoz's tone as he says this is so mocking and cutting that Antoine doesn't know how to reply. He suddenly feels ridiculous for having interrupted this private get-together and barging in uninvited. His cheeks start to burn and he can't stop himself from stuttering as he asks their forgiveness.

"Please continue; what I mean is, please forgive me."

The new guest looks at him with mocking severity, but as Antoine clumsily starts to back away, Guillaumet extends a hand and grabs his forearm.

"Saint-Ex is a pilot too. He'll soon finish his probation in the workshops."

Guillaumet could have said that Antoine was a mere assistant mechanic, or said nothing at all and played along with his arrogant friend's taunt, but Antoine is beginning to understand what sort of person Guillaumet is.

"Saint-Ex, let me introduce Jean Mermoz, one of the pilots on the Africa route."

"Africa . . ."

Antoine can't help echoing the word as his eyes widen. To him, "Africa" evokes never-ending light over an immense country. His reverie is such that the two pilots exchange a glance.

"Do you know Africa?" asks Mermoz less disdainfully.

"A little. I was posted to Casablanca for a few months during my military service."

"I can't wait to get back to Casablanca. For me, it's like coming home."

Madame Márquez informs Mermoz that soup is being served.

Guillaumet smiles.

"When you're here, Mermoz, the rest of us become invisible!"

The three of them sit down together at the table and Guillaumet asks his friend about his eardrum. Mermoz explains to Antoine that while he had recovered from his visible injuries, a subsequent infection and high fever had led to the surgeon cutting open his ear and finding sand in his auditory canal. "He said I had half the desert in my head. He was convinced I would lose my hearing, but said that I could still have a normal life, and I was lucky to be alive! But if I was deaf in one ear, I'd lose my pilot's licence, so I told him to operate again, because I don't want to live just a 'normal' life; I want to fly! The only risk I have of a relapse now would be one of Daurat's yells."

"But Daurat doesn't yell," Guillaumet contradicts him.

"He yells in a whisper," Antoine points out.

"Yes! That's it! He yells in a whisper!"

They eat and talk without pause. The weaving of an invisible thread of friendship has begun.

CHAPTER 25

★

Casablanca (Morocco), 1926

Jean Mermoz

When Mermoz steps inside the Emporium, two of the girls throw their arms around his neck and his colleagues stand up to give him a hug. Even before he's sat down, the waiter has brought a bottle of champagne inside an ice bucket. Marcel Reine, who has already drunk half a bottle of whisky by himself, disappears, and comes back a short while later, his eyes sparkling.

"Come out to the patio, everyone. There's a friend who wants to take part in our party."

It's a horse in the courtyard at the entrance to the establishment; no one knows where he's come from. Reine grabs a bottle of champagne, pours it into a container, and lets the animal drink. It leaves not a drop. When all is gone, the horse whinnies with exuberant joy. And when it takes a somewhat clumsy step, its hooves skid a little. Reine laughs so hard that he slips too and falls on top of a flowerpot. Two of the girls come out and take him in hand. He grabs one of them by the buttocks and heads inside, drunkenly singing "La Marseillaise."

Music and drinks flow all night long as they beg Mermoz to repeat again and again the tale of his crash, capture, and rescue, which he does with comic embellishments that make them all laugh.

There comes a moment when he puts his hand over his empty glass as the Moroccan waiter indicates that he'll fill it with whisky again. The waiter gives him a look which suggests he'll never understand these Westerners who squander their money and are not afraid of their God.

"That's it for today."

Ville, Reine, and two other pilots, along with several girls with long fingernails and short skirts, show how devastated they are at his words. One of them, a very slight Egyptian girl with a wasp waist and eyes outlined with kohl, wraps her arms around his neck in an attempt to detain him. Mermoz laughs and gets up from his seat with the girl dangling from his neck like an amulet.

"I have to leave early tomorrow for Cabo Juby."

His companions don't insist. They know it would be useless. He takes hold of the girl by her waist and effortlessly deposits her on the table. At that moment, Érable, another pilot, arrives.

"Mermoz, I've been searching for you all night."

"You weren't looking in the right spot."

"I want to ask you a favour—that we swap shifts: I'll do yours tomorrow and you do mine next Friday. I know it's last minute, but, you see, I have a date . . ."

"No need to explain. It's done."

Érable thanks him effusively and leaves. Mermoz turns toward his group who, thanks to the chaos in the establishment, couldn't hear the conversation even if they'd wanted to. He puts his hands on his hips.

"Ladies and gentlemen . . ."

They all open their eyes wide in anticipation.

"The night is young . . . and so are we. Waiter! Let's finish what we started!"

Cheers, hats, and even a garter are tossed up in celebration. Before he's leaned back in his seat, the heads of two girls are resting on Mermoz's chest. Reine raises a glass of pastis which he drinks as if it were water from a well, and toasts life. Mermoz doesn't yet know just how significant that toast will turn out to be.

Their laughter will precede a lengthy silence.

But before that silence, noise. The deafening roar of the twelve-cylinder Renault engine throbbing in the belly of a Bréguet 14 as, the next day, November 11, Gourp the mailman, with Érable as escort, an Arab interpreter, and Pintado, the Spanish mechanic, take off from Casablanca. As they're flying over Mogador, still in Morocco, Gourp realises his engine is failing and is forced to land. Érable lands next to him and they transfer the mail to his plane. Pintado thinks he can fix the fault in a few hours and Gourp insists that Érable leave so they don't delay the handover of the mail in Dakar.

But fate always has its own plans.

As Gourp walks away from his colleague's plane, a group of armed Bedouins emerge from behind a rock formation. Their leader, Ould-Aj-Rab, is an Arab trained by the French Army. He understands Érable's words perfectly, as he begs them not to shoot in the language Ould-Aj-Rab has ended up hating after so much humiliation by those white men who treat Arabs worse than dogs. At the leader's signal, the guns fire at point-blank range. Pintado and Érable drop down dead onto the desert sand. The interpreter throws himself at the feet of the leader of the party and, in a pitiful voice and with an exaggerated display of feeling, requests the favour of a dignified death rather than being dispatched

148

like an infidel. At a sign from Ould-Aj-Rab, one of the Bedouins takes out his huge scimitar and, as the translator prays with his head bowed, raises the blade and then lets it drop forcefully onto the man's neck. His head rolls over the sand leaving a trail of blood. Gourp, terrified, shouts out and one of the Bedouins shoots at him without hesitation, but at a signal from his chief, he doesn't finish him off. They might be able to collect a ransom.

The pilots haven't arrived as expected at the stopover in Villa Cisneros in the Spanish Sahara. The alert goes out when they've exceeded the number of hours they could fly with the fuel they were carrying.

Few things can shake Mermoz, but when he realises that he was the one who ought to have escorted Gourp that day, who ought to be missing, he feels his legs give way. His shock lasts only a moment, and then he slams the door of his apartment shut and races through the centre of Casablanca to take part in the rescue operation.

An envoy of the renegade Ould-Aj-Rab has brought a message that the sole survivor of the massacre is being held prisoner while they await the payment of a ransom. He is, in fact, half dead. The bullet wound has become infected, and gangrene is spreading up his leg like a damp patch as he spends days on the back of a camel, lurching through the desert under a blazing sun. Gourp is in such agony that he has drunk all the bottles of iodine and carbolic acid he was carrying in his pocket in an attempt to end his suffering as quickly as possible.

In Toulouse, Daurat's assistant arrives in the office of the director of operations with a telegram containing news of the deaths of Pintado and Érable as well as the kidnapping of Gourp. Daurat reads it in silence. Bouvet remains standing on the other side of the desk.

"What do you want?"

"There's more, Monsieur Daurat. We've received a message from

Port-Étienne. The pilots haven't taken off with the mail while they await instructions."

Daurat walks over to the window and looks out into space.

"Take down this note: 'If the mail doesn't reach Casablanca at 1500 as expected, the manager of the airfield and the pilot in charge of flying that leg will be fired.'"

His assistant wrings his hands.

"The pilot is Lécrivain, monsieur . . ."

Daurat turns around and, without abandoning his cigarette, gives Bouvet a look. The assistant leaves, mumbling a jumble of apologies.

The director is on his own, yet again. He continues to stare fixedly beyond the overcast afternoon and the little swirls of dust above the empty landing strips.

Blame isn't what concerns Daurat. He made a pact with his conscience some time ago. Many men from the airline have died since he became director. He's the one who orders them to fly in extreme conditions, who penalizes them if they are late even when the conditions are adverse, who reprimands them if they are daunted by a questionable weather report. He pushes them skyward and some of them fall down.

That's his mission, and he doesn't blame himself. He doesn't forget either. He remembers in precise detail every one of those pilots who has died under his leadership. He can see them all in front of his desk full of urgent life-presence. The list of their names is branded on his skin with a red-hot iron. He lives with that.

Daurat orders the ransom paid. During the days that follow, he goes home only to change his shirt. His wife doesn't ask him any questions; he looks at her and she knows: work, responsibility. She doesn't even feel bitterness anymore. She sees him coming and going like a guest. He's turned his house into a hotel, because his real home is the office.

The light in his office is on day and night. It has been impossible to recover the bodies of Pintado and Érable and there's no news of the interpreter. But the mail continues to travel between Dakar and France, as it should.

Everyone thinks that Daurat never wavers, and he allows them to believe this. It strikes him that men need to believe in something above and beyond themselves. Daurat thinks about the dead pilots, and those who will die. He looks at his reflection in the windowpane and silently asks it: *Is it all worth it?*

His reflection doesn't reply.

He doesn't know if it's worth risking the lives of these young men to carry the messages in the letters to all parts of the globe, but he does know that the sacrifice, the effort, and the delivery makes them better people. He thinks of them as the soft, unformed dough that comes out of the kneading machine. It only turns into bread when it's put into the oven and is subjected to intense heat. The soft, sticky dough is useless, but bread sustains all of humanity.

A few days later, Ould-Aj-Rab's answer to the deal arrives. There have been so many requests from Mermoz to take part in the rescue that Daurat orders him to be the one to be present at the handover of Gourp.

Mermoz and Ville travel eighty kilometres from Cabo Juby to meet up with the caravan in the middle of nowhere. When they get there, they realise how rash they've been to go without a big escort, but it's too late to turn back. Mermoz has a revolver he bought in the bazaar in Casablanca tucked into the waistband under his shirt, and Ville has a German pistol in his jacket pocket.

An emissary pulls away from the caravan, which has stopped some hundreds of metres away. He comes toward them, pulling along another camel which is carrying a weak, wasted Gourp. Mermoz tosses the bag of money to the Bedouin, and the two pilots very carefully lower their friend from the camel into their arms. Mermoz thanks God that his friend's heart is still beating, but his skin has been flayed by the sun, his leg is putrid, his face is swollen, and his lips are deathly blue. Gourp is at death's door. The Bedouin scrutinises Mermoz from atop his camel and Mermoz clenches his jaw until his teeth grind. He doesn't care if his teeth break, but what he won't do is give that bastard the pleasure of seeing him cry.

Mermoz walks away, carrying Gourp in his arms as if he were carrying a bride across the threshold into her new life. It's only when the Bedouins have started to move off that he allows his tears to forge a path down his dusty cheeks.

Gourp will die in hospital twenty-four hours later.

CHAPTER 26

Toulouse, 1926

Antoine de Saint-Exupéry and Henri Guillaumet

In the past few weeks, Antoine has come through his baptism of fire as a pilot in front of Daurat's expressionless gaze, and has performed a couple of test flights around the airfield. He's even gone along as a passenger on the Spanish route, but so far, he hasn't received either approval or disapproval from the company to work as a pilot. On this particular afternoon, Daurat comes into the workshop and walks over to where Antoine is preparing a washtub of potash so he can submerge a rusty engine in it.

"Saint-Exupéry . . ."

"Yes, Monsieur Daurat."

"Tomorrow at 0600 you'll take the mail to Barcelona."

"Do you really mean it?"

The director looks at him without moving a muscle in his face.

"My apologies, Monsieur Daurat, of course you mean it." And since the silence hanging in the air is making him uncomfortable, Antoine asks: "Do you have any important advice to give me?"

"Yes."

Antoine hurries to take out his small leather notebook so he can jot it down.

"Yes?"

"Pedal and joystick."

Daurat hands over a map, turns around, and moves off without any further explanation. He hasn't even asked Antoine if he considers himself capable of doing it. *Of course he feels capable!* But right then and there, he starts to be seized by doubt.

As soon as he's finished his work for the day, he hurriedly removes his overalls and walks to the workshop's main entrance to smoke one nervous cigarette after another. He examines the sky with more interest than usual: Twilight smudges with purplish clouds until the sky turns into a solid black curtain. A sky with no stars is a bad night for pilots.

Guillaumet strolls by and pauses.

"I've already heard, Saint-Ex . . ."

Antoine nods anxiously.

"It's easier than it seems. You'll have no problem."

"And the Pyrenees?"

"Easy."

"Easy?"

Guillaumet points toward the hangar.

"Come on, let's go over the whole Spanish route."

Antoine follows Guillaumet to a small, soulless room. He'd follow him to the centre of the earth! Guillaumet turns on the light that's hanging from the roof, and under its feeble light, Antoine unfolds the large map on top of the wooden table. *There's France, there's Spain, the sea, the mountain ranges.*

"Look . . ."

Guillaumet's hands are exquisitely clean and his fingers run over the map as if they were reading it by touch. He's searching for something that isn't included in the legend or among the symbols that denote cities, towns, capes, and gulfs. The tip of his finger moves over the Iberian Peninsula until it has leaped over the Sierra Nevada and landed in an empty zone near Guadix.

"There's an excellent field here for an emergency landing, but it's more dangerous than it seems. Beware the three orange trees that border it. You can only spot them when you're nearly on top of them."

"Three orange trees . . ."

"Mark them on the map."

Antoine obediently makes a note on the map like a diligent student. Guillaumet continues to run his finger over the map, and it stops near Málaga.

"Another landing field?"

"No, you must never land there. From above, you can see beautiful grass which makes you want to touch down there. You think it will be like landing on a feather mattress. But that high grass hides a stream that snakes around the field. If you put your plane down there, you'll inevitably tip over, perhaps with deadly consequences."

The two of them are so immersed in the map that they don't notice a shadow moving silently through the darkness in the hangar. Daurat's tiny eyes watch them. He listens attentively to Guillaumet's whisperings. He also takes on board Saint-Ex's studious silence. Daurat nods and leaves as quietly as he came. He knows the aristocratic would-be poet will be a pilot.

When Antoine lies down on his bed in Le Grand Balcon, he can't sleep. He goes over Guillaumet's warning about the field on the side of a mountain which looks idyllic for an emergency landing, but requires landing with care because a herd of about thirty sheep lie in wait and they could wander into the path of the wheels at any moment.

Guillaumet has also pointed out other slopes which are less obvious but ideal for a landing, and he's even marked with a round dot a place in the middle of the countryside in which Antoine will find a farm where they'll lend him a friendly hand. And the field with the three orange trees. Those three orange trees are crucial!

It's the best geography lesson he's ever received.

He thinks about the treacherous stream hidden in the field mentioned by Guillaumet and shivers. In his imagination, the stream snaking its way secretly through the tall grass is a serpent.

That image brings to mind a book he read years ago in the attic of the house in Saint-Maurice, *Histoires Vécues* (*True Stories*). It was about a jungle and there was a picture that used to distress and attract him at the same time, with the result that he couldn't stop looking at it. It depicted an enormous boa constrictor coiling itself around a terrified wild animal, its huge wide-open mouth about to devour it. The book explained that boas swallow their victims whole without chewing them and then sleep without moving for the time it takes to digest them. He tosses nervously in his bed at the mere thought. *How is it possible for an animal as slender as his arm to swallow another ten times its size? How large could an animal it swallows be?* Sleep becomes impossible, so Antoine turns on the light on his bedside table, grabs a pencil and one of the pieces of paper accumulating there, and tries to draw a snake that has swallowed an enormous animal . . .

An elephant . . .

It's not easy to draw a boa that's swallowed that sort of mouthful. The first light of day filtering in through the window finds Antoine drawing serpents and elephants. That's how his first day as a postal pilot begins.

CHAPTER 27

Dakar (Senegal), 1927

ANTOINE DE SAINT-EXUPÉRY, JEAN MERMOZ, AND HENRI GUILLAUMET

FOR ANTOINE, IT'S BEEN MONTHS of intense service in Spain: Barcelona, Alicante, Málaga . . . He finds Alicante particularly appealing: the warm nights, the bronzed women, and the seafront esplanade lined with palm trees make him feel as if he's part of one of the stories from *A Thousand and One Nights*. Barcelona, on the other hand, strikes him as a grey, industrial city. He's amazed that its exquisite, bourgeois opera house is right in the middle of the red-light district, where prostitutes and criminals hang out, spending their days strolling up and down the Paseo de las Ramblas, which leads to the docks.

Two weeks ago, he crossed paths with Mermoz in Málaga during an exchange of mailbags. His friend walked toward him hands on head:

"A catastrophe has struck Guillaumet!"

"What's happened?" asked Antoine anxiously. "An accident?"

"Much worse! He's getting married!"

During Antoine's most recent encounter with Guillaumet at the Barcelona airfield, Guillaumet had told him something about a young Swiss woman, but not a great deal.

"Jean, we'll have to give them a present."

"A straitjacket!"

Just when Antoine had started to get used to the climate in Spain and its cuisine laden with olive oil and garlic, he was posted to Dakar in Senegal, the colonial capital right in the heart of French West Africa.

Spain seems like Finland compared with the heat of Senegal. But the worst aspect isn't the heat, or the flies, or the smells produced by people cooking outdoors, nor the streets without asphalt that mean living in a constant cloud of dust. It's that he can't get used to the colonial lifestyle in Africa. But everything is better because Guillaumet is there. His honeymoon consisted of a return to work.

Guillaumet somewhat timidly introduces Antoine to his new wife, Noëlle, as if he were afraid Antoine wouldn't give his approval. When she goes into the kitchen to get more tea, Antoine leans in close to Guillaumet and tells him that she's the most enchanting woman on the planet.

He loves seeing Henri happy. Henri and Noëlle are one of those couples who hold hands when they sit on the terrace of a café for Europeans in the company of other people. There's nothing feigned in their love for each other. Antoine is delighted for Henri. He could be the only pilot Antoine knows who's cut out for marriage.

The Guillaumets introduce him to the city's social circles, although they themselves are a quiet couple not much given to night life. Antoine, on the other hand, likes the night. Reality rules the day; dreams take over at night. Insomnia, too. Sometimes he feels like an owl, doing the rounds of cabarets full of smoke, a great deal of noise, and women, but he never finds what he's looking for. There are pretty legs and lips painted red, so plump you could fall asleep kissing them. But seen up close, these hostess girls infect him with sadness.

They certainly smile, but it's hard to smile with sincerity if you're being paid.

He can't find his place in this city of mediocre public servants and business representatives who play at being millionaires. In Paris, with their medium-sized salaries, they'd lead humdrum lives, but here they have big mansions with a cook, a chauffeur, and two or three maids. The sticky heat seems to have impregnated the social relationships of this colony of people with delusions of grandeur.

Initially, Antoine is assigned few flights and has a lot of free time. More than he'd like. He finds the city's dance halls crass, brothels in disguise. He's often to be seen in the midst of the noisy music in one of those nighttime establishments, sitting in an isolated corner carefully reading a book by Nietzsche or *The Dialogues of Plato*. Plato would be fascinated by this cavern in which music resounds and shadows dance.

Guillaumet picks him up every day for a walk around this city of dusty streets, followed by a lukewarm beer. He listens patiently on those days when Antoine's voice is like a cat-o'-nine-tails which never stops cracking as it tells a thousand tales, real and imaginary. And Guillaumet remains by his side with the same loyalty on those days when his friend seems to have fallen down a deep well.

A break of a few days between flights results in his acceptance—to overcome boredom—of an invitation to join a lion hunt. They race across the savanna in two noisy cars which would scare off any animal or human in the surrounding kilometres. They raise a great deal of sand, cause considerable uproar, and burn a great deal of fuel in vain. Then one afternoon, when Antoine stays behind on his own to read inside one of the open-top cars while the others go off on reconnaissance, a lion appears in front of him without warning. The feline walks toward him and Antoine nervously searches for the mechanism which closes the roof of the car, but he can't find it. He decides to confront the lion in a very unorthodox way—by loudly sounding the horn. Faced with this unexpected blast, the imposing king of the jungle turns tail and flees in terror. Antoine jots down in his leather notebook that he has just played the leading role in one of the least courageous episodes of lion-hunting in Africa's history.

A forced landing near the Sénégal River leads to an encounter with friendly people who have never seen a white man—perhaps the reason for their friendliness—and this results in a horseback ride over dozens of kilometres amicably led by two Senegalese men. Antoine loves to come across kindness in his travels. But he's not prepared for the squadrons of mosquitoes. By the time he reaches Dakar, he has a fever and is admitted to the hospital which is, in reality, a scrapyard for human bodies. Yellow fever wreaks havoc. The heat is filled with destructive coughs and the stench of decaying flesh. He spends a month there, surrounded by people dying daily. The body of the person in the neighbouring bed has been colonised by lines of worms which crawl up and down its length like a little toy train. Or so it seems to Antoine in his feverish state.

Guillaumet turns up one afternoon, turns pale, disappears, and then returns with someone dressed in a medic's gown that was once white, who never stops gesticulating wildly. He reluctantly signs Antoine's release.

"We're going," Henri tells Antoine.

Antoine doesn't think he'll have the strength to get up, but he obeys. Guillaumet helps him to his feet and Antoine puts an arm on Guillaumet's shoulder to help him walk to the exit. He feels relief as soon as he senses the fresh air on his face. His friend takes him back to his apartment and puts him to bed on a pallet in the tiny living room. Noëlle prepares some chicken broth and puts cold compresses on his forehead.

Two days later, Antoine is feeling much better. He takes advantage of his first day out to go to the only florist in town, and buys up all the flowers in stock. They're delivered to the home of Noëlle Guillaumet together with a card with neither words nor signature; it only has a horizontal moon which looks like a smile, surrounded by childlike stars.

As soon as he reports his discharge to headquarters, he receives a telegram from Daurat. He is to report to Daurat's office immediately. And so he travels all the legs of the mail route to Toulouse as part of the luggage. He's filled with wonder as he crosses the Strait of Gibraltar— from the air, it's identical to the way it appears in all the school maps! The Iberian Peninsula ends in a pointed chin. Africa and Europe are so close they look as if they're going to kiss each other. He regrets that they don't.

Monsieur Daurat doesn't kiss him either, but at least he gives him a few days' leave, and a delighted Antoine goes to Paris, his head full of a thousand plans after being away for so long.

In Paris, however, he doesn't come across any of his friends. They're not in the city, or else they're busy. No one seems to have missed him much. He wanders past the bookstalls along the Seine like a foreigner and buys mystery stories to take his mind off his loneliness. He sits down to watch the pensioners fishing in the river's turbulent waters while the steam barges discharge smoke which darkens the afternoon.

He walks past Notre-Dame Cathedral and heads into the Jewish quarter, where business is booming in the narrow streets full of butchers' shops; produce stores where the fruit is displayed with mathematical precision; small jewellery shops full of bracelets, earrings, and silver rings; and somewhat antiquated hat shops. He likes the Hebrew script on the store signs. He goes into a bakery and buys a sweet pastry twist sprinkled with sesame seeds.

As he reaches a corner, a taxi stops a few steps away and a woman carrying two bags jumps in. The hair is longer; it's a light reddish colour—*her* hair!

Lou-Lou . . .

Antoine is on the verge of shouting out to catch her attention and starts to raise his arm, but something paralyzes him. His arm freezes midair. His pastry twist drops to the ground and the sesame seeds scatter over the sidewalk. When she turns sideways to climb into the taxi, Antoine realises that Lou-Lou is pregnant. He watches the taxi move off and get lost in the traffic.

He stands motionless on the sidewalk, and irritated pedestrians have to walk around him. He stands on that corner for so long, it feels as if he's grown old. When he starts walking again, he walks slowly, and he senses that he's left his youth behind forever.

As soon as Antoine returns to Toulouse, Daurat receives him in his office wearing his raincoat and hat. It might look as if Daurat has just arrived, but he's been in his office for hours. Maybe he just hasn't had time to remove them yet or maybe they remind him of how temporary everything is.

"Saint-Exupéry, you're the new manager of the airfield at Cabo Juby."

"Manager of the airfield?"

"Correct."

"But Monsieur Daurat, I'd prefer . . ."

"I haven't asked you what you'd prefer."

"I don't know how to be a manager."

"When you arrived here, you didn't know how to be a pilot either."

Antoine shrugs. He's brought a heavy burden of sadness with him from Paris and he doesn't care much about anything.

"Good. Well, then, you're the new manager of the airfield at Cabo Juby. But you'll do more than supervise the movement of the mail through your stopover. You have to establish the best relationship possible with the Spanish military, who authorise us to be there but don't trust us at all. In addition, you must also establish the best relationship possible with the chiefs of the Moorish tribes in the region. We have many forced landings in the desert. We need as many allies as we can get."

"And how will I do that?"

"Your job consists of finding that out."

"When will I start?"

"You'll leave with the mail tomorrow morning. At 0600."

CHAPTER 28

Cabo Juby (Morocco), 1928

Antoine de Saint-Exupéry

THE SPANIARDS, WITH SOMEWHAT EXCESSIVE patriotic fervour, call this territory the Spanish Sahara. But the Spanish presence is, in fact, limited to a few tiny forts scattered across thousands of kilometres of a desert they find alien. At dusk, flags are lowered, the fortification gates are closed, and the messes are opened to allow the soldiers to drink bad wine, play dominoes or the card game known as *guiñote*, and, propped on the bar, to sort out the world. They rarely wander beyond their bases in this land they call Spanish. Hostile tribes lie in wait. So too sandstorms, and the barren, rocky ground which spreads out before them. The region in which they are located—from Cabo Juby south-ward to Cabo Blanco—is a deserted area which, with their love of gran-diloquence, the Spaniards call Río de Oro. It contains neither river nor gold, just sand.

Cabo Juby is a curve between two deserts, one of dry land, the other of sea, water that doesn't relieve thirst. The Spanish base rises up in the middle of this solitary place, buffeted by the wind. When seen up close, it's not so imposing: flaking walls, chipped windows, corrosion decaying the metal finishes.

A kilometre away, located about a hundred metres out to sea, there's another square stone building covered with a beard of moss and mussels which drips when the waves break over it. It was originally a warehouse built by a visionary Scot called Mackenzie who wanted to make his fortune buying the ostrich feathers, dates, marble, and gold transported by the caravans that crossed the desert. He thought that by building the warehouse on top of large rocks out in the sea he would avoid looting. The idea was as shrewd as his plan to flood a section of the Sahara and convert it into a garden. The wind blew away his dreams, just as it blows everything away. When the Spaniards found the building abandoned following the constant looting it had suffered, they turned it into a prison out in the sea which they called Casa del Mar.

Antoine walks slowly toward the entrance of the Cabo Juby barracks. The Spanish soldiers are dressed in shabby uniforms, and the whole place has an air of neglect: rusty drums, broken boxes, flagpoles with no flags. The commandant of the base, Colonel de la Peña, is expecting him in his office. It's Antoine's second visit. His first reception, a few days earlier, could hardly have been described as warm.

When he had explained to those at his farewell meal at Le Grand Balcon that, as station manager, he was going to intercede with the Spanish, one of the mechanics suggested he'd have a good time, because the Spaniards were real party animals. But by then, Antoine had been doing the leg between Barcelona and Alicante for months and had some knowledge of things Spanish. From his occasional flights to Málaga, he learned that in the south of Spain they liked the strumming of guitars and companionship, but that in the centre of the country there was a type of Spaniard who tied in more with the image of that old nobleman Don Quijote, a type who walked very upright so he seemed taller, and refused to believe that Spain's glorious empire went up in smoke a long time ago. Pride intoxicates Spaniards more than wine.

This handful of African desert and these unruly, at times blood-thirsty, tribes is all they have left of that empire of theirs on which the sun once never set. But here in this fort, the officers with their impeccable uniforms and thin, waxed moustaches pretend not to be aware of this. The enlisted men, on the other hand, look like a bunch of beggars: torn, dirty uniforms; feet dragging along in dusty boots. Someone explains to Antoine that soldiers are posted to this remote base as punishment.

An officer takes him to a lieutenant, in front of whom the officer stands to attention with little grace. The lieutenant knocks on the door of a captain's minuscule office and opens it without waiting for an invitation. The captain is smoking and gazing out the window. He examines this French pilot from head to toe with a look of irritation, as if Antoine is interrupting an important task. Perhaps he is. Smoking is one of the main activities in this fort.

The captain walks out and signals to Antoine to follow him to the colonel's office. Doing things by the book is crucial. Here, soldiers smoke and follow proper procedure—that's what they do all day.

Colonel de la Peña indicates that Antoine should sit down. A photograph of King Alfonso XIII and a dark wooden crucifix observe them from the wall behind the desk. There are no papers on the colonel's desk; he's not doing anything. And that's his authority. It's likely that no one has anything to do here, but his command consists in covering this up.

"I've brought you the schedule of landings and takeoffs for the coming week, as you requested."

The military commander nods, his expression neutral.

"I reiterate once again our wish to collaborate. I'd like you to see us as friends." Antoine becomes a little nervous as the colonel raises his eyes and looks at him with total indifference. "The French and the Spaniards, lifelong neighbours, we're one and the same."

The head of the post lifts his chin and says not a word, but Antoine can almost see what he's thinking:

What's this business of us Spaniards being the same as these Frogs who look down their noses at us, eat cheese that smells like sweaty feet, and drink their wine warm?

"Our airfield is your home; please come whenever you like," Antoine insists.

Colonel de la Peña stretches his neck and answers with one of those set phrases that Spaniards have by the bucket load. "Señor de Saint-Exupéry, let each of us keep to his own home."

Antoine feels relieved when he leaves the bare office in which there is almost no furniture, hardly any filing cabinets, and no sign of warmth. He strolls over to the airport hut next to the army base which is now his home. Lou-Lou would probably have thought it disgusting, although she might have seen its charm. Lou-Lou wanted to be a poet, and this rough spot contains the secret of its own beauty: everything is original; nothing has been altered.

It's like being present on the first day of the world.

In terms of places to live without Lou-Lou, Antoine prefers the arid simplicity of this desolate place to the mirages of Paris.

CHAPTER 29

★

Casablanca (Morocco), 1928

JEAN MERMOZ AND ANTOINE DE SAINT-EXUPÉRY

MERMOZ'S FRIENDS PREFER A THOUSAND times over to go up in a plane with him in the middle of a gale to being passengers in his car. Mermoz puts his foot down hard on the accelerator of the red Amilcar he's driving recklessly through Casablanca as if the world were about to end.

He reaches the airfield with lots of time to spare before he has to take off for Cabo Juby with the mail. One of the ground crew holds out a newspaper in which there's an article about Latécoère Airlines. It tells of the rescue of some Portuguese aviators in which Mermoz played a part. They see him as the symbol of this generation of pilots who are putting France in the vanguard of aviation worldwide, and they're requesting that he be given the Légion d'honneur. Mermoz scrunches up the paper and angrily throws it away.

"Rubbish! I'm just doing my job! Those journalists make me look like a peacock! An idiot!"

He gets over his indignation as he flies south because he has other, more important, things to think about. For a long time, he's been asking to be part of the South America section of the airline, which is now named the Compagnie Générale Aéropostale, or simply Aéropostale. He's also been asking Colonel Denin, one of the main people in charge of French aviation, to convince the government to provide him with a machine that's capable of crossing the Atlantic. They've taken so long to reply that Charles Lindbergh, the American, has beaten them to the first transatlantic flight to continental Europe. Bureaucracy and political manoeuvring drive him mad.

And now these journalists . . . "The Légion d'honneur." How stupid! I don't want medals; I want a plane!

When he lands at Cabo Juby, he jumps down onto the runway with a caseload of wine. The manager of the airfield—a big man in a rather grubby djellaba—is waiting for him. Antoine's appearance brings the smile back to Mermoz's face.

"Saint-Ex! Have you changed religions?"

"Never! I'll never stop believing in women and Burgundy wine."

Mermoz roars with laughter.

"Dammit, Saint-Ex. You have no idea how much I needed a laugh. Have you read the papers recently?"

"I only read philosophers."

"That's my man!"

Mermoz stays two days waiting for the mail that's coming from Senegal. He takes over the kitchen and revolutionises the menu, doubling the size of the portions. Kamal the cook informs Antoine that there's no chicken.

"Kamal, that's tragic."

"There isn't a single chicken in all of Río de Oro?" asks Mermoz.

"Only on the Spanish base," sighs Antoine. Before he can look up, Mermoz is already heading out the door.

"Where are you going?"

"To the base."

Fifteen minutes later, Mermoz, Antoine, and two of the Spanish cooks are immersed in a game of cards. Lying on the table are three chickens and an aviator watch that cost Mermoz a fortune in a specialist shop in Paris. Antoine is concerned. It's a valuable work tool for Mermoz! But his friend's expression demands that Antoine trust him. And sure enough, they leave the kitchen with the chickens.

When they return to their hut, Kamal asks them how many chickens he should roast.

"How many?" asks a scandalised Mermoz. "All of them!"

Antoine eats one entire chicken. Mermoz eats the other two and anything left on his friend's plate. He drops into a hammock and asks Antoine to read him something as he starts to doze.

"Anything."

Antoine starts to read the speeches of old Zarathustra after his descent from the mountain. And to the accompaniment of his singsong voice, Mermoz falls asleep. Antoine, engrossed, continues to read. He has the book in one hand and a fly swatter in the other.

While Antoine writes up the reports which Daurat incessantly demands of him, Mermoz heads to the beach. He exercises zealously: he does sprints like a horse, one hundred push-ups, and swims naked in the sea until he's exhausted. Then he drops onto the sand to sunbake until his body is roasted and his skin has turned golden.

At night, the two of them play hangman with a paper and pencil while they argue about literature: Mermoz defends poetry as the highest literary artform and Antoine replies that it's in the novel and the essay that ideas take shape. They argue over which are the most beautiful names for women. They even learn to be quiet together and smoke in silence.

The time for Mermoz's departure arrives all too quickly. Antoine is busy writing a meteorological report. Mermoz comes in and puts a hand on his shoulder.

"I'm going."

"The mail awaits!"

"It's not that. I'm off to the new South America route."

There's a moment's silence.

"I'll miss you."

"Time passes quickly."

"I know you'll ignore this completely but—be careful, if you know what that means."

Mermoz laughs with that guffaw of his which resonates in his chest.

"Careful people get to be old. Those who are not careful get to the end of the world."

They look at each other. There's nothing more to say.

When Mermoz takes off at first light, silence settles over the runways and furnishings like the desert dust.

CHAPTER 30

Rio de Janeiro (Brazil), 1928

JEAN MERMOZ

THE NEW MAJORITY SHAREHOLDER OF the company, Monsieur
Marcel Bouilloux-Lafont, orders that an air race be organised from Toulouse to Saint-Louis in northern Senegal, with no stopovers. The first
ever flight in aviation history from the heart of Europe to the heart of
Africa nonstop. Mermoz is designated to pilot this flight before he takes
up his post in South America.

In Montaudran, they work day and night for ten days to fine-tune
and run final tests on a plane equipped with all the latest technical
improvements.

Mermoz takes off from the Montaudran airfield at dawn with little
formality. Daurat doesn't even come down to the runway to wish him
luck. Luck has nothing to do with a pilot's responsibilities.

Mermoz has to cross the Pyrenees, fly the long Spanish route, jump
over the sea at the Strait of Gibraltar, traverse Morocco, fly over 1,000

kilometres of hostile desert without an escort, conquer the night, confront the harshness of the weather . . .

And he'll do it, though it will be in a Latécoère 26 plane, a Laté, as it's known to the pilots, a new single-wing machine constructed from wood, steel, and canvas. Twenty-four hours later, as dawn breaks over Africa, the Laté 26 born in Toulouse lands smoothly at the Saint-Louis aerodrome. Mermoz is exhausted, even replying somewhat grumpily to the congratulations from the airfield employees.

"I did what I had to do," he tells them.

Some repairs delay his departure and he flies back unaware of what awaits him in France: cameras flashing, receptions with armies of waiters, medals from aeronautical clubs. It both pleases and annoys him. He hates speaking in public; his rarely seen shyness surfaces in those situations and he really dislikes showing his weaknesses. But the company asks him to accept all these honours because they increase its prestige, and this will help its expansion in South America.

High class young women, who only drink lemonade in public, discreetly slip messages into his jacket pocket with their addresses and suitable times for a rendezvous. The game amuses him for a few days, but Daurat doesn't allow him to become too distracted and urgently summons him to his office.

"Mermoz, you're going to have new responsibilities in South America."

"Responsibilities?"

"You'll be our manager of pilots."

"Manager of pilots? No way! There must be some error, Monsieur Daurat. I'm no good as a boss. Absolutely not. Office and paperwork aren't my thing. I don't want an office, I want a plane. I'll only go to South America to be a pilot."

Daurat, unfazed, drags on his cigarette.

"You leave for Rio de Janeiro tomorrow morning."

"But I'm a pilot and that's what I want to be!"

Daurat looks at him with his badger eyes.

"You'll fly till you're sick of it."

"I'll fly?"

"You'll fly until you have feathers growing out of your armpits."

Mermoz crosses the ocean by boat accompanied by the Laté 26 lashed to the stern deck. He disembarks in the port of Rio de Janeiro and is welcomed by Pranville, the director of operations in South America. He's nothing like Daurat, and not simply because he's taller and heftier. He invites Mermoz for dinner at an establishment overlooking the city's wide bay, and talks nonstop from the time the waiters bring the menu until they are finishing off their third coffee and the waiters are already starting to sweep the dining room floor with samba-like movements.

He tells Mermoz about the new route from Buenos Aires to Natal in Brazil's northeast which must be opened urgently to prevent the Argentinian and Brazilian governments from revoking their licence. A weekly mail service has to be guaranteed.

"That doesn't seem too hard . . ."

Pranville removes the cups and spreads out a map on top of the tablecloth. He runs his finger along the route between Natal and the Argentinian capital: 5,000 kilometres of thick jungle, a temperature difference of almost thirty degrees between these two points, flying in open planes in the hope that new models with cockpits might be introduced down the track.

"For now, we have to go with the old Bréguets."

"They'll hold up."

"In Natal, we'll put the mail from Buenos Aires on board one of the company's packet boats. It will cross the Atlantic by the shortest sea

174

route to Dakar, three thousand kilometres away. There, our pilots will be waiting to fly the mail stamped in Argentina to France in astonishing time."

"A beautiful operation."

"But we have to get from Buenos Aires to Natal and back again."

"When do I start?"

Pranville looks up from the map.

"We don't need a pilot, we need an entire route. We have to organise a team."

"But I made that clear to Monsieur Daurat. I won't be a boss and I won't manage anything; I don't want to be drowning in paperwork. I want to fly."

"If there's no route, nobody flies. Monsieur Daurat says that you're the man who can get that going."

"Daurat promised me that I would fly."

"You'll fly as much as you want. You'll assign yourself the services you want. Patagonia, Chile, and Bolivia await us. There's thousands of kilometres of airspace to cover; it's all waiting to be done."

Mermoz follows the pencil lines on the map which trace the multiple routes they want to open up throughout South America. If he was looking for challenges, here's one bigger than he could ever have dreamed of. He's not yet twenty-eight, and to organise all this he'll have to impose discipline on war veterans and proud bureaucrats sitting in their offices with one eye on the clock.

"Pranville, it's a very tough job."

"That's why Daurat picked you."

Mermoz takes another look, and eventually agrees.

CHAPTER 31

Cabo Juby (Morocco), 1928

Antoine de Saint-Exupéry

THE RADIO RECEIVER AT CABO Juby emits more noises than words. Having radio is an enormous advance and many planes have started to include this innovation. But the voices it carries hiss, messages cut out, words are buried under atmospheric storms.

"Toulouse, Toulou . . . ouse. Agadir call . . . Confir . . . arriv . . . mail J29 . . . hour. Over."

"Agadir, A . . . dir, Aga . . . the mail . . . 29 has . . . ed as expec . . . at . . . ven forty-five . . . ver.

The route pulses with those fragile voices which ricochet along the 4,000 kilometres.

There are still two hours to go before the flight arrives. The pilots will stay overnight at the airfield before continuing on to Villa Cisneros in the morning, so Antoine uses the time to sit down at his desk. It consists of two large empty fuel drums on top of which he's put an old door.

The pages of his story "The Aviator" which was published in *Le Navire* are scattered across the board.

Bernis is the aviator Antoine dreamed up in Paris when the greyness of his days was pressing on him like a wet blanket: a flight instructor who does the rounds of the nightclubs in his leather jacket, dragging along with him the air of loneliness typical of a person who's been ploughing the skies. Antoine finds it curious that two years later, he's managed to fly further than his imagination and he's now an aviator who has reached beyond any point he thought he'd have Bernis get to.

Every writer carries inside him a vain person who possesses varying degrees of courtesy and craftiness. What Antoine published in the magazine back then seemed sublime to him. Now, however, it seems like rubbish.

He reads the first sentence: powerful wheels, the runway . . . He snorts impatiently.

It all sounds like a death knell!

He's often thought about converting Bernis into the main character of a much longer tale. A novel. He sets about rewriting the first few paragraphs dedicated to flying, but after a few lines, he slams his hand down angrily on the table.

No, that's not right!

He can't start with propellers and wheels. Mechanics is important, of course, expertise is crucial, but what really matters is the sky. So he decides to start his story by telling what it's like to navigate among stars that are like the lights in a house in the middle of the night, with the moon making the desert dunes shine like gold.

No, no, no!

He scrunches up the paper and throws it to the ground.

Light doesn't illuminate the dunes; it invents them.

Bernis is an introverted pilot in love with an inaccessible girl in the same way that small children fall in love with the wonderful cakes on display in the window of a pâtisserie, but when they reach out for them, their hands collide with the glass.

He devotes entire pages to explaining Bernis's youthful flirtations with that girl, who drifted away from him like a bubble of soap. Aviation has been the horizon for Bernis. The years have passed and Bernis pretends to be happy with his life as a pilot, but he's deceiving himself. He hasn't stopped thinking about her one single day in all those years.

Antoine wonders if it's possible to fall in love again with that sensation of vertigo that comes with a first love.

He applies the same patience with which he removed carbon deposits from engines to cleaning and lubricating the old Underwood typewriter that he uses to write his reports for the company, and the tale of Bernis, which is also his story. He likes the round keys which respond to his fingers. Accompanied by their clatter, he starts to write the story of Bernis's youthful friendships. One sheet, two—he stops on the third. He reads over what he's written. He lights a cigarette. He inhales deeply and rips the page out of the typewriter's carriage. He doesn't want things to be explained as they are in a serialised story: first A, then B, followed by C. He wants things just to happen as they do in real life—no introductions, no logical thread, no knowing exactly why. Life doesn't give warnings, it just mows you down.

His tools as a writer provide him with tempting power: He can't fix what's been twisted for him, nor can he make Lou-Lou come back into his life, but he can give Bernis the gift of a better future than his own. He can make this pilot he has created with words fulfill the dreams that have escaped him.

He's not going to describe the woman whom Jacques Bernis loves— let each reader give her the hair colour, height, and voice of the woman or man they most loved.

The plot places us in the moment when the girl, whom Bernis has known since adolescence and with whom he's always been in love, is married to another and has a son. Antoine will add to this real-life libretto something of his own making: She's unhappy in her marriage.

He stretches in front of the typewriter, and drags so deeply on his cigarette that all that's left between his fingers is ash.

Is Lou-Lou happy in her marriage?

He blushes as he admits that he'd like her marriage to fail. He feels really callous but, at the same time, he smiles. He knows that wishing this on someone he loves isn't rational.

Love isn't rational . . .

That's how he feels.

I can't change my feelings as if I were changing my socks.

In his story, the breakdown of her marriage will present a new opportunity for Bernis and that first love of his which got left behind. Bit by bit, Antoine starts to furnish his emotional, egotistical impulse with justifications he'd like to think are rational—if truth be told, given his knowledge of Lou-Lou, the idea that her marriage isn't going well is not so ridiculous. He's well acquainted with how easily she becomes bored with everything. She never used to eat more than half a plateful of food, even if it was the most exquisite delicacy cooked by the best chef. When asked if she wasn't hungry, she'd reply that she'd tired of the flavour. Lou-Lou and routine were incompatible. *How was she going to put up with seeing the same person brushing his teeth at the same time for the rest of her life?*

His thoughts continue to unravel this thread. *And if she were to look for consolation in an old aviator friend when her marriage broke down?*

Why not?

He smiles like a mischievous child. *It's tempting.*

He places his fingers on the typewriter keys and pushes down hard. The connecting rods move speedily, the keys go up and down. His fingers do a tap dance.

Antoine opens his eyes wide as globes and lets himself go, because for him, writing is another way of flying. Both have to do with vertigo and vibrations.

The story—he doesn't know why—takes off at night, in the cold, dark air under an infinite, star-studded ceiling.

Bernis, that privileged, imaginary being, is going to have the second chance Antoine never had . . . at least for now! If Bernis triumphs in this tale, it will, in part, be Antoine's own triumph. If Bernis achieves this, what's to say Antoine couldn't do it too?

He writes feverishly as if he were writing his own destiny in these pages. But with equal fervour, he again yanks the pages from the machine's carriage, scrunches them up, and tosses them onto the floor. He lights a cigarette, goes off to listen to the radio, pores over the meteorological report, comes back, and bends down to pick up the ball of paper. He carefully opens it out, wanting the words still to be there, intact. There's one paragraph he can rescue! He doubts, he hesitates. He writes; he tears up.

He knows that an author tends to be indulgent toward his own words; no father is as overindulgent with his children as a writer is with his sentences. They all delight him, even if they're stupid; they all seem beautiful, even if they are grotesque. He knows that a writer who is totally satisfied with his work is an imbecile. The writer is a farmer sowing virgin land. Effort, determination, and many days dedicated to the task guarantee nothing; sometimes, the harvest turns out to be riddled with maggoty, rotten words.

Light is fading and the mail from Agadir arrives with the sunset. The mechanics are waiting for it outside, lazily sitting on the wooden boxes they've turned into benches. Their overalls are so stained it's hard to tell what colour they really are.

"I'll ask head office for some new overalls."

"Oh, that's not necessary, Saint-Ex! It would be better if you asked them to pay us more."

Antoine grimaces. The two mechanics often disappear in the direction of the Moorish town—if you can use the term *town* for a few adobe houses, lean-tos, and grubby tents grouped together a couple of kilometres from the fort—a town the Spaniards call Villa Bens in honour of one of their generals. Totó spends virtually his entire salary on drink, and the rest on women; Jean-Louis spends his on women, and a little on drink.

The two Bréguets appear in the airfield's line of sight but the two mechanics continue to sit placidly.

"Let's go! Let's go! The fuel!"

The mechanics grunt. They get up unhurriedly, grudgingly.

The plane is buffeted about by the wind gusts and lands with a few hops.

Antoine rushes to the machine and reaches it just as Riguelle is jumping down from the cockpit.

"Welcome to Cabo Juby!"

"The fuel!"

"It's on its way."

But Riguelle doesn't hear the reply because he's rushed off a short distance to relieve himself. He returns soon after, somewhat more relaxed. The escort pilot who landed right after him joins them as well.

"You've got ten minutes. I've prepared coffee and honey cakes."

"Just coffee, Saint-Ex. We have to take off in five minutes; we're late."

Antoine consults his watch and makes a dismissive gesture.

"You know what Monsieur Daurat is like," insists Riguelle. "Two weeks ago we arrived in Casablanca an hour late and he docked me four days' pay."

"That's a bit excessive."

"A bit? It's an outrage! I risk my life every day to deliver the mail and thanks to a very strong headwind I arrived fifty damn minutes late. Is the wind my fault? What can I do if the wind slows me down?"

"Did you tell him that?"

"Of course."

"What was his reply?"

"That if the wind is strong, I should leave earlier. Dammit! Don't we already do more than enough?"

Antoine nods, and Riguelle realises he's running late.

"Let's go; let's go! The fuel! What's with your mechanics? Are they asleep?"

The planes take off and disappear into the heavens. They leave behind the sound of their engines backfiring, the smell of gasoline in the breeze, and a slight reverberation in the air. At the airfield everything falls silent and the pace of life slows down again.

The afternoon still stretches out before Antoine and his head feels heavy. So he decides to pay a visit to some of the Tuareg tents or jaimas in an area to which the Spaniards rarely go. He's learned that when you spend time walking in the desert, you start to distinguish the subtle paths.

When you first arrive, all you see is sand and camels. To the north, the south, the east, and the west, it all looks the same—monotony! Bit by bit, you start to distinguish certain signs. There aren't the street names of a big city, but there are rocks eroded into a particular shape, a small promontory rising up from the sand like a camel's hump, or the bleached skeletal remains of a camel lying in the sand, its jawbone pointing toward the east. Remnants of caravan trails form paths which cross and divide. Here, any trace is important. It can last days or weeks, depending on the sandstorms, and its line is a thread in the labyrinth of nothingness.

There's one sheikh in particular whom Antoine likes to visit, a Tuareg called Abdullah Mukhtar who traded with a French garrison in Algeria for a while and speaks French. To reach his territory, Antoine must get to the skeleton of the camel, turn from there toward the west, and walk fifteen minutes until he reaches three very high dunes. He then walks another fifteen minutes, leaving the dunes to his right, and arrives at a greenish patch in the middle of the expanse of ochre. A goatskin jaima is pitched there, together with a small garden protected by a stone wall and the parapet of a well. A few goats graze among the dry shrubs and some children run to give warning of the stranger's arrival.

"Salaam alaikum!" says Antoine by way of a greeting.

Abdullah Mukhtar emerges. He's tall, lean, and dressed in blue from head to toe in the manner of the Tuaregs.

"Alaikum salaam!"

Antoine smiles. He recalls his first visit. He had been told that Mukhtar was one of the region's most influential people, a settled Tuareg who possessed the two items indispensable for survival in the desert: a well and common sense. He was a sheikh, the leader of a fluid community of small settlements. Among the missions Daurat had given him was the need to establish good relations with the local tribes in order to prevent planes from being sabotaged and to minimise hostilities toward the pilots who might crash in the middle of the desert. The records showed that a Bréguet engine broke down every fifth flight. Forced landings along the route were constant and the risk of being kidnapped, high.

The first time Antoine arrived at the venerable Tuareg's jaima, he was asked to put down his weapons before he approached. The sheikh was really surprised when Antoine said he didn't have any. He'd never come across an unarmed Westerner. He was also pleasantly surprised that this burly European spoke a few words of Arabic. He could have sworn by Allah that he'd never heard the words of this language so badly pronounced, but, prudent man that he was, he knew to value the foreigner's effort and courtesy in attempting to speak to him in his language. Only after that moment had the sheikh spoken to Antoine in his very proper French. Antoine had arrived absolutely exhausted from his walk, because he'd lost his way twice, and he asked the sheikh if he could drink a little water from the well.

"I'll pay you for it," he said.

The sheikh looked at him and in his eyes Antoine saw reflected the life experience of many generations of desert dwellers.

"Pay me with your blessing."

Antoine was still ignorant of the codes of the Tuareg at that stage. There are two sacrosanct norms. The first is that hospitality is a sacred obligation. If your worst enemy, whom you want to see dead forty times over, is in your jaima and at that moment, a third person arrives who wants to attack him, the Tuareg will risk his life to defend his enemy because that enemy is under his roof. The second norm is that water belongs to God: it is never denied to anyone who needs it.

"It's a joy to see you, Abdullah Mukhtar." Antoine says now, placing his hand on his chest in greeting.

"It's a joy for me to see you too, Saintusupehi."

"I've brought a little sugar for your children."

"I thank you for it. You will take this goat's milk back with you."

If Antoine were to refuse this gift, even if it was the only milk in the camp, he would offend the sheikh.

"It will be so. I have come, with your permission, to have a sip of water."

"Why do you come so far to drink this muddy water?"

"The water the tanker brings us from the Canary Islands tastes of metal and detergent."

"But this water tastes of the earth."

"That's why I like it. All things come from the earth."

The sheikh nods slowly.

"You talk like a wise man. You don't seem European."

They both burst out laughing.

When it's time to leave, Abdullah Mukhtar gives him a special gift—a djellaba. Plain, somewhat frayed along the seams, not entirely clean. In Paris they would laugh at such a rag; they would know nothing of its significance. With this garment, the sheikh is saying: We accept you as one of us. When he goes to visit other tribes, they'll ask him where he got the garment and when he says it's a gift from his friend Abdullah Mukhtar which he wears with pride, it will open many jaimas to him.

Antoine looks at the sheikh. A sea, a continent, a God separate them. They look at each other and they understand each other. Nothing separates them.

CHAPTER 32

★

Buenos Aires (Argentina), 1928

Jean Mermoz

MERMOZ PUTS HIS HANDS IN the pockets of his coat before he enters the company offices on Calle de la Reconquista. Two young women stroll past in long, slightly ruffled skirts, and he flashes them one of his smiles.

These past few months, there have been reconnaissance flights: landings in the middle of mosquito-infested marshes; on the Pampas, so extensive that his eyes got tired of looking in front of him; and in remote settlements in the middle of the jungle populated by indigenous people who knelt down and prayed when he climbed down from his plane.

But of all the mountains he's had to negotiate, none has seemed as arduous to Mermoz as the pile of files rising on the desk assigned to him as manager of pilots. He snorts.

It has been weeks of feverish work—the arrival of machines from France, always late; the reconnaissance flights to check out airfields on the route between Argentina and Brazil; the runways often threatened by an exuberant Nature which voraciously grows over the open clearings in the jungle; and the rainy climate which converts the soil into mud. But the worst part has been giving orders to the pilots, several of them more experienced than he is. And the budgets, the invoices, the reports, the repairs . . . When all this weighs him down, he turns to the map hanging on the wall on which the red lines crossing South America link Paraguay, Chile, Brazil, Bolivia, and Patagonia . . . A tangle of threads, for now just lines on a map, runways in remote places that are merely mud puddles, planes to be fitted out, airfield managers to be trained, hangars that look like junkyards.

The work is exhausting, but he feels strong. In the grill house where he goes at midday he devours enormous chops three at a time followed by a beef roulade or a tray of meat empanadas for dessert.

He receives a torrent of radio-telegrams from Daurat in Montaudran. Daurat demands reports and verifications of everything. Mermoz is delighted that his boss is thousands of kilometres away.

In March, after weeks in which he has been multitasking in order to be at the airfields in the jungle without neglecting all the paperwork in his office in Buenos Aires, the great day has finally arrived. If the route holds up, Aéropostale may make history: the first delivery of mail between South America and Europe via a postal air service.

For this first run, there's a lengthy initial leg—normally flown by two pilots—from Buenos Aires to Natal.

But nothing can fail on this first run and so, although Mermoz hasn't slept for two days, he climbs into the open-air Bréguet by himself and takes off on the inaugural flight. He leaves at first light, but the heat in Buenos Aires makes the air dense. He leaves Argentina behind and arrives safely at the Montevideo aerodrome. The only novelty is Mermoz shouting at the mechanics to hurry up with the refuelling.

"The mail! The mail! The mail!"

That's why he's beside himself when there's a water leak in Brazil which delays that leg by several hours, and he has to make an unexpected overnight stop in Jaguarão. He eats by himself, angrily chewing the rice and beans. No one even dares to speak to him.

His expression lightens when they tell him early next morning that the plane is fixed and he takes off for Rio de Janeiro as fast as the plane will go. They're waiting for him with another plane's engine running at the final stopover before Natal.

A few hours later, they inform him by radio that the mail has already been transferred to the company's packet boat for the sea voyage to Dakar.

In a far-away office on the outskirts of Toulouse, a man with angular features, on the lookout for radio-telegrams, finishes off a cigarette. He's been receiving notification of each stage of the route unmoved. Only thick smoke emerges from his mouth. No comment, no change of expression. Legend has it around the hangars and the lounge room of Le Grand Balcon that Daurat is a man of ice who lacks feelings, who's only inspired by punctuality reports. Nobody knows that today he's smiling on the inside.

The letters written in Buenos Aires reach Toulouse within a week, having travelled 13,000 kilometres, with an ocean and a sea in between. Mermoz has inaugurated the longest air route in the world.

Mermoz is congratulated in Buenos Aires. At the embassy, they want to seat him at huge tables and offer interminable speeches. After the third banquet, he sends them all to the devil. At one such celebration, as soon as the required toasts have been drunk, he gets up from the table and hurriedly makes his farewells. He grabs his hat and coat from the hands of a waiter.

"Where are you off to so hastily, Señor Mermoz?" ask the disappointed guests.

"To fly."

Everyone congratulates him, but he knows there's no reason for it; he's done nothing yet. Over the next few months, Mermoz opens another front. On some routes, what the planes gain over transportation by train during the day, they lose at night while they rest in the hangars. Daurat has been hatching a plan in his head for a long time, and has infected Mermoz—night flying is the next step that has to be taken.

Mermoz begins the rounds of the airfields on the Brazil route, personally giving instructions to each of the people in charge about how to outline their landing strips with beacons. He sees raised eyebrows, attempts to answer back, looks of astonishment, even outrage. He cuts them off with an emphatic gesture and the sense of conviction he radiates.

"We're going to fly at night."

"But that's not possible."

"We'll do it."

"But Señor Mermoz . . ."

"We're going to do it."

He takes off from Buenos Aires on the morning of April 14, headed for Montevideo. He refuels and flies on. The sun slowly starts to go down on the horizon and he keeps flying. Night falls and he flies on. All points of reference are lost, the ground has disappeared and the clouds have erased any trace of the stars. And he flies on.

Collenot, the mechanic, remains seated in front of him in silence. The roar of the engines and the wind allow for little conversation during flights. They've got used to communicating with signs.

A few days earlier, Mermoz had asked Collenot if he wanted to be his mechanic.

"Of course, Monsieur Mermoz."

"We'll be flying at night . . ."

"Yes, Monsieur Mermoz."

"We'll be trying out a night flight so we can incorporate it into the company routes."

"Seems fine to me, Monsieur Mermoz."

"It will be like flying blind."

"I trust you blindly, Monsieur Mermoz."

So far, only the military have flown at night on exceptional missions. No one has had the temerity to establish a regular route at night. Technically, it can't be done. Technically, the brain is a mass of flesh, and dreams don't exist.

The two of them fly through the night. It's raining. The cockpits in the Bréguets are still open to the sky. Even though the biplane's upper wing serves as a roof, the squally weather soaks them and the moon as a point of reference is periodically lost. Mermoz relies on his compass with absolute faith. Flying at night is an act of faith. If the engine fails, he'll have to land blindly and the possibility of his killing them multiplies. He doesn't want to think about that. Each mile they advance is a triumph.

When they reach the location of the Porto Alegre airfield, they detect the pinpoints of light, and circle above the landing strip until their presence is detected and the ground crew light up the runway: a dozen empty fuel drums full of burning wood bordering each side of the strip which form a path of beacons.

Twenty-three hours after they took off from Buenos Aires, they complete the route to Brazil. Frozen, drained. Mermoz, exultant; Collenot silent, displaying the serenity of the humble.

Mermoz bursts into the airfield office like a tornado, dripping water from his flying suit onto the carpet, and calls out for a connection with Montaudran.

"It's very late in Toulouse, senhor," says one of the administrative assistants condescendingly, without raising his eyes from the cashbook in which he continues to jot down numbers.

"Late?" Mermoz slams his fist down on the counter and all the trays containing forms jump in the air. "Connect me with Monsieur Daurat immediately."

A minute later, he's connected with Montaudran.

"The first night flight on the Brazil route has been completed, Monsieur Daurat! The night route is a success!"

Silence, broken only by the noises of the underwater cable, reaches him from the other side. Finally, Daurat replies with his customary neutral tone:

"Complete twenty without any mishap and we'll start to talk about success."

Mermoz perseveres. He carries on with his weekly night route, which saves almost a day on the movement of the mail. For four weeks, he takes off and lands with no mishap. Daurat follows the developments on a daily basis. Mermoz calls Toulouse at any hour of the day or night and Monsieur Daurat is always on the other end of the line. He wonders if the director has anything like a private life.

Colleagues from other companies, hoping to acquire Aéropostale's licences for the transportation of mail by air, label Mermoz's attempts to standardise night flights as absurd. There'll be clear nights, but there'll also be overcast nights, where there'll be no points of reference beyond the compass, and it will be impossible to land in the dark should there be a breakdown. The newspaper *La Tarde* publishes a strong article by a veteran Argentinian pilot who asserts that flying at night is suicide.

One day, when Mermoz walks into the pilots' canteen at the Pacheco airfield on the outskirts of Buenos Aires, the veteran aviator Quedillac confronts him.

"You can't fly at night, Mermoz."

"You can't? Well, I'm doing it."

"But that's suicide. It's madness! You're putting all of us in danger."

"Night flights will be voluntary."

Quedillac, a veteran of the Africa route, with landings in the desert, breakdowns in Spain, and dozens of trips across the Pyrenees, looks at Mermoz with barely contained anger.

"If you fly . . . how can the rest of us say no?"

Mermoz shrugs. That's not his problem.

They stare at each other. Quedillac sighs.

"What's the purpose of this whim?"

At that, the anger swaps sides. The veins on Mermoz's neck swell.

"Whim? Do I strike you as a capricious imbecile?"

Quedillac falls silent at the boss pilot's anger.

"No, it's not a whim, Quedillac. Our damned duty is to get these letters to their destination in the shortest time possible. We can't go on losing at night what we gain by day. We've already accumulated thousands of flying hours; we know the route. I know it can be done with a reasonable margin of safety. There's danger, of course. But we're pilots! If anyone wants a job with no risk, he can become a florist. Do you want to be a florist, Quedillac?"

Mermoz's face is so close to the other pilot's face that he can count the hairs in his nose. One of them has to back down. Quedillac swallows his anger and clenches his teeth so hard they grind in his mouth. He turns and marches off. Mermoz stays put. Backing down would be to lose what has already been gained.

In the weeks that follow, the empty fuel drums light up the night and Mermoz completes ten more night flights in a row without a single incident.

On one of those occasions, when he gets back to Buenos Aires at night and turns up at the offices on Calle de la Reconquista to do the paperwork after three hours' sleep, he finds two men in suits standing in his office waiting for him, and someone sitting in his chair smoking a cigarette.

"Mermoz, you have an untidy office. You arrive late. I haven't received the costs for the first two weeks."

"Monsieur Daurat! When did you arrive?"

"Eighteen minutes ago."

He has a bundle of files under his arm, as do the two inspectors awaiting his orders.

"I want a detailed report on the night flights."

"It's all going smoothly!"

"I don't want your opinion, Mermoz. I want a report."

"Yes, sir!" He says it a little rudely, but with such a smile that Daurat's facial expression changes ever so slightly, to what could almost be one of satisfaction. Theirs is not the only visit. That same morning, Quedillac turns up in his office. They exchange a brief look, silently sizing each other up. Quedillac volunteers for the night flights.

Mermoz leaps up from his chair, walks round the desk, and before the pilot—who is of short and slim build—can escape, gives him a hug which lifts him a few centimetres off the ground. Quedillac is resolved, but not happy. He's never confessed it to anyone, but ever since he was little and could hear his father's yells and his mother's crying from his bed, he's been afraid of the dark. He always sleeps with a light on so he won't be disturbed by the memory of his father returning home at dawn, drunk and violent. The boss of the pilots looks at him overjoyed, and grabs him forcefully by the forearms. They both know that while they're both resilient, they're also fragile.

Another pilot arrives after Quedillac, and then another, and another. Soon the rest of the pilots in the Argentinian company make themselves available for night flights. Mermoz accepts, content.

And nobody laughs any longer at Aéropostale's ambition to establish civilian air routes that fly at night. Some companies in other countries even begin to consider the possibility. There are those who see it as a road to suffering which will bring with it more accidents and more tragedies. Others see it as a solid step toward the future for commercial aviation, still in its infancy.

Neither side is wrong.

CHAPTER 33

Cabo Juby (Morocco), 1928

ANTOINE DE SAINT-EXUPÉRY AND HENRI GUILLAUMET

IN THE TIME LEFT TO him after monitoring stopovers, rescue missions, and his work as a diplomat with the Spaniards and the indigenous tribes, some of them hostile, Antoine continues to scribble. Sometimes he wants to write so quickly that the Underwood's little rods become entangled in the middle and the machine jams. On other occasions, he sits in front of the keyboard for minutes or hours, incapable of typing a single letter.

There are times when his imagination takes flight; at other times, he's dragged along under the weight of the responsibility of writing his own destiny.

Bernis, the desert pilot seasoned by a thousand adventures, who is as indifferent to his life's daily risks as he is to shaving each morning, is nervous at the prospect of flying to Paris to meet again the woman he has never forgotten.

Geneviève . . .

The name reminds Antoine of Geneva, the city where he and Lou-Lou were happy. He smiles as he recalls how they evaded Madame Petermann's vigilance during that trip which was so long ago it now seems like a dream.

He thinks about Lou-Lou's husband, a rich North American he hasn't even met. Antoine already knows that the man is not the least bit to blame for his pain, but even so, he detests him. It's not logical, but that's how it is. He believes that if hate were logical, it would stop being hate, in the same way that if love were rational, there would be no love.

The husband's name will be Herlin, Antoine decides. And he generates an absolutely devastating description of him: mean-spirited, false, decadent, ignorant, sadistic . . .

He enjoys himself as he types. He even forgets to smoke.

A waiter goes by and Herlin sticks out his foot so he'll stumble. After he's dropped his tray and the china has smashed on the ground, Herlin even tells him off for his clumsiness. The manager fires the waiter, who has a wife and four children to support, and Herlin laughs coarsely. Antoine types the scene rapidly, caught up in a delicious trance.

And then he stops. He sighs. He lights another cigarette and watches the tip burn.

He knows it's a ridiculous scene. Herlin can't be like that. Lou-Lou would never have married someone so gross or vulgar. Although, he thinks, she did fall in love with him, at least for a while, despite him being the most uncouth person in the world.

But I am a count.

And he smiles sadly as he's thinking that.

The poorest and most insignificant count on the planet!

He becomes serious again. He can't turn Geneviève's husband into the villain in a radio soap opera. He can't make the husband an enemy of humanity, not even an enemy of Bernis. Life can sometimes be ludicrous, but novels have their own rules. Herlin will be a well-brought-up man, respectable even. That said, he can't stop seeing him as an opponent, someone who builds a wall in front of Antoine's happiness. Two men who love the same woman can't be friends, because what unites them is also what divides them.

Eventually, he decides that the husband will be a gentleman of good standing, cultivated and worldly but a little arrogant, polite but inflexible.

Bernis attends a meal with a group of acquaintances of Geneviève and her husband in the discreet role of an old friend, someone who's passing through and is there that night quite by chance.

He rewrites the restaurant scene over and over again.

Jacques Bernis sees everything as if he were flying over it in his plane. Geneviève sparkles in this group of dull women without making any fuss. Her brilliance blinds her fellow diners and doesn't allow them to see her as she really is. They see her beauty, her impeccable manners, her knowledge of how to behave, her adorable frivolity. But they don't see the essential Geneviève, the important things invisible to the eye.

Bernis knows her from before, from when she was little more than a child, and that's why he detects certain invisible vibrations in the flawless movement of her gestures. He notices particular inflections in her voice when she speaks briefly about her son. The guests at her dinner adore her but they quickly change the topic. They're not interested in motherhood; to them, it's a boring, conservative subject. They feel it's a waste for this intelligent, sophisticated woman to devote time to such domestic chores. They adore Geneviève; but they don't want to know anything about such mundane matters.

"They love her as one loves music, as one loves luxury . . . ," writes Antoine.

But Bernis, her childhood friend, has picked up an echo of concern in her brief mention of her son. He knows that Geneviève looks fragile—her waist can almost be encircled with one hand—but in reality, she's strong. Flowers can withstand typhoons. If there's concern in the timbre of her voice, it's because there's something really bad going on with her son.

He also detects a certain distance with her husband. It's all very cordial—they yield the floor to each other when they speak, they don't disagree with each other, he pours her more wine as soon as her glass is empty—but there's something stifling in that overly civilised politeness. There's a moment when the men are busy with the ritual of lighting their cigars and the women have become entangled in a conversation about hats that Geneviève turns to Bernis and asks him in a whisper to talk to her about the desert.

The desert . . .

It seems inappropriate to Bernis to fill the rooms of this opulent bistro with tonnes of sand. It could be a trivial question to fill a moment's silence. Or it could be an invitation to continue the conversation later, in another place and at another time. He doesn't know what to think. He looks at Geneviève: there are those adorably capricious eyes, but he also sees that she's trying to conceal a veil of sadness. All of her is an enigma.

Lou-Lou is unpredictable. That's why it's impossible not to love her.

The familiar hum of a Bréguet 14 brings Antoine back to the reality of the airfield. A plane sways imperceptibly in the air and lands on the runway with an unusual lightness. Plane and pilot are staying overnight. As he approaches the runway, Antoine feels his heart leap.

"Henri!"

Guillaumet removes his helmet and goggles, and the black circles around his eyes make it look as if he's wearing a mask. His smile reveals white teeth made even whiter set against his skin toasted by sun and soot.

"This calls for a celebration! Forget couscous and old camel meat. I still have three eggs. I'll ask Kamal to make you an omelette."

"No, Antoine! Keep them for yourselves. I'll be dining in Dakar tomorrow night and I'll be able to eat whatever I want, but here, you wait weeks to get your supplies."

"Keep them? What do those words mean? We're going to open a bottle of Rioja. A Spanish captain gave it to me as a gift."

"How do you get on with the Spaniards?"

"Quite well. They spend all day playing dominoes—I hate that small-town game! But some of the officers also like chess."

The two go inside the hut that also serves as a home.

"If you don't mind, could I use your luxurious bathroom?"

"Why would I mind?"

In a small room set off to one side, there's a bowl on top of a structure made of pale wood. There's also a matching shelf with moulded spaces for a shaving brush, razors, soap, and clean towels. What most attracts the attention of the dust-covered pilots who arrive at this stopover in the middle of the desert is the discovery of a large, elegant bottle of cologne with a crystal stopper.

"Where do you get these fabulous American terrycloth towels? They're better than the ones at the Ritz!"

"They bring them over for me from the Canary Islands. I exchange dates for them."

"And how do you get hold of the dates?"

"I give the Berbers a little gasoline for them."

"If Monsieur Daurat finds out that you outlay aircraft fuel to buy towels, he'll have a heart attack!"

"Monsieur Daurat ought to try drying his hands on sandpaper!"

After dinner, they grab their leather jackets and go outside for some fresh air. The wind has died down. They reach for their tobacco and matches, and smoke more than half a cigarette in silence. It's cold, but they don't mind. A shooting star crosses the sky and disappears.

"Did you do it, Guillaumet?"

"What?"

"Make a wish. They say that when you see a shooting star you can make a wish."

"I didn't have time."

"What will you ask for next time?"

"A million francs."

"Rubbish, I don't believe you!"

They fall silent. The silence makes them drowsy and Guillaumet hides a yawn. He's exhausted after his very long flight, but he likes being with Antoine, even if he asks such eccentric, childlike questions. Guillaumet prefers not to say much, only what's absolutely essential. Antoine, on the other hand, when he's in good spirits, reveals everything that's inside him, together with his most intimate thoughts, like a merchant in a bazaar, spreading out all the little treasures he has for sale on a blanket.

Antoine takes some papers and a flashlight out of his jacket pocket.

"You have to listen to this."

He starts to read the most recent pages he's written about the story of Bernis and Geneviève. He tells of Bernis's moment of fulfilment in his plane, far from earth; the dinner where he meets again the only woman he has ever loved; the way in which he reads in her what others are unable to see.

"Do you think it's plausible that a woman who's stopped loving you would give you a second chance?"

"Why not? Your pilot character also gives her one."

"It's not the same! Bernis has never stopped loving her. Nothing has cooled off inside him. What's hard is to know what she might feel. I'm not sure if love is a dish that can be reheated."

"I know nothing about such things, Antoine. I'm a happily married man."

"How would you not know! Have you never had a disappointment in love?"

"No."

"Never?"

"Never."

"My God, Henri! You were a gigolo! Women fell at your feet! None of them could resist you!"

Guillaumet smiles shyly.

"No way. I've never had a broken heart because I've never got my hopes up. I've always known that no girl would be interested in me. Luckily, I met Noëlle and, well, you know the rest."

"Enough said! I can picture it perfectly! She was the one who had to pull you toward her by your ears so you'd give her a kiss!"

Guillaumet blushes uncomfortably and his friend bursts out laughing.

"The best pilot in the company! The aviator whose pulse doesn't tremble when he lands in the middle of a desert infested with tribesmen armed to the teeth wasn't capable of asking a girl for a kiss!"

Guillaumet blushes even more deeply and looks annoyed. Antoine gives him a bear hug.

CHAPTER 34

Buenos Aires (Argentina), 1929

JEAN MERMOZ

THE SUCCESSFUL LAUNCH OF THE postal connection between South America and Europe has been celebrated with euphoria in the Argentinian newspapers. Night flights are something to talk about. Mermoz starts to be something more than an aerial postman. Radio stations and fashion magazines demand interviews with him, which he tries to avoid. A flood of prizes and distinctions pours in from France. A bar in Buenos Aires creates a Mermoz cocktail. A good salary, recognition, feasts, smiling girls—at times, all this attention flatters him; at other times, it makes him uncomfortable.

He needs exercise on the weekends and he keeps in shape by rowing and swimming in the labyrinthine waters around Tigre, a town with an expanse of wetlands at the delta of the Rio Paraná on the outskirts of Buenos Aires. He sunbathes in the nude and eats in a floating restaurant near the French Rowing Club, enjoying enormous steaks that look as if they're from a dinosaur. His body is sated, but not his mind. Ever since he got off the ship from Europe and set foot on the wharf in Buenos Aires, an idea has been buzzing around inside his head. There's one red line missing from that map of dreams in his office.

One night, he finds himself at a lavish dinner in the house of a French entrepreneur now settled in South America who has invested a lot of money in the airline to advance the company's expansion. A barbeque, robust wines, powerful men and beautiful women. He greets people left and right, shakes hands and nods politely, but he's in another world. All these people mean nothing to him. A blonde with very black eyes and full lips approaches him, catlike. He welcomes her with his "big occasion" smile and requests something from her that has her intrigued—he asks her if she has a lipstick.

"Would you lend it to me?"

She'd lend him anything. She agrees with a coquettish pout and takes the lipstick out of her bag. Mermoz accepts it and, much to her disappointment and the devastation of his hosts, announces loudly that he must leave. The organiser, a businessman used to treating people as if they were his employees, walks up to Mermoz in a very self-assured manner.

"How can you be leaving now when the best is about to begin! I'm going to order special cognac for you and introduce you to some very important people."

At this Mermoz's body tenses. He gives the man such a look that, without realising it, the man takes a step back, the result of one of those reflex reactions that used to determine survival in atavistic times.

Mermoz can't bear people who insist; no one has the right to remove him from his chosen path. He makes his farewell abruptly and leaves.

He walks along the empty streets to Reconquista. He unlocks the entrance to the company offices and walks past the stillness of the empty chairs to his own office. He contemplates the map on the wall with its already-established Buenos Aires–Natal route, and the other

South American routes that will be opened. But there's one crucial route missing from the map. The one that will unite South America and Africa and thereby stitch together the link with Europe. They can race through the air no matter how inclement the weather, the mailbags can be tossed from one plane to another at stopovers, but all these advances come to naught once the mail is loaded onto the company packet boats for the maritime crossing. If airmail really wants to be just that, it has to be able to fly over the ocean.

He takes the lipstick out of his pocket and draws a line over the Atlantic Ocean from Natal to Dakar. He steps back a little and stares at it. The lipstick has left a line so flaming-red there's something almost theatrical about it.

They'll already be asleep on the other side of the world in France. But there's one person who doesn't sleep. He writes Monsieur Daurat a very long telegram in which he asks him for a plane powerful enough to be able to leap over the Atlantic. The reply from Montaudran is rapid: I ASKED FOR IT SOME TIME AGO.

While his petitions for a plane to carry mail over the ocean collide with the walls of bureaucracy, he continues to work on preparations for the opening of another route that's very important to Aéropostale: the Buenos Aires–Santiago de Chile connection. The two cities are sepa-rated by the Andes, a wall of rock up to 6,000 metres high in its central zone. Their planes can barely climb to 4,200 metres.

Mermoz tests out a route detouring toward the south where the mountain chain is not so high and they can get over the peaks.

On one of the first of these flights, he is accompanied by the Comte de la Vaulx, a pioneer of balloon flight and president of the Aéro-Club de France, who is visiting Buenos Aires to become acquainted firsthand with the progress of Aéropostale in South America. Mermoz already has the route tied down, but on this particular trip, a mishap occurs. The engine decides to stop as they're flying over peaks 3,000 metres high. He's flying with Collenot, and the mechanic looks at him without saying a word; he leaves his life in Mermoz's hands.

Mermoz glides in to land on a wide plateau at an altitude of 3,000 metres and touches down somewhat abruptly. Only after landing does he notice the plane is on a slight slope. The passengers give a sigh of relief when the plane comes to a stop, but there's fear in their eyes when the plane starts to roll backward. The incline is making it move slowly toward a precipice.

Mermoz hurriedly removes his seat belt and jumps out of the cabin. He runs down the slope until he's ahead of the machine and plants himself in front of the tail. He stops the plane with his arms and chest.

"Collenot! Get a move on! Chock the wheels, for heaven's sake!"

The mechanic leaps out of the cabin and goes in search of a couple of rocks to put behind the wheels. The comte pokes out his head with its regal, waxed moustache and looks in amazement at Mermoz holding back the plane, with his arms extended like the statue of Christ the Redeemer on the summit of Mount Corcovado in Rio de Janeiro, while Collenot runs by with two large rocks to chock the wheels.

They make their repairs and take off with the wheels of the undercarriage dancing over stones, landing uneventfully in Santiago a few hours later.

Mermoz swoops over the Andes as if he were fording a river, and the letters travel back and forth between Chile and Argentina. It might seem a success, but Mermoz isn't satisfied.

And someone else is also mulling things over in his cage in Montaudran. The man who never sleeps looks through his window toward the sky which lies beyond the runways.

A few months later, a telegram from Daurat hits Mermoz's desk: WE'VE ESTABLISHED THE OUTLINE OF A ROUTE BETWEEN BUENOS AIRES AND CHILE. BUT WE HAVE TO FLY SOUTH MANY KILOMETRES TO BYPASS THE HIGHEST PART OF THE ANDES. WE LOSE MANY HOURS. DO YOU THINK IT WOULD BE

POSSIBLE TO FIND A SAFE ROUTE FURTHER TO THE NORTH THAT WOULD CROSS
THE MOUNTAIN CHAIN IN A MORE DIRECT MANNER?

Mermoz asks for a secretary, who notes down his telegram in reply.

MONSIEUR DAURAT, I'VE BEEN THINKING THAT VERY THING FOR WEEKS.
TOMORROW MORNING I'LL SET THINGS IN MOTION.

Planes have a flight ceiling. It's determined by reaching a level in the
atmosphere with insufficient oxygen for internal combustion engines
to operate. How can a plane that can only fly to 4,200 metres cross a
mountain range with peaks of almost 6,000 metres? For Mermoz, the
answer is as plain as the nose on his face: You have to fly through the
passes between the mountains, sneak through the giant's legs.

CHAPTER 35

★

Cabo Juby (Morocco), 1929

ANTOINE DE SAINT-EXUPÉRY

ANTOINE POUNDS THE TYPEWRITER TO the accompaniment of the whistling wind and the aroma of Kamal's lamb stews mixed with gasoline fumes.

He returns again and again to Geneviève and the shadow of sadness in her green eyes.

Geneviève's expansive frivolity when out in society is an act of generosity: instead of spreading her pain and sorrow to those around her, she prefers to keep it to herself. Her son is very ill. The family doctor, who stops by every morning, speaks with a seriousness that doesn't bode well. When he sees how exhausted she is, he encourages her to leave things to the nurse and go out for some fresh air and a bit of time to herself.

And so, one afternoon, Geneviève leaves the house. She wanders along the boulevards and even visits her favourite antiques dealers, and gets lost among the Persian carpets, the expensive violins, and the

Empire-style tables with legs that look like winged lions. She surrounds herself with beauty to create a moat to protect her castle.

That night, the child dies.

Geneviève feels so unbearably cold that her tears freeze. Crying is impossible. The little one is at peace now, the doctor tells her. It's a comfort, but such a pitiful one!

Her husband tries to rebuild what's been demolished in their relationship. He tells her they must sell the house, but her only reply is silence. Geneviève looks at Herlin and she sees he is already distant from all that has happened. As Herlin doesn't know what to do in the face of her grief, he travels to Brussels to manage some properties and asks her to meet him there, so they can start again from scratch.

Antoine shakes his head as if he were chasing away flies.

Start from scratch!

Love is like those marvellous Chinese vases, so delicate. If they fall to the ground, they smash into smithereens. You can use all the patience in the world to carefully glue the pieces back together again, but you're still left with a broken vase.

There's a knock on the door of Bernis's small apartment very early one morning and when he opens the door, who should be standing on the doorstep with a suitcase but Geneviève. She's much paler, her eyes shine more brightly, her hair is redder than ever. He looks at her; he keeps looking at her. They look at each other.

"Take me with you," she begs him.

"Take me with you" . . . Bernis has spent his whole life waiting to hear that.

Antoine writes without thinking, in a trance, tapping the keyboard as if it were a piano. He grants Bernis the wish he would have liked the genie of the lamp to grant him with Lou-Lou. He gets up and stares at the piece of paper trapped in the typewriter carriage. He nods and goes out. He leaves Bernis and Geneviève alone together. It's their moment.

He walks to Abdullah Mukhtar's jaima. He feels the eyes of the soldier on watch in the Spanish fort on his shoulders; the man is tired of staring at nothing.

His Tuareg friend isn't there, nor are his goats. The wind stirs up the jaima's awning and makes the pulley wheel holding the wooden bucket above the well squeak. The bucket is small, like the toy ones children use at the beach to build sand castles. The air also stirs the locks of Antoine's hair, and although he doesn't really know why, he doesn't feel lonely in this mineral-rich solitude. He had felt much more alone in the middle of bustling, busy Paris.

A silhouette outlined against the horizon's bare promontories drags Antoine back from his thoughts. It has four incredibly thin legs, tiny horns, and the long, slender neck of a Russian princess. The gazelle draws nearer, attracted by the frail grasses growing around the well.

Rain is scarce, but the land is fertile. When Tuaregs see clouds in the distance, they head toward them, even if that means travelling dozens of kilometres. They know that already by the time they get there, the sprinkle of desert rain will have stopped, but if only a few drops have fallen, then some blades of grass for their camels will appear immediately. Water secretly flows under the burning surface and springs burst forth in unexpected places. Rare, scanty, sometimes unhealthy, but enough to keep life going; enough for their goats and camels to survive, for a few gazelles to run around; for the survival of silent snakes, and of scorpions with their deadly sting.

Antoine is totally focused on the gazelle's elegant movements as it comes closer. It lifts its head and looks at him for a few seconds with its huge, deeply black eyes. Then it lowers its head and starts to nibble on a few blades.

He feels a presence behind him and turns. Abdullah Mukhtar is looking in the same direction as he is.

"Salaam, Saintusupehi, my friend."

"Salaam, Abdullah Mukhtar, my friend. I didn't hear you arrive!"

"She's a young gazelle. It's unusual for her to have separated from the herd."

"She has tiny horns. She looks so defenceless."

"Are you thinking of hunting her?"

"No! I want to protect her! I'd like to be her friend."

"In that case, you have to tame her first."

Antoine looks at his friend, whose lively little eyes are staring at the animal.

"What does that mean, to tame her?"

"To create bonds."

"Create bonds?"

"Yes, that's what it's about. To the gazelle, you're nothing more than a strange being that walks on two legs, just like thousands of other two-legged beings. And she's nothing more than a gazelle, like any one of the many gazelles there might be in a herd. She doesn't need you, nor do you need her. But if you tame her, you'll develop a need for each other: to you, she will be the sole gazelle on the planet, and to the gazelle, you will be the sole man on the planet."

"Fine, but how do you go about taming a gazelle?"

"You have to be patient. Initially, you'll sit down on the sand at a prudent distance with a small receptacle of water. She will be aware of your movements and watch you out of the corner of her eye, but if you stay still and she doesn't sense that you are a danger, she won't go away."

"I can talk to her. I can speak calming words . . ."

"No! You Europeans place too much value on words. All they bring is misunderstandings. You all think you are very wise because you talk a lot and read sheets of paper. But you've forgotten the art of listening to silence and reading eyes."

"Fine, I sit down at a certain distance. And then?"

"Nothing else. You go often, silently, and leave behind the little bit of water. Trust is a fruit that matures slowly. You must return the next day at the same time and sit down a step closer. And the next day, you repeat the same operation, one step closer . . ."

"I see . . ."

Abdullah Mukhtar walks over to the well and drops the bucket down to the bottom. He takes a piece of coconut shell and tips a few drops of water into it. When he hands the bowl to Antoine, Antoine frowns.

"That's not much water at all! The gazelle isn't going to quench her thirst with that!"

"Nor should she. There are those who think they can gain the love of people by giving them lavish presents. The gift recipients sing their praises, and the gift givers puff up like the belly of a camel at a watering hole. The recipients don't like them, only their gifts. Do you want the gazelle to like you for your water or for who you are?"

"Well . . ."

"Do you know why we desert people offer our visitors such small glasses of tea?"

"No, I don't."

"It's not because we're miserly, but because it's not our intention to satisfy our visitors. If we were to do that, it would be like throwing in their faces the fact that they are so poor they don't even have a few tea leaves. Our intention with this tiny glass of tea is not to give them a drink, but to show them our friendship."

Antoine nods and moves a little closer to the gazelle, carefully carrying the small piece of coconut shell with its drops of water. Then he backs away a few paces. The creature immediately raises her head and watches Antoine until she sees him sit down and remain still. She continues to graze and only after some considerable time does she go to the bowl and have a sip of water. Antoine follows this same routine at dusk for a week, sitting a tiny step nearer each time. And each day, the gazelle lifts her head and briefly looks at him. Nothing more.

One afternoon, while he's sitting there silently watching the gazelle, the name Nefertiti comes to mind, perhaps because of the bust of her with her long, slender neck that he has seen in Egyptian prints. Or perhaps because she is the queen of the desert.

On the eighth day, the gazelle comes so close he can hear her chewing. That day, the gazelle doesn't even lift her head to look at him. She doesn't need to; she knows who he is. Antoine is tempted to approach her and stroke her brown fur, but he controls himself. After a while, he gets up and heads off toward his hut. When he reaches the entrance, he feels a presence behind him, similar to what he felt the day he turned around and Abdullah Mukhtar was suddenly just centimetres away. On this occasion, when he turns around, he discovers the gazelle. She has a beautiful face: two bands of white frame her nose, surrounded by fur the colour of the desert, and her eyes are black marbles. The gazelle gives a half turn and breaks into a contented run.

The barrack door opens suddenly and Totó the mechanic comes out in his underwear.

"Did you see that?"

"What?"

"An animal that came right up to the barracks."

Antoine shakes his head. "You're the animal. She is Nefertiti!"

CHAPTER 36

The Andes (Chile), 1929

JEAN MERMOZ

THE MANAGER OF THE COPIAPÓ aerodrome, in the northern part of Santiago, capital of Chile, has grey eyebrows above eyes half closed from having seen too many things. He notices that Mermoz is looking through the window toward the mountain range in the same way he himself would look at a very tall woman who was fuelling his desire.

"You're looking for the impossible."

"What else is worth searching for?"

The airfield manager nods in agreement. He continues to stir his coffee as he watches the pilot chief head off toward the Laté 26 followed by Collenot, his silent mechanic, clutching his bag of tools. He doesn't know if Mermoz is a hero or a madman.

It's hard to pinpoint the boundary.

He takes a sip of coffee but sets the cup aside with a look of distaste. Just for a moment, he envies Mermoz, who never drinks his coffee cold.

Over the noise of the engine, Mermoz shouts at Collenot that they're not flying over, but through, the Andes.

After friendly flatland, an army of mountains blocks their way. They fly parallel to the rocks, perform pirouettes, and buzz around like flies confronted by a closed window. There are small, deceitful openings, like dead-end streets where the only way out calls for acrobatic reversing. The peaks are white with virginal snow and the sun makes them glint like marble. But their immaculate whiteness and peacefulness are the peacefulness and silence of cemeteries.

Mermoz detects a promising pass, but it's higher than his altitude ceiling. The Laté can only climb to 4,200 metres and the opening is at least 4,500 metres. It can't be done.

It can't be done?

His head says no, but his heart says yes. He'll make it doable. During his hours of flying and observation, Mermoz has discovered that the sky is a sea of air. There are whirlwinds, eddies, and also currents. He reads the wing vibrations in the same way that a sailor reads the flapping of a sail. A strong northeast wind is blowing, but it's variable. No wind is ever totally constant. It's a question of doing what the Hawaiian surfers do in one of Jack London's tales of adventure that Mermoz read in his youth, when he preferred reading about life to experiencing it. They waited on tops of their boards until the right wave arrived. Mermoz waits for his wave at an altitude of 4,000 metres. A surfer has to start paddling before the wave arrives, if he wants to ride it. Like a surfer, Mermoz manoeuvres, the plane drops a few metres to get a better thrust, and then, as he points the nose skyward, Mermoz feels that thrust. He mounts an incredibly strong gust, and the updraft lifts him in the midst of violent turbulence. They climb: 4,300; 4,400—there are no more numbers left on the altimeter. The engine stutters and

Mermoz grabs hold of the joystick so hard to steer the plane that his knuckles turn white. There are sheer, rocky outcrops on either side of them; they can't alter their course. A wing making contact would mean eternal snow and life everlasting for them.

They hold their position in the middle of the air flow, propelled by the gust.

"Just a little bit more . . ."

They're almost through the highest peaks; they can already see the end of the tunnel.

Then the wind direction changes capriciously and the current that was lifting them up, now takes them down. Violent downdrafts push them toward the ground and they plummet unrelentingly in the direction of some jagged peaks a few hundred metres lower down.

"Impossible to climb again!"

If you can't fight the wind, join it. Mermoz allows the plane to be pushed downward while trying to redirect the Laté's descent, but he's surrounded by mountains like enormous saws. He's got ten seconds to decide. Then five. In full descent he forces a turn toward a steep slope in the middle of the rocky tips.

"Collenot, hold on tight!"

Rather than landing, they drop heavily onto the rough slope. The impact is severe and the plane gives a few nervous hops before settling down for good to the sound of metal crumpling. A rod gives way on the undercarriage and the machine comes to a halt, the side of the fuselage sparking along the ground. When silence falls, they look at each other. They've come out of it unscathed, but the plane hasn't.

Once on the ground, they study the disaster: landing gear twisted, ironwork on the tail bent, various engine parts broken. It's a miracle they were able to land on this platform, hemmed in by immense walls, but that will be of little use to them if they can't get out of there.

Mermoz's voice shakes as he tries to speak, not because of their desperate situation but because it's 15°C below zero.

"Collenot, we have to repair the plane."

"That's not possible, Monsieur Mermoz."

"Then we'll have to do the impossible." And Mermoz's hand gesture takes in the walls that surround them, and their location at an altitude of thousands of metres in an inaccessible spot where they'll never be located. "We can't stay and live here. There are no girls!"

Collenot doesn't laugh. Nor does he reply. He goes in search of his bag of tools. Their lives are now in the hands of the industrious mechanic.

Collenot is an instrument maker. With few spare parts available, it's only a person like him, capable of building an entire aircraft by himself, that makes the repairs possible. He strips down nonessential pieces to obtain metal plates and screws. He concocts a paste of glue, wood chips, and old rags to plug the broken pipes. He fabricates a spare-parts warehouse in the middle of nowhere.

Two days of nonstop work and two freezing nights sleeping inside the plane's cargo hold huddling as close together as possible. They've shared all the provisions they were carrying on board—an orange and a packet of mint caramels. Water, in the form of snow, is plentiful. A pair of condors nesting in the crags in front of them witness everything, and watch them with menacing concentration.

Mermoz, following Collenot's instructions, acts as the metalworker, using an adjustable wrench and his hands like pliers to straighten the landing gear rods.

On the morning of the third day, the mechanic looks up from the engine. His expression is as impassive as it is on any working day at the airfield.

"Monsieur Mermoz, I've done all I can."

"But will it work?"

"Maybe. We won't know until we give it a go. And if it does work, I'm sure it won't be for long."

Collenot has used bits of rope to hold together iron fittings, substituted wires for connecting rods, straightened parts with hammer blows using a rock as an anvil.

"I only need it to hold up for ten minutes so we can get out of here. I can land in the valley in my sleep."

The two men look upward at the incredibly high walls in front of them. The sight is daunting. Flying out of there will be like climbing out of a grave, but Mermoz doesn't allow the mechanic to know how dark his thoughts are.

"Move it, Collenot! We're off."

They get settled in the plane. Mermoz rubs his hands together to recover movement in his fingers, opens up the fuel line, switches on the ignition and . . . it starts!

"It's working."

The Laté's engine roars like an aging lion defying the vast silence, and even Collenot smiles, but an explosion spoils their party.

"What happened?"

"The radiator's burst."

"Then we'll have to fix it."

The mechanic nods.

He resorts to glue, bits of leather, and old rags. He spends hours plugging the holes. If the master mechanics could see what he is doing, they would grasp their heads in their hands. Collenot has never done such a shoddy piece of work, but it's the work of a perfectionist. He places the bits of glued leather with the precision of a surgeon. Monsieur Mermoz has asked for it to be done in ten minutes. He'll have it done.

Daylight fades and the temperature drops even lower. Their hands are stiff, hunger eats at their innards, their lips crack from the cold.

They're surrounded by extraordinary scenery, but beauty means nothing in the face of their distress.

Mermoz and Collenot have exchanged no more words during these days than they usually do when they're flying. Short sentences, lengthy silences.

"The radiator's fixed now, Monsieur Mermoz. Or so I hope."

Mermoz looks up to the heavens.

"We'll leave in the morning. For home or for hell."

News of their disappearance has resonated the length of the route like a funereal drumbeat.

Someone in the desert is also looking heavenward. Antoine wonders if his friend is still alive somewhere in the Andes. He's consoled by the thought that if Mermoz doesn't return, he'll have been defeated by a giant; it will have been a duel between equals. He regrets not having spent more time with Mermoz, not having opened the great Mermoz's suit of armour wider and delved deeper into his tenderness.

In the cordillera, dawn breaks over a tiny plane, an insignificant speck in the middle of a labyrinth of mountains. Fortunately, it hasn't snowed. The machine sits on a narrow strip of sloping land a few metres from the edge of a precipice, without enough room to build up the necessary momentum to take off. They've realised their only hope is to drag the plane higher up the slope, then let it roll down the incline to build up enough speed, although the slope isn't even half the length of a regular runway.

They have to clear the path rock by rock. Then, having endured three days of no food, and putting up with altitude sickness and the cold, they have to push the plane up the slope. They empty the excess fuel from the tank, take out the rear seats, leave behind a large drum containing four hundred litres of gasoline and all but the absolutely necessary spare parts. They strip their dirigible of all unnecessary ballast.

"And the mailbags, Monsieur Mermoz?"

Mermoz walks over to the cargo hold and strokes the bags' rough fabric.

"The mail goes with us. We're mailmen, Collenot."

They move the plane like beasts of burden. Within a minute Collenot has blisters on his hands from the rope; Mermoz does the work of two. He doesn't seem to feel the cold. Each step is a victory. Collenot's nose starts to bleed. He's dizzy from altitude sickness and hunger, so exhausted he's crying.

"Collenot, I need you to do something more important than pulling. For every tug of the rope I give, you chock the wheels with a rock so I can have a rest."

It takes eight agonizing hours to advance a few hundred metres. The condors, impassive above the chasm, observe the whole thing like notaries. It's growing dark when they succeed in lining up the plane at the highest point, facing the longest stretch of plateau. It looks like it will be long enough, but the downward slope includes two drops. One is six metres and the other, somewhat bigger.

"Monsieur Mermoz, it will be a miracle if the landing gear absorbs those bumps."

"We've become experts in miracles."

They can't think about it. Thinking is a luxury.

"Up and at 'em!"

Collenot looks dreadful—his face burnt by the sun, the blood from his nosebleed trapped in the beard he's acquired, his clothes in shreds.

They don't know if the engine will fire up after all these hours of being jolted while they've dragged the Laté up the slope. Mermoz turns the ignition key and a roar startles the cliffs. The condors take to the air, terrified.

218

"It works!"

Mermoz and Collenot exchange a look. In this moment, Mermoz feels an everlasting affection for Collenot, but they don't say a word. Everything's been said; everything is known.

"Collenot, we're going home."

"May God protect us."

When Mermoz gives the go-ahead and they start to move forward, Collenot covers his eyes with what little is left of his leather jacket. Mermoz launches the plane down the slope and they reach the first ledge. He has to be very accurate in making the plane drop onto the rock's flattest surface. The Laté hops abruptly, but the landing gear holds, and the plane continues to roll. The other ledge: more than six metres, more like eight. Mermoz doesn't think, he just jumps and concentrates on landing as stably as possible. The wheels withstand this new hop and continue to roll toward the huge precipice. When they reach the void, Mermoz pulls back on the joystick with all his strength and instead of falling, they rise.

We're flying.

Flying always seemed wonderful to Mermoz, but right now, it seems sublime. Cold doesn't exist; pain doesn't exist. The machine gains height, and he presses the joystick against his inner thigh so the nose will lift up in the air, as there's an immense wall in front of it. But that strikes him as a minor maneuver, casual almost. He puts the plane into a vertical position and climbs through the air. They breach the top of the peak and they're back where they were three days earlier. There's the gap between the mountains, a few hundred metres above them. This time, the wind isn't as strong. He waits for the gust, which isn't as violent as the first time but powerful enough to give them the push to get to the pass. The wings wobble in the air and they enter the rocky gorge. They come out on the other side into brilliant sunshine that wipes out all the shadows.

A few minutes later, as Collenot had predicted, the tubes explode and water pours out from everywhere. The engine stops, but from a height of 3,000 metres and with the mountain range behind him, gliding down is a minor matter for Mermoz, almost a game.

He switches off the fuel line and aims for Copiapó airfield, already visible at the bottom of the valley. He performs a wide, elegant turn and lines up the landing so precisely that the airfield operators don't even notice the engine is off.

They stampede from the offices. Word spreads and the radio operator burns the wires. They're puzzled at the sight of Mermoz and Collenot returning out of the blue after being given up for lost, together with the plane and even the thirty-nine mailbags. The news reaches Cabo Juby in fits and starts. Each word is anguish once Antoine manages to understand that the message is about Mermoz and Collenot—until finally, he explodes with joy and uncorks a warm wine to celebrate.

Sitting in the pilot's seat, Mermoz studies his mechanic. He looks even more emaciated than usual, and he's as white as snow. He hasn't opened his mouth throughout the entire journey.

"Look happy. We've done it!"

Mermoz stretches out his hand and places it on the man's shoulder.

"Collenot . . . ," he says gravely, "I'd go to the ends of the earth with you."

"Monsieur Mermoz, we do that every week."

The Chilean airfield employees can't believe the story of what happened in those peaks. They shake their heads, incredulous. The cordillera doesn't give men back. Planes aren't repaired with wires and rag balls. Landing gear hanging together with bolts doesn't withstand drops of several metres. The director of the aerodrome knows that pilots like to embellish their stories and notes everything with a degree of disbelief. An expedition including mules, organised the next day, reaches the place described by Mermoz. To the amazement of the director, the caravan returns from 4,000 metres with the seats, the fuel drum, the oil can, and the sleeve from Mermoz's bomber jacket.

The story spreads like wildfire. Jean Mermoz, the blond pilot, is favoured by Providence. They call him the Archangel; poor people bless themselves when they hear his name. When he arrives in Buenos Aires after recuperating, a tremendous reception awaits him. He's invited to all the important dinners; there are balls in his honour; perfumes, chocolates, and even a brand of cigarettes are named after him.

A transoceanic call reaches him from Daurat.

"You're late in arriving. But I'm happy to have you back."

"Thank you, Monsieur Daurat."

"We must officially inaugurate that route from Buenos Aires to Santiago before summer. Turn down all invitations and celebrations. We'll propose you for a medal from the Aéro-Club de France."

"I don't want medals, Monsieur Daurat! I want a plane with which I can cross the Atlantic!"

CHAPTER 37

Cabo Juby (Morocco), 1929

ANTOINE DE SAINT-EXUPÉRY

BERNIS AND GENEVIÈVE, FINALLY TOGETHER. They get out of the taxi which leaves them at the gate in the wrought iron railings of a property in the Périgord region. A magnificent country house, which Bernis inherited from a spinster aunt, rises up a hundred metres in front of them. It has large white picture windows and wine-coloured bougainvillea. The white river-stone path leading to the entrance is flanked by flowering magnolias. Together, the two of them walk along the fragrant path on their way to the imposing entrance to the mansion. Geneviève offers Bernis her hand and he takes it enthusiastically. They stroll toward a new life, wrapped in a happiness that makes them float above the ground . . .

A paw pounces on the sheet of paper and abruptly rips it out of the typewriter. Antoine holds it in his hands for a second and then tears it into a thousand pieces. The empty paint pot that serves as his wastepaper basket is already overflowing.

It's the seventh draft in which he's telling what happens after Bernis and Geneviève get together again. Antoine has spent weeks trying this and that as he flies over the Río de Oro on maintenance flights or waits for one of the Spanish officers with whom he plays chess to make a move.

He's thought through many versions of the outcome of their reunion, each one more passionate than the previous one. He's described them living out their love among artists in Montmartre; on a flight over the Normandy breakers with Geneviève's hair blowing in the wind; looking at Paris from the Eiffel Tower. All these ideas have been piling up until finally, he takes the pages and rips them up in a rage.

They're false!

Antoine's story is fiction, but fiction must be truthful.

He thought he'd be able to give Bernis the destiny that is being denied him. A novelist can generate stories and unfurl them as if he were rolling out a carpet. He can create an imaginary life where there was nothing but a blank piece of paper. But he shouldn't come up with ridiculous illusions; he is only a small-time god. Antoine lights a cigarette, props his feet on the table, and stretches his neck backward in an attempt to soothe his headache and the constant bombardment of ideas.

Dishonest writers create perfect characters: either excessively happy and heroic or excessively unhappy and downtrodden. They write stories for puppet theatres. They think they own the characters, but the characters only belong to their own stories. That's why the story of Bernis and Geneviève can't be perfect. No story is.

He hunts through the remaining sheets of paper for the most recent version of the dawn arrival of Geneviève at the door of Bernis's apartment. He tears up everything else and starts again from this point.

"Take me with you."

She's asking him to take her with him. Bernis doesn't say a word, because no word can improve on silence. Geneviève has left behind her house, her husband, and her exquisite world, and has come to his modest apartment decorated with Moorish amulets hurriedly bought from cheap stalls in the Casablanca bazaar. She's come to find him, as in his best dreams, and yet Bernis knows that something is wrong. A basic ingredient is missing—joy. He wants to believe that what has brought her to him is love, but when he looks at her and sees that she's adrift, he knows that what has brought her to his beach is a shipwreck.

It's raining, and it's hard to make out the road. They've driven hundreds of kilometres with no precise destination. "Far from Paris," she had told him. No other instruction; nothing more. And then only silence. Beside him, Geneviève shrinks into her seat, trying to curl up into a ball. She's worn out, and she's shivering. Condensation fogs up the windows. The outside cold and darkness have made their way inside, too . . .

Antoine would like to stretch his hand out to the typewriter, rip out the sheet, and write something else. But the story has taken its own course. It's like planting a tree: You don't know in which direction the branches will grow. You can try to tie it down and prune it, but then you'll convert your tree into a bush. Antoine doesn't want his story to be a small, petit bourgeois garden plant.

After searching in vain for a hotel and with the icy rain still falling, what they finally find in a humdrum little town is a grungy guesthouse. The sheets in the room smell of the sweaty travelling salesmen who have slept on them. Geneviève is exhausted and feverish, and falls asleep in this soulless room while Bernis spends the night watching her doze fitfully. In this dump of a room, there's nothing that belongs to her or to which she can belong.

At first light, when Geneviève wakes up, Bernis still hasn't slept. He gets up out of the chair to walk toward her and Geneviève gives a brief backward start. She looks at him with the confusion of someone who has awoken with no idea of where she is.

Geneviève turns toward the window. The glass is so dirty that the light filtering through makes it seem like dusk rather than dawn. Bernis thought his love for her would heal everything, would illuminate every-thing. He was wrong.

That disdainful, even contemptuous, tone in her voice when she asks him to "Take me home" is still floating in the charged air in the room. Geneviève needs to construct her own world, surround herself with beauty and smiles, even if they are false. She desperately needs to go back to believing in the truth of those lies, invent her own summer.

They barely exchange a word on the return trip to Paris. Geneviève, in her grief at the loss of her son, sits upright, wanting to show defi-ance and dignity despite her suffering. She's been hurt by the world, by everyone. By Bernis as well, for being part of that universal conspiracy of mediocrity, for not being a magician and changing the earth's rota-tion to make time go backward and save her son.

Geneviève only emerges from her silence and looks at Bernis when they reach the entrance to her house on the boulevard and he rushes to get out and open her door. She briefly brushes aside the veil of her confusion and slowly strokes his cheek with the back of her fingers. It's her parting gift . . .

When Antoine writes the final sentence and adds the final full stop, he senses that Geneviève and Bernis have walked out of his life and taken his entire baggage of mixed-up dreams with them.

That night, after the mechanics have escaped to Villa Bens, Antoine eats some dried-out couscous by himself. In contrast to what he had always believed, there is no euphoria when a book is finished. He has not only failed to save Bernis, but he has failed to save literature, too. He discovers that a writer is not at all satisfied when he reaches the end.

He can't be. What he had in his head when he sat down in front of the empty pages was music and rapture, but what he has achieved is merely a pile of pages filled with words. It's the same unbearable difference as the one between the music that transfixes and the staves on the pieces of paper which trap the notes as if on a clothesline.

CHAPTER 38

Bahía Blanca (Argentina), 1929

JEAN MERMOZ

THESE PAST WEEKS, MERMOZ HAS fled from journalists as if they had leprosy. After flying to Bahía Blanca, south of Buenos Aires, he stays there for a few days. An acquaintance invites him to a dinner with families of the city's French community and he accepts. He wears his double-breasted houndstooth suit and dark grey tie, and walks into a restaurant which has the aesthetic pretensions of a bistro. It even has a picture of the Seine encircling the Île de la Cité hanging on a wall, but then you immediately walk into an inner patio with a smoking grill loaded with barbecued ribs and steaks. His friend Bertrand introduces him to a couple who have lived in Argentina for many years, and their daughter Gilberte.

There's something about Gilberte that immediately captures Mermoz's attention. She's not the prettiest young woman, nor the cleverest, nor the most sensual. At age nineteen, she has a serious air about her, solemn even. But there's a natural elegance to her; there's nothing affected in the way she gestures, smiles, falls silent. As Monsieur Chazottes speaks to him, Mermoz nods without really taking on board what he is saying. He notices something unusual: For the first time he feels the urge to be alone with a woman while she remains fully dressed. It strikes him as very rare, a disorder of sorts. Perhaps it's due to the stress of the past few months. He doesn't hear a word of the conversation and notices that he's sweating. He wonders if he's become ill. Malaria, maybe.

Because he's not used to it, Mermoz confuses love with the flu. He's only twenty-nine, but he feels that the moment has arrived for him to take a break from the chase. After so many temporary and even desperate relationships, he sees his future in Gilberte's tranquillity, a more settled future where he can focus on the important things.

She looks at him sweetly, with no fuss or faltering, without any attempt to capture his attention, and that attracts Mermoz even more. While Monsieur Chazottes talks and talks about his strategies in the bridge championships held at the French casino in Bahía Blanca, Madame Chazottes says nothing, and that's why she knows more. With a glance to her left and another to her right, she knows everything.

"Ernest," she gently interrupts her husband, "Monsieur Mermoz will have to go and meet other guests right now. Why don't you invite him to our house tomorrow morning for a cup of tea and you can continue your conversation?"

Monsieur Chazottes gives his wife a puzzled look. She isn't given to inviting people to the house, and it's rare that she would do so with someone they've only just met. It doesn't even seem very appropriate.

"But Marguerite, Monsieur Mermoz must have dozens of engagements."

"I'll cancel them all, Monsieur Chazottes. It will be a real pleasure to visit you tomorrow."

Gilberte smiles happily. As does her mother, and Mermoz, too. Only Monsieur Chazottes seems somewhat surprised that an aviator would be so interested in bridge.

CHAPTER 39

Cabo Juby (Morocco), 1929

ANTOINE DE SAINT-EXUPÉRY

AN OFFICER FROM THE SPANISH fort descends from his car in the middle of a cloud of dust outside Antoine's office at the aerodrome. It seems ridiculous to use a chauffeured vehicle to cover the fifty steps that separate Antoine from the entrance to the fort, but these are the regulations that govern an official visit.

The officer, Lieutenant Fardo, has come to ask a favour, but he wants to disguise it with military-speak: Would Antoine intercede with the chief of a tribe with whom the Spaniards are incapable of reaching an understanding?

Antoine isn't surprised. The soldiers arrive in the settlements carrying their weapons openly, with an aloof and arrogant attitude. They refuse to learn the local language: They represent the Crown, the law, hierarchy; they're not going to lower themselves to speak the language of these goat herders, as they see it. Antoine, in the months he's been here, has made an effort to learn something of their language, only a few phrases, but it pleases them.

The Spaniards want to inform the tribes that a military convoy with an armed escort, headed for La Güera to the south, will be crossing through their territory. The want the sheikh to know that it's neither an invasion nor an attack, just a transport passing through, and to order his people not to attack the convoy.

It's a hot potato, but Antoine can't refuse.

He puts on his djellaba, as he does on other occasions, and makes his cook come along to interpret. Along the way, Kamal warns him that the sheikh is ill-tempered, but Antoine doesn't lose his good humour. If he's learned anything during these months, it's that if you want to be well received, the international language to use is a humble smile.

When they reach the camp, the Tuareg guard, covered from head to toe in blue, comes out to meet them. After conveying to him their wish to confer with the sheikh, the guard asks them to wait. A short time later, he comes back and tells them that the sheikh is busy.

"We'll wait."

Antoine indicates to Kamal that they should sit down where they are, some fifty metres from the nearest jaima. Some of the old people and children who herd the goats steal glances at them. The man who's come out to meet them disappears. A considerable period of time goes by and they see the settlement guard taking a sly peek at them from behind one of the awnings, but they give no sign of calling him or complaining. They continue to wait patiently.

After an hour, another Tuareg comes over to them. They can see his black eyes shining between his turban and his veil.

"The honourable Abdul Okri will receive you in his jaima."

He's waiting for them, seated next to a hookah which emits a mint and hashish vapor. Antoine touches his heart with the palm of his hand, brings his hand to his lips, and his forehead, and then raises it to the sky.

"Salaam alaikum."

"Alaikum salaam."

The chief's expression doesn't alter, but something in his look indicates that the respectful manner in which the stranger has introduced himself pleases him. One of the sheikh's assistants courteously extends the hookah mouthpiece to Antoine. Back when he frequented the cafés on the Boulevard Saint-Germain, Antoine would hand a glass back to the waiter if it wasn't spotless. If one of those waiters had seen him accept this mouthpiece, drooled over by several generations of Berbers, they wouldn't have believed it.

Antoine happily shares the hookah although the hashish makes his head spin somewhat. He knows that the mistake Westerners make when they come to negotiate with desert tribes is that they want to get straight to the point and settle the matter quickly. This irritates the person they're addressing and predisposes them toward an adverse decision. Any agreement requires a few introductory remarks. The direct route that pleases European rationalism so much, leads nowhere here. Theirs is a culture of the curved line. Like the half moon. Like the blade of a scimitar.

Antoine listens with utmost respect to the tales of wells wiped out by extreme drought, and camels as stubborn as camels are. When the sheikh considers himself satisfied, he turns the floor over to his visitor. Antoine, in turn, talks about the amazement caused by some animals and tells them the story of a dog they had at home when he was a child which, whenever someone in the town died, and the bells were rung to announce it, wouldn't eat that day, wouldn't touch anything they gave him.

The sheikh and his assistants listen attentively. A few of them remain silent, as if they are pondering this extraordinary event; others nod; the occasional person gesticulates wildly and is adamant that this is impossible, because dogs don't have souls. They get caught up in a

232

debate, until the sheikh settles it—he'll consult with a wise interpreter of the Koran who lives a day's journey away. A beautiful girl, her face uncovered, brings in a bowl with goat's milk. The chief has a long drink first, and then passes the bowl to his visitor who drinks and returns the bowl to the chief so that he can pass it on to the others in attendance.

Then Antoine speaks of his work as a pilot.

"We don't like planes. We've seen planes drop bombs on settlements," the sheikh tells Antoine.

"There are also camels that kick and dogs that bite, but that doesn't mean that there aren't good camels and noble dogs."

The sheikh listens gravely to the translation and signals to Antoine to keep talking.

"Our planes don't carry bombs; they only carry letters."

"Letters?"

One of his assistants whispers in his ear and the chief nods.

"Words written on a piece of paper?" He ponders this, because the only written words he's ever seen are those of the Koran on the façades of the grand mosques. "So what you carry back and forth are sacred words?"

A worried Kamal translates. If his French boss answers in the negative, the sheikh will think that they work for a trivial, even ungodly, company, because only the words of the prophets are worthy of being written down. If his boss replies in the affirmative, he'll be lying to the sheikh, and lying to someone as dignified as his host is an offense which, if they perceive it as such, will lead to their heads rolling along the sand.

"Are they sacred words? Of course they are!"

Kamal translates, trying to prevent his nervousness and his sidelong glance at the sharpened curved daggers hanging at the entrance to the tent from being noticed. The sheikh displays his satisfaction.

"I would be greatly honoured, noble Abdul Okri, if one day you were to accept my invitation to fly in one of our planes."

The sheikh stares at him and then turns toward the oldest man. Kamal translates his words in a whisper.

"Does the Koran accept that men can fly through the air?" he asks him.

"The Koran speaks of Solomon. I've heard the ancient peoples tell that Solomon flew on a green silk magic carpet with all his court, and there were more than two hundred of them."

"But infidels don't have Allah's protection," another intervenes. "It would be very dangerous. You shouldn't accept this risk."

The sheikh nods and it's not clear if he means yes or no. Since silence has fallen, Antoine says that he belongs to the French tribe, and that camped next door to where he lives is the Spanish tribe.

"The Spaniards have asked me, noble Abdul Okri, that I humbly request your blessing for a convoy of trucks escorted by armed soldiers to cross your lands in peace, in order to reach the south."

The chief thinks about this briefly.

"If they travel peacefully . . . why will they be armed? Displaying arms in my territory is an insult."

"I understand your words, Sheikh. But they are from the warrior caste of the Spanish tribe, and they cannot relinquish their weapons, as they form part of their honour. It would be like asking an honourable man to walk about naked."

The sheikh frowns, outraged by the idea that an honourable man would show his nakedness in public.

He remains silent for a moment, then speaks again, and Kamal translates:

"Accepted. They don't have to disarm. But they must not display their weapons, they must keep them hidden as a sign of respect."

"That strikes me as a magnanimous solution, which shows you for the wise and honourable man that you are."

The advisers nod in agreement and the sheikh, looking satisfied, signals for tea to be served.

They leave the jaima much later, with effusive greetings and forceful slapping of hands on hearts.

When they have moved off a few metres and started their return journey, Antoine gives a sigh of relief. Kamal does likewise.

"We diced with death," he says to Antoine.

"Why?"

"When the sheikh asked you if you were transporting sacred words you answered 'Yes.' You lied to him! And you made me lie! May Allah forgive me! If they had realised it, we'd be dead right now."

"You're mistaken, my friend. I did not lie to him. Our great spiritual leader, Monsieur Daurat, made it clear to us from the first day: The mail is sacred." And after saying this, his serious expression changes into a sly grin.

"If the honourable Abdul Okri finds out that you were mocking him, he'll cut off our heads as if we were chickens."

Antoine puts his hands on his hips, waggles his elbows in an exaggerated manner, and starts to cluck like a chicken. Kamal ends up laughing too.

Antoine leaves his cook kneeling on the desert sand praying in the direction of Mecca in the hope of purging so much sacrilege, and slowly heads back to the fort. Dusk is falling as he reaches the entrance. The soldiers on guard duty, who are sitting on a bench, weapons in hand, allow him to pass with no formalities. They'd let the devil through as long as they didn't have to get up.

Lieutenant Fardo, the one who paid him the visit, and Captain López escort him to Colonel de la Peña's office. When he enters, a soldier offers him a cup of bitter coffee and a chair. The naked walls and the crucifix high overhead give the room the appearance of a sacristy.

"Will they let us pass without giving us any problems?" the lieutenant asks him point-blank.

Antoine knows that some things here aren't so different from the jaima: If the leader says "Yes," the rest will agree; if he says "No," the rest will refuse. He explains that to a Tuareg chief, it shows a lack of respect for armed soldiers to cross his territory.

"Utter nonsense!" shrieks the lieutenant with the audacity of youth.

The colonel glares at him.

"Would it strike you as nonsense if a battalion of armed English soldiers walked through the middle of Madrid?"

The lieutenant blushes and answers more meekly: "But this territory belongs to us. This is Spain."

"They don't read the *Gaceta de Madrid*," the colonel resolves abruptly. "Carry on, Saint-Exupéry."

"After arduous negotiations, they've agreed to allow the convoy safe passage under one condition: The weapons must not be visible."

The colonel frowns.

"That's not possible. Weapons must be at hand to defend the convoy in case of an attack. Why should we trust them?"

"He hasn't requested that the weapons not be at hand, only that they not be seen. You have to understand him. He's a chief, like you; he has to safeguard his dignity before his people."

"How dare you compare our colonel with a damned Moor! You French have always looked down your noses at the Spanish!" the captain shouts.

Antoine moves uncomfortably in his chair. He'd forgotten about Spanish pride.

"It was not my intention to make any sort of comparison, Captain. If I've offended you all, please forgive me. You asked me to intercede and the only thing they are requesting is that the weapons not be visible. They don't have to be far away, just somewhat camouflaged. It's enough for the sheikh if the weapons the soldiers are carrying over their shoulders are covered with a piece of cloth."

"A piece of cloth? So we're going to submit to the whims of one of these crazy djellaba-wearing grandees?" the captain pompously wonders aloud. "If we do that, we'll prove that he rules more than we do. It's a humiliation for Spain!"

"And if we cross his territory no matter what he wants, Colonel, sir?" the lieutenant asks anxiously.

"If you would allow me, Colonel," Antoine interrupts, "I'd like to make an observation."

The colonel accedes with a wave of his hand.

"Everyone knows that here, you are the ones in charge. The sheikh knows that you'll cross his territory whether he authorises it or not. He knows that your weaponry and your military training are far superior. He neither can, nor does he wish to, humiliate you, absolutely not. He only makes this small request, asking for a magnanimous gesture on your part, so that he will not lose honour among his tribe."

Everyone turns to their superior, who remains silent for a few seconds before speaking:

"If it is as Saint-Exupéry says, this chief seems to be a negotiator, and it suits us to have chiefs in hostile territory prepared to reach agreements. If we ride roughshod over them on our way through and cause any injuries, this chief could fall out of favour and be replaced by another, more radical one who would cause us even more problems. If covering our rifles allows us to get to La Güera without mishap, as High Command orders, I see no reason for not doing it. If anyone asks why the weapons are being covered, they are to be told that it's to prevent sand from clogging the mechanisms, thereby ensuring that the weapons are in the best possible condition to be fired should that be necessary. If anyone lets on that this was the idea of a Moor, I'll put him in the Casa del Mar prison for ten years."

The others agree meekly.

"Yes, sir!"

Antoine leaves through the fortress gate sighing with relief.

CHAPTER 40

Buenos Aires (Argentina), 1929

JEAN MERMOZ AND HENRI GUILLAUMET

DUE TO A SWITCH IN pilots, Mermoz couldn't be waiting for Guillaumet at the port of Buenos Aires yesterday, as he would have liked. Now he turns the corner at Calle Valdivia at full speed and leaves his car double-parked at the entrance to El Siglo restaurant. He throws the keys to the parking valet and rushes in. Air turbulence, yelling at lazy employees, disappointment at the meanness of bureaucrats, the cold, the rain, exhaustion . . . it's all left behind when he sees Guillaumet at the table down the back.

Mermoz embraces him and almost knocks him over. He checks out his friend's peeling face, his forehead burnt as if it had been put on a grill.

"Guillaumet, you sunbake too much." And Mermoz roars with laughter.

"You're looking fantastic. Argentina suits you."

"You'll see. You'll like it here. You'll live very well in Buenos Aires. They have wonderful meat!" He winks at Guillaumet mischievously.

"It's such a delight to have you as my boss."

"If you say I'm your boss again, I'll fire you!"

They both laugh.

"There are lots of challenges for us here, Henri."

"That's good, isn't it?"

"It's the best!"

The waiter arrives with two gourds of maté and Mermoz puts on a comic look of disgust.

"I don't want that grandmother's drink!" he says in rudimentary Spanish. "Bring us coffee and a bottle of cognac!"

Mermoz tells Guillaumet that he needs a pilot like him to secure the new section of the route to Chile, and that his office is under considerable political pressure too.

"Government licences to allow foreigners to fly over this country's airspace require in return the establishment of certain complicated routes like Buenos Aires–Santiago to connect Argentina and Chile, and also the route under consideration to Patagonia. That one will probably be loss-making because of the scant population, but it's very much on the wish list of the Argentinian government, which is having enormous difficulty providing essential services in that immense territory which stretches down to the South Pole."

Mermoz moves the dirty plates aside and unfolds a map of South America in front of Guillaumet.

"We have to fly from Buenos Aires to Santiago, the capital of Chile."

"How far?"

"Over a thousand kilometres. But the real problem is crossing the Andes. I've found an air corridor."

"Some fright you gave us."

Mermoz stretches out his arms and smiles. He indicates the spot on the map through which to fly.

"I know it's dangerous."

Guillaumet looks at him, somewhat intrigued. Something doesn't stack up.

"Why me?"

"You're the best."

Guillaumet raises his eyebrows, faking incredulity.

"What are you up to?"

Mermoz bursts out laughing and Guillaumet shakes his head. *Mermoz, the manager of the pilots who assigns the routes, isn't keeping the most dangerous one for himself? Impossible.*

"Henri, I have a really serious problem, but I don't know if you're going to want to help me . . ."

"You know perfectly well you can count on me."

"It's very serious." Mermoz's pause is intriguing. "I've met a special girl. Very special. I think I've fallen in love with her."

"Wow! That's fantastic news."

"The problem is that I've flown to many different cities over these months . . ."

"And what's the problem?"

"I have girlfriends throughout South America and I don't know what to do with them. You wouldn't like to have the odd one? They're all enchanting! María Helena in Mendoza, Hallina in Natal, Flavia in Santiago . . . or is Cucha the one in Santiago? If I could at least not mix up their names when I see them!"

"Are you serious?"

"About handing over my girlfriends? No way! Noëlle would beat the living daylights out of me."

"So there's a special girl."

"Very special. I'm going to ask her to marry me."

Guillaumet's eyes open wide. Noëlle won't believe him when he tells her. As a matter of fact, he doesn't believe it himself.

Guillaumet fills their glasses with cognac and they drink a toast to their women.

"Well, Jean, I still don't believe you're going to hang up your pilot's helmet. Are you going to tell me why you're giving me the most entertaining route in South America instead of keeping it for yourself?"

Mermoz laughs. "I now have sufficient influence finally to secure a plane which will fly the mail across the Atlantic. I have to dedicate all my energy to that."

They drink another toast to the challenges of the skies.

Guillaumet goes along as Mermoz's copilot on his first crossing of the Andes. They take advantage of the wind currents and the gaps between summits. Mermoz shouts from his seat. His voice isn't loud enough to overcome the noise of the engine, but Guillaumet nods. The route is obvious. And after several satisfactory test flights, in July 1929, the regular airmail route between Buenos Aires and Santiago is inaugurated, with Guillaumet as mailman.

Mermoz focuses on his efforts to acquire a machine which will cross the ocean, avoiding the delay in delivery of the mail caused by the company ships having to traverse the 3,000-kilometre-wide puddle. They'll need a plane with the range and stability for a twenty-four-hour hop once a week. Daurat is on his side, but the French Air Ministry is reluctant. There are still those who believe they're just dealing with sporting deeds, to whom only military flights are serious. It irritates Mermoz to have to fight for the obvious: France can't be left behind in the race to establish new civilian air routes.

Writing letters to Gilberte is the only cure for his bad humour. Her replies come in very elegant envelopes with blue borders and her handwriting looks like a schoolgirl's, which softens even Mermoz's elephant hide.

He regularly flies the route between Brazil and Buenos Aires. Every Wednesday, he takes off from Pacheco right at midnight and lands in Rio at four in the afternoon on Thursday. On Saturday at dawn, he sets off again with the mail on the return flight. In Rio, he can sleep for two nights to recover. But sometimes he doesn't sleep at all; the Brazilian women hypnotise Mermoz with the samba sway of their hips. But he also experiences an agitation of his own: pilots to supervise, new routes to open, his own personally assigned route to fly, future routes that have to be developed, night flights which are starting to become the norm . . . But it's not enough.

He's been sending reports and petitions to Marcel Bouilloux-Lafont, the president of Aéropostale, and proposals to the embassy and to his contacts in the French government, but Paris doesn't want to authorise international air routes until there's a tried and tested machine. They don't want any fiascos which will endanger their political careers. They've rejected all his petitions.

When an undersecretary of the French Air Ministry passes through Buenos Aires, Mermoz asks for a meeting but his request is denied because of a full diary. So he wangles an invitation to a reception at the embassy and makes an important businessman introduce him.

"Monsieur Jean Mermoz, head of pilots at Aéropostale in Argentina . . ."

"You!" the undersecretary exclaims in disgust at the sight of him. He's already received three of his pigheaded requests for support for the Atlantic crossing.

"There are no guarantees of success; right now, that route is unviable. The Argentinian press always keeps an eye on you, and so, to be certain that you won't do anything that might cast serious doubt on the good reputation of French air safety, we've banned the sale to you of more than fifteen hundred litres of fuel."

He adjusts his glasses and brings the conversation to an end. Or so he believes. Mermoz's face becomes so inflamed with anger that the undersecretary's glasses fog up.

"The only thing that casts serious doubt on France's reputation is its lack of courage."

Mermoz turns and walks out on the politician, scandalising the ambassador and his guests. A formal complaint against Jean Mermoz, Aéropostale's head of pilots, reaches the desk of Monsieur Daurat in Montaudran two days later. Following Daurat's instructions, his assistant puts it away in the filing cabinet.

CHAPTER 41

Cabo Juby (Morocco), 1929

ANTOINE DE SAINT-EXUPERY

NEFERTITI NOW HAS AN ENCLOSURE. No lion will be able to attack her, neither will Berbers, nor bored soldiers. Antoine approaches the gazelle, and when he stretches out his hand, she comes over tamely and lets him stroke her nose. He's never seen anything look at you with the intensity of this fragile herbivore. He feels that we humans have much to learn from the wisdom of gazelles. In the dark crystal of her eyes, a wise man could read the history of the earth.

Lou-Lou pops into his mind.

Antoine remembers with surprising accuracy one of Lou-Lou's mannerisms in particular: the way in which she used to lower her head slightly, like a gazelle, and then slowly open her eyes. For him, happiness is round and escapes by rolling down the street. In contrast, sadness is square and sticks in the throat.

He puts eleven different records on his turntable, and the dust and scratches on all of them make the needle skip. He picks up a pen to make some corrections and the ink is dry. He picks up a pencil, but all he can do is scribble in the margins of the page—figures, women with their hair blowing in the wind, the *L* of *Lou-Lou*, a child dressed as a prince.

A suffocating fog sits over Cabo Juby, erasing everything. The voices of the guards at the fort sound like a ghostly echo.

"All quiet at post four!"

"All quiet at post five!"

"All quiet at post six!"

They can't see a thing. Never has their guard duty been more futile, but they remain at their posts.

After two days of dead calm, the fog in Cabo Juby lifts, although a sort of warm murkiness still hangs in the air.

Antoine wakes up feeling gloomy, and when he stands in front of the mirror in his luxurious bathroom, his hand drops because he has no one to shave for. Totó comes into his hut and tells him he has a visitor.

"A visitor?"

He imagines that a beautiful girl with long blond hair has crossed the planet to declare her love for him. Not that it would matter if she were a brunette, or a redhead, or chestnut . . . or even bald! And he laughs. He sees that mocking Antoine in the mirror, looking out at the solemn, melancholy Antoine and blowing raspberries. The visitor is probably some Spanish officer, but just in case, he puts on a clean shirt.

As soon as he steps outside, he knows already that his visitor isn't a sophisticated young woman wearing Chanel perfume. Sitting on the ground, his straight back resting against the wall of the hut and maintaining his stately dignity despite his position, Sheikh Abdul Okri is looking at him.

He doesn't say a word, but they both know: He's come so that the man belonging to the tribe that flies will keep his promise.

Antoine puts a helmet on the sheikh's head and adjusts the goggles,

246

all without a word of protest from the sheikh. He allows himself to be handled just like the child standing still while his mother combs a perfect part in his hair before he heads off to school. Antoine indicates that the sheikh should make himself comfortable in the front seat of a Bréguet.

The engine thunders and the plane rises into the air with the smack of a clumsy swimmer. As it gains altitude, Antoine notices his passenger tensing, and senses that he's clenching his fists. It must be a terrifying experience for a man who has never been higher than the rump of a camel, but Sheikh Abdul Okri doesn't say a word.

The plane stabilises and the sheikh's shoulders start to relax. Eventually, he turns his head down in the direction of the ground. For the first time he's crossing the desert without feeling the burning heat of the sand under his feet. Slowly, he spreads out his arms. The wind pushes back the sleeves of his tunic and turns them into banners. Antoine can't work out what he's doing until he remembers a conversation they had a few weeks earlier about what it would be like to be a bird. Sheikh Abdul has turned the dream of his ancestors into reality: to be an eagle flying over the desert. He doesn't know if the chief is laughing; the deafening noise of the engine prevents him from finding out. They fly for hours, flouting all protocols. When Antoine sees a flock of seagulls floating lazily near the never-ending beach past Cabo Bojador, he descends and frightens them with the propeller like a mischievous boy. The birds suddenly take off and the dance of life bursts over the sky as if it were the first day of creation.

They leave behind the dunes and small ranges. The chief points with his finger now and again, maybe signalling a place he travelled to once with some caravan after walking many days. Then he brings his hand back in and remains silent. He's never been so far into the interior. The desert he thought he knew turns out to be a great deal bigger than his long life, than any life.

They catch up with a small cluster of clouds when they reach Cintra Bay. He gains altitude so he can frolic with them a little and the sheikh tenses in his seat when he sees that they're going to crash into them. Antoine laughs. *What does Sheikh Abdul think clouds are made of? His knowledge of clouds is the same as a newborn's!* The Bréguet reaches the white cumuli and he flies into them like a spoon through a plate of Chantilly cream. The world disappears from sight, a slight tremor shakes the plane, and threads of gauze run along beside it. He sees the sheikh stretch out his hand to try to touch the clouds and shake his head in wonder. For the rest of his life he'll sit next to his hookah at night and tell how once he touched the clouds.

They pass Agadir and the desert becomes coloured by a small covering of scrub and other vegetation. They head toward Saint-Louis de Senegal and the colours of the landscape change. Sheikh Abdul points to the first trees. There's one. Another two over there. Further on, a cluster of them—ceibas, palm trees, acacias, enormous baobabs. And he starts to run out of fingers for pointing. Until he finally stops gesticulating and stays still, hypnotised by the landscape.

The rivers widen, and the ground has a greenish tinge. The old Saharan hardened by the desert, the intransigent chief, the fierce warrior, sheds tears behind his aviator goggles. Antoine looks at him bewildered and his passenger points insistently toward the ground below.

Antoine can't see anything unusual. There's just a tiny forest. Nothing special. Until it dawns on him.

A forest . . .

Sheikh Abdul Okri could never imagine that there were so many trees in the world. Maybe at this moment he's remembering the dusty bushes growing next to his jaima and feeling pain for them, lost in the middle of the sand. Antoine feels tenderness toward this man and his people, people in a harsh land, scattered throughout the desert like the sand itself and yet, still proud.

Antoine never thought he'd see a sheikh as proud as this one cry. Antoine sighs, caught up in the emotion. Humankind—egoistic, hateful, mean, capable of the greatest atrocities—can also be a creature capable of becoming emotional at the sight of the ancient peace of the trees. He leans forward and puts his hand on the Saharan's shoulder.

Antoine believes every person is a miracle.

CHAPTER 42

★

Brazil, 1929

Jean Mermoz

THE DIRECTOR OF OPERATIONS OF the company tells Mermoz that he has to be patient in his desire to set up the mail link by air between Europe and South America, that political matters have their own timetable; but Mermoz can't bear the wait.

He lands in Rio de Janeiro in the dead of night, exhausted, fifteen minutes earlier than indicated on the timetable—a gift of fifteen minutes for the pilot who is taking over from him, heading for Uruguay. As he's walking to the hut, the manager of the airfield comes to meet him.

"Bad news, Senhor Mermoz."

He hands Mermoz a telegram: Mallo, an Argentinian pilot who was working on the new stages of a future Paraguayan route, has been killed in a crash half an hour from the Paraguayan capital.

The two men exchange a look.

"The boy wouldn't have suffered. You're too busy trying to straighten the machine to be worried about dying."

Mermoz nods in agreement.

"It's the family who suffer. I once saw that boy at Pacheco. His parents brought him to the airfield in a mule cart. Very poor people, Senhor Mermoz. As he was heading for the runway, I could see them crossing themselves. Now they won't even have the consolation of burying their son."

"His body will be repatriated."

"The train doesn't go that far, and in this heat, nobody's going to wait for the paperwork to be done. They'll send the family a watch, if some scoundrel doesn't pinch it along the way."

"Give me a map. I'm leaving for Paraguay. I'll transport him by plane."

"The coffin won't fit through the Laté's narrow door."

"We'll see about that."

The airfield manager knows that nothing will make Mermoz change his mind.

"Will you leave first thing in the morning?"

"Prepare a plane for me, filled to the brim with fuel, and some scrambled eggs and coffee. I leave in fifteen minutes."

"The weather report . . ."

Mermoz has already started to walk toward the pilots' hut.

Twenty-four hours later, a 400 hp engine buzzes over Pacheco. The personnel on the ground watch a Laté line up the runway in a very stiff wind, wobbling dangerously. From a distance, the plane has an unusual profile. As it gets closer, the mechanics, the office staff, and the main-tenance workers all come outside to watch this strange thing coming down from the sky. On one side of the fuselage, a coffin is tied to the wing struts in a vertical position making the machine tilt dangerously. One of the shifts in wind causes the plane to lean in the opposite direc-tion and Mermoz supports the box with his shoulder as he steadies the plane. He lands on an angle which almost has the wing touching the runway, but he completes the manoeuvre successfully and, after braking with a zigzag, comes to a halt with his strange cargo.

When the astonished faces peer into the cockpit, Mermoz removes his helmet.

"Get in touch with Mallo's family. Tell them his colleagues have brought their son home."

CHAPTER 43

Cabo Juby (Morocco), 1929

ANTOINE DE SAINT-EXUPÉRY

ANTOINE WALKS OVER TO NEFERTITI'S enclosure. He's been so busy with rescuing downed pilots that he's ignored her. She's become a big, slender gazelle. As he gets closer, he notices she's pushing against the wooden fence logs with her forehead and trying in vain to barge her way out with her tiny horns.

"Nefertiti!"

But she doesn't react to his call. She pushes her head against the fence insistently.

"Don't be mad! There are hunters out there. There are venomous snakes, foxes, maybe even the odd lion. Here, you've got food, water, safety."

He notices that he sounds like Monsieur Charron, the chief accountant of the tile factory when Antoine told him he was resigning. He walks over to the gazelle and strokes her despite her continuing stubborn headbutts. He looks at the horizon where, at this late hour of the day, the light is beginning to soften.

"You've felt the call . . ."

He strokes her nose and she looks back at him with a deer's beautiful sadness. He goes over to the barrier and raises the log that secures the crude wooden gate.

"You'll suffer out there, you'll have to flee from terrible felines, you'll have to find your own food with the effort of your horns . . . But you want to be free."

Nefertiti looks at him.

"You're a brave girl."

As soon as he raises the barricade, the gazelle gallops off at the speed of light. She doesn't hesitate. She doesn't stop. She doesn't look back. Soon, she's just a tiny dot that's merging into the distance, running in search of her own destiny.

Antoine stands there gazing at the spot to which she's headed until night falls and he feels a little cold.

And what of my own destiny, he wonders. *This airfield far from everywhere. Isn't it also a pen protecting me from real life? What has become of love?*

Lou-Lou escaped as swiftly as the gazelle. Should he gallop after her? Or should he run in the opposite direction and look for a new love? He doesn't know the answer. He asks himself if he should settle for writing about life or throw himself into living it.

The sun sets behind the dilapidated prison in the sea where only sharks now stand on guard, and he feels that the hour to return to France has come.

In the morning, he sends a telegram to the director of operations requesting that he be relieved of his position as manager of the airfield at Cabo Juby.

Although Daurat doesn't tell him—he never does, so his employees won't drop their guard—he is satisfied with Antoine's work and knows he won't find a better replacement. Antoine has managed to gain the trust and respect of the Spaniards, he's established cordial relations with the tribes in the area, and his personality has converted one of the most hated stopovers—which had the pilots horrified at the prospect of spending a few days stranded in that arid plain—into a better appreciated one. Nobody has lasted in the desert at Cabo Juby more than three months, but Antione has been there for a year and a half. Daurat has been expecting his letter of resignation for months.

Daurat's reply doesn't take long: POSTED TO THE EXPANSION OF AÉRO-POSTALE IN SOUTH AMERICA AS MANAGER OF THE SERVICE.

Antoine jumps for joy and asks for the last bottle of wine in the storeroom. He immediately sends a reply to Daurat: COULD YOU GIVE ME A MONTH'S VACATION TO VISIT MY MOTHER AND SISTERS BEFORE I LEAVE FOR SOUTH AMERICA?

Daurat's reply is just as swift: ONE WEEK.

His replacement arrives a few days later, a veteran pilot whom he embraces effusively and brings up to date on everything. He packs his djellaba, two pairs of trousers, and a couple of shirts that have survived the desert. The most precious item in his luggage is the two hundred typed folios of the novel for which he doesn't yet have a title.

He goes to say goodbye to Abdullah Mukhtar.

"Do you remember the gazelle I tamed?"

"Yes."

"In the end she wanted to be free."

"That's how it must be."

"But all my effort to tame her served no purpose."

"Of course it served a purpose. Now, you'll always love gazelles, all gazelles. Because you'll see your gazelle in each one of them."

At the Spanish fort, the soldiers who shared afternoons of chess with him say friendly goodbyes. Even the officers who treated him with disdain become sentimental, and they all pay for one round of drinks after another in the canteen, because Spaniards can't conceive of a celebration without drinks. Colonel de la Peña offers him an unexpected farewell gift: As Antoine heads out the fort's gate, weaving his drunken way, the guards stand to attention and he's saluted with full military honour as if he were a major-general.

Antoine arrives in Toulouse as a passenger accompanying the day's mail. On setting foot in Montaudran, dressed in his one dusty but decent suit, he watches the comings and goings of the employees with the mailbags, which sit briefly on the ground awaiting a trolley, and he notices the label stamped onto the burlap: COURRIER SUD—SOUTHERN MAIL. He decides this will be the title of his novel.

He feels like a phantom in Paris. Most of his friends are absent, either travelling or living outside Paris. The city is full of people, but he can't find his place among them. He waits on a terrace in Place de la Concorde for Jean Prévost, the editor of the literary magazine which published his first story and the man who has done the most to encourage him to write. He can't avoid looking with some annoyance at the men passing by in their dark hats, and the women in their patterned dresses.

When the jovial, stocky Prévost arrives, he plants himself in front of Antoine in a boxing stance, waiting for Antoine to take up the same position. He does, but half-heartedly.

"Disgruntled on your first day back in Paris?"

"Look at those people going from their burrow at home to the one at the office."

"And that's bad?"

"Terrible! That's what Paris offers? Life as a bureaucrat?"

"Let's drink to that," teases Prévost. And he makes Antoine smile.

"I take myself too seriously at times, don't I?"

"And sometimes as too much of a joke! But what does that matter!"

Prévost proposes another toast, to Antoine's return. Then Antoine proposes one to women with small feet. Prévost toasts the mail aviators and Antoine replies with another to all those they haven't yet toasted.

The Calvados provides a bandage for Antoine's melancholy.

That night, Prévost enthusiastically reads *Southern Mail* and recommends its publication to the publisher, Gaston Gallimard. He knows it's not a well-put-together tale, even disjointed at times, and it's steeped in a lyricism that transforms Geneviève into a fairy queen. But there's something hypnotic in those pages.

CHAPTER 44

Buenos Aires (Argentina), 1929

ANTOINE DE SAINT-EXUPÉRY, JEAN MERMOZ, AND HENRI GUILLAUMET

ANTOINE BOARDS A SHIP IN the port of Bordeaux, headed for Buenos Aires. He's bought several suits, two Borsalino hats, and a Benrus wristwatch with an independent seconds dial. With the money he saved in Cabo Juby and his rise in salary as manager of the airline in South America, for the first time ever he feels that money is spilling out of his pockets. But despite the mountains of cakes and pastries he bought for his family and the ones he's carrying in his luggage, the most valuable items with which he's leaving France are his mother's caresses and the publishing contract with Gallimard for *Southern Mail*.

He spends the eighteen-day crossing smoking on deck, undertaking a do-it-yourself cocktail tasting course and amusing the children on board with his card tricks. He looks at the young women in the salon, and suddenly he doesn't feel so young. His hair has started to thin and he has difficulty keeping his weight under control.

"If God had wanted the French to be thin, he wouldn't have invented croissants!" he exclaims ecstatically at the breakfast table to the amusement of his fellow diners.

In the course of the daily ups and downs, Antoine spends a lot of time leaning on the railing of the ocean liner watching the waves dance. Some people look in astonishment at the impeccably dressed, but somewhat solitary, burly man with the snub nose, who is engrossed in watching the swell and occasionally applauds the ripple of a wave as if he were watching a performance.

During these days, his memory of Lou-Lou is like the fluctuation of the waves. It comes and goes, rises and falls.

On one such afternoon, he mulls over the dedication in *Southern Mail*. He has, of course, dedicated the novel to Lou-Lou. She, however, hasn't replied to his letter asking her if she accepts having her name appear in the book. He wonders if it might be inappropriate now that she's a wife and mother. He hesitates for some time, but in the end, he decides to telegraph the publishers and ask them to remove the dedication. It doesn't really matter, anyway. She'll know. The whole book is dedicated to her.

A few days later, they sight land. The vast Río de la Plata slowly leads them to the port of Buenos Aires which stretches out along the edge of a patch of murky water.

The terminal is on an isolated wharf with rather dilapidated sheds. The squawk of the seagulls strikes him as a bad omen. A large group of people is waiting for some of the passengers and he gloomily watches the passionate greetings, the shining eyes, and the effusiveness of those welcoming and being welcomed. Arriving in a place and not having anyone waiting for you is always a little sad.

A young porter follows him through the terminal pushing a cart loaded with his suitcases. Antoine notices a soldier of the Argentinian army throw his kitbag on the ground and start to run toward an adorable young woman with childish fringe who's running toward him. When they come together, they stop a few centimetres apart and look at each other with such joy that they don't dare touch in case they shatter the moment. Antoine feels as if he's a guest at an improvised wedding at the end of the wharf. Better than a wedding. He's so absorbed in watching them that he doesn't realise someone has approached the boy with his suitcases, signalled him to get lost, and handed him some money. The porter pushing the cart has turned into a different person, taller and stockier. He asks Antoine in Spanish with a heavy French accent:

"Where does the damned gentleman want his fucking suitcases?"

Antoine jumps and turns around startled. The porter is wearing a tweed jacket and a red scarf. He's backed up by another henchman. Antoine's cigarette drops from his mouth.

"Any further orders?"

Mermoz gives his usual explosive guffaw and Guillaumet runs to embrace him.

"Dammit, Antoine, this cart weighs a ton. You've brought more luggage than a troupe of Russian dancers. What the hell are you lugging in these suitcases? Desert sand?"

"Something better."

He removes a suitcase from the cart and puts it down on top of the wharf's wet cobblestones. He opens it, and to the amazement of his friends, it's full of bottles of Krug champagne. Before they have recovered from their astonishment, he removes a set of glasses from a wooden case and pops the cork on one of the bottles. People turn to watch them out of curiosity.

The champagne is warm, but tastes divine.

Two of the people who have stopped to watch them are the soldier and the girl with the fringe. Antoine picks up another bottle and walks over to them. In his rudimentary Spanish, he begs them to accept it.

"My wedding present."

"Spot on, señor! But how did you guess that I'm going to get married?" the soldier asks him naïvely.

Antoine looks at the amused, blushing young beauty.

"Because you'd be mad if you didn't!"

The three pilots clamber into a taxi loaded with suitcases. They've booked a room for Antoine in the Hotel Majestic.

That night, Mermoz leads an expedition into the noisiest dance halls in Buenos Aires.

"But, Jean, haven't you settled down?" asks Antoine.

"I have—in my head. But not in the rest of my body!"

Along the way, Mermoz tells them that when he travels to Bahía Blanca, he goes to visit Gilberte and it's as if the world calms down; in her, he's found the peaceful love he's needed in his life. But Mermoz is so insatiable that it's not enough for him to live only one life.

In establishments with tenuous lighting and bottles of liquor, women madly throw themselves into his arms and he roars with laughter. It must be the whisky and soda that makes Antoine feel the world is spinning around him like a carousel. Once Mermoz is buried under women, some of them turn to his companions with coquettish smiles. Guillaumet says "No" with a friendly smile. Beneath their makeup and their never-ending eyelashes thick with mascara, the women hide a fragility which is moving. To Antoine, they seem like wildflowers growing along the edge of a road. He falls in love with all of them as soon as he sees them, and walks out of the establishments with red tattoos all over his forehead.

When the cocktail bars have closed, they walk to Agüero and turn into Corrientes until they come to the humble bars around the Mercado de Abasto, where the truck drivers kick-start their working day before the sun comes up. Precariously balanced on a stool, Antoine points to an old mirror that hangs behind the counter, on which the proprietor writes the daily specials. Three somewhat blurred heads are just visible among the list of prices for stews and soups.

"Those characters over there are us."

"A great discovery!" Mermoz mocks Antoine.

"What I mean is that the real 'we' aren't the ones sitting here, but rather the ones looking at 'us' from the mirror."

Guillaumet looks at him out of the corner of his eye. He doesn't understand, and at this hour, he doesn't really want to make the effort to do so. Mermoz, on the other hand, looks at him with an intrigued expression that's overly dramatic.

"If those people in the mirror are the real ones, who the devil are we?"

"That's the question, Jean; but I don't have the answer. I don't know how to explain it, but each time I look at myself in a mirror, I see another person who isn't me. Because I'm not him . . . Do you follow me?"

"Dammit, Antoine, you're driving me mad! I think I'll ask for some brandy."

Mermoz sees a group of young women walking past the front door; they're going to set up their fruit and fish stalls. He gets up from his stool, goes to the door, and bows to them.

Guillaumet wrinkles his brow. "They'll think he's mocking them."

"No way!" remarks Antoine. "They realise it's genuine veneration. Mermoz feels devotion toward women, all women."

The oldest woman frowns disapprovingly, but the youngest ones laugh flirtatiously, blush, and walk on more quickly.

Dawn finds the three of them stumbling along the street. Arm in arm. Humming boleros badly translated into French.

A few days later, Mermoz takes Antoine to the ranch of an Argentinian pilot friend, where kilos and kilos of grilled meat are on display, alongside litres of beer, wine, and cognac, cigars, and the fervour of banal conversations, all done to impress some señoritas perhaps willing to be impressed.

A melancholy *bandoneón* and the alcohol encourage the guests to burst into song with an emotion as fervent as it is out of tune. Mermoz himself starts to sing, his tie around his head like a headband. Antoine is trying to engage a young English woman in conversation. She's very blond and very drunk. He tries to advance his flirtation, but she just touches his snub nose and laughs. For one happy moment, he believes he can conquer her with his wit, but she just keeps laughing. In reality, she doesn't understand a word of French. Still giggling, the girl walks out on him, just like that. Mermoz appears on cue. He still has the tie around his forehead, but, as if he'd already left the party and in all seriousness, he asks:

"Shall we go?"

"Where?"

"To head office."

Head office at this ungodly hour seems unreal. When Mermoz turns on the lights, Antoine can't help feeling that he's on a movie set: empty chairs, tables covered with papers, inactive calendars, sleeping telephones, clocks going round for no one, a collection of dispatch notes, files and folders.

Mermoz escorts him to his own office. He takes a shiny object that looks like a cigarette lighter out of a drawer and walks over to a large map of South America. He slowly traces a vertical line with the red lipstick from Buenos Aires toward the south, a very long line, 1,500 kilometres long, to Comodoro Rivadavia.

"What's that?" asks Antoine.

"It's Patagonia. Right now, it's just a painted line; you have to convert it into an airmail route."

Antoine walks over to the map. The line Mermoz has drawn has the dramatic colour of blood, but the smell of a woman's tenderness.

"I've done a few flights and verbally agreed on some plots of land, but as of now you'll have to take care of the bureaucracy. You'll have to supervise the aerodromes, fire the useless employees . . . and then sign them on the next day because it's impossible to find trained replacements."

He takes a crystal decanter from a cupboard and pours two glasses of whisky.

"A toast."

"What are we toasting, Jean?"

"You decide . . ."

"Let's toast red lipstick!"

CHAPTER 45

Patagonia (Argentina), 1930

ANTOINE DE SAINT-EXUPÉRY

PATAGONIA IS SYNONYMOUS WITH DISTANCE, almost exile, even for the Argentinians themselves. A million square kilometres, one-and-a-half times the size of France. An immense territory battered by winds strong enough to make the stones fly.

Antoine has been flying back and forth from Buenos Aires to establish the route: Bahía Blanca, San Antonio Oeste, Trelew, Comodoro Rivadavia, Puerto Deseado, Puerto San Julián . . . ending with Río Gallegos, not all that far from the Strait of Magellan.

For his work in this solitary place, they've named him Chevalier de la Légion d'honneur. But when he's up in the skies, honours from Paris are as useless as a flute with no holes.

He looks down as he crosses the Río Negro region, eight hundred kilometres from Buenos Aires. Sheep with curly wool move across the immense, semiarid plateaus as if choreographed like schools of white sardines. The yellowish-green plains are a huge, never-ending dry garden. Antoine is carrying a small bag in his lap because the San Antonio Oeste runway developed cracks not long after it was inaugurated, so he can't land. The head of the San Antonio postal service called him, devastated.

"They can't wait for their letters!"

There's no runway, but that's no reason for the mail not to arrive. And so a mailman on horseback is waiting for Antoine's plane on the dirt path that leads to the airfield. Antoine descends in the Laté until he's not far off the ground, and the mailman gallops behind the aircraft. Antoine throws down the bag, and on this particular morning, the letters rain down over the pampas from the sky. He turns and the mailman salutes him with his hat.

After refuelling in Trelew, he heads into the deep south, a zone where nature is intimidating: the wind sweeps the snow off the peaks, and lakes hide among the mountain cirques where condors fly. Antoine buys the *La Razón* newspaper every morning before he takes off from the Pacheco airfield, not so much to learn about the never-ending shambles that is Argentinian politics, but rather to put the sheets of newspaper inside his undershirt as soon as he's past Trelew. Nature rules in Patagonia and the wind is her most despotic minister. Antoine feels very insignificant in the midst of this vastness made to the measure of giants.

He refuels in Comodoro Rivadavia and Puerto Deseado. The world becomes more isolated as he flies further and further south. He lands on the tamped down dirt runway at Puerto San Julián.

The mailbags are small, but expectation is high. There are people awaiting his arrival and as soon as the plane comes to a stop, they rush toward him barefoot and full of wild enthusiasm. When he climbs down from the cockpit, they form a semicircle around him, not daring to get too close, as if he were one of the Three Magi. The manager of the airfield, Señor Vitoco, appears immediately, together with a policeman as barefoot as the rest of the residents, and invites Antoine to join him for a hot maté. He asks Antoine to stay longer and he'll take him to the La Catalana brothel where the bravest women in Argentina reside.

"A few years ago, they sent a gang of soldiers and their butcher of a colonel from Buenos Aires to put an end to the workers' strikes. The soldiers shot many peasant mothers and fathers, and they were supposed to be rewarded with a good time at the brothel. But the five women refused to service the soldiers. There was no way they'd relent. Imagine how humiliated those idiots felt!"

"And what happened?"

"The soldiers arrested them. But then they released them so there wouldn't be an even bigger row. Those women were the only rebels who managed to twist the arms of those shitty people from Buenos Aires. You have to meet them, hombre!"

"I'd love to . . . But the mail has to keep on flying, Señor Vitoco!"

He takes off thinking about those wonderful women. The trip from Buenos Aires to Río Gallegos takes a tough eighteen hours through constant turbulence.

But Antoine's tiredness evaporates when he reaches some long, desolate grey beaches covered with the white guano of cormorants. There's something disturbing yet hypnotic about these uninhabited coasts, as beautiful as they are unfriendly. As he's flying over the sea, he's briefly greeted by the huge tail of a whale, before it disappears into the inky waters where mystery resides.

A dense population of tiny figures loiter on the sandy shores and volcanic cliffs. The penguins remind him of the Little Tramp, Charlot— he loves Charlie Chaplin's films. When he arrives at Punta Loyola and turns toward the arm of the river that leads to Río Gallegos, he thinks about that town, with its streets, uncommonly wide for the precarious wooden houses, the two cafés, with their thick planks which allow the cold to slip through, and the cabaret, where the girls dye their greying hair. It reminds him of the Yukon, as portrayed by Chaplin in *The Goldrush*. Decades earlier, there was also a goldrush in Río Gallegos that ended up attracting a handful of adventurers and go-getters to these inhospitable latitudes of little rain and much wind.

As the end of the line, the airfield in Río Gallegos is the most completed of the route; they even brought sheet metal by boat from France to build the hangar. When he lands with the wobble of a tightrope walker buffeted by gusts, there's a retinue waiting for him. Even the municipal band has come: A barefoot *chacarera* band of three musicians—clarinet, trombone, and bass drum, all dressed in the trousers and red dress coats of a Napoleonic admiral—are interpreting noisy marches.

He'll spend the night in the Paris Hotel, where they serve delicious grilled fish. When he's about to hand over the small mailbag to the head of postal services, who has come in person in his uniform of flat hat and grey dust coat to pick up the mailbag, a tiny woman with a chin sporting a few wiry hairs and a mouth with very few teeth plants herself in front of him. He barely understands what she's telling him, but she does so in a very resolute manner. Since he doesn't understand her, she drops to her knees to implore him, as if he were a god dropped down from the heavens.

"What does this woman want, Señor Erasmo?"

"She wants you to see if there's a letter from her son in Buenos Aires. Ignore her! She's just a madwoman!"

But Antoine bends down and delicately takes her by the arm to help her get up.

"You have to wait until the mail is sorted in the post office. If there's a letter for you, they'll bring it to your house."

The woman's face is weather-beaten by the climate, which turns skin into leather, and her eyes show an intense strength. She doesn't move a centimetre.

She speaks to him slowly, so he'll understand her.

"Please, Señor Aviador. My son. His name is Lucho. I haven't heard from him for a year. I don't even know if he's among the living. You can't imagine my pain."

Antoine looks at the head of postal services.

"Señor Erasmo, could we make an exception? There aren't many letters. It would take just a moment to see if there's any mail for this woman."

"Señor Saint-Ex, that's not in the regulations . . ."

"Neither is waiting for a year without knowing anything about your son."

The mail official raises his arms like a Patagonian Christ and then points to a wooden board serving as a table at the entrance to the hangar. Antoine walks over to it with the mailbag, followed by the woman, the *chacarera*, a barefoot policeman, and half the town. He sits down on a bench behind the table.

"What is your name?"

"Mecha González, señor."

A neighbour speaks out from behind her. "It's Señora Mercedes Agregación Galeano González."

Antoine opens the leather bag and starts to search among the letters, all of them bearing a red stamp with the word AEROPOSTA. The woman watches him, her hands holding on to her skirt. Antoine is afraid there'll be nothing for her, but sometimes, very rarely, life is kind. He holds up a letter:

"Señora Mercedes Galeano . . ."

He holds out the letter but her hands keep holding on to her skirt.

"Take your letter, señora," Antoine insists.

She doesn't move. The same neighbour takes a step forward: "She doesn't know how to read."

"Well, then, please read it for her," Antoine asks him in his rudimentary Spanish.

269

The man looks down at the ground. "Neither do I, señor."

"You bunch of illiterates!" The head of postal services takes the letter. "Come over here. I'll read it to you."

Señor Erasmo opens the letter with professional care and begins to read the few badly handwritten lines. Her son is telling her that he's working in a paint factory, that he's eating well, that when he's saved enough money he'll come home . . . The woman keeps nodding her head and tears of joy run down the furrows in her cheeks.

"Forgive me, Señor Aviator!"

Another local walks up. "Could you possibly check if there's something for Leandro Luchetti Sánchez?"

Antoine glances at Señor Erasmo, who shrugs. So he starts to hunt through the mail with energy. A line forms in front of the table and it becomes an impromptu post office. Antoine doesn't understand many of the words they're saying, but he understands all the gestures. These letters contain something more valuable than gold. Sitting at this wooden table, rugged up in his leather jacket at the southernmost aerodrome on the planet and whipped by a breeze as sharp as a knife, he sees people of all ages and stations laughing and crying, cursing and becoming emotional. He feels his life connecting with these lives, and as he hands out the letters, he too is moved.

CHAPTER 46

Buenos Aires (Argentina), 1930

ANTOINE DE SAINT-EXUPÉRY, HENRI GUILLAUMET, AND JEAN MERMOZ

WHEN ANTOINE GETS BACK TO the Pacheco airfield, as he removes his bomber jacket, helmet, and goggles, he gradually rids himself of the vibrations of Patagonia. His double-breasted suit appears from underneath his flying gear. As he lights a cigarette, his taxi arrives. He hesitates for a moment before giving the address. He's tired, and the most sensible thing he could do is go straight home. But solitude tires him even more. He gives the Guillaumets' address.

Noëlle and Henri go together like a nut and its bolt. Once, in Senegal, when Guillaumet left a bar early because Noëlle was expecting him, a loudmouth pilot began to make fun of him:

"Gone home, so he won't be told off for being late! Sundays, he goes walking arm in arm with his wife to buy meringue tarts. Could you be more conventional?"

Antoine almost choked on his martini. He had such a strong coughing fit that the olive from his cocktail flew out of his mouth and landed in the middle of the table. Some of his companions started to laugh, but as soon as they saw his furious face, they stopped.

"You know nothing about love! Not even the *l*," he shouted, getting up from his chair.

"I'm married," the prickly pilot replied, "but I don't have a bourgeois life like that."

"I'm married too," added another pilot.

"And what do your partners say about you being pilots?" Antoine asked them.

"That I should find a land job!" replied one of them.

"Mine," offered another, "doesn't complain, but she bursts into tears every time I'm on duty."

"And my girlfriend becomes ill whenever I fly."

Antoine shakes his head. "They love you a lot, but they don't *truly* love you."

"Not so!"

There are sounds of protest, but Antoine asks them to hear him out.

"Noëlle truly loves Guillaumet: Each time he has a flight, she bids him farewell with a cheerful smile."

"Must be because she doesn't care if he crashes!" someone jumps in, trying to raise a laugh.

"You know nothing about Noëlle! If Guillaumet died in an accident, she'd be miserable. That's why many wives reproach their husbands when they fly. Because if their husbands kill themselves, it will make them miserable. But very few of them do what Noëlle does: She encourages him to risk his neck because then she knows her husband won't be miserable. She exchanges her happiness for his; that's true love. Anything else is just background music."

He didn't convince them. It's impossible to convince a person who doesn't want to be convinced, but Antoine knows that's how it is.

He also would like to have someone like Noëlle by his side. He's gone out with a few young women over the years, but they've always been disjointed dates, prayers without belief.

Love seems incomprehensible to Antoine. There have been days when he walks along the street, sees a woman with a feather boa, a cloche hat, and black eyes which seem mysterious to him peeping out from under the brim. And he feels an impulse to stop her in the middle of the footpath and ask her to share her life with him. He's also fallen in love for days or weeks with some of the Aéropostale company secretaries. Bibi was one of them. She was very tall and buxom, with a figure she took care to accentuate with tight-fitting dresses. He thought he had fallen in love until they went out to the movies a couple of times. She asked for soda water, and while she noisily sucked her drink through a straw with a rather grotesque expression, he looked at her and wanted to be anywhere else. What had seemed sexy, he now found common. He suddenly realised that she bore absolutely no resemblance to Lou-Lou. And it was all over then and there.

He has tried not to think of Lou-Lou. He knows she is his undoing: If he looks for Lou-Lou in every woman, he'll end up paranoid and, worse still, he'll end up alone. He's not afraid of loneliness, but the thought of a life without being loved causes him anguish.

Many nights when he hasn't had to fly the next day, he's gone as far as Calle Palermo and dropped into Les Ambassadeurs, an upmarket cabaret which offers a restaurant and cafeteria service for six pesos a person. There are also private rooms and young ladies who make kindness their business. A young French woman works there with whom he has had some good times. The doorman is no longer surprised at the sight of Antoine arriving with a spectacular round hatbox or enormous bouquets of flowers. Occasionally, he crosses paths with other pilots and he notices that they elbow each other mockingly. He doesn't care if they laugh because he's treating a bar girl as if she were his girlfriend.

As far as he's concerned, she's his girlfriend for the time booked on his ticket. He already knows that it's a patch to put over his broken heart, but such patches manage to keep wheels turning and prevent them from going flat.

Before he reaches the Guillaumets' apartment, he makes the taxi driver stop outside a liquor store, where he asks the employee for a bottle of red wine.

"Which one do you want?"

"The very best!"

Guillaumet and Noëlle aren't expecting him, but that doesn't matter. They've already had dinner, but that doesn't matter either. While Noëlle reheats a bowl of soup for him, Antoine makes himself comfortable on the three-seat sofa next to Henri and pulls a handful of folded sheets of paper from his pocket.

"You have to listen to this. I've started to write a novel about the night."

"About the night?"

"I've never experienced anything interesting before nine o'clock at night! Actually, it's a book about night flights."

Antoine begins to read. The first paragraphs don't mention flying. They talk about nights in the Saint-Maurice house where he spent his childhood. He recalls the movement of the candles in the darkness of the enormous house like the shuffle of torches. As children they would stare hypnotised at the ghostly shadows the flames threw onto the walls.

The homely warmth of the Guillaumets' modest apartment reminds him of his childhood in Saint-Maurice. The corridors were freezing cold, but in the room where the siblings slept, a sturdy iron stove kept the cold and the ghosts at bay.

Henri smiles with fond resignation. "But wasn't this a book about night flights?"

"That house at night, badly lit and full of shadows that danced everywhere, was as mysterious as the heart of Africa."

Noëlle warns him that his soup is getting cold. He ties a serviette around his neck over his suit and tie, lays out the sheets of paper next to his plate, and continues to read out loud between mouthfuls.

These are threads not yet sewn together; that's how Antoine likes to tell stories. Rather than recounting them directly, he likes to kick them around. He approaches writing in the same way he approaches an airfield at night, circling above it. Henri listens to him indulgently, and after finishing his meal, Antoine moves back to the couch and carries on reading until even he starts to yawn.

Guillaumet has to take him down to the front entrance. And it is Guillaumet who provides the taxi driver with the address of Antoine's apartment on Calle Florida, because Antoine is already snoring peacefully in the back seat.

The demanding work of their flights has prevented the three friends from getting together for weeks. Finally, one Saturday, Mermoz tells them that they must urgently gather as he has something to tell them, though they have to be sitting at a table so they can drink a toast.

He takes them to Tigre on the immense delta where the Paraná and Uruguay Rivers form a labyrinth of channels; a Venice of wooden cabins and modest barges that transport fruit and vegetables among the brown waterways.

In the café at the French Rowing Club, to which Mermoz escapes whenever he can, he tells them with a smile on his face that when he got back to his office after a recent mail run, he found a cable from Monsieur Daurat waiting for him on top of his desk: CATCH THE FIRST BOAT. WE'RE EXPECTING YOU IN MONTAUDRAN TO HEAD UP TESTING OF A LATÉ 28 WHICH HAS BEEN MODIFIED AS A SEAPLANE TO CARRY OUT THE FLIGHT ACROSS THE ATLANTIC.

"I'm taking a boat to Europe . . . but I'll be flying back."

CHAPTER 47

★

*Seaplane Base, Berre Lagoon
(Southern France), 1930*

JEAN MERMOZ

MERMOZ ARRIVES AT THE SEAPLANE base driving a fiery red convertible he bought as soon as he set foot in France. Three double hangars are lined up facing the calm waters, and a soldier shows him the building where the main offices are located. He also points out where he can park his car, but Mermoz doesn't hear that. He goes through the barricade and drives up to the entrance to the offices. He gets out of the car, now surrounded by soldiers dressed in work clothes and civilians in grease-stained overalls, and he's certainly noticed in his cashmere coat and dark blue suit. A lieutenant is expecting him.

"Monsieur Mermoz?"

"Present, and ready to fly."

"You know that you need a commercial seaplane licence to fly a seaplane."

"They had mentioned this formality to me."

The lieutenant is a young man, only a couple of years older than Mermoz, but he looks severe.

"It's not a formality, Monsieur Mermoz. A seaplane is very different from a conventional plane. You'll have to do the requisite course and pass the exam.

Mermoz frowns.

"Can I do the exam right now?"

"It's obligatory to do the course first. Those are the rules."

"How long does the course go for? I have to fly out with the March full moon!"

"That depends on the student. Some people take three months."

"Three months?"

Mermoz abruptly removes his coat and throws it on a chair, as if he were spoiling for a fight. He does want a fight. He has to win a battle with history.

"Can we start right now?"

That same morning, he climbs into a seaplane with an instructor who explains how it handles. An hour later, the seaplane lands, piloted by Mermoz himself. The instructors are astonished at the capacity of their new student to adapt within minutes to the differences in the handling of the machine.

A week later, he has his commercial seaplane pilot's licence. But a few days before the March full moon, a storm blows in, making aerial navigation dangerous. Mermoz isn't frightened by the weather; he's used to delivering mail, which has no understanding of weather. But he knows that many eyes are watching his attempt. If he fails, the authorisation could be cancelled and cause serious harm to his airline company's image. *To wait* is one of the verbs he hates most. But he has no option except to think about the April full moon.

Word reaches him of a deadly accident involving a mail plane on the

Barcelona-Alicante leg. Only a week earlier, another plane had crashed crossing the Pyrenees.

In Montaudran, Didier Daurat chews on his cigarette and looks through his window toward infinity. His most experienced pilots have been posted to the African and South American routes, but it's the leg between Toulouse and Málaga, supposedly the easiest one, that is turning into a graveyard. He has a couple of pilots to replace the two who died, but they're still pretty green. He wants them to spend a few more weeks in Montaudran practising takeoffs and landings.

"Bouvet."

His assistant, his glasses sliding down his nose, comes running in with an enormous notebook.

"Send the following telegram to Mermoz at the Berre Lagoon seaplane base: 'Be in Montaudran tomorrow. You'll cover the mail in Spain for two weeks. Daurat.'"

He already knows that Mermoz won't be pleased. He already knows that he'll arrive at full speed, his car raising a cloud of dust on the road to the airfield, and angrily brake in front of the administration offices. That Mermoz will come into his office like a bolt of lightning and stand to attention like a giant toy soldier and tell him in a respectful but tense manner that he's preparing for the most important crossing the company has ever undertaken. Daurat knows that he'll simply tell Mermoz that no deed is as important as maintaining the stability of the mail route. He knows that Mermoz will then clench his jaw, go and find his goggles, and ask for the flight plan.

And that's exactly what happens.

The Spain route experiences two weeks of impeccable punctuality, with no delays or accidents. They are two weeks during which Mermoz doubles his normal daily workload and does the work of two pilots. He insults lazy mechanics, yells for fuel, claws back minutes, eats paellas for four in Alicante all by himself, and tears apart storm clouds.

In his Montaudran office, Daurat receives daily radio reports from the airfields: The mail is on time; nothing special to report.

Two weeks later, Mermoz lands at dusk in Montaudran after flying 1,300 kilometres from the south of Spain. There's a light on in Daurat's office and his thin figure is silhouetted against the windowpane.

"You're relieved of the Málaga-Toulouse route. Return to your previous task at Berre."

The two men look at each other. Mermoz has a defiant glint in his eyes. He would like to ask the director to say "Thank you" for once.

"Have a week's break."

"I'll take a day. The day after tomorrow I'll be at the seaplane base."

Daurat puts his hand in his pocket, takes out his cigarette case, and extracts a cigarette. Before he can put his hand in his other pocket, Mermoz holds out his golden cigarette lighter sporting the jet of a flame-thrower. A seemingly polite gesture, but one which is on the verge of singeing the eyelashes of the director of operations, who says nothing. When Mermoz leaves the office, he comes across Bouvet, the assistant, in the corridor.

"I'm going to tell you a secret," Mermoz says to him between laughs. "The only way to get Daurat to lower his head is to offer to light his cigarette with the flame from your lighter."

Mermoz has lost two kilos in two weeks and needs a good meal and a soft bed. He lodges at the Brasserie Nantes in Paris. When the head waiter approaches his table somewhat nervously to ask him if he'd like an herbal tea as a digestive after his three fillets with vegetables and potatoes, Mermoz bursts out laughing and gives him a slap on the back which almost makes him lose his little moustache. He asks for two bowls of custard and four coffees.

His old friend from Syria, Max Delty, fully recovered from his illnesses and ether-free, comes to pick him up, accompanied by a girlfriend aglow with makeup and sequins. The girl has brought along a

279

friend, Sylvine, whose lively eyes are outlined with mascara. Her flirtatiousness is on full display.

When Mermoz is smoking as he gazes at the ceiling with Sylvine resting on his chest, he feels balanced. The memory of Gilberte doesn't cloud the moment; on the contrary, it complements it. They are two separate spheres for him. There have been times when he's had four girlfriends on the go at once. According to his code of behavior, he has deeply respected all of them, he's been entirely theirs, he's adored them all, held nothing in reserve, with only one caveat—a different girl each day.

He leaves Sylvine sleeping peacefully, and catches the early morning train to Perpignan so he can get to Berre Lagoon as fast as possible to start preparations for the leap to South America. He's already lost too much time. He's set himself a departure date of May 15, no more delays, no matter what happens, no matter the weather.

His machine, a Laté 28, is much bigger than the Laté 26. It's a plane with an enclosed cockpit for a crew of three, and a powerful 650 hp engine. The one he's going to fly has floats attached to convert it into a seaplane. At first sight, Mermoz's plane, named *Comte de la Vaulx*, resembles an enormous, ungainly bird, and the floats hanging from its wings remind him of crutches. But it contains all the state-of-the-art advances of French aeronautics.

A military pilot accompanies him to the slip beside which the plane sits rocking.

"It's not an easy machine to handle, Monsieur Mermoz."

"So much the better! It means I can tame her in my own way."

CHAPTER 48

Buenos Aires (Argentina), 1930

ANTOINE DE SAINT-EXUPÉRY

ANTOINE KNOWS BENJAMIN CRÉMIEUX FROM a gathering in Paris at *La Nouvelle Revue Française*, the great literary magazine of the time. He remembers him perfectly, with his centre part and his slightly messy, somewhat Assyrian-looking beard. It was at the magazine's headquarters on Rue Saint-Lazare, a place overflowing with manuscripts and reams of paper, where André Gide acted as host, although the person who was really in charge was the editor, Gaston Gallimard, whose taste was as refined as his business skills.

On the ship taking him from France to Buenos Aires, Crémieux had met a unique woman, the widow of the Guatemalan journalist, writer, and politician Enrique Gómez Carrillo. She was Salvadorean and her name was Consuelo Suncín. She was a woman of lively social aplomb combined with a look of helplessness, an exhausting energy in the body of a sparrow, a capricious yet passionate way of behaving, always intense, like an inquisitive child who never grows up and needs a new toy every five minutes.

Crémieux arrives in Buenos Aires and, as the president of the French PEN Club, the international association of writers, one of the first things he does is locate Consuelo and invite her to a cocktail party organised by the Association of the Friends of Art.

At Crémieux's friendly insistence, she accepts his invitation, but she knows hardly anyone in the enormous salon with its ostentatious crystal lamps. She finds the ladies overly bejewelled and the gentlemen excessively pompous. They're talking in their cliques about the country's tense political situation. Consuelo has only been there for five minutes, but already she's getting bored. Luckily, she has arranged to have a coffee with a Spanish pianist who has come to Buenos Aires to perform a series of concerts. Ricardo Viñes, together with Manuel de Falla and Claude Debussy, were members of the artistic gatherings organised by Consuelo's late husband when they were all in Paris. She decides not to say goodbye to Crémieux, in case he wants to keep her prisoner in this mausoleum, and discreetly goes to the cloakroom to reclaim her fur coat and disappear.

Just as she's leaving, she's crushed by a human wall: a burly, clumsy man who almost knocks her over. She shrieks like a cat which has had its tail stepped on.

The man bends over so his eyes are level with hers.

"Forgive me! Please, you must forgive me!"

"It was nothing, I just got a fright."

He looks at her appreciatively with his bulging eyes.

"But you can't leave!"

Consuelo looks perplexed.

"Why can't I leave?"

"Because I've just arrived!"

And he says it in such an excited tone that he sounds to her like a schoolboy who has just heard the lunchtime bell ring. She shows no interest, but he doesn't move one centimetre, blocking her path.

"Excuse me, some friends are waiting for me."

"Please stay a few minutes!"

Just then, Crémieux arrives.

"I'm glad you two have met, Señora Suncín! As a matter of fact, I wanted to introduce you to each other. This is Comte Antoine de Saint-Exupéry. Writer and aviator. And I'd say that he's also something of a philosopher."

"Delighted," she replies grudgingly. "But now I have to leave."

"Aren't you having a good time, Señora Suncín?"

"Don't take it to heart, Crémieux, but I think I'd have more fun in a Franciscan monastery."

From anyone else, this would have sounded rude, but from her, it sounds like a child's inoffensive tantrum. Antoine laughs.

"I'll help you have fun!"

Several people in the room turn to observe the commotion with somewhat patronising looks on their faces.

"I'm telling you that I want to go. I'm bored."

"Fine, then let's go! The three of us will fly in my plane and we'll see the sun set over the Río de la Plata."

"Listen here, Comte Whoever-You-Are! I don't like flying at all! I hate speed!"

The more unfriendly she shows herself to be, the more adorable she seems to Antoine.

"Buenos Aires from the sky is a different city. You have to see it!"

"Maybe another day," Crémieux intervenes tactfully.

"That can't be," she explains. "There are some friends expecting me."

"Wonderful! We'll give them a call. They can come too!"

"It's a pianist and his group!"

"Let them all come too. Mozart will never have sounded so close to heaven."

A tiny laugh escapes her. His proposal for her to get into a plane with a stranger is madness but, even so, she is intrigued by him. After Antoine insists she fly, a waiter brings a phone with a very long cord on a tray, and she calls Viñes. He and another friend accept the invitation.

A couple of musicians, the president of the French PEN Club, a young widow, and a hefty aviator who doesn't stop telling stories about Patagonia travel together in the direction of the Pacheco aerodrome in one of the company cars, driven by a chauffeur smoking a roll-your-own cigarette.

There's a Laté 28 on the runway with the capacity to take passengers. The first passenger flights will be introduced shortly. Antoine puts the musicians and Crémieux in the passenger section, closes the little dividing curtain, and signals for Consuelo Suncín to sit in the copilot's seat.

He takes off and reaches altitude quickly, then descends rapidly to follow the coastal railway, and reaches the turbulent waters by Tigre. Consuelo feels her stomach becoming upset and turns pale, but Antoine is ebullient. The child inside him is in charge today: He's not flying, he's playing. He transforms the plane into a merry-go-round in an amusement park, and his passengers into his playmates.

He gains altitude again and performs several zigzag maneuvers. Complaints can be heard from the rear section. Someone says that Monsieur Crémieux is vomiting. Antoine laughs.

When they reach the edge of the clouds and Buenos Aires lies below them like a toy city, he turns to Consuelo. Her paleness makes her eyes even blacker. It amuses him that she is so stubborn and doesn't want to admit that she's frightened. He cranes his neck and brings his face close to hers.

"Please, give me a kiss."

She gives him a mock angry look. "But what can you be thinking? I'm a widow."

"I'm only asking for an innocent kiss."

"Where I come from, you don't kiss strangers. You only kiss people you want to."

Antoine looks sad and then helpless. "You don't want to kiss me because I'm ugly." He teases.

She sighs impatiently again. Then Antoine lets the engine cut out, pushes the joystick forward so the nose will drop and allows it to go into a downward spin. Shouts can be heard from the cabin behind them.

"What are you doing? We're going to crash!"

"I'm waiting for her to kiss me . . ."

Consuelo throws her hands in the air.

"You're mad!"

"Maybe I'm just in love."

Consuelo grins like a mischievous little girl. Her eyes sparkle with excitement, because there's something about this big passionate pilot that hopelessly attracts her: Like her, he loves to play and hates the vulgarity of life.

The needle on the altimeter is moving in a scarily speedy fashion and the plane continues on its downward spiral. Consuelo cranes her neck and gives him a fleeting kiss on his cheek. Antoine lets out an ecstatic cry, and, carried by his jubilation, the plane climbs, making Consuelo herself smile, pleased with the game. Antoine believes he detects a promise of something in that smile.

The next morning, he stops at La Central florists and orders four bouquets of flowers to be sent to the hotel where Consuelo is staying. He thinks it's not enough, so he orders two more. It still seems paltry to him, so in the end, he orders a total of ten. He walks out with the gift of a gardenia in the buttonhole of his blazer. He stops a taxi and heads for Pacheco to cover another pilot's leave.

He can't stop drumming his fingers on the car door's armrest. He wonders if he really has fallen in love or if it's just a Sunday afternoon passion. He thrusts those thoughts aside. You can't "think" love. And anyway, thinking is the worst thing he can do, given that his trunk of memories has a lid that won't close. He can't allow himself to think about Lou-Lou; she's a scar that hurts when it's rubbed. He's thirty years old and believes that from this point onward, his life is headed into a downward spiral. He thinks that a life without love is like eating the skin of an orange and tossing out the segments.

But he's thinking again! Feeling is more important; it's a step further forward.

Consuelo's temperamental reactions, heavy with flirtation, move him. He's fascinated by her French, with its invented grammar, and by her unwitting daring in climbing into a plane with a stranger. There's something about her that ensnares him.

The first thing he'll do when he lands back in Buenos Aires is ask her to marry him. It might be a bit hasty, but time never stands still. Everything has to be now.

He must introduce her to the Guillaumets as soon as possible. Hopefully, Noëlle will like her! And he needs a new suit. And a haircut. He must try to get Consuelo and himself invited to the party at the embassy next week. She'll be an exotic bird in the middle of a mob of magpies!

Love brings so many tasks with it! As he feels in his pocket searching for a cigarette to calm his nerves, he comes across some crumpled papers: his notes for *Night Flight*.

When he gets back to the airfield, there are three urgent messages from Montaudran. They all scream the same thing: YOU SHOULD HAVE SENT LAST WEEK'S REPORT ON FLIGHT PUNCTUALITY THREE DAYS AGO!

Antoine grimaces and reflects that his boss is obsessed with bureaucracy. He thinks about Daurat the last day he was in Montaudran.

286

When Antoine arrived, Daurat was on the runway with his gabardine suit and his wide-brimmed hat, smoking. When he heard the sound of the plane from Barcelona in the clouds, he returned to his office and abruptly told Bouvet to note down a fine of ten francs to Canotier for being late. When the pilot landed and got down from the plane after a tough crossing over the Pyrenees, he would be met with a fine from Daurat. The pilot would hate his mean, intransigent boss. He'd never know how eagerly Daurat had been waiting for him in the loneliness of the runways.

Right then, Antoine decides that the protagonist of his book about night flights won't be the person who flies but the one waiting for him on the ground. Now that he himself has to carry out administrative tasks and supervise flights, he's aware that a pilot's uncertainty, even taking into account the thousand and one incidents and dangers, is nothing compared to the anxiety of the person watching the slow movement of the hands of a clock.

By afternoon, he still hasn't heard from Consuelo, so he turns up at her apartment with the flower in his buttonhole. The maid who opens the door associates his flower with the mountains of bouquets that were delivered, and smiles complicitly as she asks him to wait.

Consuelo appears in a typical Central American dress, heavy with flounces. "My mad aviator!" And she gives an amused laugh.

"Come on, we have to hurry."

Consuelo pretends to be angry. "I have no intention of going up in a plane ever again. Least of all with you!"

"We have to go to the Vauban jewelry store."

"But why do you want to go there, monsieur?"

"Can we address each other less formally?"

"I suppose so."

"I want to buy you a diamond."

Consuelo theatrically grabs her face with her hands. "But why?"

"It's my proposal present."

"What proposal?"

"My marriage proposal." Antoine looks at her with infinite tenderness and Consuelo's black eyes open wide.

"But we only met yesterday!"

"That's why we have to hurry. We've already lost a day!"

"You're the craziest madman I've ever known. I can't go anywhere right now! I have a dinner date with Viñes and Crémieux."

"We'll pick them up and have dinner. They can witness our engagement."

"My God! I thought this was all a joke! You really are mad," she says, laughing. Everything is a game.

Antoine and Consuelo pick up the two men, and Antoine brings them up to date on the way: He wants to propose to Consuelo. The pianist, the tips of his moustache turned up in the manner of a Spanish gentleman, looks at Consuelo in amazement. She laughs, not taking it seriously, as if it were a carnival.

Antoine takes them to a beer hall called the Münich, one of the three or four gastronomic "offices" where he can always be found. He loves their white sausages flavoured with nutmeg. As they're sitting down, a waiter informs him there's a call for him, and he comes back to the table looking worried.

"It's raining a lot and there are problems at the airfield. I'm afraid we'll have to move our dinner there."

They think he's joking, but children take their games very seriously.

A waiter loads up the trunk of their taxi with an abundance of oysters, Rhine wine, and sausages. They head off for their nighttime picnic at Pacheco in a torrent of rain. For a moment, he feels like Bernis during his night journey, but Consuelo is cheerful and that changes everything. Tonight, melancholy hasn't been invited.

Antoine converts his office at the airfield into a private room at the Münich. Instead of art nouveau lamps there are gooseneck office lamps, and they shuck the oysters with letter openers. The golden German wine fills their heads with Valkyries. Antoine starts to tell them the story of a flight over Patagonia near Puerto Deseado where the wind was so strong that instead of moving forward, he was going backward and flying in reverse.

The sound of telephones ringing and Morse code tapping out messages from all points of the compass along the route on this wet night give an air of underwater unreality to their worldly meal.

"This is the ideal place for us to get engaged, Consuelo. This is the world to which I belong."

"But how can we become engaged! We've only just met. It's madness."

"You tell her, Crémieux. Tell her she must marry me."

"But you already know that Señora Suncín is not someone who's easy to convince."

"She hasn't said no!"

"You talk as if this were all a game," Consuelo complains. "Marriage is a serious matter; I'm a widow. It can't be treated so lightly. I think you're teasing me, Antoine."

"I'd never do that! I'm absolutely serious!"

Just then, they hear the sound of an engine, and a light appears in the dark sky.

"I knew he'd come back. The pilot who left an hour ago with the mail has returned because of the rain." Antoine replaces his party smile with a serious air of responsibility.

"Raúl! My gear!"

The person in charge of flying equipment arrives with what Antoine needs.

"And where are you going now?" asks Consuelo.

"To deliver the mail."

"But it's pouring!"

The returned pilot arrives at the door, dripping with water, and shaking. "The storm, Monsieur Saint-Ex . . ."

"You mean the downpour, Monsieur Mercier. There's no sign of a breeze, and there hasn't been a single flash of lightning."

The pilot's head drops. "Are you going to fire me?"

"A good boss would. Unfortunately, I'm a really bad boss. Off to bed with you, Mercier. Tomorrow is another day." Antoine turns at the door and shouts to Consuelo and her companions: "A thousand apologies! Carry on with the celebration of my proposal and drink a toast to the occasion. My assistant will drive you back to the city."

Consuelo gets up and walks over to him. She looks at him with tenderness for the first time. "Be careful."

"I'll be very careful. I now have a good reason to return."

Antoine takes off in the rain and flies safely through the downpour. It's a matter of luck, and also of faith. One without the other is nothing.

Exhausting weeks follow. Antoine has to juggle attending to his scheduling tasks, his own flights to Patagonia, and ensuring that every rendezvous with Consuelo is special. He assumes they are engaged. At least she hasn't refused, although she hasn't accepted either.

He climbs out of a plane and starts removing his leather jacket on the way to the airfield office. He grabs his blazer and hat from the coat stand and rushes out.

"Señor de Saint-Exupéry," one of the secretaries calls out, unable to keep up with him, "you have to sign the fuel delivery notes!"

But he's already getting into the company car and telling his assistant to drive him home. He must at least change his shirt and shoes. The assistant informs him that the radio chatter has been incessant all afternoon: The mail from Chile is late.

The party at the home of a millionaire art collector friend of Consuelo turns out to be very crowded. The mansion, on the outskirts of the city, has sumptuous gardens through which uniformed waiters circulate with trays of spicy empanadas, pork kebabs, and glasses of wine. A jazz orchestra livens things up from a brightly lit bandstand, and the music mingles with conversations and laughter. Consuelo is radiant. She's at the head of a group of six friends and admirers, laughing as they follow her, with Antoine at the front. Despite her short stature, she can detect her acquaintances as if she had an inbuilt sixth sense, and makes a beeline for them so they can introduce her to everybody.

Antoine enjoys the energy she displays. She generates a magnetic field which results in more and more people following in her wake. There's already a dozen of them moving after her through the gardens like a flock of birds.

Antoine makes an effort to join the elegant commotion fed by Consuelo the whirlwind, but something is unsettling him. It's nothing, and yet it's everything.

He tells Consuelo he has to use the bathroom. She laughs and makes an offhand gesture as if he were a lackey whom she was benevolently authorising to withdraw. He walks to the house looking for a butler.

"I must make a call."

The butler, lean and with a prominent chin, doesn't move a muscle or say a word.

Antoine knows an infallible method of softening a butler's stiffness. He places a ten-peso note in the pocket of the man's uniform. As if he were an automaton at a fairground that had swallowed a coin, the butler bows slightly and points to a side room with his gloved hand.

Antoine asks the switchboard operator to put him through to the Pacheco airfield. He's sure there's nothing wrong, but from the moment his assistant told him that the plane from Santiago hadn't arrived, he's felt an inner cold.

"Saint-Exupéry here. I need information about the arrival of the flight between Rosario and Santiago."

"It's delayed."

"Delayed? When should it have arrived?"

"Five hours ago, señor."

"My God."

He leaves the house and strides across the garden without even saying goodbye to Consuelo. He takes one of the taxis waiting on the other side of the gate.

"To Pacheco."

The drive seems interminable to him. He draws a lamb on the window.

The delayed plane is Guillaumet's.

CHAPTER 49

Santiago (Chile), 1930

HENRI GUILLAUMET

BEFORE GUILLAUMET LEAVES SANTIAGO, THE manager of the airfield hands him the weather report that has just arrived from Mendoza, Argentina: "Cloudy, with clear patches."

Guillaumet shrugs. "I'll fly in the patches."

He has the most modern plane in the fleet, a new model capable of flying above 6,000 metres and leaping over peaks that were previously invincible.

At the altitude he's flying, the peaks of the Andes pierce a sea of clouds, and an archipelago of snow-covered islands emerges on top of the white ocean. Everything is perfect this day until the engine coughs.

The plane starts to lose altitude and becomes submerged in a thick, cloudy layer. The clouds hit him in the face with their ice crystals, and the engine stops among the jagged outcrops and cliffs. Through a gap in the clouds, Guillaumet makes out a dark mass lower down, a bluish

293

patch in the snow in the middle of an enormous mountain cirque. He unfolds a mental map in his head.

The Laguna del Diamante . . .

He might have a chance to land. The shore of the lake is smooth and if the snow is hard enough, the plane might taxi. He manoeuvres so he can line up for the landing. The wind gusts buffet him badly and he grips the sides of the joystick with all the force of his anger so the plane will yaw to the left. He succeeds with difficulty.

Come on, come on . . .

He manages to land at the edge of the lake, but the plane taxies with a violent shuddering that threatens to break it apart, until it reaches an area where the snow is softer and comes to a stop so suddenly that the nose is driven down and the whole aircraft performs a spectacular somersault.

Despite the rough landing, which has left him sitting upside down in the cockpit, held in by his seatbelt, an exploratory feel of his body suggests that all his bones are where they should be. There's only some light bruising. Relieved, he closes his eyes and thinks of his wife, Noëlle. He thanks God he hasn't left her a widow.

When he crawls out of the plane, a freezing wind hits him in the face. The lake spreads out a few metres away and reflects the steel grey of the sky. He's heard tell that in the summer, hundreds of flamingos and guanacos come here to drink, but right now, with winter about to begin, a cold whiteness and a daunting solitude dominate this landscape nestled at an altitude of 3,000 metres among the colossal mountains.

He's already very cold and it will soon be dark. He decides to take advantage of the remaining light to remove his parachute, wrap himself in it, and shelter under one of the wings, since it's starting to snow. The wind whistles menacingly as it filters through the gaps in the fuselage and raises clouds of snow. Taking refuge as best he can, he holds on until the next day.

A saying common among experienced Chileans and Argentinians goes round and round inside his head: "The Andes don't give men back in winter."

It snows silently all that day, and Guillaumet keeps as warm and sheltered as he can. He tries not to fall into a deep sleep so his body won't chill until he dies of hypothermia. When the snowstorm calms down on day two, he gets rid of the parachute and stretches his stiff muscles. He's hungry and it's cold.

The blizzard has left the plane half-buried in snow. He looks around him: The huge lake reflects the colours of the sky, more blue than grey now that the sky has cleared after the storm. He can finally see his surroundings clearly: Half a dozen mountainous formations create an imposing cirque. He thinks that the closest mountain rising up on the other side of the lake could be the Maipó volcano.

He hears a distant rumble above and looks joyfully at the sky. He has trouble finding the plane among the patches of cloud and, when he does locate it, he's surprised at how tiny it is. Pilots consider their aircraft to be powerful machines, but seen in the distance, a plane is like a fly lost among the clouds. He immediately lights a flare. But in such vastness, in daylight, and surrounded by such gigantic masses of rock, the flare looks like the thousands of other reflections from the ice. The plane disappears among the layers of cloud. Guillaumet can tell that the sound of the engine hasn't changed, nor has its direction: The pilot hasn't seen his flare.

He starts to walk quickly in circles to get warm. He's got a little condensed milk, the odd tin of meat, and a bottle of rum. There's no lack of water. He could hold out inside the plane for a few days, but something tells him they won't find him. They have hundreds of square kilometres to scan, thousands of nooks and crannies. And the plane that flew off without seeing him will eliminate this zone quickly in the pilot's eagerness to cover other, as yet unexplored, areas.

Before he took off, he had glanced at the week's weather forecast. After the blizzard that's just blown over, there will be three or four days of decent weather, a window of good conditions for the planes searching for him. Perhaps it might occur to another rescue plane to descend specifically to check out this very lake among the dozens of lakes, valleys, screes, high plains, and hidden corners in this cordillera maze, and it might find him. *But if that doesn't happen?*

If it doesn't happen, the window of good weather will close, and since it's the beginning of winter, normal conditions are snowfalls and blizzards. The rescue planes could be grounded at both the Mendoza and Santiago aerodromes, or take off but lack any visibility. And in winter, bad weather can last weeks, maybe months.

Guillaumet reconstructs the map of the region in his head. He knows he's already crossed the bulk of the cordillera and he's not more than sixty kilometres from the Argentinian plains. It's not an excessive distance, but to head in that direction means he has to negotiate the wall of mountains. The lowest one must be 4,000 metres. Tackling the ascent with no knowledge of mountain climbing, no ropes, no boots, no detailed maps of the routes, is impossible.

The Andes don't give men back.

He stores his supplies in a small leather pack, together with some matches, the one flare he has left, a flashlight, and a small portable spirit stove. A pencil is a lucky find in the bottom of a pocket in his bomber jacket. Pressing as hard as he can, he writes a message on the fuselage in case they get to the plane: "I'm heading east." His hand is shaking: No question it's cold and his fingers are numb. He adds a few more words: "Goodbye, everyone. My last thought will be of my wife." He shakes all over as he thinks about Noëlle. He can't even write her name.

He starts to walk and with each step he sinks into the snow up to his knees. Up to his waist. Up to his belly button. He advances laboriously, knocked about by the lack of oxygen at this altitude. He's barely progressed a few hundred metres in an hour. When he stops for a few moments to catch his breath, he uses the time to turn around and look at the plane turned upside down, half buried in the snow, increasingly indistinct. He's tempted to return to his shelter, but he's begun his walk and must go on. He hasn't even done a kilometre yet and already he's exhausted.

His difficult and arduous progress in the foothills of the lake seems like a stroll when he reaches the foot of the mountain blocking his way. He can't even see the peak, hidden in the clouds. He's not a committed believer, but when he grabs hold of a rock and climbs the first step, he starts to pray.

Beyond the first steep gradient, he finds another slope covered with ice. His hands ache from the cold. But he has no other tool to try to hold on to and crawl toward the top. He gets almost halfway up the slope by clawing the ice, but he slips and slides facedown until he lands just where he had started his climb. His joints ache but, with extreme care, he starts to climb again. He slips again and falls back down. He starts again for a third time. A fourth. A fifth. He has no feeling in his fingers and his face is stinging from contact with the ice. He succeeds on his seventh attempt. He's exhausted when he reaches the top of the slope. He tries to eat something, but the meat is frozen, his fingers are stiff, and he can't get the spirit stove going. He has a swig of rum and carries on. Night finds him climbing like a trembling snail.

He reaches a parapet totally drained of energy, his eyes heavy and tiredness demanding its due. The cold is also inviting him to curl up. He knows that if he falls asleep, he'll never wake up again. But he needs a break. He takes off the backpack and places it on the ground as a pillow for his head. He stretches out and feels better. He changes his mind a moment later—*too comfortable*. With an effort, he stands up and leans against the parapet, with his back pressed against the rock's uncomfortable surface so he won't fall asleep, and his head resting in his hands.

Sleep softens the stones, but when he dozes off, his arms give way, his head drops, and he wakes up. A few hours pass in this drowsy state, dozing off and waking up suddenly every few minutes. When the moon is high in the sky, he stretches with difficulty and continues on his way with the occasional help of his flashlight.

The night is too long, but Guillaumet keeps walking. He's very tired, but he keeps going. The cold is intense, and his survival depends on the connecting rods in his legs continuing to function. He knows that if he keeps walking, he'll maintain his body temperature at a level that will keep his heart beating. But if his legs stop, his heart will stop, and it will all be over.

He thinks about death. About Noëlle. About God. He thinks about everything you don't think about on ordinary days, too busy with the avalanche of trivial things that, at the time, seem important. What Guillaumet longs for most aren't extraordinary things, but rather, the most day-to-day and seemingly routine things: hugging his wife when he gets back from a flight; having a hot cup of coffee on cold mornings at the airfield; biting into a stick of crusty bread . . . what he wouldn't give right now for something as modest as a piece of bread! The image of the bakery in his town pops into his head, and a smell, that smell croissants have of toasted wheat and butter. The pain in his feet, the effort of taking one more step which seems like it will be his last. He wants to curl up, and lie down, not suffer from the pain of a thousand needles in his feet, not feel the burning sensation in his icy hands.

No, no, no.

Life is too beautiful to stop fighting for it. Life smells like warm bread. Life is Noëlle's smile, when she sees him coming through the door of their home. His thoughts start to become confused, as if exhaustion and fasting were making him delirious.

God is a loaf of bread; Noëlle is a crumb.

He's going out of his mind. He notices a sharp pain in his head which is drilling through the middle of his forehead. But mad or sane, he doesn't stop walking. The frozen ground crunches, and he goes on, because life must go on crunching.

Dawn finds him shuffling his feet as if he were wearing snowshoes. Daylight reveals a meseta in front of him, dotted with small ponds, and he crosses it leaving the sun behind his back as he keeps heading east. The wilderness is magnificent, but nature's spectacle doesn't console him; beauty can be heartless.

He suffers as he crosses a patch of melted snow which has turned into a quagmire. *Not good*. His feet are wet, but if he stops for a few minutes, they'll freeze, so he must keep going. He makes progress among the crags, feeling as if he were in a labyrinth, but he can't allow himself to have doubts; he advances. At the end of the valley, he hopes to find a pass between the mountains that surround him, but when he gets there, all he finds is an immense rocky wall.

He stops. He closes his eyes and sighs. He can't even allow himself the comfort of despair. He knows he has to retrace his steps, retrace several hours of the path he has trudged with so much difficulty, until he gets back to an earlier fork. He doubts if he'll be able to last. He knows that at any moment, his body may fail him, his legs will fold, he'll drop into the mud, and he'll be incapable of getting back up. He turns. And he goes on, he must do so, even if he wants to collapse onto the ground and merge with the snow. He owes it to Noëlle, he owes it to his friends who will be out there searching for him.

The only Potez 25 capable of reaching an altitude of 6,500 metres like Guillaumet's own plane is being flown by Deley, who's scouring the Chilean side of the mountains. Antoine flies over the Argentinian side of the Andes in a Laté, which can only reach 5,000 metres. In desperation, he tried to convince the leader of a band of smugglers—the only people capable of going through the least suspected passes in the cordillera—to mount a rescue expedition. Without even consulting

Monsieur Daurat, inside a tavern with a tin roof, he offered the man an astronomical sum to do it. And the smuggler had shaken his head a thousand times: "Why risk our lives to go in search of a dead man? The Andes don't give men back in winter."

Antoine has spent two days wobbling among the peaks in his Laté, but he's returned to Mendoza shivering from the cold and the worry. Every day, every hour, winter advances and the flame of hope diminishes. Deley informs him that the Chilean employees are asking them to abandon the search because there's no point. Antoine refuses. They advise him from the office at the airfield in Santiago that Señor Mermoz is calling him on the radio. He doesn't feel he has the courage to tell Mermoz that there's no news, but they insist, saying that he has called seventeen times.

"Jean . . ."

"I'm going to come, Saint-Ex."

"There's not enough time for you to get here, Jean."

"Don't give up. Fly for me."

"I won't give up, Jean. I'll double my flying, so that you are looking for him too."

Guillaumet also tries not to give up. He walks in his own footsteps as he retraces his path. The hollow made by his boots has already become faintly ice-encrusted and crunches when he steps in it. He attempts to think about pleasant moments, luminous days, to chase away the gloomy thoughts in his head, but even his memories have become frozen.

His feet ache. The blisters burst. Blood soaks his boots. He stops briefly and takes the clean shirt out of his little backpack. He cuts it into strips with his knife to make bandages, and has trouble wrapping them around his feet. The cold makes his hands shake; they're so stiff that it takes a gigantic effort to tie the knots.

He can't really walk, but somehow he does. He reaches the fork that will take him along the other path, which doesn't head as much toward the east as he'd like. He doesn't even know where he's going, but he has no choice. He convinces himself that pain isn't bad, because the wounds make him feel alive. It's almost afternoon when he sees another mountain in front of him, blocking his way. He knows what he's going to find in an hour's time, but he doesn't stop. *Stopping? Never.* He can't do that to Noëlle.

He arrives exhausted at an enormous pile of rock, a vertical wall higher than 1,000 metres obstructing his path.

That's it.

He hasn't got the energy to get over a peak like that. He realises now, too late, that he should never have abandoned his plane. But what does that matter now; at least he'll die knowing he tried.

Finally, he sits on the ground with his back against a smooth rock and closes his eyes to wait for death. He feels relief at the thought of the life insurance policy he bought; at least it will help Noëlle to get by for a while. No doubt she'll go back to Switzerland and rebuild her life. It seems strange to think that she could have another life without him. He'd like it to be the case, but equally, that she wouldn't be able to do so. They're odd feelings, contradictory, though not so much. Love and selfishness are old friends.

Suddenly, he feels a wave of anguish: In order to collect the insurance, they have to find his body. If they don't, he'll be deemed legally disappeared, and it will be ten years before they certify him as deceased. Years of uncertainty and suffering, because Noëlle will cling to the belief that he's still alive. In these parts, any winter storm could cause a tonne of rocks to fall on top of him and he'd never be found. That thought motivates him. He looks up, and a few metres above him, he spies a ledge.

On that ledge, he would be more visible; it might be easier for them to find his body in the summer. It won't be easy for him to get there. He has no experience as a mountaineer and his energy level is very low. But he'll spend what little energy he has left doing it. His last gesture of love will be to die there for Noëlle to ensure her future.

He clenches and unclenches his fists several times to recover some blood circulation, and takes the bottle of rum from his pack to have one last gulp. He doesn't like rum. To him, it's like drinking kerosene, but it briefly warms his stomach. He takes advantage of that momentary warmth to stand up and try to reach the ledge. He starts to climb.

He manages to reach the ledge, and a few metres higher up, there's another more spacious one where his body would be easier to find in the summer, but it's harder for him to get to. He'll give it a go.

He slowly makes his way to the second ledge with just enough strength and a strange calmness, with no fear of falling and smashing himself against the rocky crests, because his death is already assured. With each effort to climb and hoist himself over the rocks, he thinks of Noëlle to give himself momentum. Half an hour later, he finally manages to climb onto the ledge.

He's got this far. And if he were to continue?

A small hum in the sky makes him lift his head. A speck in the sky. A distant plane recklessly grazing the pinnacles of this immense cathedral of infinite snow.

Saint-Ex! . . .

A second later, the clouds obscure the plane, erase it. Antoine's looking for a needle in a haystack.

Guillaumet keeps climbing.

As he climbs painfully, he tries not to think of his wounded hands and wonders what makes us keep going. *Where do we get the strength that prevents us from being flushed down a drain like an ant? Why do we fight so hard for a life which we're going to lose no matter what?* He doesn't know.

He's out of breath. He stops for a moment on an outcrop and a squall blows grains of ice into his face. And it's then that he understands with absolute clarity that it's enough just to look at life from the edge of the final precipice, and he smiles the smile of the moribund. You fight against the impossible because each minute of life is all of life. Each second is an eternity.

He eats his last biscuit. He only has two small tins of meat left. Tears flow because he'd like to open the tins but his fingers are swollen and he can't. It grows dark and he climbs up in slow motion, holding his flashlight in his mouth. His feet are burning. Everything hurts, but he struggles on.

The Southern Cross is above him. When the moon goes down, he can only count on his flashlight and the icy comfort of the stars. The stars are his friends; they're the sign that the small squall has moved on and there are no clouds. It's colder when the sky is clear, but a snowstorm when he's climbing in the dark would be deadly. That's why he looks up and feels that the stars are protecting him from the snow. But what's going to protect him from falling down any precipice when he's climbing blind? He prays to the Southern Cross.

He stops to rest on a ledge. He feels he's losing consciousness for a moment, and then it starts to grow lighter. The darkness takes on a blueish tinge. There's something grandiose about dawn over the Andes. He's shivering in this below-zero dawn in the middle of a mountain dotted with patches of snow, and yet a strange calm infects him. It makes him feel part of the awakening mountain and planet.

A wave of well-being encourages him to curl up and close his eyes. He leans against the wall. A shiver runs through him and, at the same time, a slight warmth as he wraps himself in his arms, together with a deep serenity, as if his head were stuffed with wool. *If this is death, it doesn't seem so bad; it's soft cotton wool. It's like a dream.* It is a dream. He sees Noëlle looking at him tenderly, she's beside him. He doesn't know how she's reached the mountain, but she's come. His mother's here too, and Mermoz, and Saint-Ex. Noëlle strokes his hair and he

303

slips into infinite softness. With what remains of his willpower, Guillaumet bites his tongue as hard as he can until the sharp pain makes him start, causing him to open his eyes, and dragging him out of the trap of drowsiness. He tries to sit up but he can't; he's numb, his body is that of a corpse. Then he feels the full force of the cordillera's cold and starts to shiver uncontrollably. It's a horrible sensation, unpleasant, painful, an epileptic fit of cold and physical and nervous exhaustion. He convulses, his heartbeat races, he has difficulty breathing, but he puts up with it because the pain that is tearing him up inside is the blood circulating through his arteries, life returning to his body after it had briefly crossed the line. He puts a fistful of snow in his mouth.

He shouts.

It's a wordless shout, but he shouts. The mountain hears him and sends back an echo, as if there were a dozen Guillaumets accompanying him.

He sets off, lurching like one of those peddler's carts pulled by an old nag. He slowly continues to climb.

He crawls up a slope on all fours, scraping against the rock, and the palms of his hands are raw. A weak sun is high in the sky. Then the incline becomes gentler and more manageable. The air becomes richer and swirls. *The summit.* It's an irregular plain from which it's impossible to see the end of the sea of rocky peaks toward the north, clouds shrouding the valleys between the summits. A semi-frozen stream flows down the mountain and facing him there'll only be another mountain. But there's no other option.

Descending is more difficult than climbing. He slips, and bangs his elbow. He slips again and rolls a few metres until he smacks against a sharp rock which opens a cut in one of his thighs.

He reaches a narrow pass through which the stream flows. The gap is very narrow and forms a natural tunnel, with only a few centimetres between the water and the rocky ceiling. The only way to get through is for him to become a stream, too. He climbs into the freezing water, which comes up to his knees. He squats down and moves forward with the water up to his neck. The water is thawed ice, and it bites. He has trouble breathing. He stumbles and is about to fall. He can't feel his limbs.

He advances virtually submerged through the canyon until he reaches a wider section. When he can finally stand up, it feels as if he's being stabbed by a million needles. He needs to dry his clothes because if he doesn't, they'll freeze on his body, and he'll die. He takes them off. His pale body exposes all his vulnerability in the face of the harsh Andean countryside. Here, a naked man is a defenceless pup. Guillaumet makes use of the first shrubs he's seen in a long time, and some rocks, to spread out his bomber jacket, sweater, trousers and spare clothes. He performs clumsy exercise movements to keep his blood flowing. He decides to eat something to help warm up and takes out the spirit stove, but it has become wet and unusable. He'll eat the tinned meat even if it's frozen. He takes out his knife and manages to cut off a few frozen shards. In his eagerness to break apart the meat, his elbow knocks his glove off a rock and it falls toward the edge of a drop. Since he can't chew the frozen meat because it burns his tongue, he swallows pieces of it.

He re-dresses and continues to descend. The wound in his thigh is throbbing, and the blow to his elbow really hurts with the cold. Exhaustion makes him even clumsier. He falls again and has to hold on with his nails to prevent himself from sliding down a slope which ends in a void.

He gets up and keeps going. He's no longer capable of asking himself metaphysical questions. His brain is like the frozen meat he ate which is now making him retch. He just keeps going. He no longer remembers why.

The sun starts to go down. He won't be able to take another night. He knows that. His body is at the point of imploding. And despite that, he continues to allow his body to descend the mountain. He senses that the path is somewhat less steep, but he's not sure. Everything is becoming hazy. He doesn't know if dusk is falling or he's dying. And then he sees it on the ground—or thinks he sees it. He's not sure. He has to stop and look twice because his eyelids are so swollen. He doesn't squat down because he thinks he wouldn't be able to stand up again. But he was raised in the countryside and he knows: Those dark lumps are donkey droppings. The dung makes a sort of path and he follows it mechanically. He's like a character in a fairytale following his own trail of black crumbs. He can barely stay on his feet. But a few hundred metres further on, he sees it. *A donkey!*

"*Âne!*"

His voice is unreliable when it emerges. And as he follows the donkey with his eyes, he sees her. From the other side of a stream, a woman is looking at him more in amazement than apprehension. A man with dark skin and black hair appears right behind her. Guillaumet extends his arms toward them in the instinctive gesture of a universal language buried in his brain.

The man comes toward him, and then everything collapses. He drops like a marionette that's had all its strings cut.

After another fruitless morning flying around in circles above empty mountains, Antoine and his plane return to Mendoza, his spirits at rock bottom. He doesn't feel like talking to anyone, so he goes to a bar next door to the airfield for a coffee. He already knows what the Argentinians will say to him: "The mountains have kept him." And he lacks the strength of his own conviction to disagree with them. He's still stirring a bowl of soup without any appetite when the door suddenly opens and a mechanic sticks his head inside.

"They've found Guillaumet!"

306

His fellow diners stop chewing. The disappearance of the aviator has been front-page news in all the papers all week, and photos of him are already appearing with a black edge around them.

They see the burly Frenchman in his double-breasted suit hurriedly get up, drop his plate of soup on the ground, and almost knock over the table. He races out to the runway, the angry-looking waiter rushing after him with the bill.

At the airfield, they explain that there's been a call from the police station in San Carlos, a small settlement further south.

"But is he alive?"

Confusion abounds. Nobody knows. There are no maps to get to San Carlos, but they show Antoine a straight road which leads directly there, and he gets ready to follow it, flying at low altitude. He climbs into a plane with a mechanic and they take off.

Antoine follows the road from the air, praying to all the gods he knows that Guillaumet is still alive.

A few kilometres from San Carlos, he sees a convoy of cars coming toward him, and some gauchos wave at him. He doesn't like this procession of cars; it looks like a funeral cortège. He has to land wherever he can. He flies over a row of poplars, touches down on a tiny area of open space, and almost ends up with the plane in a ditch, which would have been disastrous. But he rights it in time, and they hurriedly climb down from the plane.

The cars have stopped in the middle of the road. The driver of the first car opens the back door of his ancient Ford. A man with sunken cheeks, burnt skin, cuts and bruises, gets out of the car with great difficulty, holding on to the door.

"Henri!"

Antoine and Guillaumet embrace. They cry. They cry like children. They are children. The mechanics respectfully doff their caps, as if they were witnesses to a miracle.

"What I have done," Guillaumet whispers laboriously, "I swear to you, no animal would have done."

Antoine carries him carefully to the plane with the help of his mechanic, to the accompaniment of "Hurrah!" and "Viva!" for the aviator who has achieved what no one else before him had. They settle him into a seat and Antoine fastens the seatbelt. Guillaumet, his face drained, looks at Antoine and, before he dozes off, manages to whisper:

"Saint-Ex, I saw you up there . . . but you couldn't see me."

"There were other planes searching for you . . . How could you know it was me?"

"Nobody else would have flown so low over the peaks."

CHAPTER 50

Berre Lagoon (Southern France), 1930

JEAN MERMOZ

MERMOZ WALKS AROUND THE COMMUNICATIONS exchange at the barracks with his hands in the pockets of his overcoat. He's done so many circuits that he's wearing a groove into the ground. The news about Guillaumet's rescue is confusing; it's not known in what state he's been found.

A soldier leans through the doorframe.

"Monsieur Mermoz! Monsieur Saint-Exupéry has sent a telegram for you from Santiago, Chile."

"For heaven's sake, what does it say? Read it to me!"

"It's a very short message. All it says is: 'Jean, put some champagne on ice, and get three glasses.'"

Mermoz's guffaw is so loud it throws the birds in the sky off-balance.

The good news allows him to focus again entirely on getting the seaplane ready. The letters he sends across the ocean to Gilberte keep his spirits on an even keel. He writes bits of poetry he remembers or invents, while, on her fancy paper with its rose perfume, she writes to him about the wedding preparations, the colour of the flowers next to the altar, and the menu for the wedding banquet.

At the beginning of May, Mermoz carries out a test of the *Comte de la Vaulx*, a circular flight which sets a world record for flying time. The machine is set to go. Everything is ready for the crucial day, Tuesday, May 14, when there will be a full moon.

On the chosen day, an unexpected passenger joins the flight. Daurat will travel with them as far as Saint-Louis de Senegal and take advantage of that first section of the flight to inspect the stopovers.

The *Comte de la Vaulx* conquers the Pyrenees as if it were simply levitating over the peaks, then flies across Spain, crosses the Strait of Gibraltar, and covers the section of Morocco and the Sahara Desert, until it reaches the greenness of Saint-Louis, where they land safely. The moment of truth has arrived and Mermoz feels comfortable at the controls of the Laté 28, ready to make the great 3,000-kilometre leap across the ocean. This transoceanic flight has been completed successfully on four previous occasions but, for the first time, it is not being undertaken as a competitive activity, but to establish a regular civil aviation route, carrying 130 kilos of mail.

Just before noon, Mermoz pulls on the plane's joystick and the five tonnes of machinery lifts off over the Sénégal River, leaving behind drowsy barges dozing on muddy waters. The crew, Dabry and Gimié, sit quietly, each in his own seat.

Mermoz is focused. His head is full of latitudes and longitudes. The *Phocée*, a company rescue boat, is a tiny lifeline in case there's an emergency landing at sea. They don't fly with compasses anymore: radio signals picked up by Gimié are converted into navigational data which Dabry can use to calculate the correct direction in the middle of this blue desert.

The first hours are accompanied by the monotonous sound of the engine. When he's on land, Mermoz hates routine, but when he's flying, the steady turnover of the Hispano-Suiza 650 hp engine is glorious music to his ears. He marvels at the perfect symphony created by the pistons moving at 650 revolutions a minute.

Their tranquillity ends in the afternoon when they reach the Inter-Tropical Convergence Zone which generates the low-pressure troughs sailors refer to as the *Pot au Noir* or Doldrums, and they fly into a squall. The plane enters the turbulence and starts to rattle like a ride at a funfair. Mermoz is calm. He's flown hundreds of hours in the *Comte de la Vaulx*, he's checked the plane from top to bottom, he's passed all the tests and feels in full control of all his faculties. Flying is a game of poker, but he arrives at the table with a handful of aces.

They are wrapped in about five hundred metres of cloud—a wall which reaches to the roof of the heavens. The buffeting caused by the changes in pressure fills the atmosphere with air pockets. They spend an hour riding on a roller coaster. The heat is suffocating. Since he can't fly above the cloud, Mermoz decides to go down and fly fifty metres above the surface of the sea. He removes his helmet and jacket. His shirt is sticking to him, but nothing makes him lose concentration. After more than three hours of buffeting, heat, and concentration in the middle of a purée of clouds, he sees a flash of brightness toward the northeast. Even though he'll have to deviate eighty kilometres from his route, he knows it's the sign of an advantageous inversion. He finds a corridor to take him to the place where he saw that brilliance, which turns out to be treasure. They are met by the moon's reflection which throws silver threads down to the sea. Mermoz feels a strange intimacy with the night. This moment of plenitude makes up for the three hours of suffering. It is compensation for everything.

Then, more hours of flying, of pampering the engine, of resisting tiredness after so many hours of concentration. At last, just after daybreak, a headland. *San Roque! Brazil! South America!*

And finally, Natal. From the cockpit, the fast-flowing Rio Potenji is a narrow alley of water that runs into the Atlantic Ocean. An elegant turn over the Fortress of the Three Wise Men at the tip of the city and a gentle landing on the river: twenty-one hours from Saint-Louis de Senegal. The 130 kilos of mail loaded on board in Toulouse has taken less than forty-eight hours to reach Brazil. The letters are hastily transferred to another plane. After 13,000 kilometres, and 180 hours and 45 minutes, the mail will reach the end of the route in Santiago, Chile. They've destroyed all the world records for airmail delivery. All the demons of civil aviation have been dispelled. The era of commercial aviation has begun.

Mermoz sighs as he switches off the ignition and the propellers start to slow down.

Gimié gives a jubilant shout: "Mermoz, we've done it!"

"We haven't done anything yet," Mermoz replies taciturnly. "The mail has to fly back. A letter without a reply serves no purpose."

When the boat which has picked them up from the middle of the river deposits them on the pier, the governor is waiting for them with a band playing popular marches. He has a white moustache and huge sideburns shaped like axes, no longer the fashion in Europe. He steps forward to shake Mermoz's hand, to the applause of the entourage of onlookers who have followed the official party.

"I'd like the Municipality of Natal to be the first to congratulate you all in the name of the government of Brazil."

"Thank you, senhor."

Mermoz feels drained, as if he's suddenly noticed the fatigue brought on by so many emotions, the weight of so many expectations on his shoulders. They've prepared banquets and fanfares, but he pleads extreme exhaustion, and despite his hosts' disappointment, walks off to his hotel, alone and in silence.

CHAPTER 51

★

Natal (Brazil), 1930

JEAN MERMOZ

A REPRESENTATIVE OF THE GOVERNMENT appears in the doorless bathroom of Mermoz's hotel room the next morning as he's shaving. He has come to inform Mermoz of the program of activities they've prepared for him, including receptions and speeches. Mermoz expresses his regret, but he has an unavoidable appointment with the woman he loves more than two hundred kilometres away.

He heads off to meet the packet boat *Mendoza*, which has a stop-over in the port of Recife before sailing for Europe. He has a date there with Gilberte, who's travelling on the boat, headed for France to start preparations for their wedding. While the sailors are descending the gangway to remove luggage, an impeccably shaved blond European in a dark-grey suit and dark tie is making his way in the opposite direction to the deck.

Gilberte meets him with tears of happiness in her eyes and he embraces her tightly. She's so small that she almost disappears in his arms.

"I was so worried about you!"

Mermoz looks at her in astonishment. His confident smile suggests that any concern is unnecessary.

"I'm starving!"

"The captain has invited us to have lunch at his table. He's keen to meet you."

"Then let's go and see this captain . . . and clean out the ship's supplies!"

The boat gets ready to sail the next morning and Gilberte gives Mermoz a handkerchief impregnated with her perfume.

From the wharf, Mermoz waves goodbye with the handkerchief.

"When you get to France, I'll be there, waiting for you!"

Two days later, flying from Florianópolis, Ville lands with 150 kilos of mail, collected from the various staging posts along the route and destined for France.

Mermoz wants to leave immediately. He wants to show that a weekly airmail route between South America and Europe is not only possible, but essential. A light breeze stirs his hair. The breeze wants to tell him something, but he doesn't hear it. A barge tows the *Comte de la Vaulx* beyond the railway bridge. The wind is light, but it's a crosswind. It's not suitable for taking off, but waiting for a wind change could mean a delay of days. Gimié and Dabry are in their seats and a clear sky, immaculate blue, awaits them. Mermoz opens the fuel line and the plane starts to glide on top of the Rio Potenji, but it doesn't lift off. Mermoz pulls on the bridle. But the horse doesn't jump. When he increases speed, a float on the left-hand side detaches in a spectacular manner.

The float is repaired quickly and Mermoz gets set to start the manoeuvres for takeoff. Again, the *Comte de la Vaulx* accelerates, but it doesn't lift. With no headwind, there's no support to hoist its five tonnes into the air.

An aeronautical engineer in Montaudran recommends that they wait for a wind change. But Mermoz isn't an engineer; he's Jean Mermoz. He tries a third time, against the current. A fourth, changing directions. A fifth. A sixth . . . At two in the morning, he makes his eighth attempt, unsuccessfully. His curses resound along the entire route. After eight failed attempts, he has to refuel and have the machine inspected.

In the morning, the crosswind is still blowing. He tries towing the seaplane to another part of the river and restarts the manoeuvre at full power. By midday, they have made sixteen attempts and they haven't been able to take off. It's already dawn by the time a furious Mermoz calls a halt for the day. The coastal breeze performs pirouettes above his head like an impertinent joker.

Later that morning, the two crew members are having breakfast in silence. They've tried to take off thirty times and the wind isn't shifting. Dabry and Gimié have had a discussion. They think it's pointless to keeping hitting their heads against a wall and risking a takeoff which conditions have proved is impossible and could lead to an accident.

Typically, the south wind they need blows twenty out of every thirty days, but a faint breeze from the west, virtually nonexistent, insists on appearing. They keep trying and all their attempts fail. On Mermoz's final attempt with a gust of wind and gliding at a hundred kilometres an hour, they're on the verge of overturning. The following day they do it all again as if they were in a recurrent nightmare.

Mermoz is sitting on a rock, his eyes fixed on the calm water he's beginning to hate. He doesn't even hear the sound of a car's engine and the arrival of an employee bringing a cable from HQ. Monsieur Daurat informs him that fifty-three attempts is excessive. That they can't delay the transport of the mail any longer. That the mailbags are to be put on the first boat headed for Europe.

The employee withdraws awaiting instructions, but none are forthcoming. Mermoz is absorbed in looking at the clouds above the lazy stands of trees. The cable is dangling between two fingers and he suddenly stares at it. Initially with anger, then with surprise. The rectangular piece of paper is moving restlessly, agitated by the wind. *The wind?* Mermoz turns his head and the wind is blowing in his face. *The wind has shifted to the south!*

He stands up and shouts: "Gimié, Dabry . . . to your places!"

Mermoz starts the engines, picks up speed, and the *Comte de la Vaulx* glides across the calm surface of the river until it lifts off effortlessly above the water.

It's a rainy night and there's only confusing darkness outside. Gimié, the navigation officer, is the ears which receive signals from the various navigation control points. Dabry is the eyes that perform the calculations to determine their position and plot their course on notes he passes to Mermoz. Hours go by, plane and crew are shaken by atmospheric disturbances. First rain and then hail land on the windscreen. And some drops of oil. Mermoz makes a mental note to tell them not to fill the tank so full, because it overflows. He can't see anything in the darkness that surrounds them, but all the needles on the instrument panel are steady and the sound of the engine tells him it's turning over smoothly.

However, an orchestra is sometimes capable of playing under the most adverse circumstances. When dawn breaks, he's stunned by what he sees on the windscreen: It's totally covered with oil. The engine is still turning at 1620 revolutions a minute, but it must be on the point of running out of oil, and when that happens, it will start to overheat until it goes up in flames. He transfers the spare thirty-five kilos of oil, but at close to 900 kilometres from the coast of Senegal, he knows they won't make land. Gimié contacts the rescue boat, the *Phocée*, which is not quite a hundred kilometres away.

They spot the boat after an anxious hour, with the temperature of the engine climbing dangerously toward 100°C. Landing on a choppy sea with two-metre-high waves isn't advisable, but they have no choice. Mermoz knows he has to set the plane down in a trough between two waves, precisely in those five or six seconds of calm before the next wave builds again. Nerves are the enemy, but Mermoz's heart only beats wildly during his nights of distraction and debauchery. By contrast, in high-risk situations, his heartbeat is slow, as if he were becoming drowsy. Mermoz descends until he has the plane steady, close to the surface of the water. He pushes forward on the joystick and lands between two waves. A small launch makes its way toward them, wrestling with the ocean.

The rescue operation at sea won't be easy. Gimié moves quickly to the cabin door, but Mermoz grabs him by his jacket.

"The mail, Gimié! Help me, both of you."

The crewmen hesitate momentarily. Loading the mailbags will take up precious time and put their lives at risk. But Mermoz, lurching because of the movement of the waves, is already at the trapdoor to the cargo hold, getting the 150 kilos of mail. He passes the bags to Gimié, who hands them on to Dabry, sitting astride one of the floats with his legs in the water. The sailors protest that they'll be overloaded, but the trio pretend that the wind and the swell prevent them from hearing and continue to pass over bags. Then the two crewmen climb into the overloaded launch. Mermoz clambers over the seaplane until he has anchored a steel cable to it, then climbs on board the launch holding on to the end of the cable so the *Phocée* can tow the plane.

The captain, astonished, sees the rescue launch arriving, dangerously overloaded with mailbags and with a pilot stubbornly hanging on to a tow cable which he hands over to the sailors before giving them his own hand.

The *Phocée* starts to tow the seaplane to the coast of Africa, but before they've gone more than a few hundred metres, an enormous wave drives the plane down into its watery kingdom and it disappears beneath the waves.

CHAPTER 52

★

Buenos Aires (Argentina), 1930

Antoine de Saint-Exupéry and Henri Guillaumet

ANTOINE USES HIS BULKY BODY to clear a path along the narrow sidewalk of Calle Corrientes, packed with men in hats and women in their Sunday best. Guillaumet follows, holding hands with Noëlle. He's more solemn than usual, something Antoine noticed when he stopped by their apartment to pick them up. Cars and trams are crowded together in a stunning chaos which also has something festive and high-spirited about it in this city which is experiencing mad growth. They leave behind the Italian hairdresser's, and a bar from which emerges the smell of fried food and, on a wobbly gramophone, the mellow voice of the popular Carlos Gardel. They finally reach the entrance to Luna Park which, like a castle in a fairy tale, raises its flamboyant, fake, vaguely Moorish columns on an empty plot of land in the middle of the avenue. A Ferris wheel turns as slowly as an old dinosaur.

Amusement parks produce a strange mixture of euphoria and sadness in Antoine.

"Roller-coaster rides are so short! You go up and down, you come back down to earth and laugh, then suddenly, it's all over. It all happens so quickly!"

There's a photo booth with a big plane cut out of cardboard. You can stand behind it like a comic actor as if you were flying in it.

"Let's take a photo of us in that plane!"

Guillaumet isn't in the mood for it this afternoon. It's also true that he, the man who conquered the Andes, panics at the thought of making a fool of himself. He threatens to resist. Antoine, whose body is so large that both the shy man and the clown fit inside it, circles around him, arms stretched out as if he were pretending to be a plane, his tiny tie looking anything but elegant. Noëlle gives Henri an affectionate, conspiratorial look. He accepts, if only to stop his friend from making a scene.

Antoine watches the understanding shared by the couple and can't avoid a certain degree of sadness. He misses Consuelo, who has travelled to Europe to sort out some personal matters. Or rather, he misses love. He longs for that thread of spider's silk that enables a person to swing in midair.

Is Consuelo his thread? She has to be. She's sensual, amusing, and extravagant. She's hardly a sanctimonious churchgoing widow! She can be volatile, vain, and adorably capricious as well. He still doesn't know if she loves him. And he? Is he in love with her, or is it his continual need to be in love? Is there any difference? He believes that love is made of fairly inflexible material: if you stretch it too much, it breaks. That's why he didn't insist more than was necessary when Consuelo told him she had to go to Paris to sign some paperwork connected with her inheritance. Nor did he insist when she said something about a suitor over there, also a matter she had to clear up. He requested her not to go and see him in person, but to deal with it by letter. And she roared with laughter as if he'd told her something really funny. Of course she'd go and see him.

What if the spark between them reignites? What if they renew their commitment?

Noëlle notices that he's lost in thought.

"What are you thinking about so deeply?"

"Trivialities."

"Trivialities? You look as if you're at a Mass for the dead."

Antoine blushes faintly.

"I was thinking about Consuelo."

"That's good!"

"I was thinking about how she's gone to France. She's got a suitor there, or some such."

"Don't tell me you're jealous!"

"Jealous?" He takes a bit too long to answer his own question to make it convincing. "Not at all!"

Noëlle laughs heartily.

"Do you hear that, Henri? He says he's not jealous, but ever since he started to think about that suitor of Consuelo's, he's had a sour look on his face!"

Antoine, feeling shy, prefers to change the topic: "Are we going to have our photo taken?"

The three of them stand behind the painted plane and the photographer asks them not to move. They can't be aware of the paradox: That cardboard cutout of a plane, the least significant these two pilots have ever boarded, will take them much further than any other plane. The flight captured on photographic paper in Luna Park that afternoon will travel through the rest of the century, and the image will remain for posterity.

They take a ride on the Ferris wheel and see Buenos Aires from a new perspective: Dusk shows them a city dotted with streetlights and splotches of colour from the new advertising signs lit by the electric glow of neon tubes which herald an era of amazing technological advances. Antoine and Noëlle convince Guillaumet to join them on a merry-go-round and sit on the little wooden horses which go gently up and down with their motionless white manes and golden harnesses. Noëlle snuggles into her jacket; the air has cooled down and they decide it's time to leave. When they're almost at the exit, Antoine hurriedly goes back to a stall to buy an excessive amount of caramelised candy which, sporting a sparkling smile, he can barely carry back to them in his large hands. Noëlle gives her husband a meaningful look.

Guillaumet shrugs uneasily in his dark suit. Antoine looks at them both, his bulging eyes giving him the air of an anxious chameleon. They want to tell him something, but they don't know how.

"Antoine, Mermoz sent me a telegram this week. He wants me to return to France to test the Latécoère prototypes. He's working really hard on the new seaplanes for the Atlantic crossings."

"That's great news! You know I don't like those seaplanes with their floats, but Mermoz is doing an incredible job." He looks at them with a smile that can't hide his sadness, just like a windscreen wiper can wipe away the rain but can't prevent it. "So . . . you, Henri, the two of you . . . you're leaving South America too?"

Guillaumet nods. "You'll stay on as the big chief in South America. Well, you are that already."

"Chief . . . ," Antoine sighs. "What's the point of being the boss and earning thousands of francs if I'm here by myself?"

"Consuelo will be back very soon," says Noëlle, trying to cheer him up.

"And if she doesn't return?"

The inability of these brave men to confront their own feelings never ceases to amaze Noëlle. She puts her hands on her hips as if she were scolding him.

"Then, if you truly love her, you'll have to go and fetch her."

322

CHAPTER 53

Buenos Aires (Argentina), 1930

ANTOINE DE SAINT-EXUPÉRY

ANTOINE HAS SPENT WEEKS FOCUSING on his work. The route to Patagonia has been standardised and there's already a list of pilots who replace each other at the various stopovers. He flies to Puerto San Julián and is received by the manager of the airfield, Señor Vitoco and his customary hot maté. Antoine knows Vitoco has a sweet tooth, so he always brings him candy bought at the specialist store on Calle Corrientes. In Río Gallegos, he shares meals and a chat with Señor Erasmo, who belongs to the Workers Cooperative and has anarchist dreams. Occasionally, he flies to the edge of the Strait of Magellan, over dormant volcanoes that make him feel as if he were crossing a remote planet.

But there's something strange in the air. Maybe it's the solitude which makes him feel uneasy. The company is experiencing financial difficulties and the magnificent expansion projects are being held up.

Antoine is working furiously on his novel about night flights. He's already written more than four hundred pages—too many words, he feels. He spends hours and hours shearing the text and removing the wool it doesn't need, as if he were one of those shepherds in Patagonia.

Antoine could never be an architect. When he renovates his house of text, he not only knocks down partitions and masonry, but also the load-bearing walls and beams of the novel's framework. But he doesn't care, because he hates literature that's measured out as if it were medicine. Life is chaotic, savage, and literature should be a reflection of that.

He flies with a radio operator, because it's now the rule that the pilot has to be accompanied by a radio operator who constantly updates their position and receives advice from the controllers of the various aerodromes over which they fly. Flying is not as solitary as it was in the past. Although the noise of the engines makes free-flowing conversation impossible, there's still an exchange of messages scribbled hastily on tiny pieces of paper and held out to him: "San Julián, light shower, wind northeast, moderate."

In his novel, he has the plane flying into the night slowly, like a barge leaving behind the lights of a port. The faint reflection from the dials on the control panel barely illuminates the pilot. Antoine looks down and watches with affection the distant lights of a dark countryside, where tablecloths are being spread out for evening meals. To him, each light is a home.

For every hundred pages Antoine writes, he tears up ninety-nine. He pardons one, more out of pity than conviction. He feels that no true writer can be satisfied with his soufflé of words.

One afternoon as he's busy shredding pages, someone rings the apartment doorbell . . . and when he opens the door a tower of hat boxes in all sorts of colours appears in front of him, balanced with difficulty by a pair of hands at its base. This being, with the legs of a man and a body of boxes, emits a "Good afternoon," and walks into the apartment. Before Antoine can say a word, a small cart appears, loaded with what seem to be canvases, or at least stretchers, wrapped in brown paper, with only the hands of the person pushing it visible.

"Hey!"

Antoine has to step aside to avoid being run over by another little cart with a wall of trunks reaching to head height.

"But . . . !"

Again, he has to step to one side because another cart is arriving, just as full, though this time, with suitcases. His bewilderment gives way to a sudden fury and he's about to go into the apartment to demand an explanation from these individuals who have mistaken his home for a warehouse, when a small glamorous figure in a huge sun hat appears in the doorway.

"Hello, darling!"

It's his little Salvadorean, with that typical expression of hers, somewhere between aristocratic and mischievous.

"Consuelo!"

"Aren't you going to welcome me to Buenos Aires?"

"But why didn't you let me know about your return?"

"Telegrams are so boring. Pay these boys!"

Bewildered, Antoine takes out a few notes.

"But what are your things doing here?"

"I forgot to write to my hotel to make a reservation. I'll tell them to come and get these things in the morning."

"Consuelo! How can you stay here? People will murmur!"

"Murmur! I love that word. Do you know that that word is almost identical in Spanish and French? Murmur! The word sounds like the noise people make when they gossip in whispers."

"Consuelo . . ."

"What, darling?"

"We have to get married."

"Right now?"

Antoine breaks into a laugh. He takes her in his arms.

"We have to organise the wedding right away. But it has to be in France."

"What haste! I'm only in a rush to have a bath and a dry martini. There was not one member of staff on the liner who had the slightest idea how to make a cocktail that didn't make your head explode."

"I've written to my mother about our relationship. She really wants to meet you. We'll get married in Saint-Maurice. It will be a dazzling wedding!"

"I'm a widow, remember. I have to get married in black."

"In black?"

"Of course. It would be inconceivable to do otherwise where I come from."

"It will be as you say." Antoine falls silent for a moment. "Consuelo . . . Do you want to marry me?"

"Oh, darling, always so unorganised! Having planned the wedding, and even the colour of my dress, now you ask me if I want to get married?"

And Consuelo starts to laugh like an exotic bird. Antoine laughs too, although he's still uneasy. He won't stop worrying until he sees her at the altar.

She convinces him there's no rush to think about weddings. If they marry, she'll lose the allowance she receives as the widow of Gómez Carrillo. In the end, they decide to rent a large house with several terraces in the north of the city, on Calle Tagle.

Weeks go by during which Antoine tries to write new pages of his story about night flights by hand while at the same time attending to Aéropostale matters. When he and Consuelo receive visitors, the guests are greeted by very unusual hosts. The house contains stuffed animals and drawings by Consuelo, furniture from antiques dealers mixed with furniture that seems to have originated in junkyards. And a mess of papers, files, and books piling up everywhere. Acquaintances let Consuelo know of the unease of some of her late husband's friends, scandalised by her improper behaviour. She's concerned for a while, and then forgets about it.

In their house, clocks are merely decorative. Meal times are when-ever. Antoine sometimes gets home very late after a four-day absence flying his Patagonia route. He's barely slept, but hurriedly removes a handful of sheets of paper from his bag, and no matter the hour, Con-suelo immediately has to listen. It doesn't matter if dawn finds them still at it, or if Consuelo has fallen asleep; Antoine continues to read out loud to the shadows.

Coming home and not finding her there bothers Antoine. Occasion-ally, she leaves him a note: "I'm at the opera. I'll be home late." He stays up waiting for her, writing. The book has taken a new turn: The aviator is increasingly becoming a secondary character, while the figure of the company director assumes greater and greater significance. Rivière is a character inspired by Daurat, a boss so demanding he's almost cruel. And yet Antoine sees in him the road to perfection: an ennobling sacrifice.

For Antoine, those weeks go by happily, even though, at times, he feels as if he is sleep walking. Everything revolves around Consuelo. She's a little planet with a maddening power of attraction. She's an explosion of ideas, no matter how outlandish they might be: starting a sculpture and leaving it half-finished in the salon; meditating on top of the dining room table; attending spiritualist sessions organised by a slightly crazy marchioness; moving the furniture around several times a day.

He tells Guillaumet in a letter that what he has isn't an engagement, but a tango. He thinks he's happy. One morning, he realises he hasn't thought about Lou-Lou for some time.

Sometimes, he takes hold of Consuelo by the waist and asks her point-blank: "Do you really love me, Consuelo?"

She gives him a seductive look, grabs him by his chin, and kisses him passionately. Perhaps it's due to the imprecise shades of meaning in her French, but she always ends up expressing herself with facial expressions, winks and exaggerated gestures rather than words. And that further heightens the ambiguity which torments and fascinates Antoine. And she doesn't only do it to him. If she's staying in a hotel and the waiter brings a bill on a small tray to her table for her to sign and charge to her room, she gives him back the tray without even touching the bill and smiles at him in a certain way. The waiter hesitates but finally gives a slight bow and withdraws. That smile is her signature.

Antoine insists that they must marry and she finally accedes. She informs him that she has to go to Europe to get things ready and her absence drives him to despair. He dedicates himself to calling her at any hour, in any place. Often, he can't find her in the hotel in Paris where she's staying. At other times, the telephone lines send back an echo of distance in the form of noises and interference which makes it difficult to understand anything. In the Aéropostale offices in Buenos Aires, the accountants and secretaries become accustomed to the voice of Señor de Saint-Exupéry loudly asking into the handset of the phone if she loves him. Now and again, when he hasn't noticed what time it is, they hear him whispering—loudly—millions of apologies for having woken her up in the middle of the night.

Finally, in one of those broken conversations, he tells her that this is no way to get things straight, and he's going to take the first ship available.

"And your work?" she asks.

Before the connection is cut, he tells her he's asked for leave to get married. "Don't move from there! We're getting married as soon as I arrive!"

"But I need a new dress, darling! Where will I find a dressmaker who works that quickly?"

"I have no idea! Order one from ten dressmakers and buy the one made by whoever finishes first!"

This time, he's the one who hangs up. He has too many things to do. He has to make one last flight to Comodoro Rivadavia as substitute for another pilot, pack his bags, write to his mother, buy presents for his sisters . . .

Monsieur Daurat has sent a brief telegram from Montaudran authorising his leave. He can't refuse: Antoine hasn't had a holiday for two years. Besides, Daurat has other concerns.

Antoine, who's never in a hurry, always ends up running at the last minute. This time, he spends so long in the cafeteria of the boat terminal drinking champagne toasts with his friends and colleagues, including several Argentinian pilots, that he almost misses the boat. On the dock, the boy who's looking after the pet Antoine has bought as a gift for his sister Gabrielle hands it over to him with relief.

"Here's your 'kitten,' señor," he says with a grimace.

On the wharf reserved for ocean liners, a heavily built individual trotting through the terminal dressed in a double-breasted suit with his shirt hanging out of his trousers doesn't go unnoticed, especially if he's got a puma cub on a leash and is signalling to the sailors at the gangplank to wait.

The voyage seems endless to him, especially as he daily has to feed and walk the feline, which is growing at a disturbing rate. On one of these walks, Antoine and the cub cross paths with one of the ship's officers and the animal can think of nothing better than to launch itself at the officer's calf and take a bite. The cub takes advantage of the confusion to escape.

Sneaking through the first door it comes across, it finds itself in the casino. When the bejewelled ladies at the first baccarat table turn around and see the beast entering, they throw down their cards and try to leave, knocking over the table in their haste, and sending the chips flying.

One of the employees appears with a club and makes a move as if to confront the puma cub, but as soon as he registers in the animal's field of vision, it jumps toward him, and he drops his club and starts to run. When the last passenger has pushed his way out, a sailor closes the door and they leave the puma locked in among the roulette wheels and green baize tables.

The puma is confiscated by the captain, to be locked up and handed over to the authorities when they dock in the Canary Islands.

That night, Antoine jots down some thoughts in his notebook. The outline of a letter he'll never send to Lou-Lou: *In a few days' time, I'm going to become a respectable married gentleman. Years have gone by since we were once engaged. An entire lifetime has gone by. I still occasionally wonder what life by your side would have been like. I know it's ridiculous, but I can't prevent myself from missing the lives I haven't lived.*

The liner reaches the port of Almería in the south of Spain, where Antoine disembarks to meet Consuelo. They hire a car, the only taxi to be found for many kilometres, and it takes them along a road where they overtake several short men riding donkeys. They reach a bare promontory in the middle of unirrigated land which reminds Antoine of an African landscape. From there, they see down in the valley the glow of an enchanted village of white houses which give off a blinding light.

They ask to go immediately to see that precious town, and drive in, frightening chickens and elderly people grasping shepherd's crooks made from olive wood, before stopping in front of the first houses. From afar, they were dreamlike with their white glow; up close, they reveal themselves to be simple, humble, in need of attention.

Antoine falls silent.

"What's the matter, darling?"

Antoine gives a deep sigh. "Dreams, Consuelo . . ."

"What's the matter with dreams?"

"If we try to touch them, they fall apart. Look at these houses which seemed to be white gold. When you touch them, they turn into lime."

"Darling! Forget about dreams! Live in the moment!"

They travel slowly across Spain. In France, they move into the house in Nice that Consuelo has inherited from Gómez Carrillo. There they welcome family and friends. Antoine's aunt, Yvonne de Lestrange, comes to visit them one afternoon, accompanied by André Gide, who is already, by then, one of France's most renowned writers.

Gide is entranced by the aviation adventures which Antoine narrates with poetic enthusiasm and is very pleased to leave with a copy tucked under his arm of the manuscript of the novel of nights and sacrifices which will be called *Night Flight*.

Consuelo gesticulates a great deal. Many times she sits down at and stands up from the table out in the garden. She tries to start new conversations, but neither Yvonne de Lestrange nor Gide pays her the slightest attention and so she becomes more and more rude. They are only interested in Antoine's work in South America, and in talking about literature. She makes her boredom obvious with vulgar yawns.

When they leave, she's furious.

"They're snobs," she shrieks as she and Antoine turn to go back inside. "I know more about literature than they do!"

"Oh, yes?" Antoine replies, amused at her temper tantrum because they haven't shown her the admiration her friends usually dispense.

"How many people do you know who have been the wife of two writers? Your aunt was looking me up and down. She's one of those women who can't bear the fact that another woman is more attractive than she is!"

The morning of their wedding day, Antoine sighs like a runner who sees the finishing line. Consuelo is dressed in black, with a veil, and holds a bouquet of carnations. Antoine, in a double-breasted suit, is elated. In the photographs, he looks more like a big child on the day of his First Communion than a groom.

He's in high spirits in the days that follow. When they visit Saint-Maurice and he comes across an acquaintance from his youth, he grabs him by the shoulder and drags him to the nearest café to invite him for a champagne and to meet his wife, who sometimes talks nineteen to the dozen, and at other times displays her boredom with shameless disdain.

Some evenings, while Consuelo is painting, Antoine goes out into the garden to smoke, and occasionally, when he's by himself, he feels overwhelmed by sadness. A deep sadness, for no reason. In the same way that other people have asthma attacks or stomach upsets, he feels in low spirits without knowing why.

He wonders where this sadness comes from. He's in the best period of his life. He's found love, his work is acknowledged, and his prospects as a writer, encouraged by Gallimard and backed by André Gide, are magnificent. He should be jumping for joy; he's the luckiest man in the world. And yet happiness slips through his fingers. He's turned thirty, and he misses the passion he had a few years ago, when he was capable of falling in love on a daily basis and nothing was settled.

When he was still in Argentina, caught up in his own thoughts, he hadn't paid attention to the conversations of the small groups at the Pacheco aerodrome, or in the offices at Calle de la Reconquista, nor to the news about Aéropostale in the newspapers. That's why he's now caught unawares. He receives a communiqué informing him of the cancellation of all expansion projects of the company's South American routes, and the sale of the Argentinian subsidiary. The ground is giving way under his feet and he hadn't realised.

CHAPTER 54

Toulouse, 1931

Jean Mermoz

MERMOZ STUDIES THE NEW LATÉ 28 on the Montaudran runway; the half-dozen windows give it the look of a small flying bus. He zips up his leather jacket and adjusts his helmet and goggles before climbing in for another experimental flight. He's spent weeks testing all the modifications with a view to doing the jump over to South America, despite the troubled state of the company.

A mechanic comes toward him carrying a bundle. It's already a small ritual. The mechanic brings him a parachute and Mermoz laughs. He doesn't want a parachute. It's uncomfortable and it seems to him that it's safer to try to land no matter what the circumstance, than to leap out from a height of hundreds of metres with that piece of gabardine. The mechanic goes along with the game until he turns around and sees the director of operations standing in front of him watching both of them closely.

"Mermoz, don't forget your parachute."

"But, Monsieur Daurat!"

"You're carrying out a test flight. And current aviation regulations require that you carry a parachute."

"It's a useless pain in the neck."

"The regulations are for everyone. Do you want them to make a regulation just for you?"

Mermoz grimaces.

The Laté takes off without even noticing the six tonnes of cargo it's carrying and reaches 5,000 metres with ease.

The machine accelerates smoothly, until suddenly it starts to shake violently, so much so that Mermoz can't even hold the joystick. The plane breaks apart as if it were a badly glued mock-up, and various bits of metal fly off the fuselage. It goes into a tailspin as it falls and Mermoz's blood turns to ice. Then he remembers the parachute, and, upside down as he is because of the plane's nosedive, he tries to exit through the opening in the roof. But everything has become twisted and his shoulders get stuck. With his head outside, he can see the ground approaching as a wing breaks off and a fuel tank detaches from the plane, which is disintegrating in midair. Pieces nearby come apart and that, combined with the strength of his shoulders, succeeds in popping off the cockpit cover. Mermoz begins to fall, just one more of the pieces raining down. The parachute opens and he is suspended in the air for a few seconds, but the falling nuts and bolts tear the parachute material and Mermoz falls heavily to the ground.

The airfield employees rush over to him with a stretcher, not knowing if he's dead or alive. They get their answer when they see him raise his arm and make a V for Victory sign.

He has to be transferred to hospital; he has a broken rib.

"You'll have to stay here immobilised for four days."

"Doctor, I got married a few months ago."

"Do you want us to let your wife know?"

"No, no! What I want is that you *not* let her know! On top of the fact that she didn't get a honeymoon because of my work with these flights, this would make her even more upset."

"Hospital protocol requires us to inform a close member of the family when a person is admitted."

"Fine, let her know. But tell her I'll be playing rugby next week."

Mermoz and Gilberte had married the previous August. The president of Aéropostale himself, Monsieur Bouilloux-Lafont, agreed to be Mermoz's witness. Off in a corner, Antoine and Guillaumet elbowed each other and pointed at him with incredulity, as if they couldn't believe what they were seeing. Even so, it wasn't the sparkling day Mermoz was hoping for. The solemn Mass and even Gilberte herself, enchanting in her white dress but with a serious smile, infected him with a degree of anxiety. As if marriage were like a trap for wild boars.

In the months since the wedding, Gilberte has been an attentive wife, always at home to welcome him affectionately. Though he can see her wringing her hands when he says goodbye, she has never reproached him over a flight, or an absence, or some of his outings for dinner that stretch till dawn, or longer. She never questions him, and she accepts any explanation he gives her without complaining. Anyone would think it's a pleasant life. But he can't stop feeling displeased with himself. She deserves a husband who's more stay-at-home, more devoted, who would not make her suffer so much. He wonders if Gilberte is happy. She sometimes appears to be, but is she really? He's not capable of truly knowing what lies behind those large brown eyes and her eternal complacency.

Several of his pilot colleagues visit him in hospital.

"Don't get up," Pichodou tells him jokingly when he sees him immobilised.

"How are things going out there?"

"Not very well."

"Those worries about Aéropostale again? I've told you many times that there's nothing to fear regarding the company. Bouilloux-Lafont is a very powerful man with infinite resources: He owns train lines, mines, even banks in South America. He treats ministers as if they were shoe-shine boys!"

Pichodou sighs. He would like nothing better than to believe Mermoz. "The court has rendered a judgement. Bouilloux-Lafont has not been able to deal with his debts; the state has confiscated the company."

For once, Mermoz's voice drops: "That's not possible."

"The company hasn't paid salaries on time for months," complains one of the pilots.

Mermoz glares at him. If he could move, he'd give him a clip on the back of his neck. "It's the government's fault. They spend fortunes on nonsense and they're not capable of extending a line of credit of eighty million francs to the company? The South American routes are in place and there are advanced projects for new routes: the Antilles, the estab-lishment of a North Atlantic route."

Mermoz shakes his head and smiles again, as if he's realised it's all a joke. "But I'm sure they're bluffing. They want to tighten the leash, put bureaucratic pressure on Bouilloux-Lafont, and then they'll authorise the credit. You'll see!"

Only Pichodou dares contradict him. "The judgement is definite, and they've ordered it to be executed immediately. Bouilloux-Lafont has had to go home, and this morning, some ministerial employees arrived at the company offices carrying black folders. The administra-tion staff say they're the liquidators."

Mermoz tries to sit up and feels a sharp pain in his rib.

"They can't throw all those years of the company on the rubbish heap! They can't dishonour the dead."

They all keep quiet. Mermoz feels a stab of resentment toward these colleagues who are prepared to give up. His lion's mane shakes with the rage of a wounded animal.

"I won't allow it!"

As his colleagues watch in amazement, he supports himself on his good arm, gets out of bed, and limps to the wardrobe. He opens it and, in the process of removing his jacket, knocks down all the hangers.

"What are you doing, Mermoz? You're injured!"

"But I'm not dead!"

A nurse who arrives just then calls for the doctors. It takes two doctors, three nurses, and an orderly to drag him back to his bed.

CHAPTER 55

Casablanca (Morocco), 1931

ANTOINE DE SAINT-EXUPÉRY

ANTOINE HAS COME BACK TO Africa, but he hasn't returned.

We can never return to a place where we were once happy.

He's thinking about this in the cockpit of the Latécoère 26, which is open to the four winds. The hot air explodes in his face, together with the taste of burnt sand and the smell of ancient minerals. The Casablanca aerodrome appears in his line of sight, with its dirty wooden hangars, piles of rusted fuel drums, and macadam runways outlined with lime.

He's dragged from his reverie by the radio operator, who holds out a piece of handwritten paper with wobbly letters on it. The readings make the flight safer, but Antoine can't avoid some despondency.

Flying has become an administrative job!

He lands somewhat absentmindedly and the wheels hop several times before settling on the flattened ground.

Consuelo's arrival in Morocco, after staying on in Paris for a few months, has eased Antoine's loneliness. Casablanca is a city that claims to be cosmopolitan, but to him, it's a provincial city where the Europeans play at being exotic.

Consuelo is always waiting for him with some plan: dinners at the homes of government bureaucrats, visits to one of her artist friends, afternoon tea at the homes of women who swish their tortoiseshell fans back and forth rapidly to scare off their boredom . . . The men joke with Consuelo and she, flattered, plays their game. Antoine wonders what she, a person in such constant need of games and activities, does during the days and nights when he's away. He wonders what she was doing all those months she was by herself in Paris, always surrounded by handsome men flattering her with their attention.

During many of the nights when he's been wandering in a dark limbo between Agadir and Port-Étienne, he's asked himself if she has a lover. Or several. Hours of silent flying lend themselves to a great deal of thinking. Some days, he discards this absurd idea and scolds himself for his ridiculous jealousy. Other days, he feels the weight of a gesture or a look he has seen her exchanging with a young officer from the fort or a very elegant English mining engineer with exquisite manners. Consuelo, small and lively, reminds him of a bird: If the door of the cage is open, she will fly out. And no one can get angry about this. Flying is in her nature.

He needs to fly too. When Lou-Lou asked him to clip his wings so she could continue to love him, he agreed. The paradox is that, when he did, she stopped loving him. He realises his tragic mistake now: You can't love a bird that stops flying, because if it doesn't fly, it's no longer a bird. He can't stop wondering if he might not have maintained Lou-Lou's fascination for him if he had remained firm and become a professional pilot, rather than a grey office worker. Although it's also true that she was a capricious fairy: She couldn't bear to be contradicted, but she reacted even worse when people agreed with her.

Antoine tries to get rid of these thoughts. He wants to think about Consuelo, but his brain supplies him instead with the voluptuous figure of the girl who does all the housework for them.

Sometimes, when Antoine is reading the paper, she's tidying up in the salon, and when she bends down to pick something up, she reveals the top of her breasts.

He thought that when he found the woman of his dreams, all other women would disappear. When he loved Lou-Lou, he was incapable of seeing other women; they had all become invisible. Now, however, he sees them clearly, his thoughts are carnal.

It strikes him that he can't be harsh with Consuelo if she has the occasional indiscretion because he's been the first to commit adultery, at least in his imagination—he still thinks about Lou-Lou.

He searches out the airfield office boy and, while he cleans himself up and changes his clothes, sends him off to buy flowers from a small stand on the Boulevard de la Gare.

"What flowers do you want?"

"All of them!" And he hands over the money stuffed in his pockets.

Consuelo adores flowers. She accepts them with the same delight with which she forgets them on top of any shelf a moment later.

Antoine arrives at the rendezvous carrying with difficulty the armful of wild flowers he bought for the price of a precious orchid. Flowers in Casablanca are like caviar. His little Salvadorean volcano is waiting for him inside Chez Zezé, a slightly run-down brasserie near the port. She's cheerful, thanks to two player pianos that she finds enchanting.

"Flowers! Thank you, Papou. They're beautiful!" She deposits the mountain of colours on top of a chair.

"How was your trip?"

"We saw a flock of flamingos over Port-Étienne. No squadron from any army, led by the strictest commanding officer, would have flown in a more orderly manner."

"We're due to dine here with the Vimeuxes."

"I like that cultured doctor and his wife."

"The Bonners and the Desrosiers will be coming too."

Antoine wrinkles his snub nose. "I don't like those government bureaucrats who think that drinking tea with a lot of mint in their Sèvres china makes them exotic."

Consuelo caresses him. "They are influential! You'll be good, won't you, and behave yourself with them?"

His expression softens. It's impossible to deny Consuelo anything. "I'll be on my best behavior."

The doctor and his wife arrive and right after them, the distinguished employees of the French government stationed in Morocco. Their comfortable social position is revealed by the pearl necklaces of the women and the made-to-measure suits and gold cuff links of the men.

Antoine wants to tell them about the flock of flamingos. But the Bonners and the Desrosiers prefer that he talk to them about the financial situation of Aéropostale. They have heard the company is bankrupt.

"I understand little of this business of bank guarantees. But what I really don't understand is how the government can allow a leading company to go under and do nothing, while their competitors in Italy, Germany, and Great Britain rub their hands with glee. We have a government to be ashamed of!"

Consuelo stares at him, trying to curb his tongue through some sort of hypnotism. She'd give him a kick under the table, but her legs are too short. He doesn't seem to realise that he's being disparaging about the government to a functionary of the state.

"Records broken, postal routes opened in the most inhospitable places, praise from the press, mountains of medals and awards for civic merit seem to mean nothing to the Air Ministry."

"Ah, now I understand!" Bonner replies with an icy smile. "Awards, the press . . . maintaining such a costly airline company is a matter of vanity!"

"A matter of vanity?" Antoine raises his voice. "It's a matter of respecting the memory of the one hundred and fourteen company people who have died. They gave their lives flying the letters of the citizens of France. But you people aren't able to understand this. The riskiest thing you've ever done is lean over the railing of your box at the opera."

"That is offensive!"

Consuelo tries to ease the tension by changing the topic to the difficulty in finding domestic staff who don't leave suddenly or end up filling the house with relatives.

As soon as they have eaten their *mechoui*, without waiting for dessert or coffee, the two government officials and their wives get up in unison, as if choreographed, and drily take their leave.

Sometime later, after the doctor and his wife have also left and Consuelo and Antoine are by themselves, Antoine puts his large hands into the oversized pockets of his blazer and sits there gravely. He can't rid his mind of the rumors of the closure of the company.

Consuelo strokes his hair. "Come on, Papou . . ."

They walk slowly to their apartment and find a yellow envelope in the letter box when they get there. Inside, there's a note from Antoine's editor, Gaston Gallimard.

Dear Antoine, the critics have been conquered by Night Flight. I can't wait to see you in Paris to celebrate. G.G.

The note is accompanied by a page from the daily newspaper, *Le Matin*, in which the literary reviewer writes: "This is not a novel; it's even better—it is a great book."

Antoine looks up in amazement, as if they were talking about someone else.

"Do you really think they've understood that it's a story about the night, and duty?"

"What does that matter! What's important is that they like it, that they've praised it, and that you are now an important writer."

Antoine is pensive for a moment.

"So, wasn't I before?"

"Well, no, darling."

He nods, not entirely sure that he understands how the world works. *You're only important when everyone else decides you are.*

CHAPTER 56

★

Montaudran Aerodrome (Toulouse), 1932

DIDIER DAURAT

THE CLOSURE OF SEVERAL ROUTES in just a few weeks means that the offices at Montaudran have lost some of their incessant bustle of administrators, secretaries, mechanics, pilots, and inspectors. The sound of typing seems monotonous and an atmosphere of after-dinner drowsiness hangs in the air. The only light that never goes off is the one in Daurat's office.

Bouvet, a look of terror perpetually in his eyes, knocks on the door and, when told to enter, finds the director enveloped in a cloud of smoke and paperwork, as usual. Daurat looks at the skinny little man with his head as bald as a tonsured friar's. He can see Bouvet's fear as he holds out a telegram, and he worries that there's been an accident during one of the mail flights. But when he looks at the communiqué, Daurat gives a sigh of relief. It's a message from the office of the company's new president, so there's no problem: in the president's office there are no planes crossing the desert, only bureaucrats crossing carpets.

MONSIEUR DIDIER DAURAT, THE COMPANY PUTS AN EXTRAORDINARY VALUE
ON YOUR TWELVE YEARS OF DEDICATION . . .

That sentence rings an alarm bell. The most dangerous sentences
are the ones that sing your praises. He skips a few paragraphs and his
little eyes open wide in astonishment.

WE REGRET THAT THE EVIDENCE GATHERED AFTER THE COMPLAINTS
PRESENTED BY TWO COMPANY EMPLOYEES REGARDING THE UNACCEPTABLE
ACTIONS TAKEN BY YOU IN BURNING ENTIRE BAGS OF MAIL AT THE MONTAU-
DRAN INSTALLATION OBLIGES US TO IMPLEMENT YOUR IMMEDIATE DISMISSAL,
EFFECTIVE FROM THE MOMENT YOU RECEIVE THIS MISSIVE, BY MEANS OF
WHICH YOU ARE NOTIFIED OF THE TERMINATION OF ALL DUTIES AS DIRECTOR
OF OPERATIONS.

There are further legal paragraphs, and at the bottom, the signature
of the new director-general.

The ever-shy Bouvet's shoulders have dropped even more than
usual, almost down to his ankles.

"Bouvet! What are you doing, standing there like a half-wit? The
quarterly fuel budget! Move!"

Bouvet happily accepts the dressing-down. *So, nothing has changed.*

But everything has changed. A few minutes before the cable reached
Monsieur Daurat's office, all the employees were summoned to a meeting by the head of personnel and informed of the immediate dismissal
of the director of operations. They all know that the accusation that
the man—who for years has taken more care than anyone of the French
people's airmail—burned entire sacks of mail like a pyromaniac is ridiculous. But they also already knew that something was going to happen,
that the current proprietor of the company, overwhelmed by financial
difficulties, had wanted Daurat removed for some time now.

It is true that, a few weeks earlier, Daurat had ordered a bonfire
be built well away from the runways, and bags made by a new sup-
plier thrown on it. The bags were filled with waste paper to check

their resistance to flames should there be a fire. But the pretext for the dismissal is not important. There's been a wind change of modernity. The new bosses wear waistcoats and colourful braces, and agree on the need to liquidate obsolete equipment, such as the director of operations who uses outdated methods.

The following morning, as always, Daurat arrives an hour before the first administrative assistant. Perfectly shaved, his hair combed back and set with brilliantine, impeccably dressed, as always, in a tailored dark pinstriped suit, a tie, restrained studs on the collar of his shirt, and a fedora.

The office boy greets him with his customary politeness and a bow, but with a hint of surprise. The secretaries, stone-faced, watch him go by, headed for his office with his leather briefcase in one hand and a cigarette in the other. As he passes in front of each of their desks, they lift their heads and their heavily mascaraed eyelashes. Not one of them dares to say anything other than a whispered "Good morning." They've been told that he's no longer the boss, that he's no longer anyone in the company . . . But how can that be true if he's Monsieur Daurat!

He reaches his office, and they all pretend they're not watching. He puts his key in the door, but it won't turn. In his absence, someone has changed the lock.

He stands stock-still for a moment in front of the door. He even takes a drag of his cigarette. The employees pretend they're immersed in their work. Only Bouvet gets up from his chair and stands upright as if he were going to say something. His chin trembles. The head of personnel pokes his head out of his office, and says angrily: "Bouvet, sit down and carry on with your work!"

Bouvet is an obedient person, which is how timid people are often portrayed. He has four children, a wife, and a paralytic mother-in-law to look after. But for the first time in his life, Bouvet doesn't sit down. Daurat looks at him. They look at each other. What his administrative assistant sees in his boss of so many years isn't anger, not even regret, just profound bewilderment, as if, for once, he didn't have an answer. Bouvet is going to say something, but Daurat raises his hand: "Please, Bouvet, sit down."

"But . . ."

"It's my last order. Sit down."

He does so. Daurat turns round. The silence is so thick that the squeak of his shoes can be heard as he walks to the exit. When the door shuts behind him, an era ends as well.

CHAPTER 57

Toulouse, 1932

Antoine de Saint-Exupéry and Jean Mermoz

Antoine arrives at the entrance to Aimé, a modest café in Toulouse. He's travelled incognito from Casablanca to Toulouse among the sacks of mail. The jolts of the Laté over the Mediterranean were nothing compared to those in his head, connected with Daurat's dismissal. The news has come as a real blow, and he feels feverish.

The new company management team had written to some of the veteran pilots, explaining to them that the changes would be for the better, and asking them to put forward their suggestions for improvement of the postal routes. Antoine immediately wrote to Guillaumet—who has been posted back to the Andes route, although there's talk of its imminent closure—and to Mermoz, to discuss how they should react to the injustice done to Daurat.

Guillaumet has been affected by Daurat's dismissal, but replies that Antoine must try to forget these political and managerial matters, that

348

they are pilots and their job is to fly. But Antoine can't extract these thoughts from his mind as you would a molar from your mouth.

He's arranged to meet Mermoz at Aimé to talk about the matter. He orders a café au lait and a brioche; anxiety fires his hunger. Mermoz is late, so he orders another coffee and another brioche. Half an hour later, a missile enters, dressed in a double-breasted suit which is far too elegant for this modest café.

"I've just heard the stupidest thing ever!" Jean exclaims with no pre-amble and no apology for being late.

He drops into an empty chair and is about to speak when the propri-etor politely interrupts him: "Would Monsieur like a coffee?"

"Coffee? Bring me some rum!"

Antoine looks at Mermoz, with his perfect blond hair and a few wrinkles around his eyes which suggest his many flights.

"What's the terribly stupid thing you've heard?"

"That there won't be one director, but several. And that the person who'll take charge of coordinating everybody is called Dautry. But do you know the best bit? The aforementioned Dautry is an excellent manager—of railway lines!"

Antoine shakes his head in dismay.

"I've also heard awful things in Paris. That shit of a politician they've put on the management board is saying that air routes are very costly."

"They've been saying that for a while, but can it be true?"

"It's all lies! With a paltry subsidy of fourteen million francs, the company could survive. And if they paid the slightest attention to me, and adjusted the tonnage of the planes, the deficit could be zero."

"What are you proposing, Jean?"

"The speed of the postal service has to be three hundred kilometres an hour. You have to provide a service that is unrivalled. People need to communicate with each other, and do it as quickly as possible. They'll be prepared to pay whatever it costs if there's a guarantee that their

349

mail will be delivered on time. With all the work that's been done on routes, airfields, trained personnel . . . what has to be done is not to divest, but to invest more in new machines, and the mail will pay for itself. And there'll be a punctual service like no other in the world."

"We have to reply to the letter from management suggesting improvements. Will you tell them this?"

Mermoz takes out a cigar and lights it.

"I already replied to them this morning. I told them that if they want improvements, what they have do is bring back Monsieur Daurat and he'll set in train whatever is required."

"I'll drink to that!" says Antoine.

"Dammit, are you going to drink a toast to Daurat with an empty cup of coffee?" He turns toward to the counter. "Bring us the bottle of rum, please!"

"I feel Daurat's humiliation as if it were my own."

"It's been tough, but we can't give up. I'm not going to do it; I have to make that leap."

"Leap?"

"The mail route to South America. After the crash of the modified Laté, the new managers want to cancel the flight program to South America because there's no budget. Cretins! They start by taking their calculators out of their drawers and crunching numbers."

"They only know how to play with numbers."

"They disgust me."

"I know."

"I've always wondered how anyone can live without pride or passion."

"They can't, Jean. They're dead; they just don't know it."

"Then let's live, Antoine!"

They exchange a look. After so many ups and downs, underneath the scars and faded dreams they recognise in each other the desire to be the naughty children they still are.

When Antoine gets into Mermoz's sports car, he already knows where they're going. They leave the traffic behind and head for Montaudran.

Mermoz has bought a secondhand Potez which the trusty Collenot has tuned to perfection. He and Antoine take off to watch the sunset, as if for the first time. They don't say a word; there's no need. The horizontal light against the brick buildings converts Toulouse into an orange city traversed by the blue ribbon of the Garonne River. When everything else wears away, they'll still be left with this buzz in the air.

CHAPTER 58

Cabo Juby (Morocco), 1932

Antoine de Saint-Exupéry

ANTOINE HAS WRITTEN A LETTER to the director-general of the company demanding Monsieur Daurat's reinstatement. But he's had no reply beyond an icy administrative silence.

One afternoon, they order him to fly as a substitute on a flight to Cabo Juby. It's been a while since he landed at the desert aerodrome that was once his home. When he sees the Spanish fort in the distance at the edge of a long beach, and the half-drowned jail which they pompously refer to as Casa del Mar, he feels he has flown back in time. Seen from the sky, nothing has changed in the blue sea, the dry land, the jaimas, and the military construction, which seems as fragile as a sandcastle from afar. Behind the fort, the precarious company hangar leans against the wall, looking like a ramshackle hut and with one grounded plane.

He lands without much attention to the beacons, his mind partially elsewhere, and overshoots the line marking the end of the runway by a few metres. He sees a mechanic he doesn't recognise coming out to greet him. A Tuareg dressed in blue who's bustling about at the back of the hangar raises his head and runs off in the direction of the desert. No one else comes out to welcome him. He walks up to his former office-cum-home and knocks on the door.

"Come in."

The manager of the airfield is a very tall man who doesn't look anyone straight in the eye.

"I'm Saint-Exupéry . . ."

He nods half-heartedly.

"You must be Monsieur Sentein. Did you know that I once held the position of airfield manager here?"

"I know, I know . . ."

Antoine detects the barely disguised irritation. Even so, he'd like to hear about how things are going at his former posting.

"How are you getting along with the tribes? Is Colonel de la Peña still in charge of the Spanish fort?"

"I don't know. I take care of my own business."

"Right . . ."

"Things have changed since you were here. Contact with the Moors and the Spaniards is no longer possible now. It's hard to tell which of them is the more savage or stupid."

Antoine listens sadly. The mechanic yells out that the plane is ready. Antoine hasn't even been invited to have a cup of tea. He has no intention of asking for one. He prepares to leave just as the mechanic comes running to the door in a real state of alarm:

"Monsieur Sentein! The Moors are attacking us! There's lots of them!"

The airfield manager nervously opens a drawer and removes a revolver.

"Hurry!" he orders, flustered. "To the Spanish fort!"

Antoine sticks his head out of the door and sees them coming—about a hundred Berbers.

"What are you doing standing there? Do you want them to slit your throat like they do to their goats?"

The two men start to run toward the Spanish fort without waiting for an answer from Antoine. The group of tribesmen, led by a chief dressed in a blue robe and carrying a spear in his hand, reaches the hut. Antoine smiles and places his hand on his chest.

"Esteemed Sheikh Abdul Okri!"

The sheikh extends an arm and orders the party to halt. Someone emerges from the group, and when he lifts the veil covering his face, it turns out to be Antoine's former translator, Kamal.

"Welcome home! Everyone has missed you!"

Several hundred metres away, Sentein has briefly looked back and keeps an eye on the greetings as he runs. The mechanic also looks back and is bewildered when he sees people lining up one by one to greet the pilot. Panting, the two men stop and observe the scene from a prudent distance.

Another old friend of Antoine's approaches, respectfully waiting his turn so that he can be the last with his greeting and, in this way, take longer.

"Abdullah Mukhtar!"

"Saintusupehi . . ."

"How is your family, my friend?"

"They are well. They'll be delighted when I tell them that you've come back."

"I've only stopped off to refuel. I have to leave right away."

Mukhtar nods impassively.

"It doesn't matter that you are leaving. People who are appreciated never completely leave. Some part of them remains with us."

Kamal translates for Sheikh Abdul Okri, who has been watching the conversation in silence. His kohl-enhanced black eyes look out over the top of his blue veil. Upon learning that Antoine hasn't returned to be the boss of the pilots, he shakes his head and frowns in disgust. His expression shifts to that of a fierce warrior, the ruthless man whose hand doesn't shake if he has to take hold of his own curved dagger to slit an enemy's throat. He fires off some words in an authoritative voice and Kamal nods submissively.

"The most honourable Sheikh says that he is the lord of this territory and that all must obey him. He orders you to stay here to be his vizier in dealings with the infidels."

Antoine asks Kamal to translate his reply as carefully as possible.

"What you are offering me is the highest honour, Esteemed Sheikh. I respect your authority and I desire nothing more than to carry out your orders, wise as always, but I cannot remain, magnificent Abdul Okri."

A trace of concern appears on the translator's face.

"The Sheikh will be offended. He must be obeyed."

"And I won't disobey him. Translate this for the honourable Sheikh: My greatest wish is to obey your orders to the letter, but the conditions for my remaining here are not favourable. On the contrary. They are extraordinarily propitious for my departure. And so it would be a very wise decision on your part to order me to leave. In this way, you would absolutely be obeyed."

Kamal translates a long shower of words in the language of the desert. Afterward, the Sheikh remains pensive for a moment. Everyone waits anxiously and the only sound to be heard is that of the choppy waves rolling onto the beach. Finally, the Sheikh speaks. There's pride in his words, and in his eyes, the brightness of the campfires that light up the night. Young Kamal translates word for word:

"I name you Flying Ambassador of our people throughout the world. I order you to leave immediately to carry out your task!"

CHAPTER 59

Casablanca (Morocco), 1931

ANTOINE DE SAINT-EXUPÉRY

THE SAINT-EXUPÉRYS HAVE INVITED BOUCHARD, an engineer who works for a powerful oil company, to dine at their home in Casablanca.

"Dear Bouchard!"

Consuelo greets him without even pausing in her scolding of a servant. It is noon, and lunch isn't ready yet. In reality, the pantry is empty. Antoine appears, unshaven and his hair untidy, as if he'd just got out of bed.

"Antoine, there's no food in the house!"

He smiles.

"Engineer Bouchard is an understanding friend, right?"

The man, feeling somewhere between amused and bewildered, agrees. Not only is there no food, there isn't a single coin in the bowl in which Antoine deposits his weekly pay. Consuelo grabs her hat and clings to her guest's arm.

"Do you like cheese?"

"Yes, madame. Very much."

"Accompany me, Monsieur Bouchard. There's a wonderful shop just next door."

"Perfect!" shouts Antoine. "I'll start opening the wine."

"There's none left! We'll bring wine, too."

Consuelo has the rare ability of knowing her way around cities, going shopping, and even eating in the most exclusive restaurants without carrying a single franc with her. She's the Comtesse de Saint-Exupéry, naturally. She's the one bestowing her honour on the restaurants and stores she visits. Her husband will be along to pay. Or, as in this case, there's always a gentleman delighted to act as husband, when it comes to a lady like her.

"Your husband's occupation as aviator is extraordinary," the engineer tells her as they return from the store.

"What I'd like is for him to be a minister!"

As they reach the apartment, loaded with cheeses, little pistachio cakes, dates, sesame seed bread, and wine, they're met by a messenger from the telegraph office. Antoine reads the telegram out loud: "'Monsieur Antoine de Saint-Exupéry, By way of this message, we inform you that your novel, *Night Flight* has been selected by the Jury in Paris as the winner of the 1931 Prix Femina for novels . . .'"

"Monsieur Bouchard!" exclaims an ecstatic Consuelo. "You'll have to accompany me again. We must toast this with champagne!"

It's a classic, freezing cold December day in Paris that year of 1931. Inside the luxurious Hotel Lutetia, a bellhop is arranging red armchairs on a shiny checkered floor, while the snooty receptionist notes down the names of the most recent guests in careful handwriting in a register. He looks up with a smile as he senses someone approaching the desk, but then the smile twists into a merely mechanical welcome. He doesn't know if the person in front of him is a guest or a vagrant: A large individual with bags under his eyes, a three-day beard blackened by a layer of soot, a blazer as wrinkled as a rag, grease marks on his trousers, and dusty, military-style boots.

"How can I help you, monsieur?" he asks suspiciously.

"I have a room reserved in my name."

The receptionist can't avoid raising his eyebrows.

"I'm Monsieur Antoine de Saint-Exupéry."

The receptionist looks disdainfully at his list. The man doesn't just have a room reserved—he has the presidential suite! He looks in amazement at this person who is presumably the guest of honour at the elegant literary gala being hosted that night by the mayor of the city.

The company has given him permission to pick up his prize, but he's had to fly from Casablanca to Toulouse on the twenty-three-hour-long mail route, buffeted by a storm over the strait, sleeping just a few hours in Alicante, shivering with cold over the Pyrenees, and avoiding storm clouds over Carcassonne. He reached Montaudran with just enough time to catch the train to Paris for the gala award ceremony.

"Send a barber to my room. And have the bellhop go and buy me two shirts with stiff collars in the largest size, and two ties. And have the housekeeper come and pick up my suit and iron it."

Someone appears in the lobby.

"Papou! You look like a castaway!" Consuelo, who arrived by train the day before, throws herself into his arms.

"I feel rescued now that you're here."

While he is being shaved, he tries to think of something to say at the ceremony. He hates this type of event. No matter how hard he attempts to memorise a few sentences, he forgets them as soon as he steps onto the podium. He has never known how to say a few polite sentences. He can spend hours telling lengthy stories, but he has no idea how to present three formulaic sentences.

He thrusts his hand in his pocket and feels something rustle. It's Mermoz's telegram. He's read it ten or fifteen times: HEARTFELT CONGRATULATIONS ON YOUR PRIZE. YOUR FRIEND, JEAN MERMOZ. The solidity of friends like Mermoz rescues him from the comedy of pretence awaiting him this evening, when he'll have to smile at people who mean nothing to him and to whom, for all their song and dance, he means nothing either.

It's a sterile tarantella!

People will drink cups of punch and listen to him unwillingly, wanting the formalities of awarding the prize to finish soon, so they can go back to their conversations about common acquaintances or business. But what is he going to say? He can't explain to them the joy he feels up in the sky. He can't, in a dining room illuminated by sumptuous chandeliers above tables with fine tablecloths, tell them how, in the total darkness of the night, after flying over 100,000 hectares less inhabited than the sea, an isolated farm appears, which seems to carry its tiny cargo of human lives in this sea of fields. Far better that he simply say thank you, that he feels very honoured, and nothing more. A book about the night, and about what makes us eternal, means nothing at this sort of ceremony for literature which is more like a sporting event.

He leaves his room in search of tobacco and finds a journalist standing guard in the corridor with a photographer. Before Antoine can say a word, the photographer takes a picture using a flash which leaves him stunned. The journalist works for a prestigious literary magazine and looks at Antoine suspiciously. With a malice born of his desire to highlight that Antoine is an amateur writer who doesn't really belong in the world of literary intellectuals, he asks impertinently:

"How is it possible to be both a pilot and a writer?"

Antoine replies with a shrug: "What's the difference?"

CHAPTER 60

★

Paris, 1932

JEAN MERMOZ

MERMOZ IS AGAIN MOVING FASTER than his dreams, which he leaves behind. The Bernard 18 cuts through the cirrus clouds as if they were butter.

After Daurat's firing, the highest levels of the company sent Mermoz placatory messages: They have great plans for his future. But as always, those in their offices who want to flatter Mermoz know nothing about him. He doesn't want positions or honours; he wants planes that cross the Atlantic. That's when the smiles and the backslapping end. They talk to him about the financial difficulties the company is going through and they give him the runaround. If they think that's how to discourage him, they're greatly mistaken.

He's moved heaven and earth until he's found an aircraft manufacturer, Adolphe Bernard, who sees an opportunity to make himself known internationally by putting his new prototype with its powerful engine in the hands of France's most famous pilot.

Mermoz returns from Algiers, that part of France which burns with white light and mosques. He wants the Bernard 18 to be officially certified, but in order for that to happen, he has to find a way for it to pass a long-distance test flight. And the ministry is not going to make it easy for him: Before it would authorise his long-distance flight from Paris to New York, he had to demonstrate the reliability of the new machine in a closed-circuit test flight around Oran in Algeria. Not only is the ministry refusing to assist him with a grant, but they are putting hurdles in his path. Rather than getting furious, he has decided that each time they put an obstacle in front of him, he'll jump over it. They wanted a test of the plane's endurance that would be internationally comparable and now he's returning from Oran with a new world record for length of flight on a closed circuit, a flight of fifty-seven hours. Fifty-seven hours of stress is a lot, but Mermoz doesn't feel tired. He's jumped over this bureaucratic hurdle and now the road to America has reopened. He's going to risk the Bernard, his record, and his own life to establish a route over the Atlantic along which letters will travel between Europe and America.

When he climbs out of the plane and jumps down onto the runway, reporters who have been informed of the new record are waiting for him, and they take flash photos. He ignores the voices asking him to pose. He's not in the mood, despite his success. For other pilots, this sort of record is the achievement of a lifetime; for Mermoz, it's nothing more than a formality in order to go further, to do something that goes beyond himself: a triumph for an entire society, for an entire country. Mermoz scares off the reporters, the inquisitive, and the sycophants with a surly gesture, and heads to the pilots' room where Gilberte is waiting for him.

As she watches him coming toward her, with his leather bomber jacket over his shirt and tie, and his blond hair mussed, Gilberte thinks he's the handsomest man in the world. Another person waiting for him next to Gilberte gets up from a bench. It's Pierre, her brother, who's already turned eighteen.

"Gilberte said I could come along with her! She told me you might show me your plane."

Mermoz doesn't conceal his irritation. He's tired and his head is buzzing with news about the company.

"Another day."

The young man nods vigorously, afraid of annoying his important brother-in-law and wanting to please him. "Of course, Jean. My apologies. Another day, of course."

Mermoz notices his excessively spruced-up hairstyle, all the hair slicked back with a great deal of brilliantine to make him look older. Whenever Pierre meets Mermoz, he asks him for stories about flying, and shyly confesses that he wants to be a pilot. Mermoz gives a deep sigh, then puts his hands on his hips and goes back to being The Great Mermoz that everyone expects:

"Pierre, don't stand there stunned. Didn't you want to see the Bernard?"

"You know something, Jean?"

"What?"

"Next week, I start my military service. I've asked to be posted to aviation as a volunteer, like you did."

"That's fantastic!"

As the two of them walk over to the Bernard, the young man lowers his head, distressed.

"You have to speak to Gilberte. She's angry with me. She says I'm too young to start flying. Doesn't she realise how old I am?"

"She's your older sister. No matter how old you are, you'll always seem too young to her."

Mermoz punches him gently on the arm, and Pierre smiles. Mermoz asks himself what sort of world awaits these future pilots given the lack of attention paid by the politicians to their workers in the skies. He recognises the excitement in the boy's eyes as he sits in the pilot's seat and strokes the joystick and dials.

"Dammit! Let's fly!"

"Do you have permission to fly?"

"I've just given it to myself."

They take off. Mermoz looks out of the corner of his eye at his young brother-in-law, whose mouth is hanging open in amazement, and he becomes reconciled again to his country. He'll fight the fight for Pierre and young people like him who don't want a country of servants and bureaucrats.

In the weeks that follow, he gets together with deputies, officials in the Air Ministry, and newspaper editors in chief. He invites them to eat lobster in expensive restaurants; he has them taste aged cognacs; he talks to them about the bridge that could be built across the ocean, of the air race which France already leads, ahead of the English and the Germans, of the school of sacrifice and service that the airmail business is to young men.

He accepts invitations to dinners with the upper class, where he pretends to have a good time. He and Gilberte attend charity raffles organised by the wives of influential politicians. He takes advantage of every opportunity to talk about what he sees as the facts. Everyone listens to him, but nobody pays attention.

Months go by, and the situation in the company is becoming more and more disastrous. Damaged planes aren't repaired, salary payments are delayed, and personnel who retire aren't replaced. Some routes stop being covered, and in South America, there are sections of routes that are on the point of losing their government concessions because they aren't being developed. The Italians, the Germans, and the Dutch are rubbing their hands with delight at the loss of momentum in French aviation.

Mermoz sends a telegram to Antoine in Casablanca: LOTS OF CON-
VERSATIONS; NO OUTCOMES. NOBODY TAKING RESPONSIBILITY FOR COMPANY.
THEY ARE LETTING IT COLLAPSE. I'M PULLING ALL STRINGS WITH MINIMAL
SUCCESS. I'M NOT GIVING UP. J.M.

Antoine replies from his forced exile in Morocco, but he doesn't
know how to write telegrams. They're too short; the required words
don't fit. He sends a letter: *Pulling the strings of those sorts of people with
little result is normal. They are puppets with rag hearts. You mustn't give up.
If you don't give up, you'll never be defeated.* He also tells Mermoz how he
feels in Casablanca, in the middle of nowhere. He sends him a thousand
embraces and mountains of small drawings: laughing foxes, wise old
men smoking pipes, toy planes.

In the midst of the mess at the company, Mermoz is posted to the
Toulouse-Alicante leg. Coming back to Le Grand Balcon is like a small
celebration; the owners welcome him like an unruly nephew returned
from distant lands. In the modest dining room, half empty because of
the reduced activity at the aerodrome, they serve him meat pies and
chicken noodle soup in tureens that look like museum pieces. Mermoz
hasn't eaten such exquisite feasts in any of the luxurious Parisian salons
where he's attended formal dinners prepared by fashionable chefs.

But nothing can rid him of his obsession of winning the North
Atlantic connection for France. He has the option of going it alone,
but when he visits the manufacturer, a distressed Monsieur Bernard
confesses that he can't make the necessary changes to the Bernard 18
for the transoceanic flight because his company is in the red. Mermoz
offers to pay for them out of his own pocket. He sells his Potez plane
and even his sports car.

Gilberte wordlessly agrees to his money management without any
objections. She also notices his restlessness with concern; he's like a
caged animal when he's at home. So, it doesn't strike her as a bad idea
that he do the Algiers route and spend some time away. Moreover, in

Algiers, Jean can visit her brother, Pierre, who is over there doing a pilot's course. Her brother tells her with excitement of the occasions when Jean comes to visit. He explains that the soldiers on guard duty stand to attention when Mermoz enters the barracks, as if he were a major. His greatest wish is that his brother-in-law feel proud of him.

Mermoz is like a coffeepot sitting over a high flame. He restrains himself, putting on a good face at social gatherings and at meetings with politicians who receive him with such politeness that it makes him even more irritated. They agree with him about everything, they say "Yes"; they tell him they'll look into doing something. But he can see in their eyes that they don't care about the company, the efforts of the staff, Africa, America . . . They don't care about history. Coffee pots sometimes explode.

An Italian squadron led by Italo Balbo, Marshall of the Air Force, majestically flies across the Atlantic, and its members are received in Brazil as heroes. Italy is waving its flag as the vanguard of international aviation, while France's Air Ministry, with its departments and subsecretariats, is taking a nap.

He asks for an urgent meeting with the secretary-general of the Air Ministry, and when he enters the man's office and is invited to sit down, he refuses; he prefers to remain standing. He's no longer there to persuade, rather to threaten.

"You are dumping years of work on the creation of commercial air routes! This is a disgrace for France!"

"The airline company which you appreciate so much is a hugely loss-making enterprise. It's a lost cause. France has other priorities."

"You have to increase the speed of the mail delivery. We could transport triple the mail, if we only renovated half the fleet. The new planes would be paid off in two years."

The politician looks bored.

"Minister Cot's plan to create an alliance with Lufthansa is a slap

365

in the face of the French pilots and mechanics and their work. They've put their lives on the line to put in place the best airmail system in the world. And you're going to hand over all that effort to the Germans as a gift?"

"That is a matter of great political importance. Do yourself a favour. Leave such strategic decisions in the hands of the experts."

"Experts?" Mermoz's gaze sweeps the office: good quality paintings, good quality mahogany furniture, good quality Cuban cigars on top of the desk. "You mean experts at living well at the citizens' expense."

"I don't have to put up with such rudeness!"

"Secretary, sir, I have to recognise that you are an expert in something—mediocrity."

Mermoz's door slam echoes throughout Paris.

CHAPTER 61

Casablanca (Morocco), 1932

ANTOINE DE SAINT-EXUPÉRY, JEAN MERMOZ, AND HENRI GUILLAUMET

THE PRIX FEMINA HAS GENERATED a storm of radio interviews, front covers of illustrated magazines, and banquets with elite associations. Antoine reacts to all this fuss with a mixture of bewilderment and goodwill. It's hard to resist the friendliness of strangers, not to mention feasts in expensive restaurants. It's difficult not to become infected by the flattery. Consuelo is delighted, and invests part of the prize money in renovating her wardrobe. When the time comes for Antoine to return to his post as a pilot in Casablanca, she tells him that she can't leave Paris.

"The dresses I have bought are only appropriate for this city!"

Antoine returns alone to Casablanca, to his apartment behind the Place de France, but during the weeks that follow, everything will get worse. He doesn't realise until the third or fourth time that all conversation stops when he walks into the pilots' room to have a coffee.

367

Everyone is suddenly in a hurry, and he's left on his own. The penny drops one afternoon when a pilot by the name of Allard is waiting for him so he can fly on with the mail to Málaga, and Antoine arrives twenty minutes late.

He climbs down from the cockpit with a smile, but his colleague has a sour look on his face.

"They'll fine you, Saint-Ex."

"Fine."

Then Allard looks at him and speaks to him with such contempt that it stuns Antoine.

"Of course, but you're an aristocrat and a writer; you can afford it."

Allard takes off, leaving Antoine standing stock-still on the runway. Once in the office, he sits down next to the airfield manager, a retired pilot, bearded and overweight, who smokes a pipe and has the air of an ancient mariner. Antoine asks him to tell him what they are saying about him. The man shifts about uncomfortably in his chair. He takes forever to choose his words.

"They interview you on the radio, your photograph appears in the society pages of the papers. You're a celebrity!"

The retired pilot is trying to compliment Antoine, but all he does is put lead in his pockets.

"But I'm not a celebrity, I'm a pilot."

"Try to understand the boys. It's not that they don't like you, it's just that they see you as different, from another world."

Antoine sighs.

He covers the Oran-Marseilles route for a few weeks. In Marseilles, he catches up again with Mermoz, who has been posted there between test flights of the transoceanic prototypes. One night, they end up together in Marseilles with no flights scheduled for either of them. They trawl through the port area, go into taverns and flirt with all the girls, recite classical poems and invent others on the fly, close the late-night bars and open the ones where the stevedores drink firewater for breakfast. They buy two dozen flowers at a florist's that opens early and hand them out to the women who cross their path. But daylight extinguishes their happiness and they feel a deep fatigue. When they say goodbye, they both feel that nothing will ever be the same again.

Very soon, Antoine is posted back to Casablanca, and, with a hint of paranoia, he thinks the company doesn't want him near Mermoz. He asks for leave to go to France to visit his mother and is refused. He again senses the coldness of some of his fellow pilots. There are days when nobody sits at his table to share a coffee. He can't understand it; it just doesn't seem fair to him.

On one of those grey days, he gets a telegram from Guillaumet to let him know that he'll be stopping over in Casablanca with a route inspector and will have a few hours to spare. Antoine feels immensely happy. He even goes for a haircut that morning, as if he were getting ready for a date. Henri's care and affection for him is one of his greatest delights.

They arrange to meet in a local café that smells of boiled mint. It's a brilliant day and the huge windows look out over a square full of stalls where the merchants cry out their wares. Guillaumet arrives in a brown suit that's too big for him. When Antoine sees him, he thinks that his elegance is of a different kind, a moral elegance, the elegance of some-one who never disappoints at essential moments. They embrace.

During the time they are together, Antoine, starved of company, doesn't stop talking.

"I wish I hadn't written that stupid book! What use are literary prizes and the flattery of people who mean nothing to me, if my own colleagues despise me?"

He tells Guillaumet, perhaps with slight exaggeration, about the baleful looks of his fellow pilots and the intrigues behind his back. "Do you believe what they say—that I'm a snob? Please, tell me the truth!"

"Since when is it a crime to be a snob?" Guillaumet replies with a smile. "Can't every person be what they want to be?"

"So you do think I'm a snob?"

"Of course not!"

Antoine shakes his head. He sighs and asks for a cognac. "Tell me the truth, Henri."

"Of course."

"Do you promise to tell me the truth?"

"Absolutely."

"The truth?"

"I've already said I will."

Antoine twirls his wide glass and watches the liquor swirling inside it. "Do you think I've betrayed something important to our profession by writing my books?"

"What nonsense!"

"But some of them think so. They think I've written this book to make myself important, as if I were better than them, which I'm not, of course. I know that any one of them is a better pilot than me."

"Don't torment yourself. They'll get over it. When they know you better, they'll know what you're like."

"And what am I like, Henri?"

"Someone who's too concerned about what others think."

Guillaumet has to continue his flight to the next stopover, so they set off for the airport, crossing unlit, windy streets where the brightness of the moon shines on the whitewashed walls.

"Henri, I haven't even asked you about Noëlle. How is she?"

"Fabulous."

"I've only talked about me. I know nothing of your current life, Henri, and now we have to say goodbye. You must forgive this egoist."

Guillaumet laughs. "My life continues to be the same as always."

"And are you happy?"

"Of course I'm happy. Why do you always ask me this?"

"Because if you're happy, then I'll also be a little happy."

One afternoon when Antoine should go to the airfield, for the first time in his life he doesn't want to do so. He's lost the desire to climb into a plane. And that definitely infuriates him: They've snatched away the thrill. And so, in his fury, he sends a letter asking for a new posting immediately, or he'll be obliged to hand in his resignation. *Those new management pen pushers will see who they're playing with.*

By return mail, management sends him a cheque to cover a miserable severance settlement, together with the termination of his contract. They've accepted his resignation with dizzying speed, when it was just a temper tantrum to grab their attention. After all these years, they farewell him with a bank cheque.

His first reaction is disbelief.

He goes to his desk to write a letter to the management of the company, to resolve the misunderstanding. But when he sits down in front of the sheet of paper, his hand is only capable of drawing sad lambs. What's he going to say to them? That his threat of resigning, if they didn't accept his demand for a transfer, was a joke? Will he beg them to rehire him? How much will he have to humiliate himself?

Mermoz and Guillaumet offer to intercede with the current management on his behalf, but Antoine dissuades them; he's too proud to accept their offer. In any event, too much has changed since Monsieur Daurat left and the company was nationalised, and directors and managers who want to know nothing about aviation pioneers, only about finances, have crawled out from under stones. Aviation was born as an adventure, but it has started to turn into a business.

CHAPTER 62

★

Paris, 1933

Jean Mermoz

Mermoz returns from a flight with the noise of the wind still echoing in his ears. It's eight o'clock and Gilberte will be waiting for him with dinner ready. He's starving! When he gets home, he's surprised to find the lights off. The house is cold, the table hasn't even been set. He calls out loudly to Gilberte, but there's no answer. A slight creak in the bedroom sends him in that direction.

He turns on the light switch and she's sitting in the rocking chair. She's rocking back and forth slowly and her eyes are open as wide as those of someone who has seen what should never be seen.

"What's the matter? Are you all right?"

"Am I all right?" Gilberte's pause is so long that it augurs nothing good. "*Now* you ask me if I'm feeling all right."

There's a hint of a smile, but it's actually a grimace of pain. Mermoz notices she's holding a piece of paper in her fingers. He holds out his hand so he can read it.

It's a telegram from the Ministry of Defence. There are polite formulas, routine expressions of sorrow, formalities. Pierre Chazottes died at the Guelma Fort as a result of an accident while undertaking a training flight.

Mermoz closes his eyes. He crushes the paper with the rage with which he would wring God's neck if He were standing in front of him. Pierre wasn't even twenty years old. Now he never will be.

"Gilberte . . ."

She holds up her hand and orders him to be quiet. For the first time ever, she is the one who is going to speak first. Her voice emerges, not from her throat, but from some cavernous other place.

"We were happy in Argentina. Pierre wanted to be a wood trader. But that all disappeared. Aviation, that damned aviation, has done nothing more than convert me into a lonely woman, and it has now taken away my only brother."

"I understand your pain."

"You understand my pain?" And she stares at him with a wild look in her eyes that he has never seen before. "You live in your own world. What do you know of my pain?"

"Lie down. I'll make you a lime-flower tea. You need to rest. I'll take care of everything."

"Take care of everything . . ."

She laughs, either like a madwoman or someone desperately sane. Gilberte begins to speak to Mermoz as she's never spoken to him before. The huge knot of silence explodes in a dark flood that obliterates everything. Reproaches, hurt, fury, insults. Mermoz withstands her words with the same icy stoicism with which he weathers a hailstorm at 4,000 metres. She throws in his face his absences, and the agony of waiting for his flights, as well as all the other waiting; the cold meals; the red stains on his clothes; and Pierre, so impressionable, so vulnerable to Mermoz's deeds.

"You could have dissuaded him from enlisting as a pilot to imitate you, but you didn't feel like doing that because The Great Mermoz knows no fear. And now Pierre is dead, and it's because of you."

Mermoz says nothing; for once, he's the one who keeps quiet. He respects her grief, but he's not prepared to assume the death of her brother as his own burden.

The rift that has opened in their marriage is a precipice. During the weeks that follow, the house is an igloo. Flying is his only escape— taking off from the runway, rising up, leaving the daily misfortunes down below and stubbornly holding on to his mission. The mission which gives meaning to everything else: opening a corridor over the ocean; forging ahead.

In Marseilles, when Mermoz gets back from a flight on the Algiers route, someone is waiting for him in the pilots' room, someone who, at 11 a.m., is drinking a red vermouth and picking at a plate of olives.

"Henri! What the devil are you doing having such an early aperitif?"

"Since when do you look at the clock when you're having a good time?"

Mermoz guffaws. He can't remember how long it's been since he last laughed.

They eat in a cheap restaurant in the port area that smells of sour beer. At one of the tables at the back, two sailors, their huge limbs tattooed with anchors, arm wrestle while other mariners cheer them on and exchange bets. The closure of the Chile route has brought Guillaumet back to Europe.

"What have you heard of Monsieur Daurat?"

"I always knew he wouldn't go under. He's a tough nut. He's suing the company for wrongful dismissal, and if he wins, they'll have to reinstate him or give him a pile of money. Old Latécoère has hired him to work as a manager in his plane factory."

"I'm delighted."

"He's not the sort to sit back and do nothing, Henri. He's not like our trivial politicians. You know something? I was in Rome last week."

"Why so?"

"Italo Balbo, their Marshall of the Air Force, sent an invitation to all the pilots who have crossed the Atlantic. It was sensational. You should have seen how it was organised . . . on a large scale! They treated us pilots like leading lights. They had me give a talk to about a hundred people through an interpreter. I spoke, and they listened respectfully."

"I don't know what to think of that Fascist Party which has assumed power."

"You can think what you like, but you should have seen the pilots' school in Orbetello, and the aircraft factories. Immaculate, all of it."

"There are good manufacturers here, too."

"The best! But here, the government spits in the faces of us pilots, while there, they set up a school and spare no expense, and the authorities show it to you as if it were a national monument. Do you know what the difference is?"

"Tell me."

"They are proud of their aviators over there. The country's top representative for aviation matters, Balbo, is a first-class pilot. Here, in the Air Ministry you only have pen pushers and the odd soldier who won his medals playing cards in the officers' club."

"You can ask for Italian naturalization. Italian women are beautiful, although they say they have fiery personalities."

"What women! They're all on fire. You should see the way they talk loudly and gesticulate like men. But you've changed the topic!"

"Is there any other topic?"

Guillaumet succeeds in getting Mermoz to laugh. They both laugh. They need to laugh. As long as they laugh, they can't be defeated.

CHAPTER 63

★

Paris, 1933

ANTOINE DE SAINT-EXUPÉRY AND JEAN MERMOZ

ANTOINE, UNEMPLOYED AND IN PARIS, hasn't flown for months. He prefers to write in cafés rather than at home where Consuelo displays the chaos of her pastimes: sculpture, painting, books, clothes . . . She's interested in everything, and everything bores her. People are always visiting their apartment and there's no way of finding a bit of peace. Compared with his home, the bustle of a café is music that helps him to concentrate. At those times when inspiration escapes him, there are always newspapers to read and customers to look at—strange men and enigmatic women for whom he invents turbulent lives hidden behind their respectable appearances.

Gaston Gallimard has given him a contract for three new books, but there's no sign of him finishing even the first one. For every page he finds acceptable, he throws out eight; for every line he writes, he does four drawings.

He has several scrunched-up sheets of paper spread out on the table alongside the leather notebook in which he jots things down. Most of his friends and acquaintances know that he spends many hours in this café and drop by to visit him. On this particular afternoon, a hand rests on his shoulder. It's a rock-heavy hand.

"Jean!"

The waiter arrives quickly with a chair.

"What will Monsieur have to drink?"

"Absinthe, please."

"Make that two," adds Antoine.

"Make it four!"

Antoine takes note of his friend's very fashionable houndstooth suit.

"You're looking well."

"I'm well on the outside, but I'm disgusted on the inside. This whole business of the company has been a dirty political trick. The government specifically didn't want to renew Aéropostale's loan so they could bury it."

"The government sinks the best aviation company in the country?"

"It has been a huge political game. Aéropostale belonged to Bouilloux-Lafont and they didn't want any one individual to have all that power in his hands."

"So who's in charge now?"

"There isn't a single boss. The management is in chaos; it's all a mishmash of departments and subdepartments, secretariats and subsecretariats. I'm trying to get to the very top to talk about your case."

"Jean! You needn't do that!"

"Dammit, how can I not do it? But they're giving me the runaround."

Antoine nods, a sudden sadness in his eyes under his heavy eyelids.

"In the end, I did speak with Faure, the deputy director-general of operational finances. It's the closest I've come to a boss who was prepared to listen to me. I've managed to extract an appointment for you from him. He'll meet you on the thirtieth in his office."

"That's great news! We have to celebrate!"

Mermoz holds up his hand. "He's not easy to get along with."

"I'll tame him."

A few days later, Antoine enters the new home of Aéropostale in Paris. The marble reception desk shines, the tile floor is like a mirror, the ceilings are very high. Everything is so new that he feels old.

Eventually, after a period of time that seems very lengthy to him, they tell him that the deputy director-general of operational finances will receive him. What surprises him most about the office to which he is taken is not the hunting scenes hanging on the wall or the huge walnut desk, but the silence. He remembers Daurat's office, the desk covered with a thousand files and reports, phones ringing, assistants entering with messages, and the noise of work being carried out on the runways on the other side of the window. Here the atmosphere of a notary's office reigns.

Faure sits with his head resting against the comfortable back of his swivel chair, looking at Antoine with undisguised indifference. "Go ahead."

"I would like you to consider my reinstatement to the company."

"The deadline for applications closed last February."

"Monsieur Faure, I have been a pilot on the airmail route flying between Spain, Africa, and South America. I have landed in the desert, rebels have fired on me, I have rescued French, Spanish, and Uruguayan pilots, I have been airfield manager in a corner of the Sahara, I inaugurated the Patagonia route . . ."

"Your old stories are very entertaining, but this is a company that looks to the future, not to the past."

"This company has been my home."

Faure shrugs.

"Send a request in writing."

"I have already sent five."

Faure shrugs again. "We have to treat every request with absolute respect for the company regulations approved by the Air Ministry, without exception. Were you perhaps expecting preferential treatment because you're a celebrity who appears in the social section of the newspapers? We take our work seriously!"

Antoine stands up, says goodbye without looking at him, and leaves. It doesn't matter that they don't want him back; he no longer wants to return.

CHAPTER 64

★

Paris-Toulouse, 1933

JEAN MERMOZ

NOBODY DARES TO APPROACH THE man at the end of the bar who is drinking whisky as if it were water. The waiter refills his glass without saying a word, obeying the man's gestures.

Mermoz shakes the ice so that it tinkles against the side of his glass and lifts it to his ear as if it were a shell. He'd like to hear a sign. He's reached a dead end both with Gilberte and his task of linking the mail between Europe and America across the Atlantic.

The Bernard 18 has been a disaster in the test flights carrying cargo. Empty, the plane went like an arrow, but when loaded, the structure became unbalanced. At 3,000 metres, it started to shake like a baby chick in winter. They would have to invest a lot of money in modifications to convert that thoroughbred into a mail-carrying mule, but the supply of money has been shut off. He has already lost all his savings on that plane, and he's now in the red. He can go back to the ministry and beg the secretaries and deputy secretaries, but that flea circus disgusts him.

He heads out onto the street. He doesn't want to go home. When he and Gilberte speak to each other, the words hang in the air like a bad smell. They've agreed he'll look for an apartment in Paris and that's what he's going to do without further delay.

In the new aviation organisational chart the ministry is putting together, they'd happily give Mermoz a position as inspector or manager of anything. The system has two ways of neutralizing anyone who rebels against it: Insignificant revolutionaries are punished, squashed; dangerous revolutionaries are given responsibility.

He's gone back to visiting people with influence, being hypocritically friendly toward people who are wealthy or well placed in the ministry, but all he's offered are cups of tea and flattery, both of which are worthless. They tell him he's a hero. He'd like to ask them why, if he's a hero, France treats him like a nobody. With every passing week, he feels the bitterness growing inside him.

Sick of Paris, he asks to be posted to the Spain route and goes back to Toulouse to fly the Barcelona-Alicante leg. At Le Grand Balcon, the Márquez sisters are getting older and have closed a section of the hotel because it was becoming too much work.

On one of those afternoons, when he's sitting in the living room at Le Grand Balcon reading the paper, Madame Márquez informs him that he has a call, a long-distance call, from Paris.

One of the administrators responsible for the expropriation of the company suggests a meeting with an aeronautics engineer who, with the government's approval, is constructing a machine that could cross the Atlantic. And it meets all the safety requirements that the new French government regulations require for the establishment of a transoceanic mail route. Mermoz stands up. For a moment, he thinks it might be a joke and his eyebrows lift. He's tried dozens of initiatives with no outcome and suddenly someone up high is making a move. The person they tell him to see is a designer and manufacturer of prototypes called Couzinet.

At first glance, René Couzinet strikes Mermoz as one of those nerdy students who is all books but little experience. He looks a bit scruffy: he's wearing old shoes that need a polish, and a good, but wrinkled, suit with shiny patches at the elbows. But when he starts to speak, Mermoz realises he has someone sitting in front of him who is even more obsessed than he is. Couzinet stirs the cup of coffee they served him a while ago, and the swirling liquid holds his gaze. At first, he seems timid, but when he starts to talk about radial engines, crankshafts, angles of attack, calibration . . . he seems possessed. He is.

Couzinet believes that there's no point in building machines for long distances that crash if they lose an engine. He has designed a three-engine plane which he has called *Arc-en-Ciel*, or *Rainbow*. Not only can it keep flying without one engine, but the design also allows for a mechanic to work on repairing the faulty engine from inside the plane.

To reach this stage, Couzinet has had many prototypes explode, he has experienced considerable penury, including being hungry, and he has had to beg for investment. But all that is insignificant as soon as he takes out a piece of paper and a pencil and begins to draw a plane of enormous dimensions. Couzinet's enthusiasm infects Mermoz. The ghosts of despondency that have filled him with shadows and darkness dissipate as this new window on oceanic adventure opens.

Couzinet insists that they go to see the plane in the hangar. The *Arc-en-Ciel* 3 is a robust machine, a silvery heavy-lifter with three propellers. Its manufacturer strokes the fuselage sensually.

"Mermoz, we can leave for South America at the beginning of January."

"We can?"

"Did you think I was going to miss the opportunity?"

Thanks to a sea change in political negotiation, the reasons for which, as usual, are subterranean, what has for months been obstruction and negativity regarding Aéropostale's transoceanic adventure suddenly turns into a wide-open door. Authorisations are accelerated, money to get everything ready becomes available, and the flight plan to connect Europe and South America is approved, resuming the France-Senegal-Brazil route crossing the Atlantic at its narrowest point.

Within a few weeks, the *Arc-en-Ciel* with its 2,000 hp engines is roaring in the skies. It's on its first test flight across the Atlantic carrying mail, with Couzinet himself as a passenger. There was no way of convincing him that he was needlessly adding superfluous weight, and Mermoz has finally agreed to his coming. After all, he is the father of this flying creature. If they end up reaching their goal successfully, they'll have opened a door that cannot be closed. It's the flight that Mermoz has spent so many years waiting for, and as he takes off, he feels as calm as when he was rowing in the river at Tigre.

1,720 revolutions on the dash. All good.

Mermoz looks around him. Several hundred metres higher up, a colossal airship is heading in the same direction, but much more slowly. He lifts both arms and his shouts rise above the noise of the three engines.

"Auf Wiedersehen, you Krauts!"

The crew look up, among them Collenot, whom Mermoz has chosen to be the mechanic on the *Arc-en-Ciel*'s first Europe–South America flight. They look through the windows and see how first they catch up with, and then they leave behind, the zeppelin owned by Lufthansa, who wants to snatch France's domination of the South America route from them.

From his seat, Couzinet raises his voice to ask Mermoz if he has ever flown one of those dirigibles.

"You call that flying, Couzinet? That's driving a tractor!"

Fourteen hours after leaving Saint-Louis de Senegal, they calmly land at Natal.

Mermoz is happy, but he rejects the parties and the celebrations. When the manager of the aerodrome arrives to welcome him with a band of musicians, he waves his hand to frighten off their concert of crickets.

"I don't want musicians, I want mechanics! We haven't done anything yet. Tomorrow we have to leave with the mail for Buenos Aires.

And the next day, the reception in Buenos Aires is tremendous, with the aerodrome chock-full of people and a swarm of press photographers awaiting their arrival.

The head pilot's serious face and concerned attitude on this first test flight prove portentous. Back in Natal to begin the return transoceanic flight with the mail, the *Arc-en-Ciel* rumbles down the runway for too long without lifting off, and then a wheel sinks into the ground. On digging it out, they discover that the whole area is riddled with ant nests and the ground is not solid. They could take off in Buenos Aires with the tank only a quarter full, but in Natal with a full tank of 9,000 litres and a weight of 1,400 kilos, the three-engine plane, so reliable in the air, is a lump of metal on the ground and requires runways that can support its dead weight. For weeks, the *Arc-en-Ciel* remains stranded like a whale in Natal, until the runway is upgraded for its use.

Some newspapers write about the failure of the transoceanic route and Mermoz is fit to be tied. Those who praised excessively what was really a test flight, specifically to find out the potential shortcomings and resolve them, now attack him with everything they've got. They draw cruel caricatures of him on board a plane which is a giant snail and threaten to scare off the volatile will of the politicians.

To distract himself, Mermoz exercises frenetically. He eats six-egg omelets. Some nights, he goes back to laughing uproariously in Natal's

Ribeira district with shots of rum and bar girls. Sometimes, Mermoz feels dizzy at his own life, as if he were still on a train moving so quickly that everything has already been left behind.

The mail has taken months to travel back and forth. It's the failure many were waiting for to block his way.

On the return landing at the Senegal airfield, after an ocean crossing with one engine not working, and producing concern among the crew until they arrived safely, Mermoz receives the news that Aéropostale no longer exists as a company. The government has ordered the merger of several companies: Air Orient, Farman, Air Union, CIDNA, and Aéropostale. The new company, solely controlled by the government, will be called Air France.

He also receives a letter from Antoine covered in stick figures, telling him that people are asking him for prologues to books, articles for magazines, and even the writing of a film script, but that what he wants to do most is return to flying. Also, that Guillaumet has been posted to the Oran route. Mermoz isn't much of a letter writer, but he sends Antoine greetings via some colleagues.

The administrative battles worsen. Mermoz is summoned to top-level meetings with the new administrators of the great new state company; they invite him to gala cocktail events where the men wear morning coats and the women fan themselves, and they award him honourable mentions as a transoceanic pilot. But they don't listen to him: He doesn't want honours, he wants planes to go further.

Eventually, they put him in charge of the postal service between France and South America, but they don't provide him with a fleet of efficient planes: They put together some seaplanes and a few reconditioned conventional planes. It's a shoddy mess. But what horrifies Mermoz most is that the politicians are thrilled with their plan for an alliance with Germany's Lufthansa. At one of those parties attended by the minister of air, Pierre Cot, he approaches the huddle around Cot and asks if he could speak to him briefly alone. When a maid closes the door to the study and leaves them together, Mermoz exchanges his worldly expression for a more bitter one.

"How is it possible for the government to consider an aeronautical agreement with Lufthansa? You're going to hand over to the Germans all the routes we have opened with so much effort over the years? That is intolerable!"

"Your tone is also intolerable, Monsieur Mermoz. But I don't hold it against you because I know that you mean well. At times, politics is complex, believe me."

"My apologies, Monsieur Cot, I have nothing against you personally. But I have spent my youth clawing through the sky metre by metre, and I won't accept that the sacrifice of so many people will be handed over as a gift in exchange for who knows what perks."

"You are free to put up with it or stop putting up with it."

Mermoz leaves the study and retrieves his coat and hat. He goes straight to the newspaper *Paris-soir* to see his friend Joseph Kessel, a journalist who was an aviator during the war. Kessel admires Mermoz and quickly takes his side. From there, he goes to *Le Matin*. He does the rounds of the editorial departments of all the newspapers and begins a campaign opposing the accord with the German company, which generates a heated debate. There are those who argue that a soldier should be in charge of the Air Ministry rather than a civilian who has learned to fly since becoming minister by taking weekend lessons.

Mermoz doesn't want debates, he just wants to fly. One afternoon, when he's in a foul mood, he crosses paths with a retired Aéropostale pilot in the Place du Trocadéro. The man seems to be in a hurry, but he stops for a moment to greet him. He tells Mermoz that he's on his way to listen to some people who have fresh ideas for the country's regeneration and invites Mermoz to accompany him. Mermoz shrugs and decides to go along. In a cultural centre on Rue Copernic, they walk past a woman crocheting at the reception desk, some tables where men are playing cards, and arrive at the function room where every seat is occupied and people are standing at the back. A man in a suit, with a high forehead and short hair carefully combed with brilliantine, is speaking from the dais.

"Who is that?"

"It's the party president, Monsieur de la Rocque."

Someone turns around to specify: "Colonel de la Rocque." Others hiss at them to be quiet.

"The dehumanization of capitalism in connivance with a corrupt parliament is undermining the foundations of social justice in this country. Why do we need a parliament which is costing us hundreds of thousands of francs if it is not capable of defending the interests of our farmers? They are taking us to the edge of a precipice. And waiting for us at the bottom of that precipice are those communists who have no conscience, who convert people into cattle, who do not believe in either family or liberty. We must demand more respect from the politicians and a firm hand against those who threaten the workers, companies, and honourable people who make this country great. We cannot allow any more corruption or distractions from these communist politicians who despise the values which have made France great: liberty, justice, and the law. Moscow has very long tentacles. If we do not convert our many voices into a single voice, and we allow chaos to take control of everything, we will be weak. And weakness is death for a nation."

Enthusiastic applause interrupts his speech for a few seconds.

"In Germany, the National Socialist Party has managed to fire up a nation that had gone to sleep. Are we not capable of doing the same thing in France? Are they better than us? Here there is more than enough talent and pride to do it, and ten times over."

More applause. Mermoz doesn't applaud. He's hypnotised.

CHAPTER 65

★

Toulouse, 1934

ANTOINE DE SAINT-EXUPÉRY

ANTOINE HASN'T FLOWN FOR TWO years. One gloomy afternoon, as he's mechanically rereading an uninspiring book of poetry, he receives a telegram which instantly transports him to the past:

TURN UP NEXT WEEK AT LATÉCOÈRE FACTORY IN TOULOUSE. YOU START AS TEST PILOT FOR NEW PROTOTYPES. YOURS SINCERELY, M. DAURAT.

He throws the book into the air. "This telegram from Monsieur Daurat with no bombastic words really is poetry!"

Consuelo, immersed in a game of bridge with her friends, comes over to see what's happening.

"Daurat demands my presence in Toulouse to be a test pilot. Will you come with me?"

Consuelo opens her eyes wide, as if she were an owl.

"Toulouse? Absolutely not, darling. You know how I hate small cities. I hate anything small."

Antoine shakes his head in resignation. Her friends are insistently calling for Consuelo from the salon.

"I'm leaving for Montaudran."

"Right now?"

"I have, in fact, already gone."

Monsieur Daurat has a few more grey hairs and has put on a few kilos. But his burning eyes are still the same.

Antoine takes off in the new Laté 290 with its 650 hp engine and the mechanic, Michelet, watches him lift off the runway. He's only flown once and he fell asleep during the trip, but he's seen all the pilots leave, he's seen a few return, and he's seen others die crashing into the runway. He watches Monsieur Saint-Ex's wobbly takeoff and shakes his head from side to side. It's a miracle that he's still alive.

Antoine is expected to mark down how the plane performs during the flight, and has a notebook between his legs for that purpose. When he lands, the engineer and his assistant, who have been watching the flight carefully from the runway, ask him for his impressions.

"Not good beyond a certain speed."

"What speed?"

"Quite fast, before reaching maximum speed."

"From five thousand revolutions?"

"Could be. And it rolls."

"We saw that."

"To which side?"

"Well . . . the left."

The engineer and his assistant exchange a look. It had seemed to them that it was tilting to the right.

"Are you sure about which side? Why don't you check your notes in the flight book?"

Antoine takes out the notebook and, to the amazement of the

engineers, can't avoid blushing. The takeoff time has been jotted down and beyond that, there's just a heap of stick figures and drawings. No sign of any technical notes. The engineer frowns angrily.

Since the development of the Latés includes their conversion into seaplanes, Antoine is sent to the Saint-Laurent-de-la-Salanque airfield located beside the Leucate Lagoon in the southern department of Pyrénées-Orientales, to test planes on which the landing wheels have been replaced by floats.

He doesn't like the saltwater lagoon where they do the tests and he's bored by the drowsiness of Perpignan. Occasionally, on a Sunday afternoon, he sits with a glass of port to listen to an orchestra and watch the girls strolling by, all dressed up for the choreographed ballet which is provincial courtship.

Antoine takes advantage of a three-day pause in test flights, to allow for modifications to the three prototypes, to catch the train to Paris and surprise Consuelo.

When he arrives at the apartment in Rue de Chanaleilles, there's no one there. Scattered throughout the dining room are paintbrushes and the pottery which Consuelo devotes herself to embellishing with the Aztec motifs she likes so much. But there's a stillness in the house, as if it has been uninhabited for some time. Antoine waits anxiously all day, but she doesn't appear, not even during the night. He begins to think she has fallen ill and is in hospital. But before he starts ringing around all the hospitals in the city, he calls some mutual friends, and one of them explains that she's spending a few days in the country with artist friends. Which friends? He can't really say, or doesn't want to. It's in fact the house of an artist who calls himself Toboggan. Antoine leaves an angry note on the table in the salon asking her to let him know when she's back from her holidays.

Two days later, Consuelo calls him at his lodgings. She tells him she's been at the house of some friends.

"Friends? You mean in the house of that Toboggan!"

"Darling, there were other people there. The Calmettes, and Louis. You have a thing about Toboggan, because he's a painter. You can't abide artists!"

"What sort of an artist can an individual be who goes by a name as uncouth as Toboggan?"

"Darling, you are insufferable!" she replies, and he sighs, repentant.

"Forgive me. It's just that I feel lonely."

"It will soon be Christmas and we'll celebrate all the parties together. Remember, I am a Catholic. My God, I have to find figures to make a Nativity scene! Or better yet, I'll sculpt and paint them myself! Our friends will never have seen a Nativity like this one."

She finally manages to make Antoine laugh.

Just before Christmas, he happily accepts an assignment to fly a new Laté 293 torpedo floatplane prototype for the military to the navy base at Saint-Raphaël, near Saint-Tropez. He loves the Côte d'Azur, as does Consuelo. He sends her a telegram and asks her to meet him at the Continental hotel in Saint-Tropez.

His marriage reminds him of the roller coaster they've built in Brooklyn in the States, the one all the illustrated magazines have written about, not just because of his and Consuelo's physical distance and those friends of hers who are always fluttering around, but also because of his own inability to be faithful to her and to refuse to stop having affairs with any woman who smiles at him. But despite their endless hot-blooded confrontations, thinking about Consuelo lightens his bad mood, because their passionate reunions compensate for the absences.

He thinks about her as he takes off from the Leucate Lagoon and heads out over the sea. He's carrying passengers—an engineer, a navy officer, and Vergès, the mechanic. Flying up above that barren area, leaving behind routine flights, and making a wide turn toward open space inspire him. The vibration of these Latés is so much smaller than in the old Bréguets. Aviation has made astonishing technical advances, and engine breakdowns in flight are now rare. He crosses the French skies as if he were sliding across the snow in a sleigh. He descends next to the navy base, lulled by the tranquillity of the flight. He manoeuvres in such a relaxed manner that he forgets that the sea is not a runway on land and that this model of seaplane, because of its aerodynamics, requires a different angle of contact with the surface of the water. When the plane touches down, it comes to a sudden stop which causes one of the floats to break and the nose to drive into the water. The seaplane does a half somersault and lands upside down.

The impact dazes Antoine. The engineer manages to escape through the narrow opening earmarked for a machine gun, but that's just the spot where water starts to gush in. Before the plane overturned, the navy officer was able to open the evacuation hatch and get out. Antoine and Vergès are still inside as the Laté slowly begins to sink. Vergès manages to get to the wing to open the emergency door. He gets out and is immediately hauled up by the sailors on the navy vessel standing by to pick them up. The plane is already three-quarters submerged and there's still no sign of Antoine.

He hit his head during the landing; and in a daze in the middle of the watery gloom, he blindly advances, holding on to the windowsills and swallowing water until he reaches the tail of the plane, where he finds an air pocket and can breathe again. The glimmer of light from the door Vergés opened shows him the way. He inhales and swims underwater through a cabin which has turned into an aquarium until he reaches the opening and swims to the surface.

When they see his balding head appear and then his mouth opening and closing like a fish desperate for air, they all celebrate his salvation, although Antoine doesn't think there's much to celebrate.

The suite at the Continental, which should have been a love nest, becomes an infirmary. Consuelo looks after him for a few days until he recovers. She orders chicken consommés and reads him the most outlandish items of news in the paper to distract him. He allows himself to be spoiled, at times even pretending to feel worse than he really is so she'll make him chamomile tea with cognac. He'd like to spend a few more days being ill, as he used to do when he was a child and a mild fever was a passport to avoiding school, staying at home with his mother all to himself while he floated between clean sheets and cough syrups with a blackcurrant flavour.

But reality arrives with his recovery, and it doesn't exactly have a blackcurrant taste. There's no way that sinking a test plane and nearly drowning several passengers because of carelessness can pass unnoticed. He feels grieved. He doesn't care about the plane and the passengers' fright. What pains him is that he's let Monsieur Daurat down.

He writes a letter to his boss. He tears it up. Then another. He crumples it like an accordion. Another. That also ends up in the basket. When the basket is overflowing and bits of paper are scattered all over the floor, he realises that he has to go to Toulouse in person to see Daurat. Travelling through France in a car is soothing. Geometric fields spread out on both sides of the road. Seen through the windows, they hide the toughness of rural life and only show cultivated land looking like ironed bedsheets. When he turns off near Toulouse and heads down the road signposted AERODROME, he has a feeling he's seeing it for the last time. He's filled with a mellow nostalgia as he passes the old Aéropostale facilities. He drives on until he reaches the Latécoère workshops, an industrious beehive where they build planes. He finds Daurat in his office. He no longer supervises an international air route but he still looks out of the window through which, at an angle, he can catch sight of the airfield runway, as if he were still waiting for the afternoon mail.

"Monsieur Daurat . . ."

His boss looks at him without a word, and it's impossible to read anything into that look. He has spent his life playing poker with human lives.

"I've come to present my irrevocable resignation, to tell you that I am truly sorry, and that the accident was entirely my fault."

The director doesn't move a muscle. Nor does he take a drag of his cigarette, which is sending out smoke signals from his hand.

But it's not an uncomfortable silence. The two share a mutual understanding of each other. Daurat isn't going to act out the drama of threatening to reject his resignation. A letter of resignation is Antoine's way of avoiding the need for Daurat to fire him, for him to be dismissed.

"Saint-Exupéry, you are a gentleman of honour to the end."

Antoine flashes one of those feeble smiles you give when there's nothing to celebrate. Women have often told him that he's a gentleman before they leave on the arm of someone else.

"I may be a gentleman, but I no longer know whose honour I'm defending."

Daurat looks at him impassively. He doesn't believe in melancholy. It's unproductive and detrimental to completing schedules and other tasks. Antoine puts out his hand and Daurat shakes it firmly. A moment later, he briskly turns his attention back to his desk and pretends to open folders, as if already busy with something else, thereby ending Antoine's visit. Antoine leaves the office shaking his head.

That old Monsieur Daurat . . .

Out of work again.

Once more, he returns to Paris with his hands in his pockets.

CHAPTER 66

★

Natal (Brazil), 1933

JEAN MERMOZ

ALTHOUGH HE HASN'T PERSUADED THE company to retire the sea-planes that are as heavy as elephants and provide him with adequate resources, Mermoz has brought together a team of pilots to maintain the postal link between Europe and South America, pushing vigorously across the Atlantic.

Once more, the Three Wise Men's lighthouse at the entrance to Natal winks at Mermoz. He greets it with a sweeping turn above the cliffs and arrives at the Potenji on time. As usual, if nothing untoward has come up, the *Comte de la Vaulx* will be refuelled, checked over during the night, and they'll leave with the return mail for Dakar in the morning.

When they land, the employees who have come in the barge to tow them to shore bring bad news. Fernández, the pilot who, together with his mechanic Nuno, was bringing the Argentinian, Uruguayan, and Brazilian mail from Bahía Blanca, has had an accident.

"How are they?"

"In hospital. But they had a narrow escape."

Mermoz grunts. As soon as he steps ashore, he gets into the ramshackle van that takes them to Natal's Parnamirim aerodrome. The Natal airport has grown considerably in recent times and Mermoz has to make his way through a dozen passengers who have arrived on a plane belonging to an Italian company that flies to Rio de Janeiro. The manager of the terminal informs Mermoz that the mail plane has indeed crashed at Caruaru, in the state of Pernambuco. Mermoz talks by radio to the Buenos Aires base. They tell him that they will send another plane to pick up the mailbags destined for Europe and held up at Caruaru, but their spare plane is under repair and it will take several days, perhaps a week.

"A week! Impossible!"

The radio operator and Collenot come in and find him pacing the office like a caged lion.

"We can't spend a week waiting here! People have paid to receive their mail on time. I'll go to Caruaru myself to get that mail!"

"It can't be done in a seaplane. Caruaru is in the interior."

"I'll drive."

"It's the rainy season. The roads are flooded. It's impossible to get through."

"Then I'll fly. Is there any company operating out of here that can take me to Caruaru?"

"I'm afraid not."

"What about the Italians?"

"I don't know . . ."

Before the man can finish speaking, Mermoz has already gone out the door like a rocket, and the others follow him.

A man wearing a cap and sporting an emblem with all the colours of the rainbow on his grubby shirt is in charge of formalities for

Trans-Nortense, the airline which belongs to the Italian consortium. Mermoz tells him that he has to go to Caruaru, but the man shows no interest and tells him that they fly to Rio, and if he wants a seat, he must sign up on the waiting list. Mermoz insists that he has to go to Caruaru, that he'll pay whatever's the asking price. But the man rudely replies that they aren't a taxi company. It's Rio or nothing.

Mermoz kicks a fuel tank and spins around, turning the air blue with his words. Then he notices a brand-new, low-winged metal plane on the runway.

"And that plane?"

It's North American. A prototype doing a test run."

"And the pilot?"

The manager of the airfield points to a pair of legs squeezed inside white overalls which are sticking out from under the fuselage.

"I think the pilot is checking the landing gear . . ."

Mermoz walks over to the plane and plants himself in front of the tips of the boots next to a checkered blanket with tools. He raises his voice so the pilot will hear him.

"Bonjour, boa tarde, buenas tardes . . ."

From under the plane, a high-pitched voice, somewhat distorted by the effort of tightening a screw, sends back a *"Bonjour"* in French with an American accent.

"My apologies for disturbing you. I'm Jean Mermoz, the head of pilots of Air France's transoceanic mail. A colleague has had an accident in Caruaru, and I need to get down there to pick up the mail as a matter of urgency. Would you lend me your plane?"

"Monsieur Mermoz," replies the voice from under the plane, "would you lend your girlfriend to the first person who asked you for her?"

Mermoz swallows.

"Well, no, I wouldn't. You're right. I'm asking for something impossible, I'm sorry. Thank you all the same."

397

"I'm not going let you borrow my plane, of course! But I haven't said I can't take you."

If the answer surprises Mermoz, it's nothing compared to the surprise he gets when the person draws in their legs and emerges from under the fuselage. It's actually a tall woman with freckles and untidy blond hair cut in a short style, a wine-coloured scarf knotted around her neck on top of her overalls.

"My apologies, I didn't know . . ."

"That I was a woman? And does that change anything? Aren't you confident that I can take you to Caruaru safe and sound?"

"Not at all. It's just that, well, I'm not accustomed to seeing many women at aerodromes."

"Well, you'll be seeing more and more of them. In the United States in 1929 only six other women had a pilot's licence from the Department of Commerce. Now that number has multiplied by ten."

"You are a country of pioneers."

"We are."

"You didn't tell me your name."

"I'm Amelia Earhart."

Mermoz's eyes open wide.

"But you set the international speed record for women in 1930! And you were the first woman to fly solo coast to coast across the United States with no stopovers."

She smiles shyly.

"I have to put miles on this Lockheed prototype. Are you still interested in a lift to Caruaru?"

"It would be an honour!"

The 450 hp engine easily lifts the plane off the runway and they fly over the swell at Ponta Negra heading south.

"It's lucky you speak French," Mermoz tells her.

"Not very well. I studied French Literature at Columbia University.

I was enrolled in medicine at the same time. Then I did a course in car mechanics. I still didn't know what I wanted to do!"

"Until you discovered flying . . ."

"Flying changed everything. You can be a pilot and lead a normal life. There are female pilots who are mothers."

"Lead a normal life! I've tried to, but I still haven't discovered how to do it."

"I'm lucky that my husband supports my aviation career. He never raises objections to any flight."

"Right . . ." And his voice becomes melancholy as he thinks about Gilberte. "Those we love don't object, but the anxious eyes of the person staying on the ground when you leave are like a harpoon piercing your chest."

"It's certainly never easy. But, Monsieur Mermoz, is there anything worthwhile that is easy?"

They travel the 400 kilometres flying over the coast of Northern Brazil. They go over lighthouses raised above dramatic cliffs, cross the spectacular Rio Mamanguape delta, and lift up over the quiet waters of the Patos Lagoon. As they pass over the estuary of the Rio Paraíba do Norte, Amelia Earhart's expression becomes mischievous as she points to the Ilha da Restinga, which sits at the mouth of the river: From their height, the island looks astonishingly like a perfect green heart sitting on top of the muddy river waters. The two exchange a smile. They know they are lucky: No matter what happens, nothing will take away the privilege of seeing all the gifts that Nature is unwrapping for them. They land in Caruaru as the sun is setting throughout the interior. At that moment, Mermoz feels at peace with himself and the world.

"Madame Earhart . . ."

"Call me Amelia."

"Amelia . . . this has been one of the best flights of my life."

"At the very least, it will have been one of the most restful!"

"Allow me to invite you to dinner on behalf of Air France."

In one of the steak houses in the city centre, the waiters arrive at the tables in a never-ending stream with skewers of every conceivable type of meat, cut in a thousand different ways. A piece of chicken hasn't even landed on the plate before another waiter arrives with a sirloin steak, and there's another waiter behind him with creole sausages. Amelia has never eaten so much meat, nor the tapioca dessert with sweet wine.

Mermoz tells her of the ups and downs of the mail routes, and she provides anecdotes from her work in the commercial department of Transcontinental Air Transport. The company thought that women would be more reluctant to fly as passengers than men, and that they had to be convinced of the benefits of air transportation, because if Mom didn't fly, the family wouldn't fly.

"My job was customer services. I wanted to be a pilot, but there were few available places."

"But you're a very well-qualified professional pilot!"

"And yet I'm always at the back of the line. I'm a woman, don't forget."

"That's impossible to ignore."

She blushes slightly.

She tells him the story of a woman passenger who asked over the phone to fly with her little dog, saying it was a tiny little thing that she loved more than anything else. The airline agreed. She turned up at the airport with an enormous mastiff, but the company was inflexible: She had paid for a single seat so if she wanted to fly with a dog weighing fifty kilos, she'd have to carry it on her lap from Cleveland to New York.

"And she did! It must have been her worst trip ever!"

A fascinated Mermoz watches her as she tells her stories.

"A florist in New York had the happy idea of expanding his business by sending flowers from one city to another by plane in record time. It was unfortunate that our personnel put the bouquet right next to a heating vent and what arrived was a bunch of dried flowers! Someone wanted to send a pony and we made him pay for two tickets. The animal travelled in the aisle and when it arrived, an airport employee put aviator goggles on its nose and took a photo."

Mermoz laughs as he hasn't laughed in a long time. Earhart falls silent for a moment.

"But the best part is wandering through the skies."

Mermoz nods. They belong to the same tribe.

They agree to leave with the mail for Natal the next day at dawn. They stay at a small hotel near the church of Santa Isabel, once Earhart has ascertained that each room has its own bathroom. They say goodnight in the corridor.

"Good night, Amelia. Sleep well."

"Good night, Jean."

"Amelia . . ."

"Yes?"

Mermoz hesitates for a second.

"If you feel indisposed during the night, I'm in room one-oh-five."

She pretends to look severe.

"Do you mean indisposed or predisposed? Please, Jean, I'm a married woman!"

"My apologies, Amelia, don't think badly of me. I was only concerned because that Brazilian grilled meat can sometimes prove indigestible during the night."

She smiles in her usual manner, like a mischievous boy.

"I'm afraid I have an iron constitution."

Mermoz laughs heartily. He doesn't mind defeat when he's dealing with a first-class player.

Once the mail has been loaded, they fly back in the Lockheed Electra, a prototype recently released by the Detroit factory which will start to be mass-produced following Earhart's test flights. Daybreak finds them flying over the sea. The pale light blurs the stands of trees below them and blends their boundaries into a never-ending forest. For a long period, the two don't speak, absorbed in the landscape.

"Amelia," Mermoz asks when the sun has started to bleach the world, "why do you fly?"

That look of immense happiness appears on her face.

"For the pleasure of doing it."

Amelia says farewell to the *Comte de la Vaulx* from the runway at the Parnamirim aerodrome with a wave of the wine-coloured scarf normally around her neck. Mermoz waves his hand and starts to taxi for his return flight to Europe. He would have loved to climb back into that metal aircraft impregnated with the fragrance of her perfumed soap and leave everything to follow that woman to the ends of the earth. But the mail is waiting. And faced with all the other fantasies, the mail is the only solid truth that gives meaning to his life.

CHAPTER 67

★

Paris, 1935

ANTOINE DE SAINT-EXUPÉRY

THE ARTICLES ANTOINE WRITES FOR the papers provide sporadic income, but his expenses are enormous. Consuelo doesn't know the word *save* and neither does Antoine. Neither of them knows how to cook beyond making buttered toast and a salad. They eat out for lunch and dinner. Sometimes, they don't have dinner and then have steak or a bouillabaisse for breakfast the next day at the Hilton. Consuelo often goes out and Antoine stays at home writing or goes out on his own. In their home, there are lumps of clay from a half-completed sculpture, an easel in the middle of the salon, sheets of paper with drafts of articles that will never be finished, packs of cigarettes everywhere, books scattered across the floors as if they formed a secret route through the apartment, and a gramophone that bewitched Consuelo and stopped working on the first day.

One afternoon, Antoine drops in on the Legrands in their mansion on the Champs-Élysées. They usually gather together sophisticated people who quote Montaigne nonstop and know all the gossip about current opera singers. And their duck pâté is the best. Going out is one way that Antoine combats the boredom of not knowing which way he should go.

The past few months have been confusing. The abnormality of his relationship with Consuelo has become the norm. Winning the Prix Femina gave him a degree of celebrity, which has an effect he would never have expected in literary Parnassus: to his surprise, there are women who are fascinated by the author of a book whose protagonists are hardened aviators. There is no other explanation for the fact that married, upper-class women whom he only knows by sight or who have been introduced to him at a cocktail party, receive him with open arms. He does not particularly like sporadic relationships, particularly now that he is married, but snubbing these ladies seems impolite. For her part, Consuelo continues with her comings and goings, some lasting an entire weekend, at the country houses of those pompous friends of hers whom Antoine finds lazy and full of a malicious sense of humour which makes him ill. They flutter around Consuelo with a servility that amuses her, and he knows that she occasionally takes them to bed. They are all artists, although he's never seen them pick up a paintbrush or a musical instrument, and he judges their sole skill to be squandering family fortunes.

Before the butler has even taken his coat, Mimi Legrand arrives to welcome him like a whirlwind, unleashing a light whiff of Guerlain perfume.

"Antoine, darling! How delightful that you've come! I'll introduce you to everyone!"

In the enormous salon, there are women with gloves above their elbows smoking tiny cigarillos in very long cigarette holders and men in suits with narrow lapels—the latest fashion. Madame Legrand steers him by the sleeve of his jacket toward the picture window where a woman is studying the hustle and bustle in the avenue at this late hour of the afternoon.

"I'm going to introduce you to Madame Hunt; you may have some friends in common."

They do have a great deal in common. Their host can't imagine how much.

When she turns round, Antoine feels dizzy and has to grab hold of Mimi Legrand's arm. Madame Hunt has green eyes, pale skin, and red hair. She smiles at him and he stands stock-still. He has dreamed during countless nights and days of the moment when he'd see her again, and now that's she's here, he doesn't know what to do. Instead of being happy, he's terrified. When you spend so much time waiting for something, and that something arrives, you feel an agonizing duty to live up to your dreams. But no one can live up to their dreams.

Their hostess looks at each of them in turn. They haven't said a word and yet their complicit silence says it all.

"So you know one another?"

"We are old friends," Louise replies with ease, given that Antoine is standing there stunned.

The doorbell announces new arrivals and the hostess excuses herself and rushes toward the entrance hall.

Louise takes a step toward Antoine as if she didn't want anyone else to hear their conversation. "How are you, Antoine?"

"Lou-Lou . . ."

She smiles that smile of hers that stops the world. "No one's called me that for years!"

"Too many years of good times . . ."

"You haven't changed! You continue to get angry with life, instead of enjoying what life provides you at every turn."

"I have a lot to learn from you!"

"You have nothing to learn from me," she replies with a smile. "It's enough if you stop feeling sorry for yourself for one day. And you're now a prize-winning writer!"

"I like you scolding me."

"You scold yourself."

"You have to tell me about yourself, Lou-Lou."

"But that's boring!"

"You haven't changed either. Being bored frightens you more than dying."

"Boredom *is* death."

"You continue to speak like a poet. Are you still writing poems?"

She doesn't have a chance to reply because a mutual acquaintance approaches, a petulant lawyer called Chardin who greets them both, but stares at her. Lou-Lou follows the conversation with apparent enthusiasm, even coquettishness. Antoine pretends to smile. A young painter from one of the best families in Paris, whom Antoine knows by sight, also joins the conversation. Within a few seconds, he's also staring at her, hypnotised.

Lou-Lou continues to be an enchantress!

Madame Legrand arrives holding a violin, and Lou-Lou takes it in her arms carefully, as if she were nursing a newborn baby. It's a gesture typical of Madame Hunt.

"Darling, why don't you entertain us with a piece?"

The remaining guests move closer with uninhibited curiosity.

"But Mimi . . ."

"You used to play wonderfully!"

"I'll play if someone accompanies me."

"I'll accompany you!"

They all turn toward the burly, somewhat ungainly pilot-writer who has a reputation for extravagance. Lou-Lou looks at him amused.

"You'll accompany me?"

He'd accompany her to hell if she asked him to.

"You play and I'll sing."

It won't be the first time. They had occasionally formed a duo, half in fun, at friends' houses, performing old popular outmoded songs.

Lou-Lou tunes the violin with a few strokes of the bow. She plays and they both sing. He feels enormous gratitude that she hasn't left him singing solo with his squawky voice. Lou-Lou stares at the neck of the violin and he looks at her. There are twenty people in the salon, but the music builds a castle just for the two of them. In that moment, he's happy.

Lou-Lou loses interest after the second song and leaves the violin on the tray of a passing waiter.

The guests applaud. Antoine is politely congratulated as etiquette demands, while Lou-Lou is enthusiastically surrounded by men and women. All the moths flock to the light. They flutter around her and construct a wall which separates her from him.

A couple who know his Aunt Yvonne congratulate him on his book and start a conversation he'd like to end as quickly as possible, but their friendliness is unassailable. Eventually, he is able to get rid of them and he moves over to the group around Lou-Lou. A gentleman whispers something in her ear and she bursts out laughing in a way that would be vulgar in any other woman, but in her is sensual. Antoine waits his turn, hanging about discreetly, pretending to be interested in the conversation of a nearby group, but never losing sight of her. He'd like to attract her attention.

He sees her saying goodbye to a couple and briefly being left on her own. This is his moment! *Now or never!* He takes a couple of impetuous strides toward her, but fails to see the waiter crossing in front of him, headed for the kitchen with a tray loaded with plates and glasses. When the two men collide, Antoine knocks over the tray, which causes a catastrophic racket when its contents hit the floor and smash. The waiter remains upright with difficulty, but Antoine loses his balance and falls on top of a sofa where two ladies are chatting. They are flattened by the hulk who lands on top of them. The squashed women make a fuss from underneath him. If he wanted to attract Lou-Lou's attention, he has certainly succeeded.

Two amiable gentlemen offer a hand to help him stand up, mainly to free the two women, who appear from under him looking disheveled and with bits of cake decorating their dresses. Antoine repeats his contrite apologies and Madame Legrand tells one of the maids to accompany the two women to the bathroom, while she supervises the cleaning operation.

"Mimi, forgive me, I'm really sorry . . ."

"It's nothing, Antoine. Please, all of you, continue to enjoy the evening!"

But the disaster has served as a signal for the guests to disperse, and the gathering breaks up.

The men go in search of their hats and the women, their shawls.

Antoine, who's beginning to recover from his embarrassment, locates Lou-Lou, who has returned to the picture window to become engrossed in the traffic on the avenue where the streetlights have come on.

"I had a slight slip."

"Going by the fuss, it was more like an earthquake."

"I wanted to talk to you. Reaching you is like climbing a mountain."

He doesn't say it with acrimony, but rather with the devotion of a mountaineer. He's committed. And that's the most assured passport to failure with a woman like Lou-Lou, who doesn't want ties, who's bored with everything except her own freedom.

"May I escort you home?"

"I'm invited to dinner here with the Legrands."

"When will we see each other again, Lou-Lou?"

"When are you going to introduce me to your wife?"

Antoine blushes. He stammers.

"As soon as there is an opportunity."

"Fine."

"And your husband?"

"He's travelling."

"Lou-Lou . . ."

"Yes?"

Antoine looks at her, and it's as if he were seeing a very distant planet through a telescope.

"I'm going," he says without being able to avoid a hint of sadness. "But I just wanted to tell you that those months we shared were the best I've ever had in my life."

She finally abandons her ironic tone and looks at him tenderly, as if right then, she's seeing him for the first time that afternoon. The hostess arrives with another woman and they take Lou-Lou over to a table to try the punch. Lou-Lou waves goodbye to him as she walks off, as if she were sailing away.

When Antoine leaves the house, he feels a cold against which he has no protection. He'd like to love Consuelo with the same intensity as he loved Lou-Lou. He wonders if he still loves Lou-Lou.

It's not possible, that would be absurd, meaningless. That was a youthful storm. To love her at this stage would be ridiculous, pathetic, stupid.

He can be ridiculous, pathetic, and totally stupid. He doesn't feel sorry for himself; it's merely a confirmation of what he is, and deep down, it doesn't upset him. Despite all his setbacks, he wouldn't want to give up being someone who dreams the impossible.

CHAPTER 68

★

Paris, 1935

ANTOINE DE SAINT-EXUPÉRY

ANTOINE WALKS SLOWLY AROUND THE octagonal perimeter of Place Vendôme. He fakes an interest in the shop window of the Cartier brothers' fanciful jewelry store, but the extreme nervousness with which he finishes his cigarette and the sideways glance toward the entrance to the Ritz betray him. He wants to be seen as just another pedestrian, but he's actually a spy.

As Antoine was having a cup of tea at his Aunt Yvonne's house recently, an old acquaintance from his student days was gossiping. His thick white moustache was like a brush efficiently spreading a storm of rumors. Some of the stories were hilarious, because tales of marital mayhem and disaster are always amusing when they happen to others.

Antoine laughed enthusiastically until the town crier started to talk about Louise de Vilmorin, currently Madame Hunt, he specified. And the sarcastic way in which he pronounced *Hunt* already augured the worst. Antoine was on the verge of opening his mouth to condemn the airing of matters related to a married woman, but curiosity makes us mean.

According to the gossipmonger, Monsieur Hunt, a rich man obsessed with becoming richer, was having serious problems with his neck. After a dramatic pause during which nobody asked him about the cause of the affliction, the man hastened to explain:

"It's because of the weight of his horns!"

Someone else in the group, happy to have his moment in the spotlight, said he'd seen Madame Hunt having dinner in a restaurant behind Notre-Dame with Guillot, a well-known orchestra conductor.

"I saw her arrive with him at a social gathering at the Antagnacs'."

"The whole world knows she's Louis Guillot's lover," the town crier with the mustache cut in scornfully. "Monsieur Hunt doesn't know that his wife, on a visit to Paris, is deceiving him with Guillot. But what Guillot doesn't know is that she is now in turn cheating on him with an American, a correspondent for *The Times*."

"Who?"

"I don't know him personally. I only know that his surname is Walker, that he's staying at the Ritz, and that women adore him."

Antoine has already heard malicious comments about Lou-Lou, but he's always attributed them to bored mediocrities who have to make up all sorts of murky intrigues in order to be listened to by the cliques at these soirées which pretend to be gatherings of intellectuals, but at which the guests find muckraking more entertaining. He could have ignored that character with his brush moustache. And yet he has spent the last three afternoons sitting on the terrace of a café with a clear view of the entrance to the Ritz hotel, or strolling like Frankenstein's monster around this octagonal square where the Chanel perfume store is unable to overcome the fumes from the heavy traffic driving around the high column, on top of which Napoleon is serving his final exile.

As he strolls along thinking about Napoleon and his fruitless empire, he sees a slender woman walking along the sidewalk in an extravagant long dress with horizontal green stripes and, rather than the usual hat, an attractively tied scarf on her head and oversized sunglasses on her nose in the manner of the American actresses who appear in the illustrated magazines. It's Lou-Lou. He sees her enter the hotel's revolving door and disappear.

He stands smoking in the street, as still as a pruned tree. Then he goes to sit down at what is now his customary spot at one of the tables at Le Midi Café and orders a rum. He wonders what the devil he's doing here. With a mix of anxiety and irritation, he watches the enormous façade of the Ritz, which takes up one side of the square, and asks himself why Lou-Lou likes so many other men, but not him.

A door to one of the balconies on the second floor of the Ritz opens and a woman comes out, removes her scarf and lets it flutter in the breeze. He's some distance away, but he makes out her dress with its horizontal, queen-bee stripes. A man leans out behind her and appears to whisper something in her ear. Antoine can't see him very clearly, but he has no doubt it's that Walker. He's considerably taller than the woman: Antoine imagines him to be athletic, perhaps with a square jaw. He would have liked a square jaw instead of his round, globe-like head.

The two people watch the traffic for a moment and then go back inside to the warmth of their five-star nest.

Antoine walks back to his apartment burning with rage. He has spent the best years of his youth loving a woman who has always evaded him. He idealised her, as if she were a fairy, when in fact, she is just a frivolous woman. He has endowed her in his mind with a virginal aura, as if she were an eternally pubescent young maiden, when her bed has been visited more often than the Louvre. He thinks that if he had married her, he would have been another Monsieur Hunt wearing the horns of a cuckold.

He never thought he would lament the day he met her. Perhaps, if he hadn't been obsessed with her, he would have been able to love other women devotedly, even Consuelo, and been a member of a dependable couple rather than riding this carousel which is their life. He'd like to go into a stationer's to buy an eraser to wipe out all his memories of Louise de Vilmorin, a girl who never existed, whom he invented to suit his fantasies—she was always right about that!

Through those twisted machinations of our brains when they are steeped in resentment, the next day, at the same hour, Antoine's feet again take him to Place Vendôme under the impassive gaze of Napoleon, and he loiters some distance from the entrance to the Ritz. Perhaps he wants to give himself a lashing, make himself ill at the sight of the happiness shared by Lou-Lou and her lover, so as to cure himself once and for all of any ember of love for her.

He hides in an arcade and this time, he sees Walker emerging from the Ritz first and walking a few metres along the pavement to where she is standing. Lou-Lou seems shorter to him. She's wearing an unusually large hat. A hat like Consuelo's . . .

My God! Oh no! It is Consuelo!

His wife and Walker head into the Ritz. Furious, Antoine walks in after them.

"Consuelo!" he shouts wildly. "What are you doing here?"

"And you?"

Antoine hesitates for a moment and looks at Walker who does, in fact, have a square jaw and doesn't appear to understand what's going on.

"I found out that you saw Louise de Vilmorin," Consuelo lets fly angrily.

"Lou-Lou? I saw her at the Legrands, nothing more than that."

"Nothing more?"

"Nothing more, Consuelo."

"But you would have liked something more. If she had beckoned, even with a fingernail, you would have left me for her."

"Consuelo, you're mad! You're trying to judge me, after I find you with a man in his hotel?"

"Yes."

"Have you slept with this man?"

"Of course, darling."

"Consuelo, you're making me look ridiculous!"

"You're the one who wanted to have this conversation in the lobby of the Ritz."

Antoine lowers his voice. "But how can you tell me that you've slept with this journalist and feel so pleased with yourself?"

Walker makes as if to go. "It would be better if I leave . . ."

"You stay right there."

"Papou, Walker isn't just anybody . . ." The journalist shrugs, pleased. "He is also Louise de Vilmorin's lover. Don't you understand? I've shown that spoiled brat of a girl that I can steal her men, too, if I set my mind to it."

Two tears run down Consuelo's cheeks. Antoine and Walker exchange a look of helplessness which unites them. Antoine is exhausted.

"Damned Lou-Lou!" he sighs. "She's ruined our lives."

He turns to his wife.

"Consuelo, let's go home."

"Of course, Papou. Goodbye, Monsieur Walker. It's been a pleasure."

The astonished American watches them leave arm in arm. He's been in two wars and three Latin American revolutions, but he's never seen anything like this.

CHAPTER 69

★

Paris, 1935

ANTOINE DE SAINT-EXUPÉRY AND JEAN MERMOZ

ANTOINE BREAKS HIS HERB OMELETTE apart with the edge of his fork. Several friends seated at the table are noisily arguing about politics, while Antoine looks out of the corner of his eye at the two wooden figures of the Chinese sages who give the name to Les Deux Magots. One of his friends at another table tries to be affable. "I've heard you're working for Air France. That's fantastic!"

Antoine raises his eyes from his omelette and looks at him. Clermont was a chubby boy in his student days and he's now beginning to display a double chin that looks like a fleshy scarf. Antoine is on the verge of saying something sarcastic, making a joke at the expense of his clerical appearance. There's no doubt the others would laugh at his remark, but at the last minute, he contains himself.

It's not good old Clermont's fault. There's no reason why he would know that, just when Antoine was in the middle of a worrying financial situation and owing three months' rent for the apartment in Rue de Chanaleilles, a representative of Air France—the company that had rejected his request to join them as a pilot so many times—had come to see him one afternoon. Before they got down to business, the bureaucrat tossed out so many words of praise that Antoine knew that what would come next would be a bucket load of shit. They offered him a position with Air France, as he had requested, but in public relations!

The worst thing about it was not that they had wiped their noses with his record of ten years' service as a professional pilot, but that, tragically, he had accepted.

"Is it true that you flew in that awesome Russian machine?" Clermont asks.

"The Tupolev!" Antoine cheers up. "An extraordinary plane, but too big. It carries eighty passengers! Can you imagine the madness? The effort now is to make national companies ever bigger. But they're mistaken. Such a big plane doesn't glide, it doesn't fly, it just hops from one airfield to another as if you were catapulting a stone from one corner to another."

Although Antoine was initially reluctant to agree to write for the newspapers, he's finally found pleasure in journalism. The editor in chief of *Paris-soir* suggested a trip to communist Russia—that country which dazzles some in Europe and repels others—to write about what he saw there.

He had been granted permission to be the first foreigner to board Russia's aerial jewel, a huge passenger plane that was leaving the entire world dumbstruck.

"A forty-two-tonne flying hotel."

He continues to talk about Russia, and Clermont, fascinated, listens to him until the light starts to fade above Saint-Germain.

As he walks home, his financial problems occupy his mind again. His salary as an employee in public relations at Air France is nothing more than pocket money. Consuelo and he, too—though his conscience pricks him when he does it—need to go out, eat in good restaurants, pay the rent for their apartment—perhaps too big—go to opening nights at the theatre, even repair the door of their Bugatti which has been attached to the chassis by a rope for weeks. He's been holding together the broken doors of his life with string for some time.

When he reaches the apartment, Consuelo is waiting for him. She has that angry look on her face which makes her even more adorable. She's smoking nervously.

"It's almost nighttime, Antoine!" she shouts as soon as he comes through the door.

"It happens every day, my love."

"I loathe your sarcasm!"

"So what's the matter?"

"Ask the caretaker to go and buy some candles. They've cut off our electricity because we haven't paid the bill. And I have a marvellous, half-finished painting to work on!"

He produces a blandishment. "I leave for Saigon in three days. That will solve everything."

She nods, and smiles. "Can't you ask for an advance in the meantime?"

"I've already asked *Paris-soir* for an advance on one article. I can't ask for another."

"I'll do it." She gives him a cheeky look.

Of course she can do it, and she'd undoubtedly get twice as much as he would have.

He's made a deal with the editor in chief to write a series of exclusive articles about his Paris-Saigon challenge to beat the aerial speed record. He's managed to get Monsieur Daurat to prepare a Caudron Simoun plane in his factory, and invested the last of his savings in it. The idea didn't please his former boss in the slightest. He told Antoine that those sorts of races were a circus, they weren't serious aviation. But Antoine insisted. He needed the money and was sure to win the prize with a Simoun, which was as light as a feather.

He goes downstairs to buy candles before it gets much later. He doesn't like to walk but he needs the fresh air. He reaches the river and crosses over on the Pont Royal. In Place des Pyramides, he spies a group of people displaying some symbols he doesn't like, and shouting annoying slogans about French pride and lying politicians. When he gets closer, he sees that they are members of the Croix-de-Feu, a party led by Colonel de la Rocque. It reminds him too much of the other fascist parties flourishing throughout Europe and is modelled on the Italian party of Benito Mussolini.

Croix-de-Feu members want to change the world, but they want to do it by force, if necessary. They erect a small dais for one of their leaders to stand and harangue them. A passerby tells Antoine that it's an homage to Joan of Arc, but everything suggests that it's one of those homages that aren't for the benefit of the person being honoured, but rather in opposition to somebody else. A heavily built man stuffed inside a double-breasted suit and wearing an armband with the black party insignia climbs up to speak to the crowd.

"We don't deserve the politicians we have. They've abandoned the working class, they've cowered in the face of foreign powers, and they're allowing this country to lose its pride. We can't allow that to happen! And we're not going to allow it!"

There are cries against the politicians, against corruption, against unemployment. Antoine is lost for words. He can't stop looking at the man who, from the improvised platform, is gesticulating energetically and talking about decency, honour, bravery, patriotism . . . He's tempted to take a few steps closer to make sure, but he doesn't really need to do so. He's looking at him up there. Messianic. Decisive.

Mermoz!

He has heard his friend speak with the indignation of those who consider politicians to be individuals hiding inside their offices; who is hurting because the politicians have allowed the great Aéropostale flying dream to die in such a dishonourable way. He has seen him punching café tables so hard that even the coat hangers shake. He has listened to all these words. But it's as if suddenly he's hearing them for the first time. Spoken to the accompaniment of banners, with all the paraphernalia of armbands and civilians with military berets, the words seem different. They are different.

He stays to the end. To the cheers for France.

As the crowd heads off behind the flag bearers who are moving on to their next destination, Antoine's friend is surrounded by supporters who congratulate him, pat him on the back, and try to take him away. Inspired by that prodigious intuition of his, Mermoz turns his head. He knows that someone is looking at him from the other side of the square.

He shakes off his admirers with gentle determination, as if he were shaking snowflakes from his coat.

"Saint-Ex . . ."

"Jean! I didn't know you belonged to this . . . group."

"La Rocque has restored the faith in France we had lost."

"Faith?"

"I've met the real France again: workers, students, soldiers, traders. The people who make this country great, unlike the politicians who have sold out and the bankers blinded by money. We'll change things."

"But how, Jean? By taking part in politics?"

"You already know that I hate politics."

"But your party is running in the elections. That's taking part in politics. You'll need money to finance the campaign and you'll have to get it from the banks. It's the same as always."

The people around them watch their leader with his black armband expectantly.

"You're an intellectual!" Mermoz replies contemptuously. "You make everything sterile with your eternal reasoning and your scepticism!"

Mermoz has never spoken to him so harshly, and Antoine, in the manner of children when they are scolded, sadly lowers his head. Several people come in search of Mermoz to escort him to the head of the retinue. Among them is a sour-faced man whose chest is covered with medals. It's Colonel de la Rocque.

The acolytes surround Mermoz like a flock of birds and rush him away. Antoine doesn't want to raise his head. He knows that if he looks up, he won't be able to distinguish Mermoz from the rest of them.

When the cloud of Croix-de-Feu members has moved off, Mermoz again breaks away from them, frees himself of some arms wanting to hold him back, and in four strides, he's back beside Antoine, who has been left alone in the middle of the empty square. He gives Antoine a bear hug. He squeezes him between his arms and doesn't let him go.

"They're waiting for us, Monsieur Mermoz!" says someone who has come to retrieve him.

The two friends exchange a look. Still holding each other by the forearms, they smile. They look at each another with the same complicity they shared in the pilots' mess, where everything that is important is communicated without saying a word.

Antoine watches him walking away and Mermoz turns around one last time.

"Antoine, pedal and joystick?"

"Pedal and joystick, Jean!"

Antoine starts to walk again, unable to stop worrying about Mermoz. He's heard the odd speech by La Rocque on the radio, and it's true that his words convey a contagious faith.

Fascism has become a religion without churches. Patriots feel they have a supreme mission and are prepared to die for their country; the trouble is that they're also prepared to kill.

Antoine just wants Mermoz to remember that the aviator's only homeland is the sky.

When he gets home, Consuelo is waiting for him in a taxi outside the door of their building, hugging her little dog.

"Where did you go to buy the candles?"

"Candles?" He had forgotten.

"Never mind! How on earth am I going to paint and you, to write, in a totally dark house? We're moving to the Pont Royal Hotel until the matter of the electricity supply is fixed. I've already made the reservation."

"The Pont Royal?"

"I know you prefer the Excelsior! But I can't stand those incredibly narrow revolving doors."

Just for a second, he thinks about the fact that they don't have the money to pay the bill, but they will be comfortable there. He climbs into the taxi and kisses Consuelo on her cheek. The two of them burst out laughing—naughty children playing in the harsh adult world.

CHAPTER 70

★

Libya, 1936

ANTOINE DE SAINT-EXUPÉRY

AIR RACES ARE A WAY to win some money and continue flying.

It's too dark even to see his mechanic, Jean Prévot, behind him. Antoine keeps tapping the fuel control lever so the Simoun engine won't drop below 2,300 revolutions. They are flying in this plane that has a cabin so tiny he's had to choose between a mechanic and a radio operator. So he's back to navigating with a compass and the stars. They've left behind Europe, the Mediterranean, the stopover in Tunisia, but for a short while, Antoine feels a bigger burden than the hundreds of litres of fuel—his financial problems, which don't allow him to thrive in Paris. Having money doesn't make you rich, but not having it does make you poor. But all that grubbiness is left behind now that he has finally started flying. He's neither hungry nor thirsty. He's flying the dark skies of Libya, headed for Egypt, and nothing weighs him down any more.

The night gives them a welcome they don't want: The little flashing red position light on the tip of the wing throws threads of red-tinted cotton wool out into the darkness. They fly through a thick mass of cumuli, and the clouds welcome them by throwing bouquets of light. Antoine is amazed: In this aerial land, they harvest rose beams.

But the garlands of light don't stop. The bundle of clouds deprives them of all points of reference. The compass shows a direction, but they don't know how many kilometres off-course they might be from their objective, Cairo, because, around that drop of water which is the city, there lies an immensity of desert. They're flying blind.

After three hours spent in the murk, Antoine tries dropping altitude in order to see something, but the clouds reach right down. It's dangerous to descend below 400 metres, but he has no alternative. When they finally emerge from the purée of clouds they are hoping to see city lights, but there's just a huge area of black; they don't even know if they're flying over land or sea.

They fly on blindly—and too low—at 270 kph in a state of uncertainty. The unknown is instantly resolved by a violent impact which shakes them like an earthquake. Antoine watches his cigarettes fly out of his shirt pocket. Everything is happening very quickly but, at the same time, he is able to take note of all the details: the bang, the abrupt braking, the grinding metal sound of the plane breaking up. The noise. The mad vibration of metal sheets. And the plane finally coming to a halt, surrounded by darkness.

When they climb out of the plane, Prévot has only a bruised knee. The crunching sound of their boots on the ground tells them they're in the desert. As do the cold night and immense solitude. The plane has crashed on a small plateau of several hundred metres, but its surface is sandy. It's a miracle they're still alive.

A quick check with a flashlight enables them to see the broken wings, bits of scattered fuselage, punctured fuel tanks. Worst of all, they realise that the spare water tanks have burst.

Dawn provides a clearer idea of their situation. They've landed in the middle of the desert between Libya and Egypt, an area covering thousands of square kilometres. Their survival kit consists of a thermos with half a litre of coffee, a quarter of a litre of white wine, and an orange. It could take days for them to be found, or weeks—or never. They check out their surroundings: sand and rocks. And a sun which, as it rises, burns everything. Dazed, they return to the plane and drink the scant liquid they have. They seek the shade of the fuselage until late afternoon.

Before they head off the next morning, they use grease to write on the side of the Simoun the direction in which they are heading— northeast. Prévot also leaves a farewell message for his wife: He asks her to forgive him for being away so much. Antoine doesn't want Prévot to see his message so he goes round to the other side of the plane to write a final note to Consuelo.

I loved you the best I could . . .

And then they walk. You walk slowly in the desert. Your feet sink, your spirits sink. Beyond one dune lies another, and then another, and then a hundred thousand more. Your body dries up. You start to miss saliva like never before. Your tongue begins to swell, and it feels like it's not going to fit inside your mouth. Your lips seal and your eyes fill with dead butterflies.

In Paris, the afternoon papers carry news of the disappearance of the pilot, Antoine de Saint-Exupéry, and his mechanic, Jean Prévot. Consuelo is at the house of an artist-friend who has asked her to be his model. The phone brings her the news and she runs for the door. He has to remind her that she's naked. She arrives at the hotel white-faced and there are already some concerned friends in the reception area, pacing up and down. There's no news; nothing other than that he should have landed in Cairo and he hasn't.

Consuelo walks over to one of the three-piece sofas in the lobby and faints into it. Friends take her to her room, which turns into a waiting room with everyone keeping an ear out for the phone. They can't imagine in Paris that 3,000 kilometres away, Antoine and Prévot are chasing phantoms through the desert.

Antoine sees a roaring waterfall and his face lights up. But as he takes a few steps toward it, it dissolves in a haze.

As dusk starts to fall, Prévot says he sees a lake a few kilometres away.

"There's no lake," Antoine tells him.

The mechanic gets angry. How can Antoine not see it? They argue, but not a great deal. They have barely any energy left. Antoine shrugs and gives him the flashlight. His companion goes off in search of his lake. Over an hour later, it's getting dark and Prévot hasn't returned. Antoine is worried; he shivers with the first strands of the night, not certain if it's from fear or cold. He stares at the point on the horizon which Prévot headed for, but now there's only an ever-deepening darkness. He's shivering when he sees several beams of light moving half a kilometre away.

A rescue party arriving with Prévot!

He waves his hands in the dark.

"Over here! Over here!"

He's surprised how hoarse his voice sounds. He stands up and, with the last of his strength, goes to meet the lights.

"Saint-Ex!"

"Prévot! We're saved!"

Their tongues feel like scourers and their words emerge thickly. Antoine finally reaches the flashlight and the mechanic's hands.

"Saved?"

"The other flashlights, where are they?"

"What flashlights?"

"There were three other flashlights accompanying you."

425

"There's no one else."

Antoine has no more saliva in his mouth. No voice emerges. He moves his head up and down forcefully, driven on by the cold night. He wants to say that of course there are more lights, that they were right there. But when he looks around, there's only a vast darkness under a sky punctured by a thousand icy stars.

They return silently to their parachutes, improvise sleeping bags from them, and try to rest. Prévot cries a steady lament of helplessness.

Antoine tries to cheer him up: Maybe they'll be able to lick a few drops of dew from the parachute material.

They set off with the first hint of the sun and three drops of water on their tongues. The heat increases at an unbearable speed. Throughout the morning, they no longer pay attention when they see a distant flock of sheep, cities with towers, caravans with dozens of camels. Antoine even thinks he see a child with golden hair and wearing a prince's cape walking over the sand on top of the dunes as if he were strolling through a field of grass.

They no longer know if they're still going in the same direction as when they left the plane. Antoine thinks about how deserted the planet is. Where are the people in this immense emptiness, he asks himself over and over. But there is no reply.

The sun crushes their heads, the sand is cast iron. They're swimming in a pool of hot air. They drag their wounded feet like automatons.

Another mirage: a Bedouin riding a camel appears on top of a rise. He advances without noticing their presence and keeps going without stopping. *What if he isn't a mirage? What if he really is a desert dweller?* As if they were in a nightmare, they try to shout, but no sound comes out of their dry mouths. All is lost. Their voices don't emerge, but something reaches the Bedouin, who pulls on his camel's bridle, stops for a moment, and turns in their direction as if he really had heard them. *It's not a mirage, it's a real human being.*

The Bedouin has learned medicine, part of that ancestral wisdom taught during desert nights around the campfire. He knows that giving a dehydrated person too much liquid could provoke death. The man of the desert has hands as rough as desert vines, but he uses them with the gentleness of a geisha. Using a feather, he trickles drops of a vegetable broth he's carrying in a *girba* to wet their tongues. Paradise tastes of lentils.

Antoine opens his eyes with difficulty. His eyelids are as heavy as wooden shutters. During these days of wandering in the middle of this emptiness, he had lost all hope. He looks at the Bedouin who is feeding them with such delicacy and feels an infinite love for this stranger. He thinks, in this moment of luminous confusion, that anyone who stops to share what little he has with two strangers is saving not just two castaways, but himself and the whole of humanity.

The news causes huge jubilation in the Pont Royal hotel. Consuelo orders bottles of the best champagne from room service. A day later, Antoine manages to call on an intermittent connection and asks her to send him clothes and cigarettes. The editor of *L'Intransigeant* sends a reporter to the hotel to make sure that when the aviator arrives in Paris, he doesn't disappear, as so often happens, but leaves a written chronicle of his wanderings in the Libyan desert.

Days later, Antoine will smile in the hospital in Tripoli where he's recuperating when he unwraps a useless package sent to him from France by Consuelo. It contains a solitary dress shirt, as if his life were nothing more than a diplomatic reception.

CHAPTER 71

★

Dakar (Senegal), 1936

HENRI GUILLAUMET AND JEAN MERMOZ

GUILLAUMET HAS BEEN LIVING IN Dakar for some time as a pilot assigned to the Dakar-Natal route. He hasn't seen Mermoz for months, and he feels a special joy as he crosses the sleeping city on his way to the Ouakam aerodrome. A low-winged Dewoitine lands gently as the sleepy mechanics lazily put on their blue overalls. Henri walks to the plane along the runway lit up by the orange sodium lights which give the night an uneven brightness. The electrification of the aerodromes has made night flights much safer.

When the cabin door opens, Mermoz is the first person to climb out. He's full of energy, impeccable in his double-breasted suit, and smiling radiantly as if it were two in the afternoon rather than two in the morning. He walks over to Guillaumet and grabs him by the arms with his strong hands.

"Jean, I'll take you for a rest until you leave for Natal."

"Rest? I've been sleeping in that plane as if I were in a bed at the Hilton."

428

The manager of the airfield comes out to give Mermoz the clipboard with the flight plan. He's leaving for Brazil in the *Comte de la Vaulx* seaplane in two hours' time. When he glances at his crew, he raises an eyebrow. There's a name he doesn't recognise.

"Who's this Lanata listed as copilot?"

He's a very capable young Argentinian pilot. You'll become good friends."

"I'm too old to be making friends."

They wouldn't normally allow a pilot to change the crew list an hour and a half before he leaves simply because he wants to fly surrounded by friends. But Mermoz isn't a pilot, he's a legend.

"Pichodou is the reserve pilot . . ."

"A veteran. Great guy! He's crossed the Atlantic several times. He's perfect."

"But Monsieur Mermoz, it's two in the morning . . ."

"Perfect! He'll be easy to find at home."

They drive to the pilot's house in Guillaumet's car. When they ring the doorbell insistently, the voice of an irritated Pichodou calls out: "Dammit! Who's there?"

He turns the key and opens the door, wearing only pyjama bottoms, his hair a mess, and ready to bite whoever it is who has ruined his sleep. He isn't expecting to find himself facing none other than Jean Mermoz.

"Pichodou, we have mail to deliver."

Pichodou smiles. From the bedroom, his wife asks what's going on.

"Prepare a thermos of coffee for me; I'm leaving on a flight."

Guillaumet himself drives the small launch that takes the crew to the slip where the seaplane is gently rocking. Apart from Mermoz and Pichodou, there's a navigator, a mechanic, and a radio operator. The night is waiting for them.

The engines roar in the predawn, and by the light of the full moon, Guillaumet watches the powerful three-engine plane take off in the direction of the ocean. He waves goodbye even though they won't be able to see him. He can't explain why, but he feels that in a way, he has taken off with them.

Up there, the night sky is friendly. Mermoz observes the trail of stars which confirms the clear sky announced in the weather report. Nevertheless, after listening carefully for a few minutes, something doesn't sound right to him.

"Lavidalie, listen."

The mechanic pricks up his ears like a gun dog.

"I hear something. It's the propeller."

The propeller is vibrating a little more than it should. Mermoz knows that bravery is built on sound judgement.

"Cruveilher, advise Ouakam. We're turning round due to problems with the propeller."

The manager of the airfield is waiting for them when they land. Mermoz asks for another machine for the crossing, but there isn't one.

"A Potez 300 is due the day after tomorrow . . ."

Mermoz glares.

"The mail can't wait. Get them to fix the propeller as quickly as possible."

Two mechanics get to work, and they take off again at dawn. They head toward the west, and the sun, reddish and lazy, chases them. The *Comte de la Vaulx* flies peacefully. The mechanic performs his checks of the various gauges with his customary calm. Pichodou dozes in the seat beside Mermoz. And yet there's something there in the background music. Something very faint. A note out of tune.

CHAPTER 72

Paris, 1936

Antoine de Saint-Exupéry and
Henri Guillaumet

THERE ARE GUESTS IN ANTOINE'S apartment. They include a couple of sculptors or painters or who knows what hovering around Consuelo. He would love to have told her not to invite them or, even better, throw them down the stairs. He looks at them with their air of long-haired bohemians who eat caviar for breakfast. He knows that it could be his jealousy which makes him see these two individuals as worse than they really are.

He would prefer Consuelo to be more discreet with her friendships and excesses. Yesterday, they had had a fierce argument. He couldn't take any more and became involved in a painful battle. He reproached her harshly for her nightly outings—those nights when she doesn't come home and he waits up, pacing up and down like a caged bear.

"Our marriage is a farce!" he told her bitterly.

She continued to concentrate for several minutes on painting a vase with a fine brush, as if she hadn't heard him. In the past few weeks she had discovered her true vocation in pottery. At least for a few months. Her indifference infuriated Antoine even more, and he began to shout:

"Have you ever heard of the word *respect*?" he screamed at her.

Consuelo examined her last brushstroke on the vase and seemed to give it a professional look of approval. Then she took the vase, raised her hands slowly, and let it to drop to the floor and smash into a thousand pieces.

"You talk to me about respect?" she began. "Who's your lover this month? Or are there several?"

At which he blushed and flinched. "It hurts me when you tell others things about our private life."

"Is that really what concerns you? What people think of the great writer? How disappointing!"

"No, it's not that! It's a question of not tossing everything out the window. Could we not stop hurting each other?" He dropped his head bashfully and lowered his voice to a whisper. "Couldn't you be my little kitten and I'd be your teddy bear?"

Consuelo looked at him. She smiled. She walked over to him and kissed him on the cheek.

An argument just like so many others.

The fact is that he does feel jealous of Consuelo's friends.

Lovers. Why not call them what they are?

But she frequently bursts into jealous attacks over his affairs too. Their relationship has become an absurd competition of infidelity. He seeks in other women the tenderness and attention he no longer receives from Consuelo. But perhaps Consuelo isn't tender, or is on the lookout for other men because he is with other women. Who knows anymore?

Among the guests on this particular evening are the Swiss composer Vigny and his wife, Nicole. Antoine likes this woman with the smooth golden hair and short fringe. She smiles at him. She shows a lively interest in his writing. She tells him that she's fascinated by *Southern Mail*, his first book. She strikes him as the most enchanting woman in the world.

He doesn't want to be unfaithful to Consuelo again. He hates being unfaithful to her. But if he doesn't pay heed to this emotional call that could give him a moment's happiness in his life's affective greyness, he would be unfaithful to himself. He wants things with Consuelo to be fixed; he wants the two of them to be a couple who stroke each other's feet in bed at night. They do have memorable nights, it's true. But they are both fickle. They lack the patience for marriage; routine suffocates them.

He thinks that perhaps, some afternoon, Madame Vigny, cultured and sensitive—and very attractive—might like him to read her some fragments of the book he's writing, so he'd know what she thinks of it. He's been jotting down notes for quite some time, but they aren't going anywhere. Since he can't channel them into a book, maybe they could serve to channel him into a conquest.

Consuelo is laying down the law. She talks about how ceramics is "the divine art" because it's made using clay, the same material God used to make humankind. Antoine grimaces, discreetly making fun of Consuelo's extravagant, liberal Catholicism. He sneaks a conspiratorial look at Madame Vigny, who smiles back at him.

The phone has rung several times. He suddenly notices it among the hubbub of conversation. He was so distracted that he hadn't heard the insistent ringing. Consuelo doesn't answer it, naturally. She has a theory about not picking up the phone after sunset, because of some sort of squeamish superstitious belief that only bad news can be passed on at night.

He lifts the receiver. The call is from a pilot friend who works in the flight control centre at Air France. It's unusual for him to call so late.

"Saint-Ex! It's Tailleur!"

"Tailleur, what's happened?"

"It's Mermoz. His plane, the *Comte de la Vaulx* . . ."

"What?"

"It's disappeared."

"How? When?"

"A few hours ago. He was flying over the Atlantic, nine hundred kilometres from Dakar. That's all I know."

Antoine comes back to the dining room already wearing his raincoat.

"I'm sorry, but I have to go to the office."

"But, Antoine," Consuelo bursts out in front of everyone, "we've got guests in the house!"

"I have to go."

"Going to the office at nine o'clock at night? It wouldn't have been one of your whores calling?"

Without a glance at Consuelo, he addresses the embarrassed guests.

"My apologies. A very dear pilot friend's life is in danger."

He opens the front door and closes it slowly. He's too worried about Mermoz to be angry with Consuelo. Deep down, her jealousy pleases him; it suggests he still means something to her.

When he reaches the Air France building, he shows his staff card to the security guard and goes inside. But on the second floor, where the operations centre is located, they block his entry.

"I'm Saint-Exupéry."

The guard examines the card he's being shown.

"I'm sorry, public relations employees aren't authorised to access this area."

"I'm not a public relations person, I'm a pilot!"

"Not according to your accreditation."

"But I have to have news about the *Comte de la Vaulx*!"

"That's not possible."

"Notify Jean-Luc Tailleur! He'll authorise me."

"I can't do that."

"Then advise the flight manager, Monsieur Travert! Or the technical director, Monsieur Vauqueline!"

"I'm afraid they're not here."

"They're not here?" Antoine turns bright red, rage makes him shout and stutter at the same time. "How is that possible? The life of France's best pilot is in danger, and they're not here?"

The guard crosses his arms menacingly and Antoine feels a huge tiredness come over him; a moral fatigue which defeats him. He moves off a few paces and slides down the wall until he's sitting with his back propped against it.

"If you won't let me in, I'll just stay here until I hear something. You can't throw me out. I'm an employee of this company, even if only an underling."

He puts his head in his hands. *Jean, Jean, Jean . . . where are you?*

There's a sound of footsteps. It's a group of men in suits, the technical director, Vauqueline, and his assistants. The minister of air, Pierre Cot, is behind them. The rest of the group walks past Antoine, but Cot stops and makes the others stop as well.

"Monsieur de Saint-Exupéry, what are you doing here on the floor?" he admonishes him.

"I'm waiting for news of Mermoz."

"On the floor?"

"Minister, I can't fall if I'm already on the floor."

Minister Cot sees the anguish in Antoine's face.

"Do we know anything, Monsieur Cot?"

"I'm afraid there's nothing new. Wouldn't you prefer to be inside the control room?"

"I'm not authorised to enter. I'm just someone from public relations."

"How is it possible that a gentleman honoured with a Légion d'honneur for his career as an aviator is not authorised?" The minister looks severely at those around him. The company directors look down at their shoes.

"If he wasn't authorised, he is now. You!" He addresses the guard sternly: "This is Monsieur de Saint-Exupéry. He'll enter and leave this room as often as he likes. Is that clear?"

"Yes, Your Excellency. As you request, Excellency."

Inside the room, the operations coordinator removes his earpiece and stands up when he sees the minister arriving.

"Your Excellency, the *Comte de la Vaulx* left Dakar with five crew members at 0710. A message was received at 1047 which said: 'Shutting down rear right engine.' After that, nothing."

Antoine does his sums: more than nine hours. Mermoz lasted two days in the Andes. He can last nine hours in the sea. Rescue missions are suspended overnight and resume at dawn, so Mermoz and his crew will have to hold out for twenty-four hours. If there isn't a big swell, the *Comte de la Vaulx* is like a big raft.

"What does the weather report have to say about the conditions?"

"Calm seas, sir. The wind will start to pick up tomorrow, and there'll be rough seas in the afternoon."

"How many are searching for them?"

"There are three Potez planes in the rescue mission and a ship with a crew of eighteen has sailed from Dakar."

Antoine, taking advantage of his height, looks over the minister's head and asks: "Is Henri Guillaumet part of the rescue mission?"

"He was the first to leave."

Antoine nods. Since he can't be there, he's relieved that Guillaumet is involved in the search. They're combing thousands of square kilometres of ocean. It's like emptying a beach of its sand with nothing more than a dessert spoon, but Guillaumet will search beneath every wave.

It's not good news that the message was cut off so abruptly. During the long wait, speculating why the radio suddenly went silent is as useless as it is inevitable. A fire, an explosion on board? Who knows?

When the minister leaves, the management retinue follows him like a herd of sheep. Antoine grabs an empty chair and sits next to the communications technician. For two hours, there are meteorological reports, messages about changes in shifts, entries and exits, but nothing about the *Comte de la Vaulx*.

"Rescue operations won't resume until the morning. Why don't you go home and rest?" suggests the coordinator amiably.

"Because what is exhausting me isn't tiredness, but uncertainty."

"But surely you'll be calmer at home with your wife."

"You don't know my wife!" Antoine tries to smile, but all he manages is a small movement of his lips. He's taken part in many rescue operations and he knows the technicians are right. Nothing can be done until morning, and in here, he's more of a nuisance than anything else.

He walks back home at a snail's pace. Every now and again he stops to look at the sky. There are no stars; no light up there.

No light the next day. No light the day after that. No light.

Antoine sleeps on the couch in the salon next to the phone. He rings the operations centre every day and the reply is always the same: "Nothing." The hope that they'll be found alive diminishes. Two more days go by. Nothing. The only outcome now is the worst outcome. On the fifth day, he gets a call from the public relations office: He hasn't been at work for days, but he hasn't explained his absence either.

"Don't expect me."

"Don't expect you today?"

"Don't expect me ever again."

On the seventh day, the phone rings. He picks it up with a mix of fear and concern, but it's not Air France. It's the editor of *L'Intransigeant*. They're calling to ask him to write an article in memory of Jean Mermoz.

At first, he doesn't understand, as if they were speaking in some foreign language. The editor gently presses him: "You know him, you can write about Mermoz's virtues, explain his significance to France."

"I'm not interested in his virtues!" Antoine shouts in reply. "Mermoz is full of defects. When we arrange to meet, he's always late and he never apologises. He's stubborn, very stubborn; he's intransigent."

There's a stunned silence from the editor at the other end of the line.

"I don't understand what you're saying . . ."

"There's no way I can evaluate him with that cold perfection of the dead!"

He hangs up indignantly. *How can those imbeciles think that Mermoz is dead.*

He stays beside the phone. He sleeps on the sofa, and uses the little side table to eat the food sent up by the Breton brasserie on the corner: savoury crêpes, mussels, and French fries. The newspapers he reads create a mountain of out-of-date news on the floor. Consuelo occasionally keeps him company. Sometimes she lies down on the sofa with him and gives him a cuddle. At other times, she paints her lips with a red lipstick so dark that, from a distance, it looks black, and goes off to the theatre or, without any explanation, to some dinner that stretches into the small hours.

A week goes by, then another. The pile of newspapers grows. Now, he only eats fillets and omelettes; he can't abide crêpes. Nothing.

Mermoz disappeared on December 7. Christmas has never gone by so unnoticed. He refuses to go out on New Year's Eve, and a slighted Consuelo goes out on her own, wearing a cheeky dress that exposes her entire back. Antoine welcomes the new year, 1937, on the sofa in his bathrobe. He hopes for a Christmas miracle, the bombshell of Mermoz turning up in the New Year. But the first day goes by, and the second. Nothing.

One evening early in January, Consuelo invites friends to the house to show them some vases she has painted in the geometric style she maintains is Aztec. But as soon as they enter, laughing and making a racket, Antoine kicks them out. He needs to be alone; he needs silence in case the phone rings.

A month has gone by. His beard resembles that of a castaway. The phone doesn't ring.

One morning, the doorbell rings. Reluctantly, Antoine gets up to open the door. He's not in a state to receive visitors: He hasn't showered for a while; anxiety has made him eat at all hours and he's gained several kilos. He opens the door and standing there, with a serious expression on his face, is Guillaumet.

They look at each other. Henri shakes his head from side to side. "The rescue mission has been terminated."

Mermoz hasn't come back. He'll never come back.

Antoine's lip trembles and hot tears start to flow as if they were coming from the centre of the earth. He embraces Henri, and finally, the two of them together can weep for their friend and let him go in peace.

Guillaumet removes a handkerchief for each of them from his pocket.

Antoine walks over to the wine rack and brings back a bottle of cognac. "We have to drink a toast to him."

Guillaumet agrees. "Mermoz hated sad farewells."

CHAPTER 73

★

Paris, 1937

Antoine de Saint-Exupéry

The apartment of the Saint-Exupérys has become a place where the door never shuts and the lights never go out. One party leads into another. There are days when guests stay and sleep on the sofas, waiting until the party gets going again the following afternoon. To occasional visitors, Saint-Ex and Consuelo seem to be one of those couples who get along better than most. Their house is full of canapés, champagne, songs, funny stories, and noise until dawn. Anyone observing them in a distracted manner, or with too much chardonnay inside them, might think they are happy.

For Antoine, the partying is a way of hiding the sadness he's carried inside him ever since Mermoz disappeared. He's totally paralyzed when it comes to writing. They ask him for articles that he never delivers. He's been paid advances for books he hasn't written. Consuelo is always on the go. His impatience with her grows.

One afternoon, they receive an invitation to afternoon tea at the Vignys. Consuelo tells him she's too busy. She's absorbed in a book about fortune telling and spends hours practising with her tarot cards. Antoine goes by himself, and when Nicole Vigny welcomes him, he explains that his wife has had to go on a trip, urgently.

"I am sorry," Nicole says politely.

"Don't be."

She asks him if he's brought any notes about something he's writing. Antoine always has pieces of paper in his pockets. In one of them, he has a few pages with some scribbles for one of the episodes he's going to write in his new book about luminous moments during the fifteen or so years he's been somersaulting through the skies. He reads, and she listens attentively.

When he's finished reading, it's teatime, and she asks if he'd like anything.

"A little tea."

"You don't want anything else?" And she gives him an intense look.

Antoine is fascinated by her golden hair and her intelligent eyes. They end up having tea in bed.

The visits to Madame Vigny's house, now that Monsieur Vigny seems to have disappeared, are an agreeable parenthesis of literature and sex to a period of anxiety.

When he sits down the odd morning, still in his pyjamas and with a migraine, to go over the correspondence from his bank about unpaid bills, he's overwhelmed by despondency. He hands the letters over to Consuelo and she throws them in the wastepaper basket with indifference. Antoine puts his head in his hands.

"A count, a writer, a gentleman of the Légion d'honneur . . . How is it possible that we're in the red?"

The only solution is to organise another of those long-distance air races so popular with a public hungry for excitement as long as the risk is someone else's. He'll have to find sponsors and sell the exclusive to *L'Intransigeant*.

"Why don't you write a book?" asks Consuelo.

"My head is full of lead."

He's pinning his last hopes on journalism. It provides an income, enables him to travel and to write. They send him to Spain in the middle of the Civil War as a correspondent. When he goes back to Barcelona, which he visited so many times while he was flying the Spanish route, he doesn't recognise it. The small rooming house facing the Ritz where the pilots used to stay has been taken over by the local militia and converted into run-down barracks. He travels to the Madrid front and is filled with horror at the sight of such a cruel and chaotic war. In his chronicles, he writes: *A civil war is not a war but a disease.*

He starts to move heaven and earth and government offices to set up the aerial distance race. He manages to convince Minister Cot of the importance of placing France back where it used to be—on the pinnacle of international prestige in the air. Where truth fails, prestige succeeds.

He proposes establishing a record on the American air route from north to south, from Montréal to Punta Arenas. France has lost its South American airmail routes. For every plane France manufactures, Italy makes three and Germany, six. Gestures such as establishing air race records are currently all that is left for France.

But this useless long-distance air race is also of paramount importance to Antoine, something of which the politicians are unaware: He needs to fly again.

The preparations are complex. Making the money stretch isn't easy either, but he does it. There's a degree of risk, and several friends have tried to talk him out of it. But no one can convince him to stay in Paris in the house he shares with Consuelo, which is more like a hostel where people he barely knows constantly come and go. He must get rid of the apathy which is eating away at him inside.

He and the plane arrive in North America by boat. He disembarks in Canada and safely completes the North American legs. At the airfield in Guatemala City he points the Simoun down the runway for takeoff. The readings on all the gauges are right and the fuel tank is full. As the plane picks up speed, however, it doesn't reach its usual power. By the time he realises that they shouldn't have filled the tank so full at an airport that's situated at an altitude of 1,600 metres, it's too late to abort the takeoff before the plane hits an obstacle at the end of the runway. Though he pulls on the joystick with all his might and just avoids hitting the obstacle, the plane immediately collapses under its own weight and slams into the ground.

The machine is wrecked, and Antoine is urgently transferred to hospital. Eight fractures, and a very ugly wound in one hand. He doesn't fall into a coma, but after a few days, the wound in his hand becomes seriously infected. The doctors decide they must amputate.

Antoine, weak and with limited Spanish, tries to refuse. But the doctors can't see any other solution.

One morning, there's a sound of voices on his floor. A familiar voice is arguing in Spanish. Consuelo enters like a whirlwind, followed by two nurses. They've been trying to convince her that the doctor can't come right now, because he's doing his rounds in another ward. Antoine only partially understands what she's saying to them, but she uses her title, La Condesa de Saint-Exupéry, and does it in such an arrogant fashion that the two nurses end up whispering their apologies.

Despite his broken jaw, Antoine smiles.

"Consuelo, don't frighten them. They're good girls. They treat me very well."

"Always thinking about girls! I thought you were dying!"

"But I already told you, in the telegram I dictated, that I was out of danger . . ."

"And since when do you say a single word of truth?"

Reasoning with Consuelo is like trying to put out a fire with a watering can. He doesn't even bother. And anyway, his jaw hurts when he speaks.

"Consuelo, explain to the doctor that I'm not going to allow them to amputate my hand."

"And why would they have to do that?"

"They say the infection won't let up, and it could cause septicaemia."

"There have been lots of illustrious, one-handed people, darling. But it really isn't very pleasant."

"It's not a question of being pleasant! How am I going to fly and write if I'm missing a hand?"

"Always thinking about yourself!"

The doctor comes in and Consuelo introduces herself. She doesn't let him say a word. She tells him that her husband is a famous writer, a celebrity in Paris.

"You cannot deprive France of one of its most illustrious pens."

"But, señora, the infection . . ."

"Give him penicillin."

"It hasn't worked . . ."

"Then rub it with an ointment of hot papaya and sage, and say ten Our Fathers. That's how my grandmother cured an aunt of mine who was knocked over by a car."

"Señora, I am a doctor."

"Then heal him!"

The doctor decides that he has visits to attend to and will return later.

"Consuelo, you've scared him off!" says an amused Antoine from his bed.

Consuelo stays several days beside her husband's bed. His fractures are mending, but the hand is getting worse. And then one morning, she says she can't stand the smell of the hospital, that she has to visit her family in El Salvador, and that when he's better, he's to join her. As quickly as she arrived, she departs. Consuelo can't stay still for long in one spot. She's a sunflower; if she doesn't move toward the light, she withers.

Antoine asks them to bring a phone to his room and he calls the Vigny household. He asks Nicole to make enquiries of the insurance company with which he took out a policy for this trip, because here in Guatemala City they can't cast any light on what he's entitled to. She notes down the details, and forty-eight hours later, a French doctor visits him and recommends that he be transferred to the United States. That requires a great deal of negotiation, but eventually, the insurance company agrees to cover the cost. The hospital is relieved to be rid of this difficult patient who doesn't want to have an operation and could collapse because of his stubbornness. He's put on a commercial flight to New York.

His shoulder has knitted together, but he'll never be able to raise his hand above his head again. He gets dizzy spells, and he's worried about his hand. An airline company employee helps him into a wheelchair when they land, and wheels him into the arrivals terminal.

A surprise is waiting for him there—Nicole Vigny herself. She's wearing a wide skirt with geometric designs all over it in the latest New York fashion, as if she'd been in the city for months, and with it, a tight black pullover and an elegant gold choker around her slender neck. She looks at him with affectionate concern when she sees the scars on his chin, his bandaged hand, and the trouble he has in walking.

"How are you?"

"Happy to see you."

Arriving in New York from the airport is a bit like seeing the work of a magician. After driving past empty, desolate fields, a forest of sky-scrapers appears from nowhere. Antoine thinks the people aren't as smartly dressed as in Paris; there are even men with no hats. The streets are busy with a stream of yellow taxis, trolleybuses, and boys shouting out the headlines from the bundle of newspapers they're carrying under their arms. For some reason that he'll never fully understand, steam arises from the covers of the sewers, adding a certain feeling of unreality and woolliness to the hurried to-ing and fro-ing of the pedestrians.

When they get to the apartment in an elegant street behind the Museum of Natural History, they are welcomed by a doorman dressed in an absurd maroon suit, a matching peaked cap, and an excessive amount of gold braid, as if he were the admiral of some impossible armada.

"The insurance company wanted to put you in Brooklyn," Nicole tells him as she opens the curtains of an enormous picture window. "But in my own way, I persuaded them otherwise. If you're not in Manhattan, you're not in New York."

"How did you make them change their minds?"

She puts her finger on his lips in the manner of a teacher telling a rebellious student to be quiet.

The American doctors are also of the opinion that the hand must be amputated. But Antoine insists that he won't allow it. In the end, they lance it, releasing an enormous amount of pus, and the wound finally begins to heal. It will take him several weeks to recuperate and he'll have to go to rehabilitation sessions every day. Nicole doesn't leave his side. In contrast to Consuelo, she's organised and decisive, exceptional at solving practical matters. It also helps that she's rich. She combines shopping in the mornings with afternoons accompanying Antoine to elegant cafés where she translates the English newspapers for him.

The letters he sends to the address Consuelo gave him in San

Salvador come back unopened. After many unsuccessful calls to the apartment in Paris, the cleaning lady picks up the phone one day, and tells him that no one has been in the apartment for weeks.

In the United States, his editors have shown an interest in publishing a new book by him, and the generous advance they've given him allows him to pay off a few debts and get by for a while. He has decided to use some of the stories he spent much of his life telling his friends at the Deux Magots and the Brasserie Lipp, and turn them into a book.

They are tales of adventures, the skies, and friendship that he's been carrying around in his pockets; and when he takes them out, he finds they have matured like fruit.

CHAPTER 74

Paris, 1938

Antoine de Saint-Exupéry

Antoine returns to France after a long absence. He hasn't heard a word from Consuelo for more than two months. He finds a letter from her in the mailbox in which she tells him that she had no idea where to contact him and so, since she felt very lonely, she's gone to spend some time in a house belonging to Toboggan on the outskirts of Paris.

That nobody!

He sends her a couple of telegrams and finally, one night, she calls him, greatly affected by the death of a cat she's been looking after.

"He used to come to the porch every night to drink the milk I prepared for him!"

"Consuelo, we haven't seen each other for more than two months and the only thing that concerns you is the death of a stray cat?"

"Papou, you've never been good with animals."

He gives up; she's impossible.

The noise of a party makes its way down the phone line and they can barely understand each other; they have never in all these years fully understood each other.

When Consuelo hangs up and opens the study door, it's as if she's throwing herself into a pool of sound bubbles in the living room: She makes her way into the smoky room through the pounding of a four-hand-piano improvisation by two of Toboggan's friends, booming voices, and roars of laughter.

A young female sculptor with fanciful ideas comes running over and urgently tugs at Consuelo's sleeve to tell her that she's going to blow away all of Paris with her project to turn the obelisk in the Place de la Concorde into a gigantic pencil. Consuelo suggests, very seriously, turning it into an Aztec totem, and adds that she could help with the colours. The artist, her eyes glassy from too much punch, screams that it is a brilliant idea, that it will be a revolution in the art world, and hugs Consuelo as if she'd just saved her life.

Consuelo decides to head for the drinks table to keep pace with her inebriated guests. She makes her way among the funny, carefree conversations. As she goes by, a very attractive young man bows to her theatrically as if she were a princess and makes her laugh. She is still laughing when she reaches the punch bowl, where the fruit floats drunkenly in the alcohol, and when she gazes through the window that overlooks the garden, she sees that darkness has fallen. As she looks more closely, she spots a tiny plane, silhouetted against the full moon, as its fragility briefly flies across its face and disappears into the night. And at that moment, her laughter dries up and the glass of punch drops from her hand, shattering on the floor into a thousand pieces. Nobody notices; there's too much commotion for anyone to notice anything.

In that moment, Consuelo would trade all the noise for a silent hug from her Papou. She already knows that he is selfish, as fickle and capricious as a child, but perhaps that's why she loves him so much, like the child she desired but will never be able to have because of a childhood illness, although this is something that she never tells anyone. She doesn't understand why, when she and Papou are together, everything immediately goes off the rails, and, on the other hand, when he's far away, she misses him so much. Toboggan comes up behind her and tells her what a wonderful creature she is. He tickles her as he gently kisses her on the neck, and Consuelo laughs. Laughter, that's what she needs. Laughter is a way of looking outward and diverting your eyes from the darkness within. She holds out another glass for someone to fill to the top with punch.

Antoine also leaves Paris on a trip to Germany to write a series of commissioned articles.

Though it looked as if it was going to be impossible to get permission to enter Germany during these days of heightened tension, Nicole has such good contacts in the most unexpected places that she acquires authorisation for the two of them, and they travel in her car. Nicole is a beautiful blond mystery: There's a part of her which is totally inaccessible, a locked door behind which she keeps her secrets.

"Nicole . . . how do you know so many important people in Germany?"

"Oh, Antoine, I even know people in Hell."

They visit luxurious houses belonging to friends of hers, fly in a rented plane piloted by Antoine, and study with concern the frantic activities of a country preparing itself for something huge. Germany denies it, but it is expanding greatly in the centre of the continent, and throwing a menacing shadow across all of Europe.

On his return to Paris, Antoine sees the same cars and trams circulating. Along the avenues, cigar smoke hovers above the terrace tables littered with glasses of Orangina and glass soda siphons with silver-plated parrot beaks. Men wearing felt hats read newspapers, cups of coffee in front of them. Shoe-shine boys carry wooden boxes with handles shaped like the sole of a shoe. The city seems the same, but it is different. Now, conversations are more heated, lovers say goodbye on street corners with more urgency, traffic officers direct traffic with more impatient gestures. There's no explicit talk of war, but the threat of it hangs in the air like the flu. Paris is coughing.

A few weeks earlier, Édouard Daladier, France's prime minister, and Neville Chamberlain, the British prime minister, had taken part in a meeting in Munich with the German chancellor, Adolf Hitler. Hitler, an insignificant figure even in the size of his moustache, was nevertheless looming over Europe. He wanted to annex the Sudetenland region of Czechoslovakia, on the grounds that the majority of its inhabitants spoke German. Hitler didn't ask; he insisted. The newspapers referred to it as the Munich Agreement, but it wasn't an agreement, it was a backdown.

When Prime Minister Daladier landed at the airport in Paris, a crowd was waiting for him in the terminal to welcome and applaud him, because they believed that he had managed to prevent war. Nobody wanted to accept what everyone knew: If you throw a lamb chop to a hungry wolf, you don't satisfy it; rather, you are showing it the way to the pantry.

Nicole provides Antoine with crucial support in this period when the atmosphere in the country is tense and his relationship with Consuelo is falling apart. He doesn't have a plan. Nicole has no intention whatsoever of divorcing her husband, although they have led separate lives for a long time by mutual agreement. Divorce is expensive and the affluent are practical people.

She and Antoine dine in high-end restaurants; they hold hands in private; she listens to him with admiration when he reads her the pages he has written, they engage in sex between laughs. It feels like love, but it's a game. A game they have to keep playing to stay alive.

1939

It starts to rain as Antoine is strolling along the Left Bank of the Seine and hears the news being shouted out by the vendor protecting his newspapers under his jacket. Hitler has declared war on Poland. It's been only six months since Hitler's army strolled into Prague, as Britain and France showed indifference. Hitler wants to keep marching. The caterpillar tracks of his tanks and the stamp of his army's boots won't stop until he has trampled over all of Europe.

Antoine reaches his apartment with the rain still falling, his wet clothes glued to his body. He throws his keys on top of the mess on the hall table and notices a letter on the floor beside the door. It's covered with official stamps. He's been hoping for its arrival ever since his trip to Germany where, at all the airfields, he saw huge numbers of fighter planes lined up outside because there was no more space in the hangars: No one builds more planes than hangars unless they are planning to move them around.

War has sneaked into his house through the crack under the door. The letter informs him that he has been mobilised and is to report to the Toulouse-Francazal military aerodrome in the uniform of a reserve officer within a week.

CHAPTER 75

★

Toulouse, 1939

Antoine de Saint-Exupéry

Since declaring war on Poland, the Germans have waited only a week to plant themselves at the gates of Warsaw. They'll knock them down with one puff.

Antoine smokes and scribbles on pieces of paper in his room in the Grand Hotel, where the officers are lodged. He used to love Toulouse, but now he feels imprisoned in the city. The doctors who examined him were reluctant to let him join the ranks: His hand might have recovered, but he is almost forty, his left shoulder is still semi-paralyzed, and he is overweight. They told him he'd have the rank of captain, but his place in the war would be behind a desk. He demanded to be sent to fight on the front lines in the defence of liberty. He became incensed, he howled, he slammed his fist on top of their desks, making the stethoscopes jump. But he didn't succeed in making any impression on the doctors.

They've posted him to Toulouse as a pilot instructor in the rear guard.

He walks around his room like a caged animal. He tosses out half-finished cigarettes and lights up others. He writes a few lines and tears up the paper. He leans out the window for the sixth or seventh time. He looks at his watch anxiously; Nicole is late. He hasn't seen her for weeks. Incapable of containing his nervousness, he goes down to the lobby to wait for her. He's wearing the shirt and trousers of his uniform, but an ordinary wool blazer. It's not regulation wear, but he doesn't care. The hotel lobby is very busy, but he doesn't care about that either. His relationship is the least clandestine of clandestine relationships in France.

Just then, Nicole arrives in her elegant hat and a tight-fitting coat with mink cuffs. A wave of pleasure invades him when he sees her, and Nicole gives him that tender smile she reserves solely for him.

"How are you, Antoine? Are you writing?"

He smiles flirtatiously and the scar on his chin seems to shrink.

"Why do you always ask me if I'm writing? Are you going to be my publisher?"

"If you're writing, I know you're well. You don't write when you're depressed."

"Right now I'm not depressed, I'm hopping mad. You have to help me."

"Invite me for a sherry."

Nicole, somewhere between scandalised and amused, takes in his messy room. She already knows that Antoine is incapable of turning his workspace into anything but a junkyard. There are sheets of paper scattered everywhere: on the sofa, on the bed, even in the bathroom. The desk, in fact, contains the fewest pieces of paper. It's covered with sunglasses, a small shaver, several books about aeronautics, a scarf, old newspapers, two dirty cups, even a flute.

Antoine clears an armchair so she can sit down.

454

"Nicole, you have to get me out of here."

"Out of this pigsty? You seem quite at home."

"I'm serious. I need a posting away from Toulouse."

"They offered you work in the ministry's propaganda department and you told them to get lost."

"Propaganda! I can't do that!"

"But writing about how dangerous the threat of Nazism is and encouraging people to enlist to defend liberty is important work."

"Dammit! Of course it's important! But how can I encourage people to fight for France if I'm taking cover in a rear-guard office, drinking sherry and smoking cigars? I don't want to be one of those intellectuals who stay safe in the cupboard like jars of marmalade. You have to help me get posted to a combat unit. I can't stay here with my arms folded."

"But your arms aren't folded. You're training young men."

Antoine grabs his forehead with the hand not holding a cigarette. He has one of those migraines which have become frequent since his accident in Guatemala.

"It's true that training is a good thing, but it's not my profession. I'm a pilot. I can't allow young people to risk their lives defending all of us while I do little drawings with chalk on a blackboard."

"But you wrote to me that you've sent requests and they've been refused."

"Can you believe it? Petitions, documents, declarations . . . I'm requesting to fight at the front for my country and they tell me to fill in a form. War annihilates everything except bureaucracy. And then they reply in a note signed by some undersecretary that my request has been denied. Imbeciles! Do you know anybody in the war ministry?"

The expression of impatient annoyance typical of adolescents when they don't get their way is reflected in Antoine's face.

"You're asking me to get you sent to the front."

"Exactly."

Nicole sighs. She reaches out and brushes his cheek with tips of her fingers. She is definitely not a fragile woman, but right at this moment, she feels as if she's had the rug pulled out from under her. Maybe that's what she finds so attractive in him: He takes her away from her control over things, makes life seem like it's made of very fine glass on the verge of shattering, so every minute is vital.

"Antoine, what women normally do is protect the men they love."

"I burn up inside that closed hall with its coal stove going from first thing in the morning. That chalk dust that gets in your throat asphyxiates me. The walls crush me. I only know how to live in the open skies."

"Are you asking me to demand that you be sent to the front so they'll kill you?"

"I'm asking you to have me sent to the front to save me."

She grabs hold of his cigarette. She inhales deeply and expels a cloud of smoke which briefly floats in the room. The two of them silently watch the smoke stretching, contorting, fraying.

"Nicole . . ."

"What?"

"Will you do it?"

"I can't tell a state secretary what to do."

"Then tell a minister. I'm certain that you can do it . . ."

She gives him a coquettish smile, and slowly nods her head.

Of course she can.

In Orconte, east of Paris, Lieutenant Laux is in a foul mood. When his boss, Major Alias, informed him several days ago that Captain de Saint-Exupéry was going to join Reconnaissance Group II/33, it pleased him as much as a kick in the groin.

Alias gave him the news personally during a visit, and the news didn't please him either. Alias doesn't trust civilian pilots obsessed with

air races and flattery in the press and accustomed to flying while playing to the gallery. And on top of all that, he's a literary celebrity. And an
aristocrat to boot.

Laux is currently in charge of the squadron, and the last thing he
needs is an arrogant prima donna further complicating a situation
which is already complicated enough. There's another matter that
makes him uncomfortable. He's the leader of the squadron because
the previous leader was transferred, but he only has the rank of lieutenant, and Saint-Exupéry is coming in with the higher rank of captain.
Alias has told Laux that he is in charge in all but rank, but not everyone
shares that view.

Lieutenant Israël pokes his head in.

"Has the star arrived yet? Has he told you if he's going to fly or
shoot a film?"

"Don't piss me off, Israël. I'm not in the mood."

"I hear he's middle-aged. Do we give him a plane or a wheelchair?"

"Get out of here!"

Laux hears the sound of a car engine and when he looks out of
his window, he sees an elegant, slightly dusty DeSoto. A burly officer
with a snub nose gets out. He hears a brief conversation with his adjutant and then footsteps escorting him to Laux's office. He stands up
to welcome the new pilot with his captain's stars. He's spent two days
preparing a speech in which he'll inform the captain in a respectful but
definitive way that he, Laux, has the confidence of Major Alias to lead
the squadron despite his lower rank, and that the captain must follow
his orders, like any other officer in the unit. He gives a quick sigh before
a man who, seen up close, has a face marked with scars comes through
the door to be greeted by him.

"Lieutenant Laux, squadron leader."

"Saint-Exupéry, pilot."

Antoine holds out his hand with a smile.

"We weren't sure if you would arrive today or tomorrow. I'll advise Lieutenant Gandard to vacate the room in the mansion for you."

"What? They have to move out a fellow officer? No way! Wherever it was he was going to be shunted to, that's where I'll go."

"But it's a tiny room in a ramshackle farmhouse . . ."

"Perfect."

During the meal in the officers' mess, everyone studies the writer in his captain's uniform with curiosity and a certain discomfort. Antoine feels as if he's back in Montaudran being watched with a degree of prejudice as he enters the veteran pilots' room. He cautiously asks these officers what life is like here and they answer unenthusiastically. When the silence becomes uncomfortable, Antoine takes a pack of cards from his pocket.

"Look at the card and don't tell me what it is."

One of the sublieutenants, full of scepticism, picks a card and puts it back in the pack, and after asking another officer to shuffle until he gets tired of doing so, Antoine turns over the top card and there it is. The rest of the officers, bored because they have nothing to do, come over and form a circle.

"Could you do that again, Captain?"

"Of course!"

During the first weeks, it's totally quiet and there are few missions in Orconte. The Germans have pulled back, but that's merely a sign they are reorganising their forces in order to hit even harder. Everything will shudder when their attack comes with all the force of their military machinery and their supremacist fury. Throughout those winter days when missions are reduced, Antoine's card tricks alleviate the tension in the officers' barracks. His proposal that they play the game of connecting words—where the last sound of one word must be the first sound of the next—also proves a success, and turns into an obsession:

"Against . . ."

"Stone . . ."

"Never . . ."

"Ver . . . ver . . . ver . . ."

"Vertical! Bad luck, it's your turn to pay for the beer!"

"But we've run out of beer," the soldier-barman points out.

"Then jot it down for after the war," Antoine calls out.

"He's already got seven on the tab."

"Even better! That way we'll drink them all in one hit to celebrate."

Now and again, Antoine tires of the comfortable officers' mess, with its padded sofas and the heat from the woodstove, which makes him drowsy. He needs to go outside and walk up and down the runways and hangars. He invites the maintenance employees for a smoke and provides them with gossip from the officers' mess. During one lunch break, he sees Sergeant Farget trying to fix a part from a smashed radiator.

"That radiator is shot, Sergeant!"

"It is, Captain. They wanted to throw it in the trash, but I'm trying to rescue it."

The mechanic clenches his jaw as he uses a screwdriver as a lever to unfold a rod. His knuckles are white, and he grits his teeth. It resists, but he persists.

Antoine watches him, full of admiration. Men like Farget are never given medals or honours, and they never appear in the history books, but they are the ones who keep the world moving.

One afternoon, the officers in the unit are sitting around waiting for night to fall with that air of restless laziness that accompanies any waiting. Conversations have stopped and there's a certain boredom. Captain de Saint-Exupéry has been away on three days' leave in Paris and his absence is noticeable. They've all become accustomed to his presence, his tales of flying in South America and the desert. The door to the mess opens and a wintery gust blows in. They all turn around and see the captain coming in with a flamboyant wooden box.

459

"What have you got there?"

Antoine goes over to the table they use to eat, play chess, write letters to family, and spread-out maps. Everyone's intrigued, and they get up and follow him. When he opens the box, they see that it's a gramophone. He attaches a handle to wind it up and the turntable starts to move. He removes a record of ballads by Tino Rossi from its cover.

The sound emerges from the small loudspeaker built into the box as if it were coming from far away. For these soldiers waiting for the German onslaught far from home, their families, and the things that give meaning to their lives, the music has the effect of activating the emotional zones of their brains which have been in hibernation. The music connects them with the lives they've left behind. Sublieutenant Aron feels his feet moving and picks up a broom leaning against a wall. He slowly, lovingly, dances with it while the rest of the airmen laugh and whistle.

At that moment, Lieutenant Laux walks in. The dancer comes to attention and there's a moment's silence, where the only thing to be heard is the slightly piercing song. It's Antoine who takes a step toward him and speaks to him with warm respect:

"Lieutenant, I brought back a gramophone and I couldn't resist putting it on."

"A gramophone in the officers' mess . . ."

"If you don't think it's a good idea, we can turn it off."

Laux looks at him.

They all watch expectantly. And Laux, usually so serious, gives a huge smile: "We'll open a bottle of cognac I was saving for a special day!"

"Three cheers for Lieutenant Laux!" someone shouts, and they all respond by enthusiastically tossing their caps in the air.

The atmosphere of lively comradeship on the base turns to silence at night when Antoine heads to the place in town where he sleeps. It's a modest room in a somewhat dilapidated little house.

The windows don't fit properly, and an icy cold comes in through the gaps. Every morning before he can wash his face with the water in the bowl in his room, he first has to break the layer of ice on the surface. He enjoys breaking it with the tip of his letter opener and making the icebergs crash against each other like tiny glass boats.

It's as if he were in a monk's cell. He feels in the silence a sense of transcendence which removes any longing for the Parisian feasts he's always enjoyed, together with the noise of the social get-togethers. He certainly has missed them occasionally. But in other moments of solitude and reflection, as he's scribbling lines on a piece of paper with his fountain pen, he has the impression that he's crossed a boundary beyond which there is no anxiety or frustration, and he feels that he is finally on the right path.

Some nights, before he goes to bed, if his fingers aren't numb with cold, he writes a few lines infused with feverish mysticism: *It isn't deeds that are important, or even people. Rather, what's critical are the knots of relationships; the connections.*

He also writes very long letters that are declarations: to Nicole, Consuelo, his mother, his friends . . . He doesn't think about Lou-Lou. He's eradicated her from his memory. He traces a cross in the air, as if he were erasing her from his life. Sometimes, his melancholy deepens. He has a bottle of whisky for such occasions, which he has to replace with increasing frequency. He tells himself it's to keep himself warm in the cold. The cold that gets right inside you.

CHAPTER 76

Orconte (France), 1940

ANTOINE DE SAINT-EXUPÉRY

BECAUSE OF THE LACK OF wintertime activity, the officers' building of Reconnaissance Group II/33 has been converted into a club for men at leisure who watch the snow on the airfield's runways. It seems that winter has put the war to sleep, just as it does bears.

Antoine has dedicated weeks to card tricks and chess, but also to considering the problem of the jamming of the machine guns on the Potez planes because of the cold during high altitude flights. And he has found a technical solution which he presents to the war ministry.

He has also had a couple of visits from Nicole during those same weeks. She has a friend who lets her use her house in the neighbouring town of Arrigny. Nicole has an ability to get anything anywhere, which fascinates Antoine. The house has been unused for months, but before they arrive, the person in the town who looks after its maintenance has filled the woodshed with logs, while a huge jug of milk and a basket of fruit give the dining room table the appearance of a tavern.

Sitting in front of the open fireplace, Antoine reads Nicole his notes for a play he's trying to write, an adaptation of some of the aviation stories he collected into a volume which has been published in France as *Terre des hommes*, and in America as *Wind, Sand and Stars*. The book is dedicated to Henri Guillaumet and includes the tale of his remarkable Andean adventure.

"And how are you going to have planes flying on the stage of a theatre?"

"Nicole, you're so pragmatic! How do you cram the peaks of the Andes into the pages of a book? Mankind's oldest invention is the imagination!"

"Mankind's oldest invention is sex!"

"I don't know how to do it . . ."

"You've forgotten how to have sex?"

"I don't know how to advance this play. It all sounds lifeless to me. I must be the worst writer in the world."

Nicole reaches over to him, holds him tightly in her arms, and cuddles him.

She is as elegant a woman naked as when she is dressed, and by the light of the fire, her blond hair looks even more golden.

"You have enormous talent, you just have to find the right way to channel it into the outcome you're after," she says as she unbuttons his captain's shirt.

"With you, life always seems simple."

"You're an expert in making it more difficult than it is."

Good news arrives one day from the United States: *Wind, Sand and Stars* has won the prestigious National Book Award (1939) of the American Booksellers Association. The French press is talking about the award at a time when good news is scarce, and this has resulted in the information ministry strengthening its insistence that he join their department in a senior position.

At the end of February, Antoine has to go to Paris at the invitation of Minister Giraudoux. Once in the minister's office, Giraudoux stresses that Antoine can best serve the nation in his ministry. He tells him that they are considering him to lead a diplomatic mission to the United States. Since his National Book Award, his is the most highly regarded French voice in North America. Giraudoux's arguments are flawless, and Antoine knows it. But that doesn't prevent his sulky refusal.

Next, he heads for another appointment on the Boulevard du Montparnasse—a meal at the brasserie Le Dôme, known as the Anglo-American café. That's not something that Daurat would have over-looked. *Since when has any detail escaped Daurat's attention?*

When he arrives, Daurat is waiting for him, with his impeccably trimmed moustache, his panama hat, his dark suit, a few extra kilos, but with the same gleam in his eyes. His boss—to Antoine, he'll always be his boss—holds out his hand. Antoine would like to embrace him, but he's well aware that Monsieur Daurat doesn't like such effusiveness.

His eyes tell Antoine that he's happy they're meeting again.

The brasserie is one of the city's most celebrated restaurants, but there are barely four tables occupied. Paris is a dejected city.

Daurat and Saint-Ex share a bittersweet past, full of tragedies and young lives lost. But they lived that past with such intensity that it erases even irreplaceable absences like that of Mermoz, who has left an immense hole. It's when coffee is served that Daurat lights a cigarette and looks Antoine in the eyes.

"France needs you here, in Paris."

"Monsieur Daurat, I'm a pilot . . ."

"You are forty years old and a pile of broken bones."

Antoine frowns. "You, too, think I'm too old to fly?"

"Yes."

There's silence at the table and Antoine takes out another ciga-rette. He's annoyed with Daurat, but only for thirty seconds. Daurat could have argued, as other friends have—including Consuelo and Nicole—that he's of more use to the diplomatic service. But it's the fact that Daurat is telling him the truth that Antoine finds most annoying: If Daurat were the leader of his squadron, he'd leave Antoine on the ground. *You don't put a pilot at the controls if he's not in peak condition.*

"You're stubborn, Saint-Exupéry. Stubbornness kills."

"What kills is not living, Monsieur Daurat."

"I'm not a man of letters, so don't give me those sorts of arguments. There are many who can fly a plane, but you are the only one who can shut up that loudmouth Lindbergh."

"A great pilot."

"And a complete idiot. He's the front man for the idea that the United States should be neutral in this war. He even says that Hitler is a man who adores order and has nothing against Americans."

"How do you expect me to go to America to ask them to sacrifice their sons in the defence of my country if I haven't done it first? With what moral authority can I do that?"

"Moralists don't win wars."

"Maybe a moral victory is the only one possible."

"What do you hope to achieve with that reconnaissance group, flying slowly over Nazi lines armed with a camera?"

"Those boys . . . you should meet them! I'm sure you'd take them in hand! But you'd like them. They are pilots prepared to do anything in return for nothing. I can't pick up my suitcase as a celebrity now, when tough times are coming, and leave those boys behind. I can't let them down."

Daurat takes a final drag on his cigarette.

"Whom do you intend not to disappoint? Them or yourself? What's more important, France or a group of boys?"

"Monsieur Daurat, those boys *are* France."

Daurat stubs out his cigarette in the ashtray even though it's only half-smoked. He crumples it as if it were a snake and stands up.

"Saint-Exupéry, I don't share your point of view. I don't even understand it. But I'll tell you something: I respect it." He pulls up the collar of his coat, turns and leaves, walking along the boulevard until he's lost among the afternoon parade of hats.

Antoine has to make a second important visit. He hasn't seen Consuelo for weeks.

He phoned her a few days earlier to avoid the disappointment of his last visit, when he went home to surprise her following an appointment at the information ministry, but no one was there. He unlocked the door and all he found was a mess of illustrated magazines lying about everywhere, scattered shoes and clothes, and half-painted vases in the room she had converted into her workshop. He spent the night there, got up the next morning, had breakfast, and left without Consuelo putting in an appearance. Three days later, she called him at the base and told him she was making a vase so he could fill it with spring flowers. She told him about friends who were asking after him, and how insufferably snooty the waiters were in the Café de Flore. Not a word about her absence. And he didn't ask for an explanation.

When he gets to the apartment, he rings the bell but there's no answer. He rings a second time; nothing. He doesn't know if he should try a third time or just use his house key, and then he hears the bolt turning and the door opens.

"My apologies, darling, I was in the bathroom."

She's standing on the threshold dripping water.

"Consuelo . . . you're naked!"

"Of course, Papou. I hate taking a bath in my clothes."

The water is running down her diminutive but very well-proportioned body and her black hair is shining.

"You've always been a very beautiful woman."

She smiles.

"Shall I get you a drink?"

And she walks toward the well-stocked drinks cabinet, saluting him with her porcelain-doll buttocks.

"Aren't you going to get dressed?"

She searches through the bottles and her small breasts move rhythmically. "Do you want me to get dressed?"

Antoine laughs. "No, not really."

"You know something? I want to collaborate with the French military."

"You don't say! And how?"

She approaches him with two Pernods tinkling with ice. Antoine laughs as she gently pushes him until he's reclining on the sofa. Smiling, he thinks of protesting, because they'd be more comfortable on the bed, but he already knows Consuelo's whims: Never make love in the same place where you sleep.

CHAPTER 77

Orconte (France), 1940

ANTOINE DE SAINT-EXUPÉRY

IN APRIL, EVIL AWAKENS. THE Nazis are so calculating they've allowed winter to go by. They've even allowed the French military to become overconfident: It has relaxed discipline because of the weeks of inactivity. But what appeared to be a lull has been cover for months of insane activity in the German factories. When their war machinery finally starts to march toward France, barriers fall one after another like dominos. War is a game played by cruel children.

The reconnaissance unit comes to a boil. High Command asks for daily reports on enemy troop movements. Flights become more and more dangerous, and more and more tragic.

Antoine walks over to the window and studies the landing strip. Major Alias, hands behind his back, walks in circles. It's cold, but he's not wearing his military jacket. He's oblivious to the icy conditions. The plane carrying pilot Charron, photographer-observer Renaudot, and gunner Courtois hasn't returned.

Their mission was to fly to Frankfurt, across enemy lines, and photograph the arms factories to generate attack maps for the French Air Force. Antiaircraft weapons don't reach a height of 4,000 metres. But German fighter planes do. Quick, accurate, relentless. The reconnaissance planes are like cows which are tirelessly pursued by hungry wolves.

When the last possible time for their arrival back at the base has passed, based on the amount of fuel they were carrying, everyone knows they won't return. Alias looks at his watch, performs one more circuit, then goes straight to the hut he uses as an office and slams the door shut. A short while later, they see his adjutant crossing the asphalt path which separates his hut from the pilots' mess. He's trawling for more bait to throw to the Nazis. He comes into the room and all eyes turn to him. Someone will become the next log to burn on the bonfire.

"Lieutenant Vinsonneau, the major is waiting for you."

Vinsonneau takes his cap and heads for the door without the slightest fuss. He's going to fly toward the German lines to roast himself on the middle of a grill, but he doesn't seem to be the least bit affected. War turns danger into one more routine, like polishing your boots or trimming your hair so it's above your ears. Vinsonneau knows he has a fifty-fifty chance of returning. It's a toss of the coin with his life. This might be the last morning he sees, but he shows no sign of irritation, never mind rebellion. Or euphoria. Neither patriotism nor exhortation is fashionable in this unit.

Alias is a major who rarely shouts. He looks into eyes a lot. He reads his soldiers' pupils. If he detects fear, he gives the pilot the opportunity to refuse a mission. When Vinsonneau comes into his office, he begins to give him precise instructions. The lieutenant watches him without moving a muscle, without drumming his fingers on the desk or smoking feverishly. He appears totally calm, but there's one detail which Major Alias doesn't miss: His nose has reddened. Vinsonneau can control his body language and order his fingers to keep still. But that hint of colour, that foreboding which silently advances from some remote corner of his nervous system tinges his nose. It's a red traffic light signal that Alias doesn't ignore. He pauses in delivering the technical details.

"Lieutenant, if you think you aren't fit enough to tackle this mission, we can replace you."

Vinsonneau shakes his head vigorously.

Alias nods and carries on with his briefing.

From the officers' mess, they hear Vinsonneau taking off with his observer and his gunner. A low altitude mission, flying between the flak and the fighter planes. One of those missions that can only be described as poison. The hours go by. Too many hours. Night falls and Vinsonneau and his crew haven't returned. There's always the hope that they bailed out with their parachutes and are on their way to a prisoner-of-war camp. Hope is a straw you clutch at so many times during wartime that eventually it snaps.

More colleagues who won't come back. There are no bodies or wakes. There's no time for ceremonies. Another reconnaissance mission will fly out the next day.

There are more and more empty armchairs in the officers' mess. Major Alias takes off to Command HQ which is moving around the region. The roads are packed with convoys which seem to come and go without rhyme or reason. There are also small flatbed trucks carrying old women dressed in black, bicycles balancing towers of suitcases, old mules reluctantly dragging carts loaded with children, pumpkins, and farm tools. They mingle with the military vehicles going in one direction or the other, getting in each other's way. France doesn't know if it's attacking someone or defending itself.

For his visit to Command HQ, Alias has put on his uniform with all his medals. He asks for more pilots, to rotate his missions more easily. There aren't any. He asks for new, faster planes. There aren't any. He asks them to explain the French Army's plan. There isn't one. But they order him to keep up the reconnaissance missions.

"We need them to identify the exact position of the German batteries on the border with France."

"Border" is no longer a precise concept. Before the war, borders were a serious matter, with barriers guarded by responsible policemen blocking the way. They were drawn on maps with millimetric precision, but the war has turned them into chalk lines. The Nazis erase France's border each day with the soles of their boots.

"You want us to locate the position of an advancing army? By the time the information regarding the battery positions arrives here and our bombers head there, the Germans will already be somewhere else."

One of the generals addresses him with irritating condescension. "My dear Major Alias, you shouldn't express such ideas. That kind of thinking undermines the morale of the troops. It is not appropriate."

High Command believes that what is appropriate is worrying about the soldiers' spirits. Their lives concern them less. It is acceptable for a soldier to lose a leg, or become deaf because of the impact of a nearby explosion, or die; it is, however, inadmissible for him to become demoralised.

Alias seethes. "To avoid the German fighter planes, we have to fly at five hundred kilometres per hour at an altitude of ten thousand metres. How are we going to detect machine-gun nests doing that?"

"You'll know their position when they fire."

Alias stares at the general. Such reports are useless. Alias knows it. The general knows it too.

It's rare in any given week for a crew to take off and return. Young men who a moment ago were happy-go-lucky are now simply decomposing bodies.

Antoine watches his comrades departing and reflects that summer is coming, with its warm breezes and the sweetness of its flowers, but they won't see it anymore. They won't see the wheat growing. They won't see their children growing.

You have to be an absolute idiot to believe that there's something epic about a war!

As the season advances with an astronomical lack of urgency, chaos takes possession of France. The roads that connect the base with Command HQ become more and more blocked, phone lines come down and nobody restores them. The joint chiefs of staff are playing hopscotch throughout the Ardennes region.

And Reconnaissance Group II/33 continues to take off with the aim of undertaking low altitude missions so the Germans can practise clay target shooting. If they're lucky, the planes return with reports that will get lost in the communications chaos. Antoine writes in his notebook with the wrinkled covers: *Men throw themselves into combat like glasses of water being thrown on a fire.*

Alias summons Saint-Exupéry into his office. Antoine likes his boss's elegant style—the impeccable cut of his white hair and his movie-star looks. He reads into the serious expression of the major, recently returned from Command HQ, that the news isn't good. Alias is standing with his hands behind his back, but he asks Antoine to take a seat. He walks over to a map of the region that is starting to show some unfortunate tears. He points to a zone some 300 kilometres to the north, near the border with Belgium.

"We're dealing with a damned awkward mission. You'll have to fly over Arras at low altitude, about seven hundred metres, to locate a column of German armoured vehicles. An observer and Dutertre, the gunner, will accompany you."

Alias has struck up a warm friendship with this captain writer and inventor. He sits down in his chair and squirms restlessly.

"Do you feel up to it, Captain?"

"What time do we leave?"

Alias nods sadly. "You have to be in the air at 0530."

Antoine nods. As he walks toward the annexed buildings, he's thinking that this might be his last afternoon. Only one out of every three regular missions returns; the statistics are worse for a "damned awkward" mission. Before leaving on a mission, there are pilots who go in search of their comrades and drink beer so they won't think about the fact that, in a few hours' time, they'll be heading out for what may be a pointless sacrifice.

Antoine prefers to dedicate this time to meditating, taking notes that try to clarify for him the logic of dying one morning over the skies of Arras. The joint chiefs of staff are moving around, signals aren't working. He's going to raffle his life to find a useless piece of information in the middle of the chaos they are all experiencing. But he reaches the conclusion that that's what waging war is all about: When it's your turn, you have to make a move, and you throw your pawn against a line of rooks and bishops. That's the game.

When he opens his eyes, still in the dead of night, it's Major Alias touching him on the shoulder. He looks at Antoine with the same grave expression he had the previous afternoon.

"If you don't feel a hundred percent ready for this mission, I can replace you."

Antoine sits up in bed. The major is like a mother who allows her sick child with a cold to stay snug in his bed instead of going to school. Children have their privileges.

"I'm ready, Major."

Alias looks at him with affectionate severity.

"Major, this afternoon, in the canteen, we'll have one of those coffees that taste like socks."

"I'll ask one of the adjutants to help you with your flying suit."

Dressing is a tedious ritual. Moreover, Antoine needs assistance because his shoulder problems make it difficult for him to put on the three layers of clothing they wear. He has to adjust the heating circuit, the oxygen tube fitted to the face mask, and the communications lines so he can talk to the photographer-observer and the gunner. When he finishes, he feels like one of those deep-sea divers with lead boots Jules Verne described in *Twenty Thousand Leagues Under the Sea*.

He wobbles his way to the plane, helmet in hand. Right then, he wants something to happen that will abort the mission, a technical issue with the plane, like the thermometer in a child's mouth which shows just the right number of degrees of fever to avoid going to school. It's not fear; fear is something else: nervousness, anxiety, fright. What he is feeling is a crushing indolence, a drowsiness which makes it his greatest wish to drop into one of those worn leather armchairs in the officers' mess, curl up, and sleep. But destiny doesn't allow for sleep. The voice communication system is working, the oxygen tubes are open, the oil pressure gauges are correct. The machine is ready, the crew are in their places, there's no possible reason to delay. They're just waiting for him to give the command.

"Take off."

"Yes, Captain, sir."

He would almost have preferred a sign of rebellion, or a sigh coming from his subalterns' headphones. But they accept the mission with an almost insane composure. They know it's quite possible they are going to die and the only thing they have to say is "Yes, Captain, sir." It might seem absurd, but he loves these men. That "Yes, Captain, sir" is not exuberant in the slightest, not even enthusiastic. They all know that their sacrifice will in no way help France in its impossible battle against Nazism. They'll take photos which will assuredly not reach their base, but if they do, they will not reach Command HQ, and they won't be taken into account in the midst of the tangle of transfers and constant movements. They don't think about Hitler or France when they accept their sacrifice. They actually think about something much less grand: carrying out their mission.

All these thoughts pile up in his head as they reach the specified altitude of 10,000 metres. The drowsiness is mild, the lack of oxygen turns his brain into jelly.

"Captain, compass."

Dutertre is right. In his lapse of concentration, Antoine has deviated a few degrees from the route to Arras. He needs to step on the pedal to enable the change in course, but the pedal is frozen. He puts pressure on it, he stamps on it to force it, but he can't. *The devil take it!* Right then, he doesn't hate Hitler, he doesn't hate the war, he doesn't hate those generals who play chess with nineteen-year-old pawns; he just hates this jammed pedal. That's all that matters. That's his war. He puts pressure on it again. The effort causes him to feel dizzy at the plane's current altitude, and he sees flashes inside his eyes. He can't unblock the pedal and he can't make another effort like the last one or he'll faint. He has to compensate with the plane's controls, moving in a slow zigzag. Exhaustion makes him even drowsier. He felt more anxious on the base; he could barely sleep the previous night. By contrast right now, when they are approaching the German lines, he feels as if he could fall asleep instantly.

"Captain, enemy fighters at forty-five degrees."

He turns his head and sees them. Six Messerschmitts. They change course. They're coming for them.

"Ready, gunner?"

"Ready, Captain."

The pantomime, again. A performance about the war in a provincial theatre would be more truthful than the actual war. They fire their token machine gun as if it were useful when faced with fighter planes armed to the teeth. A single fighter plane would be impossible to tackle with this joke of a weapon. But six . . . !

Rather than being frightened, Antoine is irritated at the inopportune arrival of the fighter planes just when the pedal has frozen. He hasn't been able to calculate how far away the fighter planes are, but he does have one advantage: He and his crew are flying 1,000 metres above the enemy. If they pick up speed, it forces the fighters to climb, and climbing slows down their progress.

"Distance, Dutertre?"

"Unchanged, Captain."

They are flying at maximum speed. The needle showing the engine revolutions is in the red zone. The fighter planes climb.

"Distance, Dutertre?"

"Er . . . yes. We've gained slightly on them!"

Half a kilometre is a tiny distance but when measured vertically, it's crucial.

Antoine grits his teeth, whispers encouraging words to his plane as if it were a Thoroughbred. They maintain their speed.

"They're being left behind, Captain!"

There's a juvenile joy in Dutertre's voice. He doesn't stop to consider that the Messerschmitts are letting them go because they have the secure knowledge that a few kilometres further on, they'll fall into the net of the next patrol. Antoine feels no joy at all; in fact he's sweating, even though the temperature in the cabin is 40°C below zero. He feels a dizzy spell coming on, which threatens to cause him to faint and the plane to go into a nosedive. He frowns. He's no longer fighting against the Luftwaffe; he's fighting against himself.

"Captain . . ." Dutertre is puzzled by Antoine's silence. His voice, as it comes through the communication system, sounds as if it's underwater.

"I'm here, Dutertre."

"I know."

Antoine smiles. Not the Légion d'honneur, not Academy recognition, but those two words are the highest praise he's ever received.

"My dear Dutertre, we're going to Arras."

"Yes, Captain."

He wants to reduce the plane's speed, which at present is running the risk of destroying the engines, but the fuel levers have frozen and he can't turn them to reduce the enormous flow. They're flying at more than 800 kph. Again, he's not affected so much by a concern that the engines will seize, but rather by his irritation at the fuel levers not functioning.

They construct planes to fly at ten thousand metres but no one is capable of recognising that at that altitude, parts freeze and become useless!

He's exasperated by that sort of slackness, the negligence of engineers who smoke cigars while pilots' lives go down the incompetence plughole.

He doesn't need to see the French High Command dossiers, classified as secret. At this very moment, when he's trying to free a stuck lever, he knows without a shadow of doubt that the war is lost. If a fuel lever in a plane flying across a map of Europe doesn't turn when it should, the entire nation will suffer the consequences.

His own exasperation enables him to draw on a strength his body doesn't otherwise have to move the lever, which finally yields. He sweats from the effort. The engine rotations ease. They begin their descent toward Arras and their objective.

They are welcomed with sparks climbing rapidly from the ground to meet them. Tracer bullets. Suddenly, there's a celebration of small explosions in the air. A tinny thud signals a hit to the fuselage. They come through that broadside, but another begins. Dutertre takes out his camera and they start their counterattack. While the Germans are firing explosive bullets at them, they reply with camera shots. Not even Don Quijote was as badly equipped, when he attacked the windmills. The bullets buzz around them and some hit the plane, but they don't hit the fuel tank.

"One more minute, Captain."

Antoine shrugs. He dances among those hostile missiles without much concern, because things are beyond his control. There's nothing he can do. It's destiny's game of roulette yet again. Red, odd number, and pass. He's put his chip down on the table; the rest is not up to him.

"Thirty seconds, Captain, sir."

He hears a sigh through his headphones. It's come from the gunner.

"Aubriot . . ."

"Yes, Captain?"

"Are you married?"

"Not yet, Captain. My fiancée is waiting for me so we can marry when I get back."

"What's her name?"

"Sophie."

"Dutertre . . ."

"Yes, Captain, sir."

"Get it done. Sophie is waiting."

"Yes, sir. The last one . . . Finished!"

"Let's go home."

Two more bullets thud into the plane's fuselage, but they start to climb. On the way back, a miracle prevents them from running into another swarm of wasplike Messerschmitts. Sometimes, destiny's roulette can be marvelous.

They land in Orconte and as they are taxiing down the runway, they see Major Alias coming out of his hut. He's proudly waiting for Antoine on the runway when he climbs down the ladder with difficulty, his body clumsy and stiff.

"Captain Saint-Exupéry, you've won!"

Antoine is in pain, and exhausted.

"Won, you say?"

They've returned, true, with a plane full of holes and the requested photographs. But he feels no pride. They have to defend themselves from an enemy who wants to turn France into a stage for blond psychopaths, but war strikes him as a colossal mistake.

CHAPTER 78

Lisbon (Portugal), 1940

Antoine de Saint-Exupéry

Lisbon is a city which smells of salt and seagulls. And exile. Antoine has arrived in Portugal's capital to wait for a boat to take him to the United States. His American publishers have insisted strongly that he come.

He's smoking a cigarette as he looks out over the Atlantic Ocean. There's a graveyard of cigarette butts at his feet. He sat down here midafternoon, and soon it will be sunset.

A few days after his Arras mission, the Germans advanced and spread throughout the country like a flood. The caretaker government, presided over by Marshal Pétain and installed in the spa city of Vichy, capitulated. To Germany. The High Command had just enough time to save as many planes as they could and fly them to Algiers, on the other side of the Mediterranean, to keep them out of the claws of the Nazis.

Retreat is a bitter morsel, but Antoine believes it was the only possible decision. He tried to cheer up those who were feeling devastated—in an Algiers crammed with headless chickens dressed in French military uniforms—by telling them that in this way, they could regroup and counterattack. If they'd tried to stop the avalanche, the caterpillar tracks of the German tanks would have crushed everything. The Third Reich would have taken the planes and become even stronger. It feels strange when you try to convince others with an impeccable explanation that doesn't reassure you yourself. They've abandoned France to the wolves.

Despondency is an iron ball attached to your feet. General de Gaulle continues to dream about an invincible France capable of destroying the Nazis on its own—an idea that only exists in his nationalistic dreams—but is now convinced that only the entry of the United States can change the direction of the war.

Antoine has been deeply depressed by the thought that in a few hours of chaos, withdrawal, and confusion, he's lost his country, now submerged in a sinister Europe riddled with swastikas. Nevertheless, sitting in the dock loading area with the ocean in front of him, that loss seems insignificant compared with the devastating news he's just been given. After all, countries are nothing more than an invention, a game for older, badly raised, and possessive children who, because they don't want to share their toys, draw lines on a world map. But that morning, he received a telegram which remains crumpled deep in his pocket, a telegram that has struck him such a violent blow that losing his country now seems trivial; he has lost an entire world.

He pulls it out and reads it again, as if in the hope that he didn't understand it properly, that it was all a huge misunderstanding. The telegram informs him that on a transport flight over the Mediterranean heading for Syria, a Farman F.220 piloted by Henri Guillaumet was shot down by Italian fighter planes. High Command has certified his death. Neither the remains of the plane nor the bodies could be recovered.

He watches the sea shaking. Or maybe he's the one shaking. The feeble late autumn sun dances over the surface and the breeze puffs out the chests of the clouds which form white sails of invisible ships. It's a lovely spot, but to him it seems horrendous. The fact that trams continue to cross the avenue with their cabaret-singer sway, boats moored to wooden poles still pitch up and down, and people still stroll lazily along the esplanade strikes him as a misunderstanding. A revolting misunderstanding. He makes as if to stand, but his legs won't push him up.

He wants to shout, but his voice has gone. He throws down his half-finished cigarette and lights another. He moves his head and studies the cobblestones.

How can it be that Guillaumet is dead and the world hasn't stopped?

He's too crushed to cry. He hasn't enough strength. Nature is so wise that she makes the heart pump blood and the lungs work without needing willpower to intervene. If Antoine had to take charge of those tasks, he wouldn't be breathing. He's been sitting for a long time because he can't stand up. He doesn't know if he'll ever get up from this cement bench facing Lisbon's inner harbour. And he finds no good reason for doing so either.

He tried to contact Noëlle throughout the morning. He had no idea what he could say to her; maybe just share the emptiness. But the phone connection failed time and again. And deep down, he was relieved. He felt mean-spirited for being relieved at not speaking to Noëlle. But speaking with Noëlle terrified him more than flying over Arras in the middle of the entire German army. How was he going to console her, if he didn't know how to console himself?

What a wretched egoist!

A very old man comes walking down the avenue, an accordion squashing his grey beard against his chest. He walks very slowly and somewhat unsteadily on his feet, wearing what must once have been boots but now look like bundles of filthy rags. He stops a few metres away from Antoine. He removes a metal tumbler from a dark leather satchel and puts it on the ground in the hope some passerby will be encouraged to toss a coin into it.

It takes Antoine a while to notice that someone is playing. The music irritates him. *How can music continue to exist if Guillaumet is dead?* The world strikes him as a stupid place.

He thinks about Noëlle again and takes a pen and notebook out of his pocket. The sheets of paper are too small for the letter he has to write to her. Perhaps he should send her the whole notebook. And yet, having written *Dear Noëlle* he can't think of a single word to put after it. They all seem hackneyed, artificial, and useless. Maybe he'll write a letter with the words *Dear Noëlle*, the date, and his signature. Nothing more. What else can he say to Noëlle that doesn't sound trivial? Hence-forth, she'll have to learn to fill an enormous hole in any way she can. And how's he going to fill it? He doesn't know. He may not want to. He prefers his friends' graves to stay open.

A few days later, he can watch the open sea. He does it from the stern of the USS *Siboney*, an American transatlantic liner, his coat collar turned up to try to fend off the freezing North Atlantic wind. The ship is crammed with people fleeing the war, but the deck is empty. Wet and empty. He gazes mesmerised at the foamy breach being made by the hull as it moves forward. The keel is ploughing the ocean. He sees his own life in those watery fields with their fleeting, useless beauty. All lives. A furrow which silently opens and closes as if it had never been. He wonders if ploughing the sea makes any sense.

Whisky and gin keep him company, but getting drunk by himself only makes the hole of his loneliness bigger. Writing is the only thing that briefly rescues him from sadness. Writing is a mirage, a way of establishing cities with turrets and pinnacles in the middle of the des-ert. The books will end up falling apart like everything else. With the passage of time, the pages will shred, the words will get lost. Nothing will remain.

And yet, everything will remain. Because Antoine wants to believe that the history of humankind, if it is anything, is a knot of relationships. A pile of insignificant grains of sand that nevertheless manage to form the wonder that is a beach.

Antoine has started to jot down notes of something that may become a book. There's a citadel and a man who governs his subjects with the strength of a tree trunk. There is in him a strict sense of justice which many might find old-fashioned. War has shown Antoine that laziness and a lack of commitment to the mission by each individual has brought the community to a state of collapse, and has allowed the triumph of evil. Because evil is always better organised than good is.

At the same time as he's working on this philosophical, rambling book which accumulates in odd notes, he's also jotting down reminiscences of the reconnaissance unit and its adventures. He writes in the small cabin he shares with a warm, somewhat chatty Frenchman called Renoir. His writing matches the speed of his smoking. Words and ashes cascade onto the floor from the tiny desk attached to the bulkhead. He needs to write many pages so he can throw almost all of them out and keep only what is essential: a sentence, a paragraph, just one word.

Occasionally, he looks through the porthole and tries to glimpse the essential, something that is beyond this temporal life and the taste of nicotine in his mouth. Now and again, in the ship's smoking room, he joins other expatriates in lamenting their exile: They criticise Germany, France, the United States, as they dine on lobster soup and take part in organised bridge tournaments. He doesn't know if he's done the right thing in leaving. The government has insisted to him so many times that he'll be more useful in America, how important it is to involve the United States in the war that, in the end, he wants to believe it. He also knows that he's not much appreciated in the French Army which has regrouped outside France under General de Gaulle. He doesn't like de Gaulle. He doesn't like his military arrogance. He doesn't trust military men who have political aspirations. They turn nations into army barracks.

He arrives in New York on December 31. Seen from the deck, Manhattan's skyscrapers rise up majestically, the towers of a futuristic castle. He's relieved that 1940, the year of the invasion, is departing. It's also the year he's turned forty, and the year in which Guillaumet has gone to the bottom of the sea and left him on his own.

New York's docks area is a hive of activity, with passengers and goods coming and going, many of the goods being stowed in round containers waiting in loading bays. Transatlantic liners arrive and depart nonstop.

Antoine sets foot on North American soil with hundreds of other passengers, disembarking in a bustle of luggage carried by porters with cloth caps, cigarette butts hanging from their lips. Some reporters are waiting for him, anxious to record the impressions of the winner of the prestigious National Book Award for the sort of book Anglo-Saxons refer to as "nonfiction" and which is not exactly the brainy, academic, bombastic essay so liked in Old Europe.

They ask him about politics, Marshal Pétain, who has formed a French government in Vichy, as ephemeral as the bubbles of its mineral water, in a German France over which the swastika flag flutters. Feeling uncomfortable, Antoine avoids their questions. He is sickened by the Frenchmen who have stayed to lick the boots of Gestapo officers, but he also loathes the ones who display exaggerated political feelings against Vichy while drinking their glasses of cognac on soft sofas in the salons of Estoril, London, and New York.

There are more than seven million people in New York, but he has never felt so alone.

He feels the same sensation in his body as years ago when he was travelling around the interior of France selling trucks nobody wanted to buy. His publishers have made a reservation for him at the Ritz-Carlton

Hotel and his bank account looks better than it ever did, but his smile is overdrawn.

During the first weeks, he's endlessly invited to parties. Everyone wants to have this writer-aviator at their social gatherings. He sometimes even performs hypnotism sessions if they beg him enough. Antoine always selects one of the more solicitous women, who are ready to be hypnotised even before his hand starts moving.

One afternoon, on returning to his hotel, someone is waiting for him on a sofa in the lobby. Resplendent in the latest fashion of a tight-fitting dress with a belt at her waist, and that penetrating look under her blond fringe.

"Nicole! You told me you were setting up London. What are you doing in New York?"

"The whole world is in New York!"

She wants him to show her his work. "Have you made any progress with the citadel book?"

"Very little."

"Don't abandon it."

"I won't."

"There's someone waiting in the coffee shop I want you to meet."

"Who is it? An exotic young woman?"

"Much better."

When they enter the coffee shop, a portly man in a white suit is drinking coffee at a table.

"This is Eric Perrot."

Antoine feels a wave of displeasure rising up from his stomach and looks at Nicole in despair. He'd like nothing better than to leave. Perrot is in charge of de Gaulle's propaganda machine. He's more Gaullist than de Gaulle himself, with all the general's defects and none of his virtues.

"Antoine, my friend. It's a pleasure to meet you."

Antoine reluctantly shakes his hand. For an interminable thirty minutes, Perrot, discreetly supported by Nicole, tries to convince him that he should join the general's group. In a style somewhere between mannered and mobster, he threatens Antoine in a veiled way if he won't come on board.

"This is no time for half measures, Antoine, my friend. You know what I mean . . ."

"You mean that you belong to those who believe that if you're not with my cause, you're against it."

"That's how it is, Antoine. He who doesn't fight for the right side is supporting the enemy. And you've made some mistakes."

"Mistakes?"

"You visited Vichy."

"Of course. The fact that I don't share the opinions of the Pétain government doesn't mean that I don't think I should talk with them and try to exchange ideas."

"You can't exchange anything with those people."

"But they are French too!"

"Antoine, my friend, those are the sorts of statements that put your prestige in danger."

"Monsieur Perrot, you can say all you like about Marshal Pétain, you can disagree with his opinions, you can hate his opinions and even his moustache . . . but you can't say he isn't French!"

"He doesn't love France."

"He was decorated as a hero of the First World War for defending France."

"Your ideas are all mixed up. Join us and we'll show you the truth."

When Perrot leaves, Antoine, alone with Nicole, is furious.

"What was that, Nicole? An ambush?"

"Antoine . . ."

"Don't call me Antoine in the same way Perrot does. Do you also think that I'm a traitor because I don't kiss de Gaulle's ass?"

"I merely wanted you to listen to his point of view."

Antoine suddenly looks at Nicole Vigny as if he were seeing her for the first time.

"Nicole . . . who are you?"

"For heaven's sake, Antoine! What do you mean?"

"Your contacts in the ministries, in the army, in Germany, with the leadership group of de Gaulle . . ."

"I know people, yes."

"There's something more than that, isn't there?"

Weeks ago, he'd overheard something that he thought was a joke, but it doesn't seem that way to him now. Someone in the group who had worked in the French embassy in Washington years earlier declared that Nicole Vigny wasn't her real name. And he added something else: that she worked for the American intelligence agencies.

"Antoine, I think you're upset. It would be better if we continued this conversation tomorrow."

Nicole gets up and half turns to leave.

"Nicole! I'm tired of partial truths. If you leave now, don't come back."

She stares at him. "What do you want?"

"I want you to tell me the truth. Is Nicole Vigny your real name?"

The most confident woman Antoine has ever known hesitates for a moment. "You're unfair," she says to him. She turns around and walks out of the hotel.

He's left deflated. He feels betrayed. He's put all his trust in Nicole, or whatever her name is. Now he no longer knows if she really did feel something for him and was interested in his books, or if that was a means of having another source of information on call. His disappointment with Nicole leaves him feeling even more alone.

He doesn't speak English; he stubbornly refuses to learn a single word for fear of contaminating his written French. But the community of French exiles is large, and rich. And it needs to amuse and desensitise itself, to forget what it has left behind. His hosts celebrate this extravagant and amusing guest with banquets and social gatherings. They don't know that he needs to talk, gesticulate, start singing, do magic tricks . . . do whatever it takes to prevent the silence and the feeling of immense emptiness surrounding him.

At one of the parties in which he takes refuge, he's approached by a young journalist with smooth blond hair and sky-blue eyes, ten years younger than him. Her name is Silvia Hamilton. She's fluent in French and feels an immediate attraction to this man full of hidden dimensions. Yet again, Antoine allows himself to be loved. He doesn't know if he's in love with Silvia Hamilton, but he acts as if he is. Antoine is still passionate about love.

His relationship with Silvia Hamilton makes him think about Lou-Lou again, even if he doesn't want to, even if he has buried her memory.

He's been receiving occasional news about her. Sometimes he hears conversations in which someone refers to her, and he feigns a routine—almost bored—interest, but takes note of every detail. Someone says that she has married again, that she still changes lovers as if they were slips in her wardrobe. She has also begun a promising career as a writer.

All these years, he has tried to understand why Lou-Lou has accepted so many unsuccessful lovers and rejected the only one who would never have failed her. He recalls how one night, he shared his conjectures with Mermoz in a dive in Montmartre that smelled of absinthe and old newspapers, and his friend let loose one of those guffaws that made the rafters shake. "You're mad. You want to turn love into a doctoral thesis!"

No thesis has worked in his relationship with Consuelo, either. Perhaps they met too late, when they were no longer of an age to make kites fly.

When word arrives that France is going to shut down transatlantic voyages, Antoine worries about Consuelo. She's living in a villa in the south of France with a group of artists—at least that's what she calls them. One of them is Consuelo's lover. Antoine doesn't feel jealous anymore. Rather, he feels sorry for her, because she needs to be admired constantly, to feel that she's the most striking flower in the garden. The two of them aren't so different in that: They both need to be loved, but are incapable of being constant. They are too passionate about love to stop pursuing it up and down mountains with a butterfly net. But they are both deceiving themselves: The more they run after love to catch it, the further away it gets from them. Einstein would probably explain it with the laws of magnetism—what attracts also repels. Pure science. *Damned physics!*

The person in charge of the tiny postal and telegraphic office at the Ritz-Carlton is a slight man with a moustache so long the ends curl up like a carpet. Antoine writes a telegram to Consuelo. Then another. And the next day, yet another. He tries to order her, suggest to her, and plead with her . . . to take the last boat departing from Brittany. In some telegrams he tells her he misses her. In others, he warns her that in New York he has to concentrate on his writing and that when she arrives, they ought to live in separate places.

One morning, as dawn is breaking, just when he's climbed into bed after correcting the pages of his new novel where he recounts his reconnaissance flight over Arras in the middle of this shipwreck that is the war, the phone in his room rings. He answers grumpily and the receptionist tells him that they wouldn't have disturbed him if it weren't a collect call from Europe from the Countess de Saint-Exupéry.

Antoine immediately sits up in bed. "Consuelo! It's six in the morning in New York!"

"They always want to be outlandish in New York." She makes him laugh.

"Consuelo, you have to come right away! There won't be any more visas or ships."

"After weeks of not hearing from you, now you want me to leave everything to run to your side? What's the matter, Papou? Are you ill?"

"Dammit, Consuelo! I'm not joking."

"So you want us to go back to living together?"

"Did I say that?"

"I don't know! You say so many things I can't remember them all! Yesterday, I finished a harlequin scarecrow inspired by one of Picasso's pictures. You'd love it!"

"Consuelo, you know that I love you, but I don't want to live with you and your friends."

"You've never liked my friends."

"They don't like me either."

"And if I come to New York, where will I live?"

"I'll find you a room in the same hotel."

Since all that follows is a silence full of interference from the underwater cable, Antoine sighs. He softens his tone a little.

"Consuelo, I don't know what percentage of intimacy I have to devote to you."

"Percentage? I'm your wife, not a bond! You're going to be an accountant now?"

"It is true that since I was in the reconnaissance unit I think more in calculations. But I'm offended that you think I want to be an accountant! In any case, my calculations are those of an astronomer."

"Accountants, astronomers . . . they're the same thing."

"How the devil can they be the same? What kind of thinking is that?"

"Do you see how intransigent you are?"

490

"Consuelo, you're not even here yet and we're already arguing."

Another aquatic silence, and this time it is Consuelo who moderates her tone. She adopts that tender way of speaking from which there is no escape.

"Papou, it's all the fault of the war, which drives us to despair. I'll come to New York, and I'll make you a marvellous remedy for confused states of minds: an infusion of maple syrup and cognac which a medical friend of mine taught me how to prepare."

"A doctor who prescribes cognac! I'd love to be his patient!"

They both laugh.

"Consuelo, I've spoken with a friend at the embassy about arranging your papers. I'll buy a ticket in your name at the shipping company."

"So, you really do want me to come?"

"Isn't that what I'm telling you?"

"One hears so many things! I'm going to hang up now because packing is an exhausting business. Do you think we'll be away from France for long?"

"Who knows?"

When he enters a café a few hours later, the head waiter in his black suit and slicked-back hair comes over quickly to lead him to the Reynals' table. Reynal, coproprietor of Reynal & Hitchcock, the company that publishes Antoine's books in the United States, has an easy smile, and his wife is a cultured woman with whom Antoine takes pleasure in talking about plays and novels.

The Palatine vermouth served with a little soda and a drop of Angostura bitters puts Antoine in a good mood. Behind Reynal's worldly, relaxed manner, his slightly almond-shaped eyes scrutinise Antoine carefully. Antoine tries to hide his inner confusion with a fiery diatribe against unacceptable behaviour.

"A few days ago, I was in a restaurant that wanted to be refined and they served me a dish of custard with caramel sauce. Can you believe it, Madame Reynal, how can they ruin custard with a sticky, burnt caramel paste? Something worse than that happened to me once in Spain: In the north of the country, where they boast of being more progressive than any other region, they burn sugar on top of the custard, and it forms a hard cover. Can you imagine an atrocity like that?"

The woman gives a slight nod, not daring to contradict him. Her husband observes the scene with his customary smile, but Antoine can't fool him. His verbosity is nothing more than a smoke screen. Reynal's been told about his author's nighttime adventures, how he distracts himself with lightweight parties far from the centres of political discussion, where he spends the night drinking, and then spends the next day dozing in his room.

His new book is already on its way to the printers. It wasn't easy for Reynal to introduce any changes to *Flight to Arras*. The story is powerful, but Reynal thinks that the pessimistic philosophical digressions diminish its appeal to the North American public who want pure action and to admire heroes with no flaws. But Saint-Exupéry wasn't prepared to make any concessions. Reynal would talk to him about the preferences of North American readers and Antoine would insist that he didn't care what the public thought.

Reynal recognises the material with which he is dealing. Writers are artists: They always say they don't care about public opinion and look down their noses at the business side of publishing, but when their publisher invites them to visit, they don't want to stay in a cheap guesthouse full of cockroaches, but at the Ritz-Carlton; and the advance always seems small to them. But Eugene Reynal keeps all this to himself. He also knows that writers are fragile.

The publisher is interested in Antoine's new literary projects. Antoine smiles and plays with the green beans accompanying his steak, taking his time, as if he were going to tell them about some childish prank.

"I've got a few pages written. Unpolished material, of course. But they are my most prized treasure." He pauses dramatically and looks up at them. "I'm writing my definitive work."

"What's it about? Is it a novel?"

"Novel? No, I'm not sure how to describe it. It's a message."

"A message for whom?"

Antoine shows that he finds it odd they're asking him something so obvious. "A message for humanity. Duty, honour, virtue . . ."

Reynal is momentarily stuck trying to find an appropriate response. People want distractions, not sermons.

"Very interesting!"

The three of them fall silent. Reynal has spoken with such exaggerated enthusiasm that nobody believes him. His wife skillfully changes the topic of conversation.

When it's time for after-dinner drinks, the waiter appears to take their order. Antoine asks for a Grand Marnier. The waiter looks at him oddly and then at the woman who has acted as translator.

"My God, a waiter who isn't acquainted with Grand Marnier. In Paris, he'd be fired on the spot!"

The Reynals deduce that he's talking about a liqueur and they hurriedly tell the waiter to list the available liqueurs, but none is suitable to Antoine, who falls silent and stares at his plate like a disgruntled child. It's an insignificant detail, but it has broken the illusion of the moment: They are not in France; France remains on the other side of the ocean.

While others are fighting with the Resistance, he's in the United States loafing around and eating in top-class restaurants.

As he does at other times when he's upset, he takes his pen out of the inside pocket of his blazer and starts to doodle on the white tablecloth. One of the pictures that he draws almost automatically is of a curly haired child with a princely cape. He also draws tree branches that look like wharves and trains like ants climbing spiky mountains. The publisher watches him out of the corner of his eye.

Reynal is concerned that this talented man is fading away through his nightly dissipation and melancholy, that he's becoming lost in metaphysics. He studies Antoine, who is focused on adding dials and moustaches to his childlike sketches, and an idea pops into his head:

"Antoine, why don't you write a children's book? We could publish it for Christmas."

Antoine lifts his heavy-lidded eyes and looks at Reynal. *I'm immersed in a book of the utmost intellectual depth, trying to turn on a light in the midst of the chaotic darkness of contemporary society, which has become entangled in two world wars in less than twenty-five years. And my publisher is proposing that I write a children's book!*

He continues to doodle, but senses a tingling rising up through his feet, atavistic, as if from another era. *Maybe it's not such a crazy idea!* He would have liked to have children and bought them lots of sweets! But it wouldn't be so simple. How do you speak to children? He'd have to consult the child he carries around curled up inside him. He tells the Reynals he'll think about it.

He walks in the direction of his apartment with his hands in his coat pocket. He's been walking for a long time; he realises he has no idea where he's going. New York is a city where nobody strolls. During the day, the streets are full of cars, and people hurry along the sidewalks, avoiding each other, always with a precise destination.

On turning the corner at Fourth Avenue, he sees a small human figure walking toward him very slowly, and in the semidarkness, the body appears to have a strange shape, as if it had an enormous stomach. As he approaches, Antoine realises that what is deforming the body is a tray hanging from its shoulders by two straps. The tray is loaded with wafers. The person carrying it is a small boy with messy brown hair who, on spotting a potential customer, puts on a smile which crowds out his freckles.

"Mister, do you like wafers. Ten cents for six."

When he sees that the burly, foreign-looking man is giving him a puzzled look, he repeats the offer in the Mexican-accented Spanish of his parents.

"But, muchacho, now very late. Is cold. What you do here?" Antoine replies in his rough Spanish.

"I'm looking for people, mister."

Antoine raises his eyebrows, perplexed. Seven million inhabitants and the pavements are deserted.

"Nobody here."

The boy sadly agrees as he looks at his tray full of paper cones with crunchy wafers. Antoine studies him more carefully. He's about twelve. He's dressed like a beggar, but his green eyes are those of a prince. This boy looking for people among the frozen concrete of a great city strikes him as the loneliest person on the planet.

"I like wafers . . ."

"Really, señor. Six for ten cents."

"I'm a real glutton."

"How many do you want?"

"All of them."

Antoine removes two one-dollar bills from his wallet which the boy stares at wide-eyed. He puts the paper cones with the wafers in his pockets, and he still has to hold a few in his hands as if they were a bouquet of flowers.

"You live far?"

"Si, señor."

"I come with you."

Then he sees how the boy frowns and takes a backward step. He moves away like those animals accustomed to living freely, who won't allow themselves to be tamed.

"Is late for you walk alone."

The boy makes as if to leave.

"Wait!"

A taxi drives by just then and Antoine stops it.

"You ever been in taxi?"

The boy shakes his head. He glances at the imposing yellow vehicle with its green light. Antoine steps up to the window and gives the driver fifty cents to take the boy wherever he tells him.

The boy, his empty tray tucked under his arm, opens the door with a giggle, as if it were a game, and hops into the back with one jump. The soft seats make him laugh. Antoine hands him a cone of wafers.

"For trip."

The boy doesn't thank him; he behaves like an aristocrat. As the taxi leaves, Antoine wonders if he wasn't actually a lost prince.

Antoine walks out of his study dressed in a wine-coloured robe, clutching sheets of paper in his hand, and walks toward the salon from which unbearable trumpet music is emerging. He finds it incredible that Consuelo's friends are so mad about that Louis Armstrong and his circus music. As he enters, he sees that no one is paying attention to the gramophone playing at full volume. They're sitting in a group around Consuelo, who's doing a reading of tarot cards for a young woman so pale she looks as if she's been bathing in milk all her life. He can't stand swindles. He thinks Consuelo doesn't believe in these things either, but she finds reading tarot cards and organising a spiritualist session so entertaining.

"Consuelo, you have to read this."

Someone imperiously tells him to be quiet. Antoine turns to him furiously. Are these lazy bums who drink his burgundy going to order him to be quiet in his own house?

Consuelo looks up from the cards for a second.

"Darling, I'm busy. You can tell me about it later."

Antoine is so angry that he turns and goes back to his study. He lifts up the handset and dials the number of one of his French friends, a sculptor called Martin.

"Martin, you have to listen to what I've written."

"Antoine?"

"It's an episode in which my character arrives in a garden . . ."

"Can it be tomorrow?"

"Why tomorrow?" Antoine asks, bewildered.

"It's three in the morning."

"Tomorrow? How am I going to wait that long?"

He starts to read at the point where the boy with the curly hair, from asteroid B-612, angry with a very haughty rose which thinks it's very important, comes across an entire field of roses. He's stunned, because his flower had told him that it was the only one in the universe, but here there are thousands of identical flowers. And he feels great pain for his rose, always so arrogant, making itself out to be the important one, perhaps only to hide its fragility. Consuelo is like that rose on asteroid B-612: capricious, arrogant, coquettish, unstable. But Antoine, at those times when she isn't driving him mad, feels the same tenderness for her as the little prince feels for his impertinent rose.

Martin mumbles that it all sounds fine to him, though in reality, he's groggy with sleep and hasn't taken anything in. Antoine hangs up, very pleased with his friend's verdict, as if it was the judgement of a great literary jury. In reality, Antoine wasn't reading to the sleepy sculptor but to himself. He's reaching a point in his life where he no longer needs the approval of everyone else as he did before, and the world around him is starting to interest him very little. He is like that little prince who is searching for a planet where he can be happy, but he can't find it. The friends with whom he could share his youthful memories are no longer around: Mermoz, Guillaumet, Pichodou . . . He's going round and round on an empty planet.

Consuelo's partying with her acolytes continues to reach him from the salon. Her lovers irritate him at times because of her lack of tact. She needs to exhibit them like gypsy bracelets which she shakes like rattles, but they don't make him jealous. He knows she doesn't love them, that she forgets them as easily as she loses her ornamental fans—everywhere! He feels sorry for Consuelo, as he does for himself. They've exchanged their small diamond of love for a tonne of costume jewellery.

CHAPTER 79

★

New York (United States of America), 1942

ANTOINE DE SAINT-EXUPÉRY

ANTOINE PROGRESSES TOWARD THE COMPLETION of the text of his little character bent on an impossible search. As he doesn't like the illustrator that the publisher has found—he asks them to let him go and decides that he himself will create the pictures of scarves, lambs, and impossible wells in the desert where the water springs from the effort of the arms turning the wheel. He manages to isolate himself for a few days on the outskirts of the city, in a house he shares with Consuelo and her friends—including one of her lovers with whom, for once, he gets on well. They even play chess together.

In those moments when he's writing and the book advances, he's happy. But a phone call or a visit bringing news immediately bursts his bubble. He feels more and more weighed down by the negative replies to his insistent requests to rejoin the defence of France as an aerial reconnaissance pilot once the Allied front against the Germans has been regrouped.

* * *

Antoine nervously paces an enormous room in the Shoreham Hotel in Washington, DC. The dozens of chairs piled up in a corner make the space seem better suited to a wedding banquet than a political meeting. But General Béthouart's adjutant had suggested that it would be better to meet in a discreet location. Béthouart is the right-hand man of General Giroux, who is in charge of the regrouped French troops in Algeria, and has come to the United States seeking armaments.

There is so much friction between the various French factions, however, that Antoine has to tread carefully. De Gaulle considers Giroux a bigger enemy than the Nazis because he believes that Giroux's initial acceptance of orders from the Vichy government, which agreed to capitulate to the Germans, is a sign of his collusion with the enemy.

Antoine has spent months trying to have them readmit him as a pilot in the armed forces. He's repeated the same refrain continuously in New York, and in the most influential Washington salons. They encourage him to become the voice of the exiled, to act through his speeches as an intellectual opposed to the war, but to the bewilderment of the pragmatic Americans he refuses: He stubbornly insists that he's not going to give lectures about morale to anyone if he himself doesn't fight on the front. The Allied Command led by the United States has informed Antoine that he is over the age limit, and that all the medical examinations reveal that his health is fragile, his pulmonary capacity is reduced, and the movement in one shoulder limited.

Antoine has spent months sending dozens of letters, undergoing physical examinations, attending tedious cocktail parties to mix with influential Frenchmen and Americans, and has achieved nothing. General Béthouart is his last hope. But as he inhales deeply in this enormous hotel room and commences the umpteenth repetition of his so-far useless arguments, General Béthouart interrupts him after thirty seconds

500

and promises that he will personally sign the authorisation for Antoine to present himself at Command HQ in Algiers as a remobilised officer. That's how chaotic everything is.

The first thing he does on his return to New York is take a taxi to a uniform store. It's not so easy to find the uniform of a pilot in the Free French Air Force. In fact, he visits the three most prestigious stores with military stock, but with no success. They suggest he can have one tailor-made, but there's no time.

So he goes into the Continental Hotel and starts to call the same friends he used to wake up in the middle of the night to read them fragments of his book. They are lawyers, physicists, and history professors. Their eyes open wide when the ear-splitting voice of Saint-Exupéry, shouting with the force of necessity, asks them where in New York, as a matter of urgency, he can buy the needed uniform. His Swiss colleague Denis de Rougemont, Consuelo's lover with whom Antoine plays chess, is one who receives this unexpected call, and his links with the artistic world make him stop and think: Perhaps the costumier who works for the Metropolitan Opera might have something.

De Rougemont and Antoine agree to meet in the costumier's workshop, a warehouse full of trunks packed with fancy outfits for the most astonishing range of characters. The costumier, slim and fragile-looking, has a prodigious memory, and extracts an enormous suitcase from underneath three trunks. From it, he removes an officer's navy-blue uniform of a large enough size for his client. It doesn't have the buttons engraved with the insignia of the French Army, and the excessive braid gives him something of the appearance of the concierge of a luxury hotel, but Antoine is delighted. After a few small alterations, he walks out dressed like a general.

When he arrives at his new apartment in Beekman Place, it's almost dinnertime and he can hear some musical chords. Consuelo has bought a harp.

"I didn't know you could play the harp."

"I don't. But I've always wanted to have a harp."

"I see . . ."

Consuelo looks up from the instrument and checks him out.

"What are you doing in that uniform? Are you going to a fancy dress party? Take me with you! I adore fancy dress parties!"

"I'm rejoining my air reconnaissance unit in North Africa."

Consuelo puts her hands back on the harp and tries to extract a few notes. "Papou, why do you have to go to war?"

"It's my duty."

"War is for youth."

"That's a ridiculous idea! Young people have their entire lives in front of them; why should they waste them? Only old people should be allowed to go to war. That would be fairer."

"You sound as if your life no longer interests you."

"I can't bear being in this stagnant city any longer. I feel like I'm rotting inside. I need to leave."

"You're always leaving, Papou."

Antoine notices the glimmer of a tear in her eyes. He runs a hand over his head. "I'm sorry I haven't been a good husband."

"You talk about being a husband as if it were a trade."

They both smile.

"I'm sailing in three days' time."

"I'll try to learn to play the harp before you leave. I want to bid you farewell with a harp concert that will be heard all over New York. We'll invite everyone! You should have given me more notice! If you don't give Falcon's at least a week's notice, they can't provide their meat and port pies!"

He watches Consuelo run to the phone to put in her ridiculous orders, and whereas at any other time this would irritate him, right now it provokes a feeling of enormous tenderness.

When he boards the ocean liner three days later, he feels like his little prince, who leaves his planet behind and goes far away from his rose. There's no way of living with her without pricking himself on her thorns, but he can't avoid a tightness in his stomach because he hasn't stayed to look after her. He asks himself if what he feels for Consuelo is love. All dictionaries fail in that moment of looking for any definition which isn't just a handful of dead words.

CHAPTER 80

Algiers (Algeria), 1943

ANTOINE DE SAINT-EXUPÉRY

ANTOINE HASN'T BEEN BACK TO Algiers for years. He's sitting in a little café where two American lieutenants are smoking a hookah, and based on their silly laughs, he deduces that there's more in the pipe than tobacco. He looks out at the winding street where they sell carpets, brightly coloured spices in huge sacks, goatskin backpacks, baskets, and trinkets. A vendor with his noisy patter is trying to sell rugs to a group of English sailors. They bargain and he puts his hands on his head theatrically, to the delight of the sailors, who have no interest in the rugs, but might end up buying one if only for the pleasure of having purchased it for half its price, as if that were not a ritual the vendor had counted on to perfection.

He orders a coffee. They make it small and very strong, because water is scarce. He can have it with a few drops of camel milk.

He stirs the cup, allowing the steam to dissipate into the city's hot sky. He thinks that Consuelo would be horrified by the grubby state of the tablecloth they put down on the table for him, and with the sediment on the cup, which they must clean with nothing more than a dirty rag from one use to the next. He is stirring a coffee he doesn't really want to drink.

In New York he dreamed of returning to combat for France and asked to fly planes which fired off snapshots instead of bombs. But things haven't turned out as he had hoped. He managed to be posted to the Photographic Reconnaissance Wing in North Africa and he even managed to survive a period of training on the complicated Lockheed P-38 Lightning planes, five of which the Americans have donated to his unit. They are very fast planes with more than two hundred controls and dials in the cockpit, advanced voice communication systems, oxygen masks, a narrow cabin like a coffin. The planes weren't in tip-top condition and one of the squadron's best pilots had died during the training flights. Antoine isn't affected by thoughts of his own demise, but the death of other pilots demoralises him.

He smiles when he thinks of his first mission with this reconnaissance group. It was exhausting crossing the Mediterranean with temperatures below freezing at an altitude of 9,000 metres on a six-hour mission to fly over heavily guarded objectives in a plane with no weapons. He wasn't flustered when he sensed the salvos being fired in his honour by the German batteries in Sicily, Corsica, and Sardinia, but when he saw the French coast from the air again, his heart skipped a beat. He felt happy to be back home. Marseilles from 9,000 metres looks like a fishing village. His mission was to photograph enemy factories and logistical centres, but he detoured to fly over the area near Lyons where he was born. And down there, on a small rise, was the Saint-Maurice mansion where he spent his childhood and that has always been his refuge. He was flying too high, but even so, he thought he could make out the path lined with birch trees behind the house. There, on many an afternoon, he had pedalled with all his might on a bicycle to which one of his older cousins had helped him attach a sail held by wires. He believed that if he pedalled fast enough, that improvised sail would make him lift off from the ground and fly through the air. It is his paradise lost.

He made one pass and then another, as if he were in a rocking chair above the territory where he had been happy. It didn't occur to him that when they developed the photographs, the American officers would frown at the sight of a pile of useless shots of a small castle among the images of airfields and factories.

On his second mission, he had mechanical problems in one of the engines and had to turn back. The improvised runway at the La Marsa airfield near Tunis was very short, barely 500 metres. The plane was equipped with a button for activating the hydraulic brakes before landing so they would operate the moment the plane made contact with the ground and could stop the plane within the necessary margins. But Antoine remembered too late, when he was already moving down the runway. Despite his efforts to press down on the brakes, he overshot the end, and the plane ran into some vineyards and ended up with a damaged wing and broken landing gear.

The American colonel in charge hit the roof. He was sick of these unorganised Frenchmen who spent their time arguing among themselves and seemed to him to be undisciplined thrill seekers. When he saw on the file card that this Saint-Exupéry character was thirteen years over the regulation age limit to fly these sorts of planes, he ordered the careless pilot to be brought before him.

Antoine arrived with his naughty-boy expression on his face. It moved some people, and drove others mad. The American colonel fell into the latter category. After kicking up an almighty fuss which Antoine endured standing to attention, he dictated the order that is now resting in Antoine's pocket. It is like a sentence. He was to be removed from the unit and sent to Algiers pending another posting. In other words, going nowhere. Antoine had already visited the Algerian capital when he disembarked from North America and had spent a few horrendous days there. It was a city that was gloomy, because of its lack of supplies, and tense because of the constant games between the pro- and anti-Gaullists.

He has two options: spend the rest of the war in the pool of intrigue in Algiers like a pariah with no destiny or friends, or return to New York where they treat him as a prominent figure, where he eats roast beef and lobster and they fight over his presence at the most select parties. He continues to stir his coffee, which has already become cold.

He plays at being undecided, but he knows that he isn't going to return to New York. He prefers suffering in the real dirt of Algiers to living in the artificial brilliance of Manhattan.

In Algeria, he's fighting against military bureaucracy, not Hitler. Finally, after weeks of stagnation, he succeeds in having his petitions dealt with, though in a limited way.

He has been granted reinstatement in group IV of the photographic reconnaissance wing, but taking into account his age and medical history, he's authorised to complete a maximum of five war missions, after which he'll be transferred to the reserves list with all the honours of a lieutenant-colonel. General Ira Eaker himself has signed the letter. Finally, he's going to take off again.

CHAPTER 81

★

Corsica, 1944

Antoine de Saint-Exupéry

Summer in Bastia, in the south of Corsica, is hot and the light is blinding. But Antoine likes to wear his leather flying jacket and his gold-framed sunglasses. He learned to do this when he was a mailman: You're a pilot no matter the climate.

He walks toward the hut which serves as the officers' block for group IV. He's where he wanted to be after spending eight months stranded in Algiers. It has cost him a huge effort to get here. And yet he doesn't feel the slightest euphoria. He's won a personal war, but now the real war begins, the one with young smiles covered in blood and parents who'll never see their sons again.

He's where he thinks he has to be, but he's not happy. No decent person can be happy during a war.

He remembers a night long ago in Paris, almost at daybreak, when he and Mermoz were watching the Seine flowing past below them and they were feeling that vague, dawn sadness when daylight dissipates the illusion of a night of laughter and alcohol. He asked Mermoz if he was happy. Mermoz turned to him in the way he always did, looking into his eyes with that conviction which was intimidating: "Of course not! That would be a tragedy. If you're happy, there's nothing left to fight for." He really misses Mermoz and Guillaumet. The world has become a desert without them.

When he reaches the whitewashed house which serves as the officers' residence, an adjutant appears and tells him he has a visitor. There's no need for him to say who it is. The Chanel perfume announces her.

"Hello, Major!"

"Nicole! You always know where to find me!" And then he hits his head with his hand as if everything suddenly made sense. "My reincorporation in Bastia, you moved it along, didn't you?"

She gives an inscrutable smile. "You overestimate me."

They walk out to the street and stroll along the avenue dotted with almond trees.

"Have you finally come to tell me who you are?"

"Antoine, you're an idiot. I'm me. My love for you is genuine, perhaps the most genuine thing I've ever had."

"So everything else in your life isn't?"

They stop and look at each other.

"Dammit, Nicole, I was starting to fall in love with you."

"Well, that's not such a bad thing."

"I can't fall in love with someone if I don't know who she is, someone who appears and disappears. Consuelo does that too, but I always know where to find her: with those idiot artists."

"You should have left that woman some time ago."

"You've never wanted to divorce your husband? Is he really your husband or is that a cover for your work?"

"I'm not a spy. Or not exactly."

"So?"

"I'm a woman who helps her country."

"Nicole, you're a box of enigmas."

"We all are. A person with no secrets is of no interest."

"I know you can't answer lots of questions, so I'm only going to ask you to answer one, and to answer it honestly, because it's very important to me."

"All right."

"What did you think of the pages of *Wind, Sand and Stars*?"

"It's the best thing you've written."

"And were you really interested when I was reading you the book I'm writing now, even if only occasionally?"

"The one about the citadel? Of course! It contains such powerful images!"

"Please, come to my apartment now."

"Do you want us to make love?"

"What I want is something much more intimate."

When they get to his room, in among the mess, from the interior of a shoebox he pulls out the manuscript of what will become *Citadelle*.

"It needs a lot more work, but I want you to keep these pages. They are the only important things I have. With the war, you never know."

She takes the folder of pages and holds it tightly to her chest. "Antoine, I never lied to you."

"You never told me the truth."

"The truth also deceives."

Antoine takes her by the waist and holds her tightly against his burly body. She's about to say something, but before she can speak, he kisses her. He knows that there's more truth in one of Nicole's kisses than in a thousand of her words.

"Keep writing. I'll be back for the rest of the manuscript!"

"I know!"

"I'll ensure that this wonderful book is published."

"I'm sure you will."

Nicole departs, leaving in her wake a trace of perfume as enigmatic as she is. Antoine feels incredibly grateful for the protection she has given him—so intelligent, so serene, so self-assured. She has given him so much encouragement to write during this despondent time, but he wonders if she has ever loved him. If he could read Nicole's thoughts, he would know that, in the midst of this masked ball that her world has become, Antoine's passionate naïveté has been a life buoy. She feels that he's the one who has protected her during this entire period, when the worst dangers have been lurking out there: cynicism, disillusionment, the absence of affection.

CHAPTER 82

★

Corsica, 1944

ANTOINE DE SAINT-EXUPÉRY

ANTOINE HAS ALREADY FLOWN TWO missions in the Lockheed P-38 Lightning. A genuine bolt of lightning! An innovative fighter plane with a twin-boom tail and two powerful engines, each 1000 hp. The Bréguets that he used to fly over the Pyrenees and across the desert had a single 180 hp engine.

But it's not all good: In his bubble-canopied cockpit, it's freezing cold at 9,000 metres. A mix of higher and lower altitudes causes pain in his patched-up joints. His big body avidly consumes the thread of oxygen transmitted by his face mask and occasionally he's scared that he'll faint. There are thousands of instruments requiring his attention. Yesterday he was at the very heart of the German lines; but flying doesn't produce the same emotion in him that he used to feel.

He strolls along the runways surrounded by field tents and prefabricated barracks, as lost in thought as if he were wandering through a forest. He walks over to a Lockheed with its engine exposed, a mechanic half-inside the machine with only his legs visible in their blue overalls. When his head appears, Antoine feels enormous joy.

"Farget, what a delight to find you here!"

A happy expression appears on the young mechanic's face, covered with black grease.

"Monsieur Saint-Ex!" Then the mechanic spots the insignia on his bomber jacket. "My apologies, monsieur. I mean . . . Major, sir!"

"Dammit, Farget, when we're alone, forget military protocol. I had the uniform made in a workshop by a tailor who makes costumes for the theatre and he asked me how many stripes I wanted. I could even have had stripes down the middle of my backside."

They both laugh.

"How are you doing, Farget?"

"Rumors never stop here: The Nazis are advancing, the Nazis are retreating, Hitler has made a pact with the Devil . . . But I can't tell you anything important, I just carry on doing my own thing: I keep myself busy with the Allison engines and have my fights with counter-rotating propellers."

Antoine nods slowly in the way he does when important things are being revealed to him.

"You know something, Farget? The joint chiefs of staff gather together, maps are unfolded on a table, different coloured pins are stuck into them, and the arguments go on for hours. But do you know what I've learned after all this time? The war is won by good mechanics, people like you."

"You always exaggerate so much! I just adjust screws."

Antoine studies the young workshop soldier with affection; tall, slim, and with a lovely smile, who can only aspire to medals of grease, but who confronts the armed forces of the Reich armed solely with a wrench. He's convinced that if all the French had individually put the same effort into their tasks with the same care as this young man, the Germans would never have defeated them.

513

"No, Farget, you don't just adjust screws. You knead the dough."

The mechanic looks at him without really understanding what he means, and watches him walking off through the aerodrome, swaying like a badly loaded trolley. He wonders what someone like Monsieur Saint-Ex is doing in a war like this. And then he wonders what they're all doing here.

When Antoine pushes open the door to the officers' mess, two of the unit's pilots who are playing a game of chess quickly stand up.

"Major, how was yesterday's mission? They say the Boche invited you in for a snack."

Antoine smiles cheekily and plays along with them.

"Hey!" shouts one of the young lieutenants to the barman. "Pull out the good whisky for the major!"

On hearing the noise, a captain who was reading an out-of-date newspaper comes out of an adjoining room and joins the gathering. Another workshop officer enters. More people keep coming in and adding to the group. With a cigarette in one hand and a glass of whisky in the other, Antoine tells them about the previous day's flight.

"When I was getting close to the lake at Annecy, the left engine started to cough like an old man with a cold. Slowly, at first, but then it turned out to be the flu. The fuselage started to shake and vibrate madly and it felt as if it was going to come apart, so I had to cut the engine."

"Bad news to be in the middle of the Boche with only one engine; if a German fighter plane catches you at a moment like that . . ."

"That's why I veered toward the Alps. There are fewer enemy bases, and I could make a getaway even at slow speed, hiding among the valleys. I had to cross the Galibier Pass and later the Mont Cenis Pass and come out on the coast."

They all nodded.

"But at some point in the Alps I strayed off course." Here, Antoine shrugs. "Instead of coming out at the coast, I came out over a plain and to my great surprise, at the end of the plain I saw a big city with lots of German landing strips . . . I was in Genoa!"

"That's impossible! Genoa is one of the cities totally protected by the Germans."

"It's a hornet's nest!"

"Well, into my head popped that map we have in the pilots' room where we mark enemy bases with little flags, and how there are so many flags on Genoa that it looks like one of those small cushions into which dressmakers stick their pins. I was headed all the way into the frying pan. When I realised it, I started shivering. Even more so when I spied in the mirror a black spot in the air behind me, a few hundred metres away: a Messerschmitt. And there I was, floating over the city at the speed of a tortoise with just one engine. I said to myself: 'This is it, it's finished, everything ends here. Now there'll be an explosion and it's goodbye.' I closed my eyes—don't ask me my reason for doing something so pointless. Perhaps to start getting used to the afterlife. A second went by, two, three, five, ten . . . I opened my eyes and the fighter plane was flying away! I couldn't believe it, but that was the case. And then I understood: From that distance, it had taken me for a German plane; it didn't even bother to come in for a closer look. It didn't occur to him that an Allied plane would fly openly over Genoa at low altitude, and at the speed of a Sunday morning stroll."

They listen totally absorbed. They've all risked their lives in similar or worse situations, but Major Saint-Exupéry has a hypnotic way of describing things.

"Saved!"

"Not yet. Overcome by the fact that I'd escaped between hundreds of antiaircraft batteries and fighter planes who saw me go by without paying any attention to me, I forgot to connect the Friend or Foe signal so that our boys could identify me, and in Borgo, they were on the point of sending out a squadron to riddle me with bullets. I gave a warning by radio to identify myself. The biggest miracle of the entire mission wasn't that I flew right in front of the Germans' noses without them firing a shot. It was that they understood my made-up English at the base."

"It seems incredible!"

"It also seemed that way to the information officers when I landed. You should have seen the look of amazement on the faces of the two American captains! The jaw of one of them dropped so far he almost lost his chewing gum. But they had to believe me, because the camera photographed Genoa at 8,000 feet as if it were making souvenir post-cards."

There are laughs, hand slaps on the table, and toasts to the major.

The weeks go by and rumours grow of troops disembarking on French soil. This would mark the final push which would, without a doubt, alter the flow of the war which, since the entry of the Americans, has changed radically. The German army has worn itself out on the Russian front, the Italians changed sides after hanging Mussolini, and after four years of war, the Allies are starting to see a light at the end of the tunnel.

Antoine has exceeded his five authorised missions, but there's no way of convincing him to stay on the ground. Major Gavoille, who fears for Antoine's life, works out a plan to stop him flying. Soldiers who know anything about the secret invasion plan that's being finalised—to launch a definitive attack with a landing on the beaches of Normandy—are retired from active duty, since they could endanger the whole campaign if they were captured.

Two officers in the unit who were summoned to a secret meeting at Command HQ because they'll take an active part in the landing have been removed from reconnaissance flying. Gavoille calls them into his office and asks them to give Major Saint-Exupéry some of the facts about the landing so that in this way, he'll have to be removed from active duty.

For several days on the Bastia base, people watch how the two officers try to take the burly major aside to a discreet place, and how he escapes, and emerges at a trot, almost running in the opposite direction with his hands over his ears.

"I don't want to know anything! I don't want to know anything!"

CHAPTER 83

★

Corsica, 1944

Antoine de Saint-Exupéry

Farget the mechanic sees Major Saint-Exupéry wandering through the workshops, and signals him to come over. Antoine approaches him with the pensive expression which, barring the odd explosion in the canteen brought on by American whisky, now almost never leaves him.

"Major, I'd like to ask you something."

"Of course. My rank has to be good for something. Do you need to be relieved of some duty? A leave request? I can take it to the people in the office."

"No, it's nothing like that! You are a person who has read a great deal and travelled a lot, so you know a lot about things. I'd like to ask your advice."

"Farget, you're never going to get anywhere that way. Everyone asks for money, references . . . no one asks for advice anymore!"

"So you think it's a bad idea?"

"I think I'm probably the worst adviser in the world. But it delights me that you trust me in this way. How do you think an old pilot like me can help you?"

"In Algiers, you see, some acid flew out of a battery onto my hands and they took me to the military hospital. I met a nurse there. Her name's Camille."

Antoine notices how the mechanic's eyes light up.

"When she'd finished putting on the dressings and giving me my medication, she came back to my bedside. I don't know why. She took a chair and sat down beside me. She told me she was from a place in Brittany called Pont-Aven. But I have a fiancée, you know. I've been engaged to Amandine since I was sixteen. We grew up together in our town; her father bought cheese from my father to sell at the market. Amandine is delightful and I love her a lot. We intend to get married when the war is over. But I've never talked with a girl like Camille. You should see her, Monsieur Saint-Ex, dressed all in white, with that smile. I felt something different."

"Different in what way?"

"I forgot the pain in my hands. I couldn't stop looking into her eyes. I couldn't, Monsieur Saint-Ex. I don't know if it's ever happened to you."

"Years ago."

"Then you do understand what I felt?"

"It's as if the world were somewhere else, and you don't care."

"Exactly! I didn't even remember that France had been invaded by the Germans!" And as he says this, he realises the gravity of a comment that's not appropriate to the patriotic spirit demanded by High Command. "Well, of course my country *is* important to me, Major . . ."

Antoine looks at him affectionately. "Carry on! Continue telling me what's important! What happened with your nurse?"

"A plane had crashed at the aerodrome. There were many wounded and the doctors started to yell. She got up quickly and left. They needed beds and a doctor came right away, took my temperature. Since I didn't have a fever, he discharged me. He almost pushed me out of the bed. I searched for her all over the hospital, but I didn't find her. People were constantly coming and going, ambulances were arriving, no one knew anything about anybody. I left."

The two men look at one another with fake gravity.

"But you went back."

"I went back."

And the two of them smile with the complicity of old friends.

"Those days—you already know what it was like—everything was a mess. I went back the next day to try to see her and the whole hospital was topsy-turvy. She was the one who saw me, and came over to me. She told me she was really happy that I'd come back, because they'd given orders for an immediate evacuation and they had trucks on the point of leaving. He boss was calling her and there was no time for anything else. We held hands briefly and gazed into each other's eyes. I don't know how to explain it . . . I felt very close to her, closer than I've ever felt in all these years with Amandine. I told her we could exchange letters and she nodded yes. I hadn't been posted anywhere, almost all the personnel were being demobilised, and the nurses hadn't been told of their destination. She opened her mouth to say something, but a medical captain in a really foul mood arrived, grabbed her by the arm, and shouted that the trucks were about to move out. I saw her disappearing in the commotion of the evacuation and never saw her again."

Farget falls quiet and Antoine joins him—both of them silent in the midst of the noise on a military base which never stops. The two of them, their thoughts far away, both watching a girl disappear in the whirlwind of war.

"And that was it," the mechanic begins to speak again. "When the war ends—because it will end one of these days, sooner or later, if those crazy Germans haven't killed us all—I'll go back to Perpignan and marry Amandine, who is a wonderful girl and will be a wonderful wife."

"Farget, you're in real trouble."

"But nothing happened with Camille! I swear, I didn't lay a hand on her. We didn't even exchange a kiss. There's nothing Amandine could reproach me with."

Antoine shakes his head and takes a deep drag on his cigarette. "The problem is what you could reproach Amandine with."

"How? She's a saint!"

"Marriage is a contract for life, which is signed when everything is fresh and brand new, and it continues to be valid when everything is becoming stale and worn out. After years of routine, you may feel tempted to project onto the good Amandine the frustration of never having gone in search of that possible love that arose during the war. You'll blame her for everything that might have been but wasn't, and you'll start to be distant with her, to sharpen the blade of reproaches. And Amandine doesn't deserve that, does she?"

"Of course not! But that won't happen, because all I have to do is forget Camille and everything will be as before. And I'll be happy with Amandine."

Antoine shakes his head again. "That would be perfect, but there's the root cause of the problem. It's not in our hands to forget, Farget. You'll never forget that enchanting nurse, and with the passage of years, protected from the wear and tear of day-to-day life, from the disappointments and small defeats of each day, her memory will remain intact, even idealised."

"Do you think so?"

"Memories don't age, Farget, they don't get wrinkles, or a paunch, or become rheumatic. I know this. Many years ago, my own 'Camille' played the violin. That melody has played in my head every day of my life. And I'm not hiding from you that it ruined my life."

"And what became of her?"

"She slipped through my fingers like a goldfish. Who knows if we would have been happy but I will always regret what might have been."

They both stop talking, their gaze lost in that place where one is alone, so remote, and where no one can be accompanied. Antoine says goodbye to Farget. He takes hold of him by the forearms and clasps him firmly.

It's already very late. He has a mission to carry out the next day. General Eaker authorised five missions and this will be his eighth. Gavoille, the commander in chief, tries to avoid giving him all possible missions and he has to stay alert in order to claim his spot on the duty roster. He's grateful that they are concerned about his life, but living isn't of much use to him if he's not flying.

Joystick and pedal!

Antoine prefers not to have dinner on the base. He orders a few calamari and some strong, spicy marinated sheep's cheese in a tavern with hardwood tables and jugs of red wine. The proprietor, her greying hair caught up in a rather untidy bun and wearing a very clean white apron somewhat worn at the edges, comes over to his table. She brings him a bottle of chestnut liqueur and a glass.

"We have faith in you all," she says, her eyes tired.

He nods. The comment makes the war meaningful; they know what they are fighting for.

It's late, but he doesn't feel like going to sleep. Common sense tells him he should go to bed so the next day he'll be rested and able to face one of those exhausting missions of several hours' duration: He has to photograph an area covering Annecy, Chambéry, and Grenoble. But there's another part of his brain that demands that he not sleep, that he not waste the night.

The half bottle of chestnut liqueur produces a heat in his stomach like the inside of a crater, as well as a vague feeling of unreality. He wanders through the old quarter of the city, along narrow streets with whitewashed houses belonging to fishermen and small businesses that remain closed. There's one establishment lit up, with its windows open to let in the fresh night air, and he stops in front of it. Inside, there are piles of pale-gold flowers and three workers in grey dustcoats are putting together bouquets.

"What are you doing, friends?" he asks them from the sidewalk with the camaraderie that overtakes strangers who find themselves awake in a sleeping city.

The oldest worker, his white hair in a brush cut, turns to him and tells him they're preparing centrepieces of dried flowers.

"At this hour?"

"When the day isn't long enough, you have to make use of the night."

"And what are those flowers?"

"You don't know the everlasting flower?"

At his expression of embarrassed ignorance, like that of a child who doesn't know the answer to the teacher's question, the man points at the door, inviting him to come into the store. There are mountains of these unassumingly beautiful flowers. The workers pause in their task for a moment and introduce themselves with a smile. The white-haired man in charge tells him it's a flower that grows wild in the fields all over the island.

"It's the most astonishing flower in the world."

Antoine looks at them in their wooden crates and what he sees are ordinary flowers of a straw-coloured yellow, not the least bit remarkable. The man notices his involuntary look of scepticism.

"Do you know why they're called everlasting flowers? Because once they've been cut, they never ever wither. They remain exactly the same forever."

Then Antoine looks at the flowers again with renewed interest.

Their beauty is discreet, but when all the flashy flowers droop, these ones remain.

"Then they really are amazing!"

He falls silent and becomes lost in one of his reflections. Initially, he discounted the flower, because it wasn't as pretty as the others, and now he finds out that it is unique. Yet again, it proves that eyes aren't enough to see what's important.

"Please, would you let me help you?"

The workers smile, amused. For the first time, they have an apprentice wearing the uniform of a major. They push over a bunch of flowers and some very fine pieces of string. He never thought that at his age, he'd spend a night learning to be a florist.

It's not long before dawn when he walks down to the harbour. Small boats rock at their moorings in front of the building housing the fishermen's guild. He can see the city spread out on the other side of the inner harbour, the buildings almost skimming the water and the two towers of the Church of Saint John the Baptist jutting above the roofs. Everything is quiet and the inky-black sky is becoming more of a bluish colour, as if it were a great theatrical performance being staged just for him. He sits on a stone wall and prepares himself to watch the sun come up over the Mediterranean. *The tangerine-coloured morning sun!* He feels fortunate to have fallen onto this planet.

As he walks through the streets of a city which is starting to fill with light, he greets the mailman and the milkman with a smile on his lips. He feels as nimble as a child on his way to school.

He appears, freshly showered, in the officers' dining room at a very early hour and there's only a captain there, drinking his coffee and dressed in the regulation bomber jacket, as if ready to fly.

"What are you doing here so early, Tosti?"

"We saw the door to your room was open but you weren't inside."

"I was making bunches of flowers."

Tosti looks at him suspiciously. "But have you slept at all? You must be tired. I'm ready to substitute for you, Major."

Antoine goes up to him and puts a hand on his shoulder. "You're a good sort, Tosti. But it's my mission."

The summer flaunts itself gloriously in Corsica. A soldier takes Antoine to the runways in a jeep. The aroma of lavender and rosemary floats in the air, the sky is a biblical blue, the stone houses on the way to the airport are covered with bougainvillea, and the smell of coffee and fresh cheeses emerges from the windows. The war is an anomaly. Men kill each other, even on the most beautiful days.

One of the ground crew helps him with the hassle of putting on his two layers of clothing. For Antoine, lifting his hands above his shoulders to put on the fire-resistant clothes and the thermal suit is torture. Climbing up into the plane with the oxygen tube and radio wires embedded in this body armour leaves him exhausted on this hot day. And he'll still have to spend at least ten minutes in stifling heat going through the check of all the controls before he can take off. A mechanic perched beside the cockpit is holding a folder with the form on which he'll be marking crosses.

"Voice communicator . . ."

"Correct."

"Oil pressure."

"Correct."

Another mechanic arrives and asks the first one for the folder so he can finish the checklist.

When Antoine, boxed into his bubble-shaped cockpit, looks sideways, he recognises Farget.

"I thought you weren't on duty."

"I am now. Oxygen flow?"

"Correct. Farget?"

"Yes, Major?"

"Is that charming nurse still in your head?"

"All the time."

"Do you know something, Farget? Throughout many years of wandering around up in the skies, I've watched the birds. Flight contains no mysteries for them; the best aviator loaded down with decorations is a clumsy apprentice next to the most inexperienced swallow. You learn a lot from them. I've seen migrating flocks heading out to sea until they disappear from sight. Minuscule, fragile birds who support themselves in the air on wiry wings above an immense ocean, flying into a constant headwind. I've always asked myself how many of them collapse and are swallowed by the swell."

"Lots, probably."

"They don't know if they'll reach the opposite shore, but images of sun and warm sand dance inside their little bird heads, and that, Farget my friend, makes them keep on flying."

The mechanic looks up from his record sheet.

"Farget, pursuing pretty illusions might not lead anywhere, but the road is full of hope."

The two men are silent for a moment.

"Monsieur Saint-Ex . . ."

"What?"

"Take care out there."

"You know something, Farget? If they take me down up there, I won't regret a thing. The termite mound of the future and its robot-like ethics worry me more."

He looks at the two-hundred controls in his plane and then at his old hands. He'll carry out his mission. He'll wage war. But he doesn't understand war. He turns toward the mechanic for a moment and speaks to him through the voice communicator for the last time, before giving the sign that everything is in order for takeoff.

"I'm made to be a gardener!"

Farget smiles at him and closes the canopy.

It's a three-and-a-half-hour flight to Grenoble. The Allied forces who landed on the beaches of Normandy have opened up a mortal breach in the guts of the Third Reich. The beast is bleeding and retreating. Given the speed at which the battle fronts are moving, the photographs he's capturing now will be given little or no consideration. But he doesn't care; it doesn't matter if they throw his photographs into the wastepaper basket. He'll complete his mission because that's what the game of war consists of, a game of chess in which victory justifies the sacrifice of all the pawns.

The sun throws blinding flashes onto the sea. He can no longer tell Mermoz and Guillaumet that the motors of these P-38 planes sound like bees, not engines. This may be his last flight. Only the absence of Major Gavoille has prevented him, thanks to his rank, from being removed from the programed schedule at the last minute by the captain who assigns duties. Antoine is forty-four. His time as a pilot is over. He could buy himself a small plane and go for joyrides on weekends, but the thought of that irritates him. Converting aviation into a Sunday pastime strikes him as offensive to his profession. People say to him that if he stops flying he'll have more time to write. He sighs inside his face mask and everything fogs up. They don't understand anything. *His writing is a consequence of his flying!*

He does have one last challenge: to finish the book about the citadel, as Nicole refers to it, the book he still has to strip of unnecessary pages to get to what is essential.

The thermometer shows 30°C below zero. The altimeter, 8,000 metres. The coast of France is silhouetted down there. He wrote to his mother a few days ago. She continues to be a strong woman who works as a volunteer head nurse. He begged her that if Consuelo knocked on her door one day asking for shelter, she would take her in. Consuelo believes herself to be strong, but she's fragile. He's touched

527

by her obstinate faith in confronting the world with her innocuous thorns.

He descends a little to see the land breathe. He recalls the first geography lesson Guillaumet gave him in that hangar in Toulouse: three orange trees, a stream hidden in the grass . . . These are the important things in life.

Out of the corner of his eye, he sees a dark spot in the sky to his left and his heartbeat accelerates. The spot slows down. It's seen him. It changes course to sit in his slipstream. It's coming for him—a Messerschmitt.

He has nowhere to take shelter, the German plane is too close. He can't see it, but he knows it's there; he senses it getting closer behind him, getting much bigger. There's no escape, he can't jump out with a parachute.

He feels an icy rod in his back. Fear paralyzes him. His first thought is to hit the fuel pedal and try to leave the plane behind, but he already knows there's no leeway. Not anymore. The German fighter plane is too close, he's approaching at high speed. He could try to do barrel rolls and perform desperate yaws in the sky, but no. He doesn't want to be hunted like a mouse running away terrified. If the curtain has to fall, let it fall. Eventually, he'll end up falling anyway. In that decisive moment when perceptions are sharpened, he has the absolute certainty that death is just a formality and that what really defeats you is fear. And then, free now of all uncertainty, his anxiety evaporates. Everything is in equilibrium.

The German pilot has him almost within range, his finger over the firing pin of the MG 20 mm cannon.

In that final moment, Lou-Lou's image appears. Her red hair, her pale skin, her green eyes. And then he has a revelation. *He's been mistaken all his life!* Now, he sees his error! He always believed that the most important thing was to be loved, but he realises in this crucial moment that the most important thing is to love. The love he has felt for Lou-Lou has lit up his life. How can he hate her? He's never hated her, no matter how much he pretended to do so. He has adored her and continues to adore her. So much looking for love everywhere so strenuously, and he now realises that he had it in the palm of his hand, because the love that saves us isn't the love we ask for, it's the love we give. The lamplighter knew it: The real gift isn't the light, it's lighting the flame.

Antoine hears the German fighter plane's engine. He's within range of the machine gun. He knows it. He feels the snake wriggling behind him getting ready to bite him with its poison. That's his destiny. He lets go of the joystick and smiles with an inner peace he hasn't felt since the nights of his childhood when his mother would come to his bed to tuck him in. The moment to depart has arrived.

A yellow flash. He doesn't shout.

He falls gently like a leaf falling from a tree.

Major de Saint-Exupéry doesn't return to the base at Bastia as expected that midday of July 31, 1944. He never returns. His body is never found.

CHAPTER 84

★

Toulouse, 1945

DIDIER DAURAT

THE REPORTER FROM A LOCAL Toulouse newspaper holds his note-book in one hand and with the other, pushes open the door to the offices of Air Bleu, a company that has closed down. Everything has a somewhat ramshackle and moribund air about it. A poster that is start-ing to curl up at the corners says:

AIR BLEU: RAPID AIR POSTAL SERVICE. FOR THOSE LOCALITIES SPECIFIED IN THE TIMETABLE PANEL (PARIS, LE HAVRE, LILLE, NANTES, TOULOUSE, AND BORDEAUX), LETTERS AND PARCELS POSTED IN THE MORNING ARE GUARANTEED DELIVERY THE SAME DAY. 2,50 FRANCS FOR AN ORDINARY LETTER UP TO 10 GRAMS.

The small airline, like so much else, must have suspended its activi-ties because of the war, and the only person in the office is its instigator, a man experienced in the business. In the morning, he organises the sheets of paper, and in the afternoon, he makes a mess of them. His wife, in her armchair, brings her crochet work up close to her eyes. Her husband has nothing to do in the office, since it ceased all activity three

530

years ago, but he can't bear to be at home. So she comes to the office every afternoon to not be alone.

"Monsieur Daurat?"

The moustache is grey and the suit somewhat threadbare. But yes, it's Daurat.

"Who are you? The company is closed."

"I'm Bouffard, a reporter from the *Écho du Midi*."

"What do you want?"

"I imagine you know about the disappearance of the aviator and writer Antoine de Saint-Exupéry in Corsica?"

Daurat neither confirms nor denies it. He merely drills the reporter with his customary penetrating stare.

"I understand he was your employee for a while?"

"He wasn't an employee, he was a pilot."

"It's a tragedy!" the reporter exclaims, projecting his voice at the sight of Daurat's bad-tempered expression.

"I have nothing to tell you."

The reporter insists: "But aren't you moved by the death of all those pilots before their time—Saint-Exupéry, Guillaumet, Mermoz?"

"Not in the slightest."

"How is that possible?"

"They chose their own destinies."

"But even so, doesn't it pain you that they've thrown away their lives?"

"You understand nothing!" Daurat slams his fist on the table and the pencils jump. His wife looks up over her glasses for a second, and then continues to concentrate on her crochet work. "Get out of here!"

The reporter leaves and Daurat gets up, watched by his wife out of the corner of her eye. He goes over to the window, puts his hands behind his back, and scrutinises the darkening sky. They won't return, but it's his duty to keep waiting for them.

His wife walks over to him.

"Didier, I know you regret the deaths of your boys."

"Perhaps."

"Was it really worth it?"

"They lived each year as if it were ten. They conquered their fears, they reached amazing places where no one had been before, they overcame challenges that seemed impossible, they sacrificed themselves so that people could receive their mail in remote places. I don't know if it was worth it, but I'm certain of one thing: They made their lives extraordinary."

EPILOGUE

★

Brittany (France), August 1945

FARGET

FARGET CARRIES HIS CANVAS KITBAG with the wing of a plane sewn onto the material. His civilian clothes feel strange and, after five years of uniforms and military overalls, his cloth jacket chafes him. He stops for a moment by the parapet of a stone bridge which crosses a narrow but noisy river in front of a watermill with an enormous wheel surrounded by flowerpots. It's one of those spots in which one would like to stay forever. The sign indicates that he's reached Pont-Aven.

On the main street, he walks a few metres in front of some houses with tiny front gardens and stops, undecided. He's standing in front of a bicycle workshop, and while he's thinking about what to do, the owner comes out, wiping the grease from his hands with a rag.

"Excuse me . . . ?"

"Yes, monsieur."

"What brings you here?"

"I'm looking for someone. A girl who was a nurse during the war. Her name's Camille."

The proprietor, close to retirement age but still strong, looks him up and down very carefully. He doesn't say a word.

"You wouldn't by any chance know her?"

"The lovely bricklayer's daughter."

Farget asks for directions and the man gives them to him.

"I don't suppose you know how to fix bicycles?"

The man points toward the workshop full of handlebars, frames, and wheels. "I need an assistant. Someone who's good with machinery. Soon, I'll have to think about retiring and passing on my business."

Farget looks over the sets of wrenches, hammers, and pliers neatly organised on the workshop shelves, and smiles.

"During the war, I fixed machines that flew."

The man nods.

"I was going to make some coffee. Why don't you come inside and have a cup, and tell me about it?"

Though he is eager to see Camille, Farget finds himself crossing the threshold of the workshop, and as he does so, that clumsy, daydreaming major who talked to him about birds pops into his head.

He'd like to be able to say to him: "Major, sir, I've started to fly."